MW01518220

THE COMPLETE ANNA SERIES

LEE ALAN

FREE BIRD

ANNA SERIES BOOK 1

Chapter 1
ESCAPE

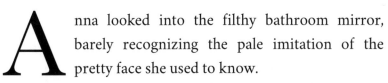nna looked into the filthy bathroom mirror, barely recognizing the pale imitation of the pretty face she used to know.

Mom said I was the most beautiful girl in the whole world.

"Don't go there," she whispered aloud, suppressing the crushing grief.

Her fingers touched a softly rounded jaw line and then traced upward over thin cheeks. She looked tired and drawn. True, her lips were still full and her nose remained petite. But lines of care had appeared on her youthful features, despite only being twenty-eight years old. They were the depressing reminders of her sadness. Most of them had been earned during the difficult days spent nursing her parents. But more than a few came from her god awful job, and him of course.

She steeled herself before the inevitable tears came,

determined not to give into raw emotion yet again. Tucking her shoulder-length brown hair behind her ears, Anna gave the reflection a firm stare, and then put the outdated waitress hat back on.

"At least my eyes are still blue," she said, grimacing at the urgent pinging sound coming from the counter: another order.

She exited the bathroom and marched through the kitchen, passing Alonso on her way. He stood at his station wearing the same grease-spattered apron from the day before, cooking the same artery-clogging crap. Anna continued through grubby swinging doors and into the bustling fifties-themed diner. She sighed inwardly at the sight of Audrey tapping her long, ruby fingernails on the white, plastic surface of the sales counter. The woman's other chubby hand remained poised over the brass service bell, ready to ring it again.

"Great—that's all I need," Anna muttered under her breath, while forcing a smile.

The fake grin formed only part of the method she'd developed for dealing with the nasty bitch. The second element involved trying to imagine which animal the oddly featured woman most resembled. This week, the new, black perm clinging to her large head gave Audrey a distinct poodle-like vibe. Anna wondered if the hair stylist responsible for the curly monstrosity had done so in a moment of spite toward the old witch.

"Excuse me! Can I get some service around here?"

Audrey demanded, making her double chin flap.

"Yes, ma'am. Can I take your order?" Anna replied with a levity she didn't feel. Audrey's eyes scanned the menu greedily. *A well-done chicken fried steak with extra gravy*, Anna thought, filling the tedium.

"I'll have a well-done chicken fried steak with extra gravy on the side, fries, and a salad with no dressing." Audrey decided finally.

"Yes, ma'am," Anna said, scribbling on her pad.

She took the scrawled message to the kitchen and placed it on the order rail next to the olive-skinned Italian chef. As always, Alonso's thick, black moustache resided in a hygiene net, giving him a comical appearance. His flamboyant facial hair had become a running joke among the staff who speculated that the net was actually a cage to prevent the hairy little beast from escaping and attacking the customers.

He took one look at the note and groaned. It read a single word: "Audrey."

The chef had developed a grudge against the woman after she'd complained about the quality of his deep fried treats on several occasions. Each of these tirades ended with an inevitable demand for a free doggy bag.

"One Audrey Special coming up," he said in a thick Sicilian accent, before removing a pre-cooked steak from the fridge and spitting on it.

Anna had made a conscious decision weeks ago to never ask how the gravy was prepared.

He slung the sad-looking thing into the grimy interior of

the microwave and turned the dial. It took all of five minutes for the chef to complete his task while Anna waited anxiously. More than a ten-minute delay would have ended with more bell-pinging drama.

After only an hour into the shift, Anna's heels already throbbed; her cheap new shoes dug into the blisters on her heels. She'd put off buying them for as long as possible— mainly, because of the cost, but also in anticipation of the torture she now endured. The fate of her poor feet had been sealed by a throwaway comment made by none other than the wonderful Audrey to the duty manager, regarding "shoddy footwear".

She carried the order to the dining area with all the grace that someone treading on a pair of cheese graters could muster, then laid it in front of her impatient customer. Audrey sucked her teeth in response before shoving the plate away.

"It's not hot enough. Do you want to give me food poisoning? Hmm?"

"But…" Anna stopped herself from completing the sentence, knowing that it would only make matters worse. "Yes, ma'am," she said instead.

She picked up the plate and headed to the kitchen while trying to hide a growing limp.

Alonso wiped his greasy hands through his hair while she explained the issue. There'd been a time when he would have reacted with typical Mediterranean fury, but today he rolled his eyes at the familiar annoyance. He paused, then put the dish back in to heat it further—probably considering one final spit garnish. Instead, he looked up at the kitchen clock and set the microwave. Without speaking another word, he disappeared out the rear door for his usual five o'clock smoke.

Following a mercifully short wait, Anna opened the microwave door and pulled out the steaming contents. The hot ceramic rim instantly burned her outstretched fingers. She hissed with pain, realizing her mistake. After just managing to avoid dropping the food, she placed the hot plate on the sink drainer and then ran her throbbing hand under the cold tap. Her thumb and feet now sang a duet of discomfort.

When the harried waitress returned with the sizzling steak, Audrey's eyes narrowed. "I've changed my mind," her voice sounded matter-of-fact. "I want mayo for the salad."

Although it was common for the fickle woman to add mayonnaise to her selection later, Anna found herself annoyed, regardless. She'd once tried to avoid the problem by bringing a bottle of it with the food, unasked, but the result had been a loud complaint: "This waitress is deliberately trying to ruin my figure." Most galling of all was the management's casual dismissal of Anna's objections to the petty bullying.

"She's one of our best customers. If you don't like it, Miss Price, look for another job," Anna recalled being told. As much as it hurt to admit, with so few opportunities in the small town, alternative work was out of the question.

And hanging around the apartment with Tony would be worse.

"Yes, of course. Is there anything else you would like while I'm getting that for you?" She asked Audrey brightly.

"No."

Anna made another tortuous round to the kitchen while clenching her jaw. The pain leapt to an exquisite peak. Worse, she suspected a smirk had appeared on Audrey's chubby face when she'd hobbled to her table a second time.

The large woman examined the mayo bottle, as usual, searching for any sign of dirt. This was another failing that would guarantee an email being fired into the inbox of Anna's employer.

"I'll also have water with lime," Audrey declared. "I said lime, not lemon, do you hear?"

Anna sighed, then pressed on in silent misery until her long shift ended.

BY THE TIME she clocked out, the young waitress felt exhausted and more than a little depressed. It wasn't the work itself that she minded so much. The pay helped her keep a modest studio apartment—and she was able to sneak extra food home most nights. The real problem lay in the daily humiliation, chipping away at any self-regard she had left. It made her fearful that one day she'd look into the dirty diner mirror and not care about the person staring back at all.

It's the little things that get you through, she thought, as she hurried to an old brown station wagon. The ancient automobile was one of the few things wearier than her. *What are those little things, Anna? Can you even remember the last time you laughed?—I can't,* came the depressing answer.

The traffic dragged, and it took almost an hour to commute to the sprawling, blue collar housing estate she called home. Her own slice of paradise, the oddly named Nightingale apartment block, was located just off Interstate 40 in Kingman, Arizona. By the time she pulled up outside the small run-down apartment she shared with her boyfriend, Anna had already stifled several eye-watering yawns. All she could think of right then was a soak under a hot shower, followed by an early night.

With a sense of relief, she stretched and then strode up the same rickety wooden porch stairs she'd been trying to persuade the landlord to paint for years. Anna put her key in the lock of the flimsy, red front door, waiting for the welcome click which would signify the end to a very long day. Unexpectedly, the motion made the cheap wood swing inward. The door was already open.

But didn't Tony say he started his night shift at the can factory tonight?

Taking a deep breath, she pushed it further ajar and looked down the dimly lit entrance hallway. The action caused the door to creak. As her eyes adjusted, Anna noticed that the two decorative angels she'd hung in the entrance the previous week had fallen from their hooks and shattered on the threadbare carpet.

The little statues represented the latest in a long line of failed efforts to make the place look less unfriendly. Somehow, they'd only served to emphasize how alien the apartment felt most days.

Is anything in your life not empty? She reflected, too exhausted and in pain to think straight about the unlatched door.

"Well, if it's a burglar, they can't torture me any worse than these fucking things," she whispered, slipping off the shiny, black shoes and kicking them to one side. Anna winced as one of the heels brushed against her raw skin, but the release of pressure felt good.

After allowing the fleeting pleasure to continue for a moment, she focused on her surroundings and crept toward the dark entrance to the living room. She stepped lightly through the gloomy archway, her gaze needing a second to adapt.

The familiar form of Tony lying face up on the couch made her sigh with relief—and then curse silently. He snored in greeting. She stared at the shadowed cheeks and scraggly, brown beard of the once good-looking man, finding it hard to believe that she used to caress those features. The memory made her search harder for any residual sense of affection to cling to. But as her gaze moved over his nose marked by the telltale veins of a heavy drinker, her deep sadness signalled that those feelings were long dead.

Of course, she dared not tell him how she felt. There were happy boozers and unhappy ones. Tony was the latter. While she contemplated her burning resentment toward the prone figure, he snorted and scratched his belly. The action caused an empty vodka bottle to roll from underneath his arm and clunk against ill-fitted floor boards. Anna continued to watch, daring herself to build enough courage to confront him, but fearing the consequences. In an attempt to distract her inner voice, she tidied the mess strewn around the room. With little remaining natural light to aid her, she turned on the lamp beside the couch.

Tony bolted upright. Two red-rimmed eyes flicked open and, after blearily orienting themselves, they fixed on Anna. His dark, blonde hair stuck out, giving him the appearance of a demonic scarecrow. Even as her senses registered the danger, she couldn't help but notice how his presence repulsed her. The glassy, flat quality to his gaze scared her, so she took a step back.

Not good, she thought, as a sinking feeling spread from the pit of her stomach.

"You woke me," he said in a deathly quiet tone, with words devoid of warmth.

"I'm sorry." She headed for the bathroom, trying to fake a call of nature, but, with a sinking heart, she heard him rise and stumble over the empty bottle.

"You bring food?" He asked, as she reached the doorway to the tiny facility they shared.

Anna paused at the pointed question, silently cursing her own stupidity. The shift had been so tiring that she'd forgotten about their evening meal. "I'm so sorry, hon, I forgot. I'll see if I can run and get something. What would you like?" She kept her voice light.

Thudding feet answered her question. Anna felt her head being yanked by the hair, along with the awful sensation of a hand wrapping around her neck. Tony quickly pushed her through the open doorway and pressed her face hard against the bathroom mirror. She got a jumbled, back lit glimpse of bared teeth next to her pale, panicked expression. The putrid chemical stench of his breath invaded her space.

"Stop," Anna whimpered, as he took her chin in his hand and jerked her toward him.

"You don't ever forget to feed yourself, huh?"

"I'll go to the store. Please, Tony…"

His reply came in the form of a fist crunching into her jaw. The terrible impact sent her flying into the shower where the body wash she'd hoped to bathe with later clattered around her slumped form. Stars danced around her vision, like angry fairies disturbed by an unexpected intruder. Through the swirling haze, she made out the figure of her loving boyfriend moving back to the living room.

A gentle wave of oblivion threatened to take her away

completely, then. Anna wondered idly if it was still too late for a shower. She'd been looking forward to it all afternoon.

When her thoughts started to coalesce again, they took the form of an image: Audrey's fingernails drumming on the table at the diner. It stuck there, floating before her mind, like the beating of a dead man's heart. The person she'd once loved had hit her, and she couldn't bear the betrayal. *After working yourself to the bone to keep him festering in this pit, here's your thanks, kiddo.* The torment exploded in Anna's mind, and she rose out of the cubicle and strode through the bathroom door.

He'd sat on the couch again. A smile formed on his unshaven face when she reappeared. "You wanna play?" His voice was low, almost a purr.

Tony shot from the couch straight at her. Instinctively, she ran for the kitchen, pulling the portable TV off its stand in passing, hoping to slow the pursuit. Without time to look back, and sensing that the desperate measure had failed, an unbidden sob escaped her throat as she realized they would reach the small kitchen at the same time. Panic struck once again in the shape of an oncoming tiled wall and the certainty of what would follow.

I will face this.

Anna pulled to a halt before she hit the surface and turned, only to be confronted by Tony, who'd already clenched a fist ready. It would lead to an unspeakable act, met by an equal rage in her. She refused to be hit again.

As he reared his fist to strike, she ducked, and his flailing arm swooped over the top of her head. Tony staggered—a combination of not expecting her resistance and the vodka.

You only have a second, hon. He won't miss, next time.

DO SOMETHING! Her inner voice roared. She reached for the nearest drawer and picked up the first thing she could find.

Tony had regained his balance and now paused to stare at the boning knife she held. He laughed. "Just another weak fucking whore!" He spat the words toward her. "You haven't got the balls!" He hefted his crotch at her luridly.

He charged, and time itself seemed to slow for Anna. His approach played like a movie in slow motion, from his hate-filled expression to his club-like raised arm. From somewhere within an instinct for survival took over and a detached part of her looked on as she positioned the blade at an upward angle. In contrast to the previous second, the next became a blur, filled with the overriding sensation of being thrown backward.

Anna lay, panting like an animal in a snare, staring at the grime underneath the white electric cooker they'd never got around to replacing. Once again, however, her will to live refused to give in. She forced her eyes toward the man. Tony stood with an open mouth, looking down at the knife handle sticking out from his crotch

A red stain spread down his dirty cream chinos.

I really must do some washing tomorrow, she thought, as hysteria threatened to wrench her away from reality.

He swayed on his feet. "What have you done?" Tony asked, before dropping to his knees.

She remained paralyzed by an awful fascination while the dark crimson patch travelled down his legs.

"Anna," he muttered, before toppling to the floor, blues eyes rolling back in their sockets.

ANNA WASN'T sure how much time had passed while she watched the pool of blood grow outward across the beige linoleum. Eventually, a kind of self-awareness returned.

Leave now, she thought.

Chapter 2

CUCKOO

ARIZONA: 1992

H azel shielded her eyes from the blazing sun while she hurried home from another exhausting cleaning shift. Heat rose in relentless waves from the pavement and mixed with the thick air, leaving her parched throat aching for water. She scolded herself for not thinking to fill a bottle before heading back from her final client of the day.

A blue Chrysler sped past, leaving a pall of dust in its wake.

What I wouldn't give for A/C, she thought with a sudden wave of envy directed toward the occupants of the car. Her mind's eye pictured them heading to a cool, shaded four-bedroom duplex in the suburbs, where they would sip lemonade and laugh at the sun burnt woman foolish enough to walk four miles during the height of summer.

Finally rounding the bend to the familiar sight of the

trailer park, she contemplated what her life had become over the years. Since leaving a pointless and unrewarding time at high school, she'd worked as a cleaner to support her son, Tony, and the love of her life, David. It was hard, degrading work, but at least they had a steady income.

She sighed, reflecting on how she looked closer to thirty-five than her actual twenty-nine years, these days. Her sandy, blonde hair had long lost its sheen, and her cheeks were now wrinkled from too many hours trudging through the desert. These sad facts led to the depressing conclusion that the future had finally passed her by for good.

That opportunity sailed, honey—just like owning a shiny, blue car.

Nothing was easy with David. He'd given up looking for work a long time ago, claiming that the small town of Salome didn't have much to offer. She suspected, however, that nobody would take on a man with a reputation for being the town drunk. So, for better or worse, richer or poorer, he relied on her for everything. She cooked, cleaned, worked a ten-hour shift six days each week, and cared for the boy. Some months, especially this one, she felt overwhelmed. But there was no getting around the simple fact that she loved her man. Sure, the son of a bitch spent most of his time wasted, but he didn't beat on her. According to the messed up wisdom of her grandmother, that's all that mattered, in the end.

"Hazel, my dear, men aren't fit for diddly shit, but, as

long as they don't whoop yer, then one's as good as another." She still recalled her exact words.

In Tony, though, lay a different story. He was her reason for living, and at only seven years old he behaved with remarkable thoughtfulness toward his mother. Each morning, he would get himself ready for school and pack his own lunch, all because he knew Momma needed to get to work. His relationship with David was more complex. He'd learned to avoid his unpredictable father for the most part, because of the few occasions when David had belted him—usually for the flimsiest of reasons. Hazel tried not to dwell on such inconvenient considerations. Instead, she contemplated with pride how Tony had developed a way with people. He had a deft, easy manner which his father would never achieve. Often, one of her elderly customers would remark on her "lovely, polite boy," before giving him a warm toffee candy or a piece of chocolate.

The prone figure of David greeted her, after opening the scratched, brown door of the run down trailer. He lay sprawled along the green couch in the corner of what passed for their living room. She sighed again. It was becoming common to find him this way, sleeping off a date with his liquid mistress, even so early in the afternoon. She counted eight empty beer cans lined up on the beige rug beside him—a handy sign for what kind of evening to expect. Three to six cans meant there would be a calm night, but anything over nine could spell trouble in paradise. More than a dozen and she would take their son to stay at her sister's.

She went to check on Tony as her routine demanded. More often than not, she'd find him in his room reading or listening to the radio. Hazel knocked, but when the expected "Hey, Mom," didn't follow, as usual, she began to worry.

"Tony? You there, baby?" No answer.

She'd learned a long time ago to trust her intuition, and it gave her a definite nudge right then. Tony should have been in there, and if not he would have been playing in front of the trailer with the Smeaton kid.

What if something's happened to him? The thought didn't stop there. *While you left him with a drunken lush of a father.* Goosebumps rolled down her arms.

"Perhaps he's hiding," she muttered out loud in an attempt to counter her conscience. That didn't sound like her little boy though. He was a serious child—some would even argue: withdrawn. Playing pranks just wasn't like her good, little boy. Despite the reservations of her maternal instinct, she entered the tiny box room and searched without luck.

Is he in the closet? Hazel thought. But, after pulling open the wooden door, she could only see a jumble of clothes and toys. Worry took root in the pit of her gut. She knew the boy could take care of himself, but something felt unsettling about the break in their shared normality.

LEE ALAN

After pacing the short span between the living and sleeping quarters, she decided to search the exterior of the property. Heading back out, she dismissed the idea of waking her husband for help. At best, it would have ended in another sulky rant about apron strings. At worst, it would be a full-on rage, and another hole would appear in their bedroom door.

The trailer park sat at the edge of a wash which flowed with water during the winter months. It allowed the residents of the park to grow a few vegetables in the arid climate rolling off the distant Harquahala Mountain. During the hottest points of the year, such as now, it lay parched and filled with stinking garbage. Spikey mesquite trees, capable of tearing through the unprotected legs of a passer-by, dotted the land around the channel.

Perfect for scorpions, she thought darkly. "Tony!" She called, as her stomach churned with fresh concern.

The only answer to her plea came from the yapping of a neighbor's dog. Disconcerted, she searched through the scrub, but it only took a moment to appreciate that the foliage was too sparse to hide a child. Hazel's mind reeled.

What if he's fallen and banged his head, left unconscious? Jesus, in this heat...

"The wash," she muttered. "How many times have I told him not play down there?"

She climbed down the dirt walls of the wide trench in a panicked rush, causing a thorny branch to rake down her left cheek. The sudden pain induced an ugly urge to punish the boy harshly if this did turn out to be a prank.

Wincing, Hazel reached the bottom and looked down the length of the channel, her feet sinking deep into the sand of the gully. Nothing looked amiss. She frantically pondered her next move, finally deciding to scout the bank on the far side. From her recollection of the unforgiving environment, there was a small clearing just over the rise. *Exactly where a child would build a fort.*

After rounding the top, she stopped dead with terror at the sight of several small, mutilated bodies. A swarm of carrion flies buzzed around the remains. But, her overwhelming sense of dread ebbed as the realization sunk in that the gruesome remains appeared to be animal. She gasped with relief and then placed her hands on her knees in a vain attempt to contain her fluttering heart. The horrified young mother inspected the grim scene with a sense of revulsion. The pitiful collection included desert birds, and shockingly, the matted corpse of a tabby cat.

"Who could do such a thing?" She asked, almost at a loss for words.

It must have been a person, she thought, noticing how the carcasses had been arranged in a pattern that no natural predator would replicate.

But why? More to the point, my dear: where is your son? And, by the way, have you considered that whoever did this could do the same to him?

She ran through the scrub, calling out for Tony. But,

after a few minutes of exerting herself in the intense heat she ran out of breath. Black dots spread across her vision. As she stopped to force oxygen into her heaving lungs, a rustling sound came from the bushes beside her. A moment later, the innocent face of her son emerged.

"Tony!" She half-screamed. The relief was incredible.

"I'm here, Mom," his sweet voice answered.

Hazel ran to the boy, snatched him up, and then started to hurry home. She wanted to put as much distance between them and the grim scene she'd stumbled upon in the clearing as she could. After retracing her steps and reaching the relative safety of the trailer park, she set him down and looked into his blue, twinkling gaze.

"Where have you been? I've been worried sick!"

"Just playing, Mommy."

"Did you see what happened to the birds?" She couldn't help but ask, fearing that such a cruel sight would damage his young mind.

"What birds, Mommy?" His voice sounded calm. Further feelings of relief ran through her.

She hooked a protective arm around Tony and led him inside, before deciding to risk waking David. Someone capable of doing such appalling things to those poor creatures was an obvious danger.

Hazel never did find out who killed and tortured those animals in such a sadistic manner. She wondered about it for years to come, unable to shake the sense that she'd missed something important that day.

Chapter 3

JULIA

The station wagon was halfway to Phoenix before starting to die. It finally gave up the ghost fifty miles after passing a solitary outpost of civilization. Its equally unhappy driver could only thud her hands against the steering wheel in helpless frustration while the engine choked and came to a shuddering halt.

Anna was left to contemplate the bleak, dusty, scrubland which stretched toward a distant horizon. A cold finger of fear ran down her spine at the prospect of being stranded in the Arizona Badlands. She decided to consult her out dated road map in the glove compartment and concluded that her mid-night exodus had brought her to a featureless location literally called Nothing.

Well, kiddo, you are in a place called Nothing with nothing left...

Nothing, Arizona. Population: one, she thought, unable to

raise even a bitter laugh at the irony of the situation.

Her mind turned to the shattering events of the previous night for the thousandth time once again causing bile to rise in her stomach. Underpinned by a sense of dread, every memory and question about their relationship rolled around her shattered mind. She found it all so hard to believe. That man was supposed to have loved her. Instead, he'd smashed both of their futures.

He must be dead. The four words refused to stop their tortuous assault on her senses.

Part of her wanted to return and face the consequences, but she couldn't do it. If he did live and, by some miracle, the law didn't get wrapped up in the wreckage of their lives, she feared that he would somehow, find a way to reel her back in. And then, the nightmare wouldn't end. She'd be trapped forever.

Oh, and he will do it again, Little Bird—make no mistake about that, she thought, forcing herself not to cry any more.

The fire in her heart burned a hundred times stronger than the desert surrounding her, but she only had the energy to sit and ride the unpleasant sensation of her chest thumping. She rested her weary head against the wheel for a second and then opened the car door. A vein throbbed in her temple as the rusty mechanism screeched. She stepped into the scorching heat.

In retrospect, it became so clear: he'd not given a single thing to her in return for everything she did. Not once did he bring her flowers or make dinner when she returned from another hard day. She found herself stunned by her own blindness. The question kept arising: why had they stayed together so long? The answer was that Tony had the ability to charm when it suited him: when he wanted the apartment which made her get a second job, and of course, sex. He could have persuaded the birds to fall from the trees so he could clip their wings to stop them from ever flying again.

She collapsed to the ground, ready to give in.

No. You have to be strong and think, Anna. If you want to survive this, you have no choice, she thought, knowing that to let go in this forbidding place risked total ruin.

Firming her resolve, she lifted herself up and breathed.

AMAZINGLY, the rested car spluttered to life on the third attempt, and she soon made her way south again, not daring to go above forty miles per hour.

Why don't you call for an ambulance, Anna? Her internal Jiminy Cricket chirped up.

It crept into her thoughts like the ultimate un-flushable turd—the number one head twister on the score board of questions best avoided.

"Too late," she whispered.

The first two hours of her escape had been a barely registered blur of dark, winding roads and numb thought processes. She'd been too screwed in the head to call for help during that crucial time. Since regaining some inner control, the narrow window to turn back or pick up a phone had receded, along with any remote possibility of rescuing the situation.

When did our love turn grey? She wondered, thinking about the way he would lie with her, quiet and sullen.

He'd never cuddle, but why? Anna didn't know. Occasionally, he would utter the word "love," but the mechanical way he said it always spoke louder than the sentence, itself. His only passion seemed to stem from a constant anger—a furious rage that lurked just beneath those pale blue eyes, ready to explode for the smallest reason.

The long drive under a scorching sun brought other thoughts amidst the sense of impending doom. Reflections on their so-called home and how it felt like more like a trap to her—a snare in which to keep a willing slave locked away and neglected. Apart from the dismal aura, the smell of rolled cigarettes had permeated the air. The stench rose from the half dozen ash trays scattered about the apartment.

It's way past time to leave that nest, kiddo, she thought, shifting in the sticky, plastic seat.

She wasn't sure how long this newfound freedom would last, but Anna knew of one person who could make any remaining time count: Julia.

Her fears of impending arrest came as a distant second to the sense of loss for what he'd stolen: the bright-eyed girl with an innocent view of the world. The person she'd used to be—the Anna who trusted others and loved life—was gone. And for that, she hated him most.

WHEN JULIA GOT her sister's call, she felt relieved beyond words. She'd watched helplessly over the years, while Anna suffered the lingering fate of a woman trapped in a loveless partnership. Instinctively, she'd not trusted Tony; he'd always left her feeling unsettled in his presence. Although she could never quite put her finger on it, something dark lay hidden behind those rugged, handsome features. Something bad. One day, she knew his rotten core would emerge from the depths and hurt the person she loved most in the world.

Of course, Julia had tried many times to persuade her to leave him, but Anna would only try to excuse his casual cruelty. "Tony just needs to find himself," or, "He needs to find a job." Whatever.

Oh, Little Bird, you silly girl, Julia thought.

Despite feeling like slapping her younger sister on more than one occasion, she'd refused to give up on her. Even when the abuse threatened to drive a wedge between them. She knew with absolute certainty that a man like Tony would finally break down—it was inevitable. Although the thought of Anna getting hurt in the process made her feel sick, Julia knew it would present an opportunity to break free.

Unlike Anna, she'd not really found the one. For reasons best known to the wider universe, after waiting decades for the perfect man to come along, it never happened. Of course, she'd been on dates and experienced passionate flings. But refusing to settle for anything less than Mr. Dream had become a challenge. Unfortunately, she was yet to find said perfect gentleman amongst a mix of momma's boys and control freaks. She didn't sweat, though—well, not much, anyhow—because at the not-quite-panic-stations age of thirty-one, she remained happy being single. Somewhere along the line, she'd also managed to build a good life, despite being a hopeless spinster.

That's where she differed from her sibling: Anna had always wanted to lose herself in a man. Therein lay the problem: learning to assert herself, rather than finding someone else to provide an emotional crutch. Julia had noticed many years ago that Anna didn't have enough self-confidence. She said "yes" when she should have been saying "no fucking way, man." With poor, sweet Little Bird, it'd always been about other people and never herself. Julia just hoped that whatever ill luck had prompted her emotional call would also put an end to her self-destructive behavior.

Silver linings, she thought, stealing another look at her wrist watch.

A pinging sound emanated from her phone to notify an incoming text: "Be there in ten."

Thrilled at Anna's message, she put some water on the

stove and planned her strategy.

We'll just have to have a little chat: Big Bird to Little Bird. "Nothing too heavy—just enough to know she's okay," Julia said aloud. *And if she's not, then I'll find that fucking son of a bitch and rip him a new one.*

Comfort food was her secret weapon to uncover the truth. Julia wanted to make this a special homecoming, so she'd splashed out on a sure winner: special shrimp enchiladas. She'd already covered the plump pink crustaceans in her own special spice recipe and mixed them with salsa, before placing them in the refrigerator. The delicacy came with handmade flour tortillas and a creamy, green chili sauce.

"You've got no chance against this menu, kiddo," she said, adding an extra drop of cream.

TWICE, Anna wondered if the car would make it to Scottsdale, and the busy highway traffic didn't make matters better, either. The delay was not entirely unwelcome, however, because of the crippling indecision tormenting her. Should she tell Julia the whole story?

Surely if the police started searching, this would be the first place they would try to find me. She didn't care though. The need for comfort overrode any other consideration.

A little after eight, she stepped from the car outside her sister's little-whitewashed bungalow, still unsure of what to do. Almost three years had passed since her last visit, and the quiet neighborhood appeared just as peaceful as she remembered. It was the kind of area where old couples strolled and people said "good morning." She took a deep breath as if the air itself could lift the impending doom sitting on her slim shoulders.

Julia came straight out and gave her a long hug before looking her over. Immediately, she fixed her gaze on the ugly mark on her sibling's cheek. Big Bird's pretty face flushed red with anger.

"I swear, I'm going to kill him," she said.

Anna tried to contain her strained emotions, but something about Julia's shocked rage brought her close to cracking. Tears welled once more. In response, the anger drained from her sister's face and was replaced by concern. They held each other tight while quiet sobs of despair escaped Anna. After a moment, she felt gentle fingers lift her chin.

"Sweetie, he can't hurt you here."

Anna stared into Julia's dark brown eyes and found love staring back. She looked good—in fact, she looked great. Compared to her own wiry frame, her sister had a perfect hour glass body, and her attractive, freckled face glowed with health. Her red lips pursed with worry.

Julia led her into the house before insisting she sit in the massive, leather recliner, which had belonged to their late father. Too tired to protest, Anna flopped down, appreciating the sensation of soft cushions against her aching thighs.

"Lemonade?" Julia asked.

"You kiddin?" She replied, managing a wan smile.

Seemingly satisfied that her guest looked comfortable, Big Bird disappeared into the kitchen. Anna's parched throat ached for the sweet liquid with an intensity she hardly thought possible. She also experienced the first smells of something delicious drifting through the cozy home.

Julia returned a moment later with two ice-filled glasses topped to the brim with hand-pressed juice. She set both drinks on the table between them, staring at her sister the whole time.

Anna lifted the drink to her mouth, swigging the bitter-sweet mix. The cool sensation felt heavenly. Julia looked on, sipping politely. It took several moments before either of them broke the silence. In truth, she hadn't a clue about where to start. It all seemed so bad that she feared even her beloved sister would reject her. Instead, she let the seconds drag by, staring at the residue left by the lemons in her glass, as if they would provide the answer.

JULIA COULDN'T TAKE her eyes off the way Anna slouched. Her thin frame hunched while her trembling hands restlessly picked at the stitching on Dad's big chair. More than anything, she looked completely exhausted— haunted even.

What the hell happened to you, Little Bird? She thought, knowing Anna was too frail to be pressed. She decided to provide simple comfort instead.

"You're home," Julia said finally, wishing the weight of the statement would sink in. But to her dismay, Anna didn't appear to hear. Although shocked at the evident level of trauma, she did her best not to show it and went about the task of setting the dining table.

They ate their food in silence. Julia resisted the urge to ask questions until they were done. After they'd finished, she observed Anna staring at her still half-filled plate. Wordlessly, she cleared away the dishes while pretending to ignore the wrongness of the situation. It broke her heart to see just how low the woman she treasured above all others had fallen. Uncertain of what else to do, she tried to distract Anna with trivial things, asking if she had any clothes or toiletries. Anna shook her head like a small, frightened child. The two dark circles beneath her blue eyes, filled with unshed tears, emphasized how close to collapse the poor kid was. Julia smiled reassuringly and placed a comforting arm around her shoulder, trying to project a calmness she didn't feel.

Within thirty minutes, she had helped Anna shower and change into a pair of Garfield-themed pyjamas.

"Night, Little Bird. Love you," she said after tucking her beneath crisp sheets.

"Love you more, Big Bird." Anna finished the ritual they'd started as children.

Chapter 4

FATE ROLLS THE DICE

Dawn's harsh light crept into Anna's little haven. She wasn't sure how long she'd slept, having lost count of the minutes she'd spent tossing on a sweat-soaked pillow. Over and over again, her mind had replayed the attack in the apartment, occasionally adding a pinch of spice from the worst imaginings of a sleep-starved mind. The dream she found cruelest was the one in which she'd arrive at the apartment, take a hot shower, and then nod off in a comfortable bed, only to wake to the nightmare of the real world.

The pattern of night terrors continued for hours until she was finally interrupted by mouth-watering smells. Her stomach rumbled in sympathy, and despite the protests emanating from the darker corners of her consciousness, she found herself rising and putting on a set of clothes, already laid out in a neat pile.

She'd barely gotten out the bedroom door when Julia approached with a heaped breakfast platter.

"Oh no, kiddo," her sister said. "Back in there."

With that, she was unceremoniously herded into the bedroom. Despite her present gloom, the fussily protective treatment brought a smile to her face.

Whatever happens, I'm glad to be here, she thought.

Seating her sister in the wicker chair beside the bed, Julia theatrically laid a napkin in Anna's lap and began to point out the various goodies before her. In doing so, she adopted the ludicrously overblown accent of a French TV chef they'd used to watch together as teenagers.

"Madam may nootice the par ev juicy meloons," Julia said, screwing her face up in a poor attempt to impersonate the odd celebrity.

"He never said meloons!" Anna replied, unable to stop herself from laughing.

"He most certainly did—outrageously big, juicy meloons!" They both giggled, this time.

Julia gave her a final smile and then left Anna to bite hungrily into a generously buttered croissant. The food had obviously been cooked with love. The melon stuffed with ham proved a refreshing contrast to the rich pastry, and Anna could actually feel the energy flowing into her over-worked limbs with every morsel. Munching away, she reflected on how even the blackest of moods could be lifted given a hearty meal cooked by a caring hand. It reminded her of the days when Mom would bring her breakfast in bed.

She polished off the tasty offerings, moved the empty plate to one side, and then lingered in the chair a little longer, enjoying the early morning warmth that bathed her. Realizing she'd begun to nod off, Anna stepped back to the bed before curling up on top of the sheets.

SHE WOKE up feeling rested and immediately noticed the serving tray had been removed without disturbing her. Rising from the bed, Anna went to the window and looked out. The sun hung low in the amber-colored sky, while shadows formed beside the other neat, white houses of the avenue. Two little girls in yellow dresses skipped together on the other side of the road.

All day? She marveled to herself.

Anna walked into the bathroom and looked in the mirror: her face appeared clean now, with the dirt of the desert washed away. The dark circles under her eyes had lessened, but the green bruise still remained—just as loud as the previous day. Thoughts of Tony threatened to drift in again, but she resisted them. It took all of her will power but, after a much-needed rest, it felt easier than it had through the fog of exhaustion which had previously dogged her.

She brushed her teeth and made a half-hearted attempt

at bringing some order to the tangled mess on her head before going to find Julia. The sight of her sister cooking up yet another food lover's delight greeted Anna on entering the kitchen. Evidently, Big Bird had opted to put something sweet on the menu this evening, as she busily conjured up homemade cookies. A fresh pot of ice cream sat on the draining board, ready to complement the naughty treats. She noticed the table looked beautifully set: a vase of hand-picked pink roses framed by a stellar white table cloth, completed a simple, yet elegant display.

"Half-melted ice cream: yup, that'll do nicely," Anna said. "Seriously though, thank you, sweetie. This is beautiful."

Julie turned while kneading cookie dough with a ferocity she clearly enjoyed. "I just want you to be happy, sis," she replied, blushing at the sudden show of affection.

They spent the next twenty minutes pleasantly baking together and chatting about trivial nonsense, just like old times. It felt great.

"Thank you for letting me come here," Anna said while surveying their finished creations with pride.

"You've got no idea how relieved I am to see you," Julia replied, looking at her with a troubled gaze.

Anna felt a pang of guilt at the worry she must be causing, realizing she'd been so wrapped up in the situation that it'd hardly occurred to her to consider what Julia must be making of it all.

"I need to talk to you, Big Bird."

"I know."

Anna couldn't bear to look at that deep concern any longer, so she flung her arms around her big sis, knocking a bag of flour over. Left unnoticed by both of them, it continued to spill its contents while they hugged.

"It's... bad," Anna sobbed.

"Shh," Julia whispered, gripping her tightly.

"I came home and he'd passed out," she began, struggling to find the words. "I'd been working all day and started to clean the place up... it woke him," she paused. "That fucking apartment is always a mess."

"You don't have to justify anything to me, hon. The lazy bum should pull his weight."

There was silence while the hug continued, but finally it felt like a great dam broke within Anna.

"He pushed me up against the wall and... and—oh, you have no idea how much that hurt," she said as tears flowed freely. "His voice sounded so full of hate, like I meant nothing to him." She could feel Julia's body tensing against hers. "He hit me." The words sat between them, ugly and raw. Oddly, she felt a sense of lifting while making the statement. Just to be able to tell another human being helped expel some badness. "I ran to the kitchen, and he came at me again," she continued.

"He hit you a second time?"

Anna gently pushed her away. "You don't understand," she said.

"Tell me."

"He went to hit me and I..." It hung there.

"You can trust me, honey," Julia reassured her, "Whatever it is."

"I, I—oh, Big Bird, I think killed him." Anna gave an anguished cry as she spoke her darkest fear.

Stunned silence followed for what seemed an eternity. With her thoughts entering free fall, a dog barked in the distance—almost as if it had been alerted to the sense of dread settling between them.

"Are you sure?" Julia asked at last.

"No, but it... it was a knife."

There was another long pause.

"You stabbed him?"

"Yes."

Anna waited for the accusations to follow. How could anyone be expected to support a murderer—family or not? She started to relax her grip.

I don't deserve her support, she thought. *You shouldn't have brought this to her door.*

To her surprise, Julia began to cling to her all the harder. "I hope you did kill the bastard." She said fiercely.

"But..."

"Listen: you protected yourself, hon."

"Julia, I..."

"It was self-defense, period. Do you understand?" After finishing the sentence, she took Anna's delicate chin in her hand and turned it until they looked each other dead in the eye.

"He might've killed you. Do you understand?" She repeated.

Anna found herself nodding, and a weight lifted with every move of her neck. *Bless you, Big Bird,* she thought as they clung to each other like children.

She felt an irrational need to change the subject.

"You have so much here, Julia. I didn't realize just how lucky you are."

"Luck's got nothing to do with it, kiddo." Julia kissed her on the forehead. "We can do this together, Little Bird. Whatever happens, I'm here for you." Julia refused to be distracted.

"Thank you," Anna replied, certain her sister meant it.

After several more moments locked together, Julia removed her arms. "There's only one way to get rid of a problem," she said, leading Anna to answer.

"Do something about it," Anna responded to the saying their parents had drilled into them for years.

"That's right." Julia reached for her handbag and removed her smart phone. For an awful second, Anna thought her sister had decided to call the cops. "Say cheese," Big Bird said, pointing the phone's camera at her sibling.

"Why?"

"Evidence, my dear. That nasty bruise will fade, and we need to make sure the whole world knows what he did, if it comes to it."

"Oh, I see," Anna replied, feeling stupid not to have thought of it before. "But I've been crying."

"All the better. They need to see what the pig did to you."

Julia took a few pictures and then placed the camera back in her bag. Her face was a picture of calculation.

"What now?" Anna asked. It felt good to have someone else to share the terrible burden with.

"That's just what I was thinking." She paused, her red lips pursing. "You're unsure if he's…"

"Dead? He looked unconscious and I saw blood." Anna said, her mind trying to shy away from the grim specter of his face drained of color and lit horrifically by the bright strip lights of the kitchen.

"It happened so fast. I couldn't think… and then I ran," she continued, searching through dark memories to find any kind of indication that Tony had survived, only to draw a blank.

"We need to find out for sure," Julia concluded. "If he's not dead, then maybe he hasn't gone to the cops. The bastard would be too ashamed."

"But how do we find out?" Even before the question had left her lips, Anna knew the answer.

"We go back."

"A man was found brutally stabbed to death today in Kingman. Police have identified the victim as thirty-one-year-old Tony Eckerman and would urgently like to speak to his partner, Anna Price. The waitress was last seen…"

The imaginary words played through Anna's head in a loop. Fortunately, they didn't become reality, as the two women anxiously listened for news while flicking through local radio stations on the road to Kingman.

After making the decision to return, they'd set off within the hour. Julia's new air-conditioned Chevy made the journey both quicker and far more comfortable than Anna's earlier chaotic flight. They pulled up outside the eerily quiet apartment just before midnight.

The sisters stared at the dark, curtained windows, attempting to discern signs of police activity. There was nothing. Just a gentle breeze stirring the dusty, deserted road.

"Come on, let's go," Julia said, gripping her door handle.

"What if he's in there?" Anna asked, putting a restraining hand on her shoulder.

Without reply, Julia opened her handbag to display its contents. Inside the purse glinted the black casing of a gun. Shocked, Anna read the words embossed into its textured grip: "Made in Austria. Glock INC. SMYRNA. GA." She felt her heart beat quicken.

"Only if we need it," Julia added.

Anna swallowed and then nodded.

The night air felt cool against her bare arms as they quietly left the car and approached the chipped, red door, all the time listening for sounds of life from within. Again, there was only silence.

Because he's in exactly the same place you left him to die, Anna thought darkly.

As quietly as possible, she slipped the key into the latch and turned it, subconsciously holding her breath. They slipped into the dark interior, gripping each other's hands tightly. The hallway was partially illuminated by a flickering street lamp behind, and Anna could immediately see that her two little angels had been crushed further, but whether from her hasty retreat, she couldn't recall. They crept onward.

The dark soon enveloped them, forcing the sisters to pause with their hands clutching painfully with suppressed tension. Anna strained to listen while her inner fears ran amok, but the only noticeable sound came from a heavily dripping tap somewhere in the gloom ahead.

Better to see him coming, she thought, trying to build enough courage to break their collective paralysis.

She ran a trembling hand along the textured wallpaper until she found the hall light switch, which she then pressed. The living room looked just as she remembered: the discarded vodka bottle still lay in the shadows amidst the same clutter she'd so fatefully started to clear prior to the attack.

Was it empty before? She wondered.

They moved silently toward the kitchen; the atmosphere was so heavy that Anna could hear the beating rhythm of her body.

Feels like a morgue, she thought, breathing heavily. To her dismay, a fetid aroma greeted her nostrils.

"The smell, Julia…"

"Shh!" Big Bird hissed urgently. "Where's the living room light switch?" Anna froze, not wishing to see the gruesome truth. "The light," Julia repeated.

With only the hallway lit, the kitchen floor appeared an ominously concealed mystery. Anna gazed into the blackness, imagining a pale, decaying corpse, its eyes staring back, forever etched with hatred for her.

Take a good look at what you did. Do you like your handy work? She imagined it whispering.

I have to be honest with you, love of my life. I'm not sure I like it.

Anna firmed herself and then pulled them both toward the nearby kitchen dimmer control. Mercifully, it'd been positioned just outside the food preparation area, which allowed her to avoid traversing the patch of unknown blackness. She reached for the dim white outline on the flower-patterned wall and her thumb touched the dial. In a moment of racing panic, however, she found herself unable to carry out the irreversible

action. All would be revealed in its hideous glory.

How many days has it been, Anna? Get a grip! She screamed inwardly before turning the switch to full.

The scene flooded with an unnatural, yellow glow. There was no body. Anna subconsciously touched her hand to her mouth in shocked relief. The blood was gone, and no signs remained of the struggle. The source of the rancid odor she'd found so jarring now became apparent as the smell emanating from the unemptied trash can.

"Has he been moved by the cops?" Anna speculated aloud.

Julia looked pensively around them, visibly at a loss. "No," she said at last. "There would be signs. This place has been empty for days."

A blur of possibilities flitted through Anna's mind. Despite the unexpected twist, she realized two other rooms remained where he could be: the bathroom and the bedroom. "He might have crawled," she suggested, her stomach tightening at the implications.

The women checked both quickly without finding any trace of a disturbance. Tony was gone.

After a few minutes of speculation, they gave up, and then packed a case with the few things Anna needed in order to leave the unhappy place for good. While driving away, her mind filled with a renewed hope for the future and a determination to never return.

Chapter 5

A NEW START?

O n a bright and already-warm Saturday morning, Anna woke and fetched a bowl of cereal from the generously stocked pantry. She found Julia in her spotless living room, staring at the screen of the home PC. A picture of them hugging at summer camp as children perched on the glass desk next to the monitor.

"What's 'firefighters with big hoses.com?" Anna teased, while kissing her sister on the top of the head.

Julia jumped at the unexpected intrusion and then laughed at the outrageously false question. "Better than your browser history, kiddo: 'hairy dudes with boobs.com,'" Julia retorted. This earned a playful slap on the same spot as the kiss preceding it.

In fact, Anna could see that the browser had been opened on two subjects: one about adult education in the area and the second was a job search.

"Just checking out the school and job situation for you," Julia explained. "There's a community college across town and it's only a five-minute drive away."

This is Big Bird code for "Time to shake your ass and stop moping around, kiddo," Anna thought.

She'd been living with Julia for over a month, each day regaining a little of her old self. They'd laughed lots and cooked together most evenings. Occasionally, the pair would visit Phoenix for some much-needed retail therapy. It had been a carefree time without the crushing anxiety caused by the prospect of being branded a killer. Anna had experienced a first glimmer of happiness, but the future also demanded a direction beyond larking around. And her big sis had obviously decided that time had come.

Am I ready?

Getting a part-time job would be relatively easy here, with Scottsdale so close to the city. All she needed was enough money to cover her classes and pay rent to Julia, who'd already made it clear that she could stay as long as necessary. College, however, hadn't occurred to Anna during the years since leaving high school.

Looking back, Julia had always been the academic one, and their parents had naturally encouraged her, rather than their shyer younger daughter. Anna really did want to learn, though, and not least because of her dream to be an author. As a kid, she'd kept a journal and had even submitted some short stories for publication in various magazines. Of course, they'd all been rejected, which stifled any resolve to keep trying.

Maybe this is the right time to change that?

The possibilities seemed tantalizing. Previously, she'd never considered what the world might offer beyond the dispiriting confines of waitressing in Kingman. These past weeks offered the hope of a different future. But, the question lingered: what form would her future take?

"Let's do it," Anna said.

THE FOLLOWING WEEKS became a heady mix of planning and unknowns. She'd found a suitable English course with the pretentious name: "The Experience of Writing." Despite Julia's reservations that the title made it sound like "politically correct bullshit," Anna liked the syllabus, which included an interesting blend of creative writing and journalism. She went with her gut and signed up.

On the day her entry exam results were due, Julia returned from the post box looking subdued. She held an official-looking envelope stamped "Private and Confidential: Arizona Department of Education." Clearly, the contents had already been viewed.

Anna's heart sank because her sister's body language spoke volumes. Suddenly, however, Julia's solemn expression changed to a wide grin. "You're in!" She said.

Anna could barely contain her excitement; she would get

her chance to be an author. They celebrated by sharing a whole tub of double chocolate chip ice cream while watching re-runs of old comedy shows.

The morning after, Anna made an early start in front of the PC. She sipped from a steaming cup of Americano while scrolling through endless dead-end waitress jobs. The depressing list only served to dredge up unwelcome memories of fat Audrey. But, ironically, they also offered her the best chance of making a successful application. Her other dilemma came from the meagre wages on offer, which would never be enough to cover her college fees, let alone contribute toward her keep.

Numerous call centers were scattered across town, making customer service another possibility. They paid better money, and she wouldn't be on her feet all day. By late morning, she'd dismissed the scams promising huge rewards for little effort, to be left with few real opportunities. The unfortunate conclusion loomed that she'd be living off her sister for the foreseeable future.

She was about to give up when an ad for an entry level personal assistant at a local attorney's office caught her eye. The hours seemed perfect, and surprisingly, they did not ask for previous experience. Hearing Julia's car pull up outside, she decided to ask her opinion.

"Hey, sweetie," Julia greeted her as she walked into the living room. She looked great today in a cream pantsuit which contrasted well with her dark curls. Her role as a real estate agent demanded a professional look.

"What do you think of this?" Anna ushered her over, pointing at the screen.

Big Bird looked over the ad and nodded. "Perfect. You can type, and you're great with people. I say go for it! Why not?"

Seizing the moment, Anna picked up the landline handset beside the monitor and dialled the number on screen. The following ring tone served as a late reminder that she'd not made any preparation for the conversation. Before she had the opportunity to chicken out, though, a pleasant female voice answered.

"Good morning. Howard and Moyer, attorneys at law. How may I help you?"

Anna's throat suddenly felt dry, and she hesitated to speak. But a pointed look from Julia soon put a stop to that.

"Oh, hello. My name is Anna Price. I'm calling about the ad on The Gazette website for a legal assistant," she said, hoping her question sounded calmer than she felt. Julia didn't help matters by pulling a comical face to signal how she felt about Anna's posh phone voice.

"Right. Well, we've had a lot of people call already. Hmm... the only time I could fit you in for an interview would be tomorrow morning at nine."

Holy shit, Anna thought. *That's all? No "Please submit your resume?"*

Without time to think further, she found herself saying, "Perfect." After noting the details of the location in town, she hung up the phone. "Nine AM tomorrow," Anna confirmed with a smile... "Nine AM tomorrow!" She repeated with alarm. "I'm not ready for an interview."

Julia, however, eyed Anna speculatively.

"Let's go shopping." They said in unison.

Julia grabbed her credit card and pulled Anna out the door without saying another word. Finally, they'd gotten the kind of challenge the Price girls excelled at: finding a good dress and a decent hair stylist.

"We're getting proper branded stuff," Julia said, matter-of-fact, during the drive into Scottsdale center.

"You're not spending that much on me," Anna replied.

"On the contrary, my dear, you're going to get the job, and I'm not going to let you walk into the interview looking like the kind of woman who gets a second dress free with every purchase."

Anna knew from experience that there was little point in raising an objection. She would be turned into a designer pin-up whether she liked it or not. The insistent nature of Julia's generosity conjured pleasant memories of Mom and her elder sister each refusing to allow the other to pay for coffee during one of their legendary—not to mention embarrassing—standoffs.

The mall seemed close to empty, way too expensive, and filled with the latest fashions—not that it mattered. Of course, her sibling organized the next hour like a well-rehearsed military campaign. Mission priority one: find a killer interview outfit. She had a theory to guarantee success, namely: picking something "tight, but not too slutty." Not wishing to curb her sister's obvious enthusiasm for the task, Anna didn't dare question the dubious sexual politics of the plan. Instead, she found herself being indulged and loving it.

They came to a fancy looking store front lined with size-zero mannequins, which made Anna feel inadequate. "Perfect," Julia said, leading them in without further discussion.

Anna's sense of being out of place wasn't helped by the immaculately presented clerk, who had the figure of an eight-year-old boy and gave her a sour look that said: "You're not good enough to be in my shop."

Julia pulled her into the corner. "You're beautiful, period. Does madam comprehend?" Her voice left no room for argument. "Don't take any notice of Miss Fancy Pants— the woman's probably a fem bot," she whispered, obviously sensing her hesitation.

"What the fuck is a fem bot?"

"Half-woman, half-robot... with machine guns for tits." Julia made a shooting gesture with her breasts, making them both giggle while causing the frown to deepen on the clerk's dour face.

"I trust you," Anna said more seriously, feeling another wave of affection for her wonderful Big Bird.

"Good. Now, come over here," Julia replied, pointing to a well-stocked clothing rack. "We're not leaving until we find something."

Anna tried a slinky, red dress first, but, after looking in the mirror, she concluded that it appeared a little too tight around her bony butt. *I wish I'd gotten a curvy frame,* she thought in frustration.

An hour later, they'd scoured the store, trying various combinations before settling on a gorgeous black pant suit. "It shouts 'look, but don't touch.'" Julia approved, before helping her select underwear and a dainty pair of platform shoes to complete the look.

Just when Anna thought they were done, Big Bird insisted that their mission wouldn't be complete without a makeover. So, clutching a half-dozen bags filled with their booty, they proceeded to find a stylist on the lower floor of the shopping complex.

Upon entering, they were greeted by a flamboyant male couple who introduced themselves as Georgios and Theo. Much to Anna's secret amusement, they had complimentary hairstyles featuring long side partings. Georgios' was colored blue and parted to the left, while Theo's was red and parted to the right.

The warm welcome put their anxious client at ease, and Anna buried herself in a style magazine, looking for inspiration from the latest fashions. But despite the guide, the sheer number of choices on offer overwhelmed her to the point that she asked for a simple trim. She noticed Julia give a slight shake of the head, though, and Theo nodded solemnly in agreement. Wimping out was not an option.

As the transformation got underway, the positive attitude of the eccentric pair became infectious. Anna began to relax and enjoy the experience.

SHE DIDN'T dare look in the mirror, but, after a few words of encouragement from her new style gurus, she found the courage to view the fruits of their labor.

It seemed incredible: the woman staring back from the mirror was not recognizable as the bedraggled creature that had fled Kingman. Her hair had been crafted into a wavy bob framing her blue twinkling eyes. Not only that, but the indulgent time spent alongside Julia's passion for good food had given her cheeks a rosier appearance. She smiled, finally, gaining an audible sigh of relief from the others.

Chapter 6

IN AT THE DEEP END

Julia's borrowed silver Chevy pulled up outside the large, nineteenth century-period building with a grace her own station wagon would have flunked completely. Thankful for the small victory, Anna gathered her thoughts.

You can do this, she reminded herself, refusing to listen to a lingering voice of doubt.

Taking a deep breath, she walked over to the heavy, black door. An embossed brass plaque on its lacquered surface, read: "Howard and Moyer, attorneys at law. Est. 1866."

She pushed against the large door-knocker, struggling against the weight of the heavy frame. With an unladylike amount of effort, the door grudgingly gave way to reveal a reception area. The walls had been inlaid with old-fashioned wooden panelling and were decorated with portraits of presumably long-dead lawyers. They stared on disap-

LEE ALAN

provingly. A faded, green carpet ran down the center of the forbidding room, completing a vision speaking of former glories.

A surly looking older woman with an unusual white streak running through the center of her jet black hair sat behind the reception desk, eyeing her through rounded spectacles. Anna suspected this was not the pleasant young woman she had spoken to on the phone.

Great: Cruella Deville. Just my luck, she thought.

"Can I help you?" The receptionist's east coast accent sounded shrill.

"I have a nine o'clock interview," Anna replied while smiling.

"The position's been filled," Cruella said, with a long, grey hair sprouting unattractively from her chin.

Anna felt crushed by the news, but she refused to give in to the old bag just yet.

"I'll take a seat while you confirm that." Her sugary composure didn't drop, despite the defiant edge to the statement.

The receptionist sucked her lips to the point that Anna expected a lemon to drop from her mouth.

What's her problem? She wondered, realizing that the petulant display went beyond common bad manners.

Five long minutes passed while the receptionist furiously typed and generally did her best to ignore the unwelcome intrusion. In the end, the acid-tongued woman rose and, with an audible sigh, exited the room via an adjoining door. She'd evidently concluded that the problem wouldn't solve itself. Shortly after, Anna could hear a muffled conversation, with one of the voices sounding male. Although she couldn't make out the precise words, the exchange was heated.

Cruella returned with a look of profound disapproval on her leathery features.

Yowzer: looks like the puppies got away, Anna reflected with growing hope.

"Mr. Moyer will see you now," the receptionist declared before sitting back at her desk, obviously flustered.

"Thank you," Anna said in a calm voice she knew the other woman would find infuriating. Savoring the small triumph, she led herself through the office door, only to find the positive vibe to be short-lived.

Bill Moyer, attorney at law, was an aging man with pock-marked skin and the most bizarre-looking dyed black comb-over. Below his red, perspiring face, he wore a geode bolo tie, just like the ones in old western movies. Anna observed him from the doorway for a moment, speculating that there was something familiar about the guy she couldn't quite place. But in the time it took to stride over to his large, cluttered desk, she recognized that he was the law cowboy from a long-running TV commercial. His signature theme consisted of declaring, "Bill Moyer: I am the law," in a heavy, southern drawl while bestride a massive, white stallion. She'd always found the ads more than a little cheesy.

Jesus, this guy couldn't ride a cart horse, never mind a regular sized one, she thought, resisting the urge to laugh out loud at the mental image of the sweaty, little man weighing down the smaller animal.

Presently, he sprawled in a leather recliner, not bothering to rise. Behind him, the heads of several stuffed creatures had been hung on the wall. Most of which, seemed to hold the same expression as the stuffy parade of former attorneys in the lobby.

Mr. Moyer looked her up and down, his expression of disinterest disappearing. "Résumé?" The abrupt command emerged from a mouth filled with bright, white dentures that appeared way too large for his face.

Anna reached into her new Calvin Klein bag and produced the document she'd thrown together the previous night. He half-snatched it from her outstretched hand before proceeding to lean back in his brown leather recliner. After giving her a creepy wink, he scanned the paper with beady, little eyes.

"Waitress, huh?" He asked, his cocky smirk irritating her.

"For six years."

The lawyer dropped the document onto his desk after a few seconds and then fixed his hands behind his sweaty head. He stared up at a stuffed deer, as if it were the subject of the interview, rather than her.

After a minute of this awkward interlude, he pulled himself forward to face Anna again. "Lucky for you, I need somebody right away," he said, talking to her breasts rather than her face. "No offense, Miss…?"

"Price. An—"

"No offense intended, Miss Price, but my clients need something pleasant to look at when they arrive. As I'm sure you've already noticed, Blanche is about as welcoming as a mule having its balls squeezed." He smiled to himself, evidently finding his coarseness amusing.

"Oh, but I'm sure I spoke to someone else when I called about the position?" She replied, deciding to change the subject, rather than respond to his repulsive manner. "Someone other than Cru—Blanche, I mean."

"Jenny only works Tuesdays," he answered, waving his plump hand at such trivialities. "Yes, I think you'll do fine," he concluded, sucking his huge teeth.

Although she felt like slapping the filthy, old toad, Anna thanked him for the opportunity. *You can handle this one,* she thought, her urgent need for a paycheck outweighing the prospect of his sleazy attentions.

"Good. You start tomorrow at nine. Blanche will fill you in with the details," he replied, dismissing her with another arrogant wave of the hand. While leaving the lawyer's toxic presence, she could almost feel his gaze on her rear.

Blanche didn't seem surprised in the slightest when Anna announced the news. "As I'm sure Mr. Moyer explained, I am needed for more important legal support work. So, a more junior person is needed to cover the reception area," she said, obviously having been spun a line by her employer.

Anna didn't bother to contradict and instead asked for

any relevant paperwork. Blanche thrust an employment contract before her in response. While Anna signed the document, she reflected on the unwanted attention of Bill Moyer. It remained a concern, but she also felt certain he wasn't fit or young enough to pose a real threat. On the plus side, the job would offer far better pay than the poor earnings of the diner, and the part-time hours fitted with the schedule for her forthcoming English course.

That evening, she celebrated in the local bars with Julia, sensing her new life starting to take shape. But, as they laughed over too many tequila shots, Anna realized that one unfulfilled aspect of her days bothered her more than she cared to admit: she felt lonely. Although she treasured the time spent with her wonderful sister, Julia couldn't replace the love of a good man.

THE NEXT MORNING, Anna barely made it to the office in time after sleeping through her morning alarm. With the help of her hungover big sis, she managed to walk through the heavy black doors of the old building just in time. It became clear, however, that her concerns about being late were unfounded, because the building appeared empty, including the reception area, which had been left unattended without so much as a note of guidance. Whoever had opened up seemed long gone.

Unsure of what to do, she decided to seek help from Mr.

Moyer. But after finding his office door locked without signs of activity inside, she slumped in front of the reception computer with growing feelings of frustration. Clearly, Blanche couldn't resist her petty torments.

"Sour-faced bat," Anna muttered. Determined not to be defeated, she turned on the PC. *I'll just have to wait until someone arrives*, she thought.

A few minutes later, the phone rang. Anna picked up the receiver, hoping for Blanche or Mr. Moyer to be calling to offer a late welcome.

"Good morning, Howard and Moyer, attorneys at law. How may I help you?" She said into the mouth piece, trying to copy the greeting she'd received when applying for the position.

"Hello, this is the office of Congressman Peterson. I'm calling to confirm his appointment with Bill Moyer at two thirty this afternoon," a clipped, female voice replied.

Not expecting a genuine query, Anna looked around for any kind of visual clue to help answer the question. Sticky notes lined the desk, but they said nothing about a congressman. And, she didn't have the details to log in to the computer terminal—not that she would know where to look on the system, anyhow.

The moments ticked by, while she fretted until the voice politely prompted again, "Hello?"

"Yes, that's correct: two thirty PM," Anna found herself saying, forced to decide.

The PA thanked her, and the line went dead. Anna

replaced the handset while puffing her cheeks out in both relief and anger. True, she'd expected some sulky behavior from Blanche, but not outright refusal to provide her with any training. Reluctantly, she decided a chat with Mr. Moyer would be needed when he arrived. Not that she enjoyed the idea of giving the perv another opportunity to lech over her.

By the time the portly lawyer strolled in at noon, Anna had taken a few other calls and given similarly awkward answers to the first. Luckily, there'd been no actual visitors.

"Good afternoon, Mr. Moyer. Could I speak with you, please?" She asked as he passed, apparently oblivious to her presence.

He waved her away. "Later."

"Congressman Peterson's office called to confirm your two thirty meeting—and I told his PA that would be fine," Anna called after him, attempting a different tactic to gain his attention.

"You did what?" He stopped mid-stride, turning in her direction. His pudgy face was a picture of alarm.

"Mr. Moyer, I've sat here since nine this morning without any training or support," she retorted, rising from the reception desk as her frustration boiled over.

"Oh. Well… er, I didn't know Blanche…" he mumbled in surprise, seemingly uncertain of how to respond to the suddenly assertive blonde. "I'll be in my office, if you need me," he added before retreating toward his room with haste.

Just as Anna was about to protest further, the phone

rang again. With an exasperated growl, she answered the call, allowing him to escape.

The next few hours became hectic. Everyone wanted to speak to Bill, but he'd locked himself in his office without giving her any idea of how to transfer calls. The fact that she could hear him having several loud phone conversations of his own through the door only heightened her annoyance. During one particularly frantic-sounding call, she heard him say to an unknown person, "Got to see Peterson at two thirty," followed by, "Tell me about it—new fucking receptionist." Embarrassment flared in Anna at the horridly unfair statement. She continued to listen. "I'm not sure. He's got me over a barrel, and we both know it." He paused, presumably while the caller pressed him further. "Okay, okay already. Look, I'll think of something. I always do," he said finally in a resigned tone. It left Anna wondering what a congressman and a lawyer could have between them to cause such obvious friction.

The afternoon left Anna dealing with a stream of annoyed clients demanding access to Mr. Moyer. When he finally responded to her repeated attempts to gain his attention, he fobbed her off, claiming he had critical work to do. Anna got the impression that the work he referred to had something to do with his unwanted meeting with the congressman.

THE DOOR to the reception area opened dead on two thirty. A heavy-set man with a shaven head strolled in, followed by another man in a very expensive-looking designer suit. The larger of the two stood to one side with his arms held behind his back. He had the certain air of a security professional. The second man held an expression exuding supreme confidence as he approached Anna. His grey-eyed gaze contemplated her with curiosity.

"Hello. Sorry, we've not met," he said in a rich voice accompanied by an engaging smile which framed his boyish dimples.

"Anna," she replied, her cheeks reddening.

"Pleased to meet you, Anna." His marvellous smile grew wider. He had a strong Roman nose, which added a quirky, yet fitting effect to his features. "If you don't mind me asking, are you new here?" He asked pleasantly. "Unless you've had a lot of work done lately, I'm pretty sure you're not the same lady who greeted me on my last visit."

Anna couldn't help but laugh at the obvious flattery. She had little doubt that this must be the mysterious congressman. "You mean Blanche? No, she doesn't work on the reception desk any more. This is my first day."

His handsome grin widened. "Well, I can't say I'm totally disappointed."

A long silence followed until it dawned on Anna that he was being too polite to ask her to announce his arrival to the waiting lawyer. "Oh, I'm sorry," she blurted, her face reddening further. "I'll tell Mr. Moyer you're here, Congressman."

"I'd appreciate that," he replied, seeming to be unconcerned by her flustered outburst.

Just as she rose to carry out the task, a smarter version of Bill Moyer appeared in his office doorway. He had an exaggerated look of pleasure on his face.

"That will be all, thank you, Annie," Bill said, dismissing her. The fact that he'd still not learned her name left Anna seething—especially in view of his other shoddy behavior.

"Congressman Peterson, it's been too long," the lawyer's voice dripped with southern sincerity.

The congressman turned to greet the lawyer with a neutral expression. "Bill."

As the young law maker was about to shake Moyers' hand, he paused and turned to her, again. "Thanks for your help, Anna." He emphasized the letters of her name, prompting a flicker of embarrassed recognition from the lawyer.

"You're welcome," she replied happily. After the men disappeared into the adjacent office, Anna let out the breath she'd held in.

This guy is something different, she mused. Polite, urbane, and powerful: it was a combination she'd not experienced before. Disappointed the fleeting banter had passed, she settled back down at the computer screen and returned to fuming about her lack of access to the stupid thing.

Her day had become so tedious that she'd contemplated

trying to strike up a conversation with the still-waiting guard. But, one look at his thick arms and severe expression discouraged her.

So, big fella, shot many people this week? It was the only question she could think to ask. Deciding that wouldn't be such a great idea, Anna sighed with boredom, before becoming aware of the rising voices coming from next door. It wasn't possible to hear everything being said, but it seemed clear that Jim Peterson was giving Bill Moyer a hard time— pressing for something. The context remained elusive, but seemed to involve pointing out a few home truths. At one point, the garbled argument became audible.

"How does a junky even run a law firm?" Peterson asked. She blinked in surprise at the revelation.

Moyers response sounded inaudible, but contained a definite note of pleading.

Peterson said, "You know what's expected." She couldn't make out the rest.

That explains a few things, Anna thought. She wondered what the congressman wanted from her new employer. *Maybe he's threatening to fire the pompous asshole as his lawyer?*

The conversation became less heated, then, with Mr. Moyer making conciliatory noises. He said something like, "Please, I need more time."

The last thing she clearly discerned came from the congressman. "Just do it, Bill. You have no choice."

Shortly after, the two emerged again, and a dark shadow

clung to the younger man's attractive features. She noticed, however, as soon as he saw her gazing at him that his expression returned to his previous affable facade. To Anna's surprise, he made straight for the reception desk before placing a white business card in front of her.

"Call me," he said.

Anna's heart fluttered with excitement when she glanced down at the official-looking card. In the top left corner was the emblem of the great seal of the United States: a bald eagle in pure gold, with wings outstretched. In the talons of one foot, it held a sheaf of arrows; in the other, an olive branch. At the center of the card sat the congressman's full title:

James L B Peterson
Member of Congress
1st District, Arizona
(2013 - 2015)

Chairman, Committee on Energy and Commerce

Shocked by the unexpected offer, Anna wasn't sure what to say. "Err, thanks," she said, her inner ego screaming at the goofy response.

James Peterson gave a final, sunny smile, and then strolled out the entrance with his stocky companion following him. Moyer gave a derisive snort after they'd left and immediately returned to his sanctuary without further comment. This left Anna alone, feeling both drained and elated.

Did that really just happen? She thought. *Wow, wait until I tell Julia about Congressman Hot Pants!* The possibilities were tantalizing.

By six PM, Anna desperately wanted to go home. Unfortunately, the sound of loud snoring coming from Mr. Moyer's office made it clear that he wasn't planning to go anywhere soon.

Stop being such a wuss—you're going to have do something, Anna realized.

With her resolve stiffened, she decided to wake the sleeping lawyer and inform him of her impending exit. But, to her further exasperation, she found the door locked again. Anna knocked.

"Mr. Moyer, hello? It's past six. Is it alright if I leave?" There was no response.

She returned to the reception, cursing her rotten luck. *Bill Moyer be damned,* she thought darkly.

After searching through the desk drawer, she found a pot full of keys. And after several fumbling attempts, the office door creaked open. Sure enough, the fat attorney sat in the recliner, hunched over a pile of folders he'd fashioned into a makeshift pillow. He lay fast asleep in a puddle of his own drool. Bill presented an oddly vulnerable figure in his currently prone position, with greasy hair sticking out wildly from his bald pate. He was hardly the image of the high-flying courtroom bruiser.

More like hopeless bum, she thought. *No wonder James Peterson is pissed with him.*

Anna tiptoed toward the slumbering man while the failing light cast eerie shadows across his creepy hunting trophies. She poked his shoulder gently.

"Mr. Moyer..." There was a snort, and then nothing. "It's past six, and I'd like to leave, please." He still gave no answer.

After trying three times, her patience reached its breaking point and the frustrations of the day exploded into fury. Without considering the consequences, she gripped Moyer by his comb-over, pushed aside the stack of documents, and then released the handful of grubby hair.

Thwack!

For a heart-stopping moment, Anna feared the result of her efforts would require medical intervention. But the lawyer's red-rimmed eyes, suddenly opened and blinked.

"Arrrgh," Bill groaned, raising a trembling hand to his temple. "Who the hell are you?

"It's Anna, Mr. Moyer," she replied, relieved that he seemed unaware of her morally questionable methods. "Mr. Moyer, can I please leave? It's late. Would you like me to lock up?" She spoke slowly as if to a child.

He appeared to mull over this challenging concept. While he did so, Anna noticed a discolored glass tube protruding from his suit pocket. Although she'd not been around hard drugs before, Anna recognized the device.

"Yes, yes," he replied groggily, giving an exaggerated royal wave, as his head already started to droop toward the leather-trimmed desk.

Chapter 7
THE DATE

J ulia watched on with a tinge of sadness as Anna scrolled down the estate agent's website, searching through apartments to rent. Although it was the next logical step for Little Bird, she simply didn't want her to go. The time they'd spent together recently had brought them closer than ever. And, to witness the incredible transformation from the broken person who had walked through the door just a few months before, to the confident, young woman blossoming in front of her had been a privilege. Still, she found it jarring. Of course, Anna was a grown woman, and the present arrangement could never be more than a fleeting pit stop on their journeys in life. She just wished it would last a little longer.

Maybe you've come to feel so maternal toward her because Mom's gone, she reflected.

Her thoughts turned to the big night ahead. Anna had

returned from her disastrous first day at the law firm in an oddly happy mood. After some probing, she explained the encounter with her unexpected visitor. Naturally, it was the duty of any big sis to hound out more information. This had produced the congressman's card and, bingo: the confession. He wanted her to call. Three long days of relentless persuasion followed until she did just that. When Anna eventually did, it had amounted to a brief anti-climactic conversation with Jim Peterson's PA. Seconds later, a window in the congressman's calendar had been identified: this evening.

Julia looked down at her wrist watch and noted the time with a small thrill.

"Okay, kiddo, it's time," she announced, trying to contain her own excitement.

"Oh," Anna replied, as if unconcerned.

Three seconds before she tries to back out, Julia thought.

One…

Two…

"Julia, I feel sick. Maybe I should call to arrange another day?"

"Nice try, Little Bird. Up you get," she replied. "You're gonna have a wonderful night. Now stop being a big pussy."

Anna let out an exaggerated sigh. "But what if it goes wrong, or if he's not interested in me?"

"Anna, he's a man. If he's not gay, trust me: he'll be interested." She'd already given the same reply on three occasions that afternoon.

The typing and clicking on the PC stopped, and Anna turned to face the inevitable. Her blue eyes were large and worried. "Let's do it," she said, with a broad grin replacing the look of concern.

The next two hours passed quickly amidst panicky wardrobe changes and intense discussion about her new hairstyle. They both had to admit, however, that the result of the frantic makeover session was a triumph. Anna stood radiant in a bateau neck, sheer, beaded, black evening gown complimented by a matching diamond necklace and earring set borrowed for the occasion. Delicate makeup accentuated the feminine curves of her face.

"Perfect. You show him, girl!" Julia declared with only ten minutes to go. The responding twinkle in Anna's eye sealed the verdict.

Eight PM arrived, and a long, black limo pulled up outside.

"It's a limo!" Julia said, pulling aside the net curtains to get a better look. She turned and flung her arms around Anna before uttering the age old Price family advice when either of them went with a new date.

"Be good, but, if you can't be good…"

"Be careful." The youngest finished the sentence, making them both giggle.

"Good luck, sweetheart," Julia added after the light-hearted moment passed.

"Thanks, Big Bird." Anna kissed her sister and stepped out the front door.

Julia watched from the window as a suited driver emerged and opened the car door for Anna. As he did so, she also caught a glimpse of the congressman.

Wow. Anna's right: he is gorgeous, she thought. A vague note of caution followed the observation: over confidence often came with good-looking individuals. "Especially men," she murmured.

"HEY, you. I'm so glad you called me," Jim Peterson said as the driver opened the limo door. "You look amazing, by the way."

Anna smiled, marvelling at the whole situation. He looked just as attractive as she recalled from their brief introduction. This time, he was wearing a slim-fitting, dark blue dinner suit. Two manicured hands clasped a bunch of sweet-smelling roses, and his intense, grey eyes scanned her dress in a way she found exciting.

"Thank you. They're beautiful," she replied, accepting the flowers.

"Not as stunning as you, though."

"Oh, this old thing," Anna said jokingly, "I just threw it on."

They both laughed while she revelled in the deep, warm tone of his chuckle. The driver helped her into the back on the passenger's side. Anna recognized him as the same large guard who'd accompanied Jim to the law office.

The interior of the vehicle dazzled in a combination of polished, black leather and gleaming chrome. In the center was a small bar stocked with various drinks presented in sparkling, crystal decanters of various sizes. Interior LEDs bounced subdued lighting off the smooth surfaces surrounding them to create an atmosphere of relaxed indulgence. Anna noticed their complete privacy had been assured by a shaded screen between them and the driver. She found herself loving the extravagance, having only ever seen the like in movies.

"So this is where my tax dollars go," she mused, partly in an attempt to break the ice, but also to hide her overwhelmed senses.

Jim laughed again, his tone the same rich coffee. "It's rented," he replied in mock protest. "No taxes, scouts honor." He chuckled, accompanying the assurance with a quick salute.

"It's great," Anna added, eager to show that her last comment had been made in jest. "So, Congressman Peterson, where are you taking me?"

"How's the Pink Coconut sound?" He ventured.

She'd heard of the place: a trendy new upmarket bar in Phoenix.

"Sounds good to me," she replied, trying to sound casual despite her excitement at the suggestion.

The following drive passed in a pleasant blend of light conversation and several chilled glasses of Chateau Laville. Although the journey wasn't a long one, she'd still had time to learn that Jim was relatively new in Congress, having previously worked as a geologist.

"You like rocks?" She'd asked somewhat naively.

He gave another warm smile. "Well, I've come across rocks with more personality than some of my congressional colleagues, if that answers your question," he jibed. "Actually, I had the responsibility of finding new mineral deposits for a major oil company."

The more he explained, she realized how modestly he painted his achievements. According to the online search she'd done on Julia's PC, he'd become a rising star within the Republican Party and associated with many major governmental industrial contracts. Most impressive of all, he chaired the influential Energy and Commerce Committee.

He also mentioned being too busy to consider another relationship since divorcing his wife years ago. Although the statement made her doubt his intentions, she guessed he wouldn't be here, if he wasn't reconsidering a single life.

When Jim asked about her, Anna tried to be as honest as possible and explained that she'd moved to Phoenix for a fresh start after a difficult split. With a guilty feeling, she realized no mention had been made of how recent the break was, or how traumatic the circumstances. Thankfully, Jim didn't press further.

ANNA HELD onto her handsome escort's muscled arm with nervous anticipation as they strolled toward the electric lights and buzzing atmosphere of the venue.

On the twentieth century art déco facade of the club, blinked a giant, fluorescent coconut, which shone neon pink against the azure Arizona skyline. Beneath the flashy entrance, a long queue, monitored by a team of uniformed door staff had developed. Despite the security, Jim ignored the line and led them to a discreet side doorway, marked VIP.

"Congressman Peterson, it's a pleasure to see you." A large African-American bouncer greeted him.

"Evening, Tylor," Jim replied. "My usual spot please."

"Yes, sir. I'll make sure it's ready for you," the doorman replied before speaking discreetly into a small microphone attached to his tux. Shortly after, he raised the rope and ushered them through.

They sauntered into an area denoted by a red carpet, which ran down the length of the darkly decorated passageway. The adjoining walls were painted a smoky black and dotted with silver sequins. After emerging from the hall, they came to a spacious bar shaped like a silver palm tree, behind which an attractive young woman in a gown offered them drinks. Anna opted for a rum and Coke on the rocks while her date requested a gin and tonic. Looking around, she noted that they appeared to have exclusive access to the swanky spot.

I could get used to this treatment, Anna thought, and took a healthy swig of rum. The fiery liquid sent a warm sensation running down her throat.

Shortly after taking their beverages, another smartly-dressed member of the Pink Coconut team appeared and led them up a marble effect staircase. This culminated onto the upper story of the venue which had been decorated in the style of an old-fashioned theater hall. Unlike the ground level, the VIP section was arranged into a series of balcony booths.

The view from their personal terrace was impressive: it must have been at least twenty feet above the dance floor, and Anna could see dozens of elegant tables below, each with a pure white tablecloth and a pink coconut motif. Numerous couples streamed across the highly-polished wooden flooring before settling. Silver cutlery gleamed and twinkled across the cavernous room in a dazzling display.

The main stage was the centerpiece of the club. It had been framed in shining blue cloth with the name of the main act emblazoned across the top of the set: The Luke Marvin Jazz Orchestra. She counted at least thirty musicians bustling and fussing around an array of instruments. The occasional sound of tuning drifted up and mixed with the hubbub to create a heady atmosphere, thick with expectation.

If the floor of the club appeared opulent, the upper floor balconies looked downright luxurious. Each booth had an individual table with a pure white cloth sporting a gold leaf version of the logo, in the same manner as the VIP area. Not only this, but each booth also had its own team to cater to the desires of their clients.

"Would sir and madam enjoy a glass of champagne while they make their selection?" The usher asked after seating them and presenting a leather-bound menu.

"Oh, no, thank you. I have a drink already," she replied, still on her first rum.

"Sure, why not?" Jim consented and downed the gin and tonic in one go.

Anna felt a little intimidated by the confusing array of listed delicacies, many of which were written in French. She did, however, find a few familiar descriptions.

"Would madam care to order?"

"Could I have the scallops to start with, and then the beef Wellington, please?" She replied, trying not to show her ignorance about the other dishes on offer.

"Excellent choice," the waiter remarked. "And sir?"

"I'll have the same."

"Very good," the waiter said, before leaving them to soak up the atmosphere.

As soon as he'd left, Jim leaned toward her. "I can't read French," he whispered.

"Me neither," she confessed with a smile.

"Thank heavens for beef Wellington, or we'd be outed by the food police," he said, conveying an infectious grin.

"I hope you like jazz," he added after a moment of silence, "Because, if you don't, I fear you're in for a long night."

"I've never really listened to jazz," she replied honestly.

"Oh," he pondered. "Well, who knows—you might like it."

"We shall see," she agreed, feeling a little giddy.

Another dazzling smile greeted the reply. "How's the new job going?" He asked, changing the subject.

"Let's just say Mr. Moyer is a bit eccentric," she answered cautiously. The mere mention of her hopeless employer prompted another long gulp from the crystal glass. The alcohol added to the growing glow in her belly.

"Doesn't surprise me one bit," he agreed. "Between us, I think the guy's losing it. That worries me."

"I noticed you didn't seem very impressed when you visited. Are you his client, Jim?"

"No, thank God. But he does represent an organization I care about: people with important work—well, important to the state of Arizona," he continued. "In all honesty, Anna, he could ruin their chances because of the state he's in." Jim took a sip of the gin, which had been quietly placed in front of him a moment before, and then crunched ice between his teeth, while shaking his head.

"Can't you just warn them, the clients?" she asked.

"I wish it was that simple," he replied with a shrug. "People think politicians spend all day meeting in smoke-filled rooms, doing dodgy deals. The truth is that we have to be extra careful not to. If I'm seen interfering…" he left it hanging.

"Deep doo doo," she finished. He raised his glass in

agreement. "So, that's why you went to speak to Bill Moyer the other day?"

"Exactly. I thought maybe I could talk some sense into him."

"He didn't listen, I take it?" Anna was already sure what the answer would be. Unsurprisingly, Jim shook his head in reply.

She'd only been working with Bill Moyer for a week, but she could already tell that the man seemed close to his breaking point. He rarely saw clients, and the paper work continued to pile up on his desk. Of course, she'd done her best to keep the office running, but he'd spent most of the time either getting high in his room, or sleeping off the effects. In fact, she had become so concerned that she'd tried to contact the other lawyer in the firm: the mysterious Mr. Howard. Unfortunately, this avenue was cut off when she'd learned that the senior partner had died over a year ago.

That left conveying her concerns to Blanche. Predictably, the rude woman had reacted with a vindictive lecture and even said the enquiry was "unworthy of a loyal employee." Clearly, her dislike for Anna left the woman blind to any other consideration, even if it was in her own best interests.

"I worry that he's totally off the rails," Jim continued. "I just wish there was a way of finding out if he's doing a half-competent job for them."

This prompted an idea to form in Anna's mind. But,

before she could share it, their sizzling starter arrived, accompanied by a booming voice rising from the direction of the stage.

"Ladies and gentlemen, please give a warm welcome to Luke Marvin and his jazz orchestra!" A grossly overweight guy in a white tuxedo announced.

A huge round of applause went up from the audience, in which Anna joined. The group of musicians on the stage bowed in unison, led by an elderly-looking man in a purple, velvet suit dotted with flashing sequins.

At first, she found it difficult to concentrate on the performance, distracted by the mouth-watering smell of the scallops. The orchestra, however, soon dropped into a mellow rhythm, complementing the meal. In fact, the food tasted so good that she had to stop from exclaiming out loud when tasting the delicate flavors of the shellfish which were mixed with a refreshing mint and pea puree.

Anna lost track of time amidst a swirl of sound, taste, liquor, and flirtatious banter from the bewitching congress-man. As she relaxed, he proved to be the perfect gentleman, always asking about her enjoyment of some aspect of the food or music. Most gratifying of all, he seemed more inter-ested in her, rather than talking only about himself. It was a courtesy that she found attractive.

AFTER THE LAST note of the orchestra played, Jim escorted

her to the waiting limo. Neither of them were too steady on their feet, and Anna felt a euphoric sense of glee. As they made their way back down the marble staircase, she reveled in a wonderful night. They both giggled and staggered out into the sultry, open air to find Dirk waiting outside the main entrance. He invited them into the shining limo and the interior appeared even more indulgent than she recalled. Everything became a delightful mix of colors and sensory pleasures. She relaxed, settling into the luxurious leather, and her mind drifted pleasantly.

"Another drink?" Jim asked, raising a decanter.

"Oh, no, thanks. This girl is all rummed out." She flapped her arm theatrically.

The limo glided into the late night traffic, and they found themselves alone again, separated from the driver by the darkened visor.

Anna suddenly recalled their earlier conversation about Bill Moyer. "You remember how we talked about the fat cowboy?" She asked, placing her head on his shoulder.

He laughed, "You mean Bill Moyer?"

"I was thinking, maybe I could find out what's happening with this client you talked about," she offered.

His hand touched her gently under her chin, and she found her face being turned toward his. "No, that's not fair. You could risk your job. I wouldn't stand for it." While his gaze held hers, she could feel her pulse quicken.

"I can get another job, and the ignorant prick can go ride a donkey," she slurred, her heart thumping.

"A donkey?" He smiled, his mouth glistening with moisture that she had a naughty urge to lick.

Jim leaned down and their lips met. The sensation tingled, giving her a shivering urge to open her mouth wider, which she did. The taste of lemon and alcohol greeted her as his tongue entered. The feeling was welcome and tantalizing. A manicured hand followed, running fingers down the length of her neck. His fingertips moved lightly and with care until they rested just above her left breast. She moaned, wanting the action to continue to her swollen nipple. The wait was short-lived, and they shared more urgent kissing.

His hand continued its sensual journey of exploration and rubbed against her aroused breast. It felt delightful, and she craved more—a lot more. Anna willed the wayward fingers to do just that. Not needing further encouragement, they moved southward, over her stomach, and then lingered. They stroked, as if building the courage to go on. Their mouths pressed hard, his lips sucking hers.

I want him, Anna thought wildly.

Her legs parted until one corner of her black dress slipped over her right knee. Jim's hand followed, and his light fingertips flickered against the flesh of her inner thigh. She found it hard not to make any sound, so great was the urge building between them. His hand continued upward until the tip of one of his fingers brushed the underside of her panties. She gasped, becoming aware of a pulsing that longed for fulfilment. His finger brushed her again, this time with greater force, and she felt herself starting to give in to the insistent call. A thin layer of lace was the only thing between them. The desire to let go of her remaining inhibitions was almost irresistible.

It's too soon, her inner voice said firmly. *You might regret it.*

Hardly believing her own action, Anna closed her legs, making Jim's arm retreat. At the same time, she placed her hand on his chest and pushed him tenderly. Even as their lips separated with one last flurry, she longed for him.

"It's too soon," she said, still panting. Jim resisted for a moment, his face full of lust, but her arm remained firm. "Not yet, Jim."

The same dark shadow she'd seen at the law firm passed over his features: a black, brooding anger. But it left as quickly as it appeared.

"I understand," he said, as he threw himself back onto his side of the limo, his face still flushed from their close encounter.

"Sorry, Jim. It's not that I don't want to, but…"

"No need to explain," he raised his hand, cutting her off. "I respect you."

A wave of relief washed over her. She didn't want to drive this attractive man away.

After their anti-climactic tussle, the remaining ride was a quiet one, with only the hypnotic sound of the limo wheels to accompany their confused emotions. Anna watched the lights of the Phoenix skyline sail by, oblivious to her passions. When she did glance at Jim, he seemed equally lost in his own unreadable thoughts, while staring at the now quiet city. In truth, she wanted him, but, deep down, she wondered if it was him she craved, or to commit a physical act which would finally separate her from Tony. The answer was a mystery that only time could reveal.

They kissed one last time after arriving outside Julia's, but this time the passion was more tentative. She made a promise to call him, and a moment later, stood alone with her soaring hopes for the future.

Chapter 8

FIRST IMPRESSIONS

A s soon as Thanksgiving was over, the two sisters launched operation Santa's Grotto. This demanded the most extravagant decorations for the little house. No bauble could be too large, and no yuletide sing-along tune too cheesy. The credit card flowed with sweet abandon while its ill-gotten gains piled beneath the over-laden spruce tree occupying pride of place in the lounge. Likewise, the porch greeted the scorching Arizona sun, festooned with twinkling snow drop lights. A large inflatable representation of father C, himself, had taken residence next to the ugly, old cactus in the front yard. They delighted at the way their particular Mr. Clause looked worried by the prospect of being impaled on the needles of the prickly plant. Both agreed: they'd created a winter oasis.

The days spent together that month turned into some of

the happiest of Anna's life. They would bake all afternoon and stay up late with mugs of warm cocoa, watching old movies. When the big day arrived, they ran into the front room like children, ripping open gifts in sheer excitement. Anna squealed with delight at the laptop that her big sis had purchased for the start of college in the new-year. Julia, in turn, shed more than a few nostalgic tears while unwrapping an engraved picture of the two of them as girls, hugging during a long-forgotten summer at camp.

It represented such an amazing change for Anna. December had been the worst time for as long as she could remember—until now. She'd always done her best to make the holidays bearable with Tony, but he'd made no pretence of sharing her love of Christmas. It would become an inevitable ordeal with his excessive drinking punctuated by her loneliness. She'd lost count of the Christmas dinners she'd spent without another human being to share the experience. Of course, he'd never allowed her time with family. That was the past, though, and Julia had appeared hell-bent on making up for every single one of those years apart.

Later, they'd speculated on what the new year could bring while lazing on the porch swing sipping hot chocolate. They let out the occasional groan at being so full after the colossal turkey dinner they'd both tried and failed to defeat. The conversation led to the subject of Jim Peterson.

"So, have you guys…?" Julia asked, giving her sister an exaggerated comic wink. Anna shook her head, cheeks coloring.

"Jesus, Anna! Do we have to have the birds and bees conversation again?"

"You can talk, smart-ass. When was the last time you had any midnight action?" Anna retorted, a little more defensively than she intended. "Sorry. I didn't mean it like that," she added.

"Don't ever apologise to me, kiddo." They smiled at each other, sipping more of the sugary drink.

"Anyhow, as I recall, that talk went something like, 'Hey, Little B, guess what? Men can put their tally-wackers in yer and make a brat!'" Anna joked, complementing the impression with an ignorant-sounding accent. This made Julia laugh so hard that she spilled the hot liquid down the front of her Rudolf, the reindeer, tee shirt.

In reality, since the first tantalizing night at the Pink Coconut, Anna had met the congressman a few times. Each date had been great, but they'd still not consummated their relationship. After asking herself why many times, she'd always come up with a blank. Some voice within her told her she shouldn't commit. The problem was that she'd come to trust that voice, however inconvenient it was—Tony had ensured it. But they'd continued to learn about each other, which was a start, at least.

Jim was obviously passionate about his job—to the point that Anna worried she'd traded a control freak for a workaholic. He loved to talk about law and his plans to revolutionise cheap energy in the state. More than that, he seemed to care. This was clearly shown by his close interest in Bill Moyer's representation of the mysterious client. To her alarm, Anna had learned that, if her employer lost the crucial environmental case, it could open up the Tonto forest—one of Arizona's most loved natural habitats —to exploitation by a company with a reputation for sloppy standards.

When Anna related her secret observations, the situation appeared even worse than Jim feared. A quick scan of the relevant computer files showed little evidence that the lawyer had even begun to build a case on behalf of his client, the forest trust. Jim voiced his frustration at the 'pathetic excuse for a man' on more than one occasion. But despite this, he wasn't sure what to do about it, due to the murky nature of the politics surrounding the issue. He did promise to find a way—a statement she didn't doubt for a moment. It felt gratifying to be reassured of how impor-tant the case was to the state, and it made her feel like a sexy female spy in an old movie.

Despite Jim's patient approach, she could sense him becoming frustrated at their lack of intimacy. Not only this, but she found it increasingly difficult to invent excuses for her reluctance.

Hell, you don't understand it yourself, she thought.

"I don't know why we haven't. I really can't explain it." Anna confided. "He's kind, thoughtful…"

"Have you discussed the bastard with him?" Julia refused to utter the name of Anna's ex. Anna shook her head again, clamming up at the mention of Tony. "I don't pretend to be Doctor Ruth, hon, but maybe that's why you can't be with Jim, yet." Julia speculated.

"Maybe." Of course, this made perfect sense, but the same inner voice of caution, which took over whenever she and Jim started to become close, nagged at her.

"Hey, listen: you're worth waiting for, kiddo," Julia concluded. "If he's even half a man, he'll wait until you're ready."

ANNA FRETTED IN THE LONG, snaking freshman's queue at the Scottsville Community College, feeling both aged and more than a little intimidated by the youthful people surrounding her. Depressingly, she realized that, at almost thirty, she was one of the oldest students passing through the college gates.

The campus was an impressive architectural achievement of glass and steel, and each building had its own theme. At present, she stood in a large dome made to mimic a giant aircraft-hangar, decorated with stencilled representations of passenger planes. It'd been given the lofty title of the Theodore Wing. The huge site crawled with fresh-faced teenagers, many looking like they belonged at a high school, rather than at college. As if to emphasize the point, she watched as a curly-haired boy shuffled past, clutching a backpack with an expression of horror on his face.

I know how you feel, kid, she thought.

Stewards handed out maps at every intersection, but when Anna tried to make sense of the colorful pictures of rockets and trains. She found it difficult to navigate her way around.

Could I just have a normal map, for goodness sake? She thought in exasperation, without any idea of where to find her class.

Walking into a NASCAR-themed cafe, she found a group of emo students lounging around in subdued contrast to their chirpy surroundings. They sipped energy drinks and munched on what looked like a perplexing mix of pizza and burritos. Hesitantly, she picked out a black-haired girl with battleship-grey lipstick and spiked, orange eyelashes.

"Uh, excuse me?" Anna asked, which to her own ear, sounded like a parent trying to 'get down with the kids.'

The kid responded by looking her up and down, her grey lips pursing. "No cigarettes and no money. Go away, grandma," she said.

Anna was in no mood for games. Her anger flared, and she threw the map in front of the startled teen. "Show me where my class is. Now, kid."

The girl's tough demeanor crumbled instantly. "Where are you going?" She asked, her tone far less confident than before.

"Woodrow Building, two J."

The girl reluctantly pointed at a location on the other side of the sprawling complex.

Twenty minutes after the official start time, Anna snuck into the large lecture hall. As soon as her rear end touched the seat of the swivel desk at the back of the room, she breathed a sigh of relief.

"As I was saying, before this young lady rudely interrupted, submit your introductory piece this Friday. Nothing heavy—a thousand words is plenty," a blonde-haired man with a short, trimmed beard stated from the front podium. With a sinking sensation, Anna realized she'd just been chastised by the lecturer. In response, the entire room turned in her direction to get a look at the rogue among them. Worse, she'd missed the description of the first assignment. The thought of asking the short-tempered tutor risked further embarrassment. She looked around to find that he'd already handed out paper copies of the assignment to the other students. All except her. With her discomfort rising, Anna tried the white board for information, only to find the name of the professor written in neat text: Professor Young.

Great. Five minutes in, and you've already fucked up, she thought.

But, to her surprise, Professor Young came up the wooden steps and stopped beside her. She braced for a further reprimand. "I need one thousand words on what inspires you to write," he whispered in her ear. A pleasant scent of expensive cologne drifted toward her.

Anna issued a quick "thanks," and then glanced in his direction. The beard made him look older than he probably

LEE ALAN

was—no more than twenty-five or twenty-six. She suspected that the fresh-faced young man had grown the facial hair to project experience. His youthful appearance looked further tempered by a scar above his left eyebrow. Somehow, the slight disfigurement complemented a strangely endearing look.

She removed her laptop from a brown, leather bag, relieved that he wasn't quite as unsympathetic as the first impression led her to believe.

"What inspires me to write?" She typed after loading the notepad.

What, indeed? She thought. *Perhaps money? Or fame?* The immediate answer eluded her.

As the introductory session continued, Anna noticed that Professor Young's keen brown gaze rested on her more than once, while he looked around the room, asking various questions of the class about their differing writing experiences. The way he kept glancing her way left Anna wondering what else she'd done wrong.

Great—he hates me. Way to go Anna, she pondered.

When proceedings neared the mid-way point, it occurred to her that their new professor wasn't the most confident speaker. He often had to backtrack on points and occasionally developed a mild stutter. So, by the time he began to cover the required reading list for the course, half the kids seemed engrossed in their smart phones. A few even sniggered at the clumsy delivery. Anna observed one chubby girl wearing a curious pink all-in-one body suit start to nod forward before falling asleep with a chewed stick of gum hanging from her mouth. The lecturer clearly wasn't having the best day. Despite their terse introduction, Anna couldn't help but feel sorry for him.

The lesson ticked on as did Professor Young's obvious discomfort.

Mercifully for some, the class was short, but he'd managed to cover an overview of topics ranging from literature to journalism. It all sounded interesting to Anna even if her opinion didn't seem to be shared by her fellow students. To emphasize the discontent, sounds of relief mixed with mockery sprang out across the hall as Professor Young declared the end of the class. Anna couldn't help but overhear some of the crueler jibes and winced at the casual meanness expressed. She looked toward the front of the auditorium and noticed that the professor had retreated to a study desk, where he sat, reading a thick textbook in front of him, doing his best to look lost in thought. In marked contrast, however, his cheeks burned red with shame.

Sensing an opportunity to rectify their shaky beginning together, Anna clutched the laptop and made her way toward him. She tried to think of an approach to convey reassurance without making matters worse. The rest of the students left, leaving the auditorium silent, other than her footfall on the polished boards. Mr. Young appeared oblivious of his surroundings, looking like the loneliest man on the planet.

"Kids—they're a pain in the ass," she ventured. His brow furrowed in response. It suddenly occurred to Anna, too late, that people didn't always appreciate their insecurities being exposed, regardless of the intention.

"A tardy approach to timekeeping is more annoying," he replied.

"I'm sorry. It's my first day, and I couldn't find—"

The flustered tutor raised his hand and cut her off. "Look—miss?"

"Price," she replied, tight lipped with suppressed irritation. "I prefer being called Anna—actually."

"Miss Price, do you require any assistance with your…" He started, finally tearing his gaze from the book.

"How do you know I'm a Miss?" She asked, widening her expression to show he was being rude.

To her secret amusement, Mr. Young's cheeks reddened again. It seemed that even a minor social rebuke was more than he could cope with. At the same moment she happened to notice the content on the pages he'd been blindly pretending to study.

"Tell me, Professor Young," she asked, bringing her hands to her hips. "Do you often relax after class by reading about the female reproductive system?" Immediately after the words left her mouth, Anna realized she'd taken the taunt a step too far.

The effect on the poor man was dramatic. He suddenly looked at the pages as if for the first time, his eyes bulging in utter panic. She could tell he'd selected the first book from the nearby shelf to spare himself from having to face the mockery of the class directly. The awkward error added to what must have been an intolerable situation for him.

"I—I, do—don't," he stuttered a protest.

Anna felt awful. He'd obviously had a terrible morning, and she'd just made it worse by petty point scoring. Under the circumstances, she opted to beat a hasty retreat.

"No need to explain. I understand," she interjected, trying her best to calm him. "Nice meeting you, Professor Young. Erm... I look forward to the next lesson." With that, she turned on her heel and marched out of the auditorium.

Chapter 9

MONSTER

He slept on hard pavement using the same rancid-smelling bag for a pillow he'd carried since being discharged from Saint Joseph's. The days had become a blur of alcohol and pain, wandering along unnamed street after unknown alleyway. Above all, he nursed a raw, vibrant hatred, which coursed through his veins, along with the agony. It forced him to exist each countless day, until, little by little, the pain lessened to become a pale twin of his rage.

They say big cities don't sleep, and he'd discovered it to be the truth. His days and nights were a procession of dimly-remembered encounters with every low life this rotten hole threw his way: pimps, dealers, and hookers, for the most part. He'd come to imagine his new neighbors as a rodent infestation deserving of extermination. But his feelings toward the local rats were nothing compared to his thoughts for her.

Of course, he could have gone back to the apartment. As soon as the thought entered his mind, however, hatred for Anna would overwhelm him and leave him unable to function. Over the years, he'd learned to spot the signs when the urge began to grow out of control. Now was such a time; the pressure was building inside, like a volcano demanding relief.

Oh, and isn't it so sweet when you finally do give in, he thought. *But, take care.* Tony nodded to himself in agreement. He knew a release would entail huge risks. *For her, any risk is worth it old boy.*

"Oh, yes, for that fucking bitch," he said out loud.

But the craving had already become unbearable. He needed relief. Something—anything—would do until the time came, and it had to be tonight. Unfortunately, the complications of his situation threatened to intrude on his plans. The vodka he'd stolen earlier was long gone, only to leave the poisonous after-effects seeping into his skull and writhing around his bowels. Bitter experience told him the inevitable withdrawal had already begun and would only worsen. The shakes would soon follow, and then a longing, which would burn almost as bright as his other calling. Pressed under the discomfort of both needs, he knew he must satisfy one to be able to carry out the other.

Tony emerged from the fetid sanctuary of the alley and stumbled to the convenience store across the busy street.

The people of Phoenix continued their daily lives, just as ignorant of him as he of them. Mothers picked their kids up from school, workmen passed in white vans, and thousands of others completed their own daily routines. Those passing the blonde-haired bum did so without giving him a second glance.

He crossed the main avenue, narrowly missed by a souped-up Chrysler. As the car swerved, a tattooed, bald head stuck out from the driver's side and hurled abuse before disappearing back into the stream of traffic. Tony ignored the danger and entered through the faded green door of the liquor store. His arrival gained the attention of a bored-looking young Asian man standing behind the sales counter. The boy observed his latest customer as if he was something he would find stuck to the bottom of his sneakers.

"Excuse me, sir!" The cashier called out. "You can't be here. You leave."

Tony walked straight over to the liquor aisle, pulled a gallon bottle of vodka off the shelf, and then walked past the sales desk on his way to the exit.

"You put that back right now!" The Asian man shouted, his voice quivering.

Tony stopped mid-stride and looked at the cashier. The flustered shop clerk halted in his tracks, seeming to be unsure of how to deal with the crazy-eyed thief's lack of caution.

"I call the police!"

Tony remained still, with his glassy, blue eyes fixed. When the clerk showed no further sign of intervention, he turned and strolled out.

TONY FELT BETTER. The vodka had sent molten lava flowing through his veins, making him feel strong again. But he yearned for the other craving. He didn't know for sure where Anna now lived although he had his suspicions. Until then he needed something tasty to take off the edge.

He found the woman at the corner of Thirty-Eighth Avenue. She had a good body with long, auburn hair and long, supple legs. Her attractive features, however, had been spoiled by the cracked, brown teeth of a meth head. The way she swayed on her feet betrayed the fact that her intoxicated adventures were drawing to a close for that evening. A faux fur coat covered her from head to toe. Instinctively, he knew she would be near-naked underneath. Drawing closer, he noted, with revulsion, that the garment looked caked with grease and dirt.

"Well, hi, honey," she greeted him in a thick Texan accent. Her smile didn't quite reach her eyes. "You wanna have some fun tonight?"

Tony suppressed the urge to smash those filthy, brown teeth down her throat. "How much?" He asked bluntly.

"Forty dollars, and you can do—whatever you like," she replied, her tone all business now.

Tony produced sixty dollars from his back pocket. He specifically made sure it was the same money stolen from the small stash Anna had hidden in her panty drawer. *Maybe I'll tell Anna how I spent her money,* he thought, enjoying the anticipation.

"Where do you want to go?" The hooker asked.

"Anywhere nearby," he replied. "I want privacy."

She nodded, took him by the hand, and then led them toward a dimly-lit parking lot that had once served a now abandoned doughnut shop. Tony hated the sensation of her coarse fingers on his, imagining them encrusted with dirt, just like the coat. As they moved into the gloom behind the building, he looked around to ensure no other soul was in sight. The light from the main street didn't penetrate this far, and all the windows at the rear of the shop had been boarded. Overlapping graffiti tags covered the cheap, rotting wood in thick, multi-colored layers. His excitement grew in the knowledge that she'd picked a good spot to allow for full indulgence.

The prostitute turned to face him and slipped the coat from her shoulders. It dropped onto the grimy ground with a lack of feminine care he found distasteful. She was, indeed, bare underneath, except for a pair of black suspenders. Her breasts were large and dark in the gloom, and a mound at the bottom of her abdomen greeted him invitingly. Tony reached out and began to feel the curve of her hips. Her skin was smooth and cool. Instinctively, he placed his lips around her right nipple and sucked hard. It reacted instantly, engorging inside his mouth.

"How do you want me?" She asked. He pressured her hip, making her turn away. "Okay, honey." She agreed, pushing her bottom toward him.

Tony became aroused at the prospect of things to come, and he dropped his pants. He entered her quickly, and she moaned without any genuine conviction. In response, his rage grew further, even as the climax in his loins did. When he vented, his anger spewed forth in union, and he grabbed her roughly by the hair. This time, her groan sounded real.

"What the—" she didn't get the chance to finish her protest.

Tony swung her face around and slammed it into the concrete wall of the building. He rubbed her fetid teeth against the brickwork, making them grind against the concrete blocks. She let out a squawking noise, dazed by the sudden violence.

He forced her to turn to look at him again, her face a bloody mess and her eyes now those of a trapped animal. Tony didn't see the hooker, anymore. Instead, he saw Anna staring back, triggering the final rush.

"Anna," he said, laying his hands around her throat. He could tell she'd become paralyzed by fear, as was often the case by this stage.

All the better, he thought. *Then I'll huff, and I'll puff, and...*

He squeezed harder. She began to fight as his full intentions were revealed. Her mouth opened to scream, but he choked off oxygen until only a gargling sound could emerge. He watched with curiosity as her eyes widened further and became bloodshot. Panic set in, and she tried to claw and gouge at him. He countered by head-butting her in the nose. The pain made her limp, allowing him to continue. Tony observed the life leave her eyes, and a tremendous relief sailed through him. The promise of how it would feel to extinguish the light from Anna heightened his bliss.

"I'll find out soon enough," he said to the dead woman before him.

Chapter 10

CLEAR WATER

Anna stared at the blinking cursor on the blank laptop screen. Several times over the past hour, she'd started to type only to produce long-winded nonsense. Visions of Professor Young and her fellow students mocking her came to mind. Frustratingly, she also found her concentration wandering to his attractive chin, or the way he'd whispered in her ear.

"Get a grip, girl!" She exclaimed.

Despite her hesitation, she felt determined to prove her literary skills. She just couldn't seem to focus. She felt guilty for thinking about the self-effacing teacher while already dating Jim Peterson. She reminded herself more than once that the dashing congressman had been good for her. Yet, here she was, getting all doughy-brained about another guy. She speculated why. Perhaps it was the attractive naivety that Jim lacked?

Jesus, did I just admit that he's attractive?

The mischievous chain of thought gave her an idea: truth. It was a quality she'd always clung to during the hardest of times. From truth came betterment, and in her view its absence led to pain.

My time with Tony proves it, she thought.

While padding out the concept further in her mind, she rose to fetch another cup of coffee. On entering the red-tiled kitchen, she noted the favored status of the room with its owner. Julia had lavished much time and money on its appearance. An expensive Aga stove formed the center piece of the area, with a brushed copper pan set hung above its six gas burners. Rows of neatly-labelled jars sat upon shining, metal shelves running the length of the back wall. As usual for this time of the evening, her sister cooked at the stove while watching TV shows on her tablet. Big Bird removed one earphone as she noticed Anna enter.

"Any ideas, yet, hon?" She asked.

In response, Anna raised a finger in a gesture that said, "Do not disturb, genius at work." Julia smiled and continued to stir the bubbling pot of spaghetti.

Returning to the blank screen, Anna considered the assignment question once more.

Why do I want to write?

In truth, she wanted to reach out to people and tell stories. It offered the potential to influence the world using the power of truth. Running with the theme, her essay title started to form.

Using the Written Word to Forward the Cause of Truth.

SHE TOOK a sip of the bittersweet coffee, reviewed the words on the screen in front of her, and smiled with satisfaction. But the feeling was short-lived, because she remained concerned that, after their disastrous conversation, Professor Young would regard her work unfavorably, regardless of its real merit. With this in mind, she resolved to speak to him at the earliest opportunity and head off any bad blood between them.

THE NEXT DAY, she arrived to the class before anyone else in the hope of talking to her professor before the lesson started. Anna laid her laptop out, ready, along with a notepad and a few sharpened pencils. This time, she meant business. After her initial block, the rest of the essay had poured out to the point that she'd struggled to fit the piece into a thousand words. It'd taken a couple of re-writes and lots of coffee to finish, but in the end, she was pleased with the result.

The class filed in without any sign of Professor Young. Anna worried that the entire lesson would be cancelled. Sure enough, a flinty-eyed woman in a floral dress entered the lecture hall and began to step with great care toward the front. This simple action seemed to take forever, due to her extraordinarily short legs. Unfortunately, the unusual impediment triggered a chorus of sniggering across the room.

"Christ, we're being taught by a friggin' oompa loompa." The unpleasant observation came from one of the same students who'd been rude about Professor Young.

After several painful moments watching the tiny lady tackle the steps, like an explorer traversing Mount Everest, she finally reached the podium.

"I'm afraid Professor Young is not well and won't be teaching until further notice," she announced into the microphone. "My name is Kendra Williams, and I will be your new professor."

The news hardly caused a stir with the audience, but, in contrast, Anna's heart sank. She couldn't be certain, but part of her suspected that Professor Young's absence had something to do with his last performance. The knowledge that she'd played a role in the situation only fueled her anxiety.

Now I'll never get the chance to prove myself, she thought.

Anna raised her hand. Kendra Williams pursed her lips with disapproval, but nodded. "Erm, Mr. Young promised to provide his email address—for our assignments."

"All assignments should come to me," the older woman replied, before scrawling her details on the board.

Disappointed, Anna made an impulsive decision to send her essay to him, regardless. And, while doing so, make it clear just how stupid she thought he'd been for giving up. Without further hesitation, she gathered her things and left. After emerging from the lecture hall, she took out her phone and scrolled through the staff listings on the college website without luck. It looked like they'd already removed his details. *Maybe he intends not to come back at all?* Cursing, she headed for the main college office.

The reception desk had been designed to look like the basket of an air balloon, with a fake, plastic canopy rising above it. She waited in line, trying to think of a way to persuade the faculty staff to give her Professor Young's personal contact information without being branded a stalker. Ten minutes had passed since her initial decision, and with only a half-baked idea to go on, the last person ahead of her concluded their query. Taking a breath, Anna put on her best ditsy female expression and approached the boy manning the desk, while wondering what the hell she was doing. Judging by his uncertain demeanor, she guessed he was a student intern.

"Hi, there," she said, her expression warm.

"How can I help you?" The student asked, in a bored tone.

"I'm in Professor Young's class," she stated, producing a radiant smile. Have you met Professor Young?"

"Sorry, I'm afraid not," he replied with a puzzled look.

"He's a wonderful teacher," she pressed on, prompting an awkward smile from him. "Unfortunately, he's really unwell. We've heard it's, well, serious."

The young man continued to look uncomfortable, and his gaze darted toward a mature-looking supervisor, who was currently in the middle of a deep phone conversation. Anna knew if she allowed him a lifeline, it would almost certainly be game over.

"You see, we've all come together and bought him a get-well-soon gift. The problem is, we don't know where to send it," she went on, grabbing his wavering attention. "So I—we, that is, wanted to take it to him in person." She paused, watching his conflicted body language. "Like a surprise to cheer him up," she added.

"Oh, I don't know if we're allowed to…"

She could tell from his demeanor that he didn't enjoy confrontation and would probably give in if pressured enough. Riding the vibe, Anna put on an expression of crushing disappointment.

They'd be right to think you're a fruit loop. She imagined Julia chastising her silly behavior.

He looked terrified by the display of emotion. "What is it?" He asked, pushing up the thick frames of his glasses. "The illness, I mean."

"What is it?" Her mind raced to think of an illness serious enough to give Professor Young without handing him a death sentence. She felt bad enough about her lies without turning them into something downright sinister.

While waiting for an answer, his eyes flickered to the

older woman who luckily remained engaged in an argument about a late delivery of white board markers.

Think Anna!

"Fibro myalgia of the kidneys," she blurted out, suppressing an irrational laugh.

"Wow. That sounds bad! What happens to someone with fibro minagia of the kidneys?"

"Myalgia," she corrected him solemnly. "Anal problems mainly." It was the first thing that came to mind.

"Ouch," the boy sympathized. "'I think I had the same thing a few years ago. It's not good." His voice was also low, matching hers. "The shits, I mean."

She stifled another inappropriate giggle. "So, you see, it's really important that I get his address, so we can deliver the gift." The kid looked unsure. "Can't you just give it to me, and I can mail it for you?" He asked.

Anna mentally kicked herself for missing such an obvious comeback. "Sorry, I can't…"

He frowned, looking toward the agitated supervisor. Apparently, the supplier had no black markers in stock until next Thursday.

"I can't, because the gift is a… Rolex," she nodded. "It would probably get stolen in the mail." The ridiculous reasoning hung between them while Anna's inner voice screamed. *A fucking Rolex, you dumbass?*

He mulled over the concept before finally stating, "Cool. That makes sense. Please wait and I'll see if I can find his file."

ANNA FELT MORE than a little surprised when the address provided by the intern specified a location in Paradise Valley - the most exclusive area in the whole state, and a favored playground of Arizona's great and good. She assumed Professor Young lived with family there, or perhaps he house sat for a wealthy friend. Without doubt, the modest wage of a college lecturer wouldn't buy a trash can in the Valley.

As her station wagon trundled down Interstate 10, Anna pondered why she'd begun this crazy wild goose chase. She didn't know the guy, at all, and it wasn't as if they'd gotten along. But something about his vulnerable nature drove her on, regardless of the illogical nature of the quest. Even to her own mind, it was hard to explain, but, despite his rude comments and obvious discomfort, he'd still taken the time to relate the topic of the assignment to her. There was a selfless quality to the gesture, which hinted at a different person. Deeper still, she tried not to think about how good he'd smelled and the oddly fetching way he'd turned red with embarrassment.

"Stop it, you silly slut," she muttered. The vision of his lips mouthing words in her ear, however, lingered.

"Argh!" She exclaimed and then turned on the radio.

The voice of Barry White boomed his super sexy tones from the speakers. Anna immediately changed the station to some good old-fashioned Christian fire and brimstone, which seemed to do the trick. It was far more difficult to have naughty thoughts while a self-declared messenger of "gaawd" screamed about demons flaying the unworthy.

She continued to follow road signs to her wealthy destination and reached the outskirts shortly before midday. As a child, she'd visited once on a school trip. She recalled being paraded past increasingly gigantic mansions. Every kind of luxury existed in the valley, from towers of glass and concrete to southern-style plantation buildings. Her overriding impression from that far off day had been the discovery of an ugly new emotion: envy.

As her modest car passed the first of the estates, Anna noted that her memories hadn't been an exaggeration. The level of sheer decadence on display was intimidating. Artificial lakes and private golf courses dotted the landscape, all attached to luxury dwellings. Resisting the urge to gawk at her surroundings like some country bumpkin, she couldn't help but feel inadequate each time a supercar sailed by. Her journey felt like the automobile equivalent of turning up to the Paris fashion show in a pair of mom jeans and a sweatshirt.

The buildings became ever grander, and she felt sure that the information provided by the college had been wrong. The smaller mansions had given way to huge estates, now, encompassing acre upon acre of perfect greenery, sculptures, and water features. The only sign of humanity was the occasional gated guard house marking the entrance to one of the grand houses. She noticed with a twinge of jealousy that many of the security posts appeared larger than her old apartment in Kingman.

She could only imagine the kind of opulence waiting behind each immaculate front because every residence had been screened from the road to provide total privacy. It also made her doubt the theory that Professor Young was house sitting for a friend. These estates were so large that they must have required a small army just to keep the lights on.

After almost an hour of driving through the incredible environment, she reached a guard station beside ornate, gilded gates with the name Clear Water Estate etched across its massive iron bars.

I'm here, she thought. I *may as well see this one through.*

Pulling up outside the checkpoint, Anna put on her best friendly, but dumb look before approaching the uniformed guard who manned the post. She could tell with one glance at his professional stance that he would present a far more challenging prospect than the naive kid back at the college.

"Good afternoon. Welcome to the Clear Water Estate. Can I help you?" Despite the polite tone, his martial bearing shouted ex-forces. He watched her intently, alert, but seemingly unconcerned.

"Hi. My name is Anna Price, and I'm a student at Scottsville Community College. I've been given this address by," she paused, not wishing to dump the blame onto the college for her own deceit. "Well, by a friend. I was told a Mr. Young is staying here."

The guard frowned. "Look, miss. I'm not sure who put you up to this, but Clear Water is a private estate."

What did you expect? She thought. But something inside her pushed aside the sensible conclusion, though. "Professor Young invited me for private tutoring," she lied, her face a picture of sincerity. *You crazy bitch!* Her responsible inner voice protested.

"Just tell him Anna Price is here to discuss her assignment," she added, her smile frozen with effort.

The guard looked surprised. "Odd. Mr. Young hasn't left any instructions to expect a visitor today."

Despite her disappointment, at least the response proved the address was correct. He did live here. *Maybe he's the son of someone rich,* she mused.

"I'm sure, if you just ask, he will confirm it," Anna said, folding her arms to signal her intention to stay until he did something.

The guard looked flustered for the first time. He was obviously more at home with shouting in the face of a six–foot marine recruit, rather than a determined, young woman. After several tense moments of twitching his neat mustache in contemplation, he picked up a small phone and talked quietly into the handset. Although Anna couldn't make out the exact words, she heard the phrase, "Are you sure, sir?" After returning the handset to the receiver, the guard looked surprised by the outcome. "Mr. Young will see you, Miss Price. Please follow the drive up to the main house and he will greet you personally at the main reception area."

Anna smiled sweetly and strode back to her car, hardly believing the ploy had worked. Before she could consider the implications any further, the huge gates opened.

If her tired little car looked out of place driving around Paradise Valley, it looked like a wart on the face of Venus, as it spluttered up the driveway of the Clear Water Estate. Unlike many of the other grounds she'd passed en route, the vegetation here looked very different. Instead of lush, green lawns, a sea of cacti dominated. The desert plants had been arranged into sweeping, circular designs, rather than the random patterns of nature. Each display was a magical array of colors from deep, dusky purples to bright, virulent yellows. Mixed with the unusual foliage was a varied collection of sculptures and columns. Roman gods seemed to be a common theme on display. But unlike the cold, white marble on view in museums, these had been painted in the most vivid colors, giving them a super realistic quality. She marveled at the perfection of the human forms and even stopped the car alongside one particularly beautiful goddess. The painted lady appeared to be lost in contemplation at the still butterfly resting on her outstretched finger.

Anna found the whole effect nothing short of breathtaking.

The paved driveway carried on uphill for a quarter mile, until it levelled onto another incredible view. Before her sprawled a structure she'd not seen the likes of: a dome, but not solid, like the roof of a cathedral or a mosque. It was more like the interwoven branches of a tree—a great living tree. It was pure white in color and streaked with green lines, which gave a stark, yet not unattractive contrast. Light twinkled off what she guessed must be glass set between each section of the remarkable building.

There were obvious differences from the wider estate. Surrounding the structure, lush vegetation thrived—greener and less adapted to the desert. A series of magnificent water features flowed among flower beds and pathways. It looked like a vision of fertility, but, at the same time, an essential part of the environment, rather than an attempt to dominate it.

Unable to contain her wonder, she drove toward what looked like the front of a massive arched entrance. It reminded her of the domed palaces of India and other eastern designs she'd seen in magazines. Anna followed the driveway around a miniature lake and observed a delicate, curving arc of pure, white stone spanning across it. The waters underneath were still, reflecting every last detail of the dome. The stunning optical illusion made it appear as though she gazed upon two palaces. One, living in the bright, blue Arizona sky, and another residing in a darker nether world.

She parked outside the arched entrance, which, on closer inspection, could be seen to bristle with life, including butterflies fluttering among the flower beds surrounding the slender supports of the structure. Bird song filled the air, while she complemented the tranquil sounds of trickling water.

Trying to focus on the matter at hand, Anna opened the station wagon door, while mentally rehearsing her reasoning for coming here. *To demand he look at your assignment like a crazy stalker?* Her conscience interjected. She expected that he would reject her, probably accompanied by a curt reminder of her contribution to his misfortune.

"What the hell am I doing?" She muttered.

The entrance looked devoid of anything resembling human activity. It was more like the doorway to a UFO, or the long-forgotten opening of an ancient tomb. The doors, themselves, if one could call them that, seemed to be a further extension of the branched pattern covering the rest of the structure. Not a sliver of steel, or, a single concrete girder could be seen.

As she neared, the two halves of the entrance parted, allowing a large, red admiral butterfly to wing into the open. The naturalistic theme did not stop outside, but continued inward. It all looked so alien; a small fountain sat in the middle of a lobby area, with benches placed around it for people to admire the view. Again, flowerbeds added patches of intense color to the astonishing picture. Moving inside, there was a definite drop in temperature—not the icily-artificial tang of air conditioning, but like a gentle breeze on a summer's day, ebbing and flowing past the skin on her uncovered arms. The glass panels high above projected dappled shade inside, reminding her of a stroll through a wooded glade. The sensation felt soothing and

Anna forgot her mission for a moment. She closed her eyes and listened to the fountain.

"I did the same when I walked through that door for the first time," a male voice said.

Anna turned to find Professor Young sitting on a bench near the fountain. He'd been just out of her line of sight as she'd entered.

It struck her what little resemblance he bore to the nervous individual she'd encountered at the college. He wore white from head to toe in a simple tee shirt without design and equally unadorned linen pants. A quizzical look on his handsome face conveyed perplexed interest at her unexpected appearance.

Anna struggled to give a coherent greeting, at first, her senses were so overwhelmed. "Nice place," she said.

The understated description brought a smile to Professor Young's face—a warm gesture she couldn't help but return. An awkward silence followed, while her mind raced to find a plausible explanation for her unannounced visit.

"I heard you're unwell?" She asked after a moment. He flushed at the question, betraying his discomfort. "Professor Young. Listen, if..." she began.

"Call me Corey. I'm not at college, anymore."

"Listen, Professor... Corey, I came because of the other day when, well, we got off on the wrong foot. I just wanted to say I'm sorry about what happened," she paused. "I didn't mean to embarrass you." The words tumbled out of her.

His cheeks reddened further in response. *Here you go again, Anna: just harass the poor guy at home, why don't you?*

"Also, I hope the reason you're not going to class anymore doesn't have something to do with what happened," she added.

Corey's expression softened at the statement. *Wow, this guy really is the sensitive type*, she thought.

"And I need my assignment grade," she added, changing her approach.

There was another long pause, and his expression was unreadable. "You'd better take a seat, then," he said finally, patting the seat next to him.

Relief washed over her. A thousand put-downs had run through her mind, ranging from asking why her new professor couldn't grade the damn paper, to flat out, "I'm calling the cops, loony toon!"

After taking the document from her bag, she crossed the short distance to the bench overlooking the stunning water feature. While she did so, a fat bumble-bee buzzed past them before settling on a spotted, blue orchid. She handed the neat paperwork over, surprised at how strongly she felt right then. The whole experience verged on the surreal. Here she was, handing her assignment to a strange man she'd just borderline stalked, who lived like the king of the hippies in a gigantic greenhouse. It wouldn't have surprised her right then if a flying pig floated overhead.

"Would you like something to drink?" Corey asked politely. "Tea, coffee, juice?" The mundane nature of the question broke her dreamlike spell.

"Water would be great, please," she replied, as the long drive had left her parched.

Rather than rising to fetch the requested beverage as expected, Corey picked out a small device from his breast pocket.

"Could I have an iced tea and a glass of mineral water for my guest, please, George?" He spoke into the gadget.

"Certainly, sir. Where would you like it?" An oddly stilted voice replied.

"By the fountain at the main entrance."

"Coming right up." The accent sounded so strange that Anna couldn't place it.

With the refreshments ordered, Corey picked up the assignment.

"You're going to look at it now?" She asked in surprise, having expected a vague promise to read it at some point in the future.

"No time like the present," he replied, already reading.

After a few minutes, he paused and gazed out at the surrounding scenery. "Truth," he said aloud, as if testing the word. He repeated this mental process several times as he immersed himself in the text. On one occasion, he looked directly at Anna, causing her tummy to flutter.

Suddenly, his contemplation was interrupted by a mechanical, swishing sound. Alarmed, Anna turned to face the oncoming noise, only to be greeted by what at first appeared to be a marching child dressed in playful plastic armour. Her perception, however, quickly changed to recognize the newcomer as a robot. It had the form of a human, but with a synthetic head inlaid with two unnaturally large, oval eyes. The body seemed to be a moving collection of interlocking white panels. Beneath its polished torso, gears moved in rhythm, propelling its legs and creating the unusual noise she'd heard. The remarkable machine carried a single silver tray with two glasses sitting on top.

Here comes that flying pig, she thought, calming her thumping heart.

The futuristic waiter stopped in front of them. Corey remained deep in thought, barely seeming to notice he was being served by an extra from a sci-fi movie.

"Ahem. Your iced tea, sir," the robot said, its voice the same stilted tone she'd heard coming from the communication device.

Corey took the iced tea from the tray, and then took a sip of the light brown liquid. Anna watched how his lips touched the lip of the rim.

"And madam?" It asked, swiveling on the spot to face her. She took the glass and thanked the robot awkwardly, feeling like a cave woman seeing a wheel for the first time. "You are most welcome," it replied flatly, the huge eyes remaining on her. "Men are like children, don't you think? You have to give them a nudge to get their attention," it asked after a pause.

Anna found herself at a loss for words, not having engaged in conversation with inanimate objects before. Corey returned his attention, noticing her reluctance.

"I'm trying to teach George to engage in gender-specific conversations," he explained. "It's quite clever, really, that he recognized you as a female and picked an appropriate line of conversation. The trouble is that poor, old Georgie doesn't seem to get the idea that he's a boy bot."

"Poor George," she agreed, still finding it a little too weird to converse with the thing.

Having performed its task, "George," the gender-confused robot, left them alone again, its legs swishing back and forth as it returned to other duties. Anna turned once again to her mysterious professor, to find him reading the last page of the assignment. Her stomach tightened with anticipation.

After he'd finished, Cory laid the work beside him and looked Anna straight in the eye, his expression unreadable. Trying to disguise her discomfortingly intense thoughts, she took a sip of water. The liquid felt refreshing as it ran down her throat.

"Well, it's obvious to me," he said, at last, with a boyish grin materializing on his face.

Anna waited for the inevitable put-down to follow. She imagined it would probably go something like, "It's obvious to me that you can't write, so quit wasting both of our time and get the fuck out of here!"

Instead, Corey stunned her by saying, "You should be a journalist."

She blinked at the handsome teacher as if he'd suggested she could be the Pope. "Journalist?" She repeated.

"Of course," he replied, his grin widening. "It's a no-brainer, really. 'Using the Written Word to Forward the Cause of Truth.' If that's not a description of someone who wants to be a journalist, I don't know what is."

Of course! It makes perfect sense, she thought, stunned by the simplicity of the concept. Even as a teenager, she'd wanted to tell tales of truth and open eyes to harsh realities.

"Of course! Why didn't I think of it?" She exclaimed, and without thinking she wrapped her arms around him in gratitude.

He smelled good, like the outdoors, mixed with something vaguely sweet and inviting. Sensing she'd gone a little too far, Anna pulled away. "Thank you," she said.

"You're very welcome. It's not every day that I get to help someone decide what they want to do with their life," he replied, seemingly pleased by her obvious joy.

"Now, could you please tell me why you are living in a giant UFO? I keep wondering if this is all some freaky dream," she asked after enjoying the moment a second longer. He laughed—a deep, unguarded sound, which she enjoyed. "And don't tell me you're house sitting, because I'm not buying it!"

"Okay, okay," he replied, holding up his hands in mock surrender. "I own it—well, my company does, anyhow."

"Holy shit!" She responded in amazement. "Did you inherit all this?"

"No. My father worked as a grocery clerk for thirty years, and Mom was a typist. This is all my own mess." He looked slightly embarrassed by the size of the implication.

"How? Sorry, but, if you don't mind me saying so, I'm guessing you're not the best-paid college professor of all time? If you are, though, where do I sign up?"

He smiled again. "Well, I volunteer at the college," he began. "Actually, I build something like solar panels."

"Are you about to tell me you've invented solar panels?" She asked, already cringing at the stupidity of the question.

Corey gave another of one those deep chuckles. "No— that would make me about ninety years old," he teased. "Solar panels were a great step forward at the time, but they didn't take into account the most efficient ways of producing energy. That's where my company comes in."

"So you make a newer kind of solar panel?"

"Yep—sort of. Here, let me show you," he said, offering his hand. She took it, and he led them toward the nearest bed of flowers. Bluebells made up this particular arrangement. "You're looking at the most efficient way of capturing sunlight on the planet." He gestured at the pale, blue buds.

"Plants?"

"Exactly. Nature evolved them over millions of years to show us the most efficient way. I just found a way to copy the cells artificially."

"So it's your invention?" she asked, surprised by his modesty.

"Yup. It's not as complicated as it sounds, though. I'm not a proper scientist, really—just a tech journalist with the Phoenix Globe who got fed up with writing about the achievements of other people. I figured, why not me?" He raised his iced tea in a silent salute. "Believe me, the results are amazing: our panels produce twenty times the energy of the last generation ones. They're much lighter and thinner, which opens up all sorts of applications."

"You sold your invention?"

"Sometimes I wished I had—sit back, get fat, and collect the dollars." He took another swig of tea. "I did it the hard way, though, like a stupid asshole, and set up my own company. I've been selling to governments and corporations world-wide for the past six years."

It started to make sense, although huge gaps remained in the story. "And the teaching?" She asked, wanting to know why someone so wealthy would choose to devote time to a community college.

"I miss the writing side of my life, and I've always wanted to teach." He sighed then. "And it's a good thing that I'm a better CEO than a teacher, or you'd be passing me in the gutter on your way to class."

"That's not true," she replied. Something was still bothering her. "Still, why such a grand building? I mean, it's beyond amazing. It's…well, unbelievable."

"It does seem a bit much for one single man, doesn't it?" He agreed. "To quote my PR team…" He cleared his throat theatrically. "Clear Water isn't just my home—it's a showcase of what our future could be. Where man and nature live as one, rather than the current destructive spiral." He pressed on more seriously with a growing passion for the subject. "If we can make a place like this work in the middle of a desert without sucking in all the resources around it, then we can do it anywhere."

Anna admired his drive, but couldn't help but challenge some parts of his plan. "Surely it uses huge amounts of energy and water?"

This prompted another enthusiastic grin. "I'm glad you asked, Miss Price, but please don't call me Shirley." He replied, dusting off the old joke. It was her turn to laugh. "The whole structure is one giant energy generator. Look," he pointed at the delicate branches of the roof above them. "Do you see the green streaks running through the sections?"

"Mmhm," Anna confirmed, shading her eyes as a beam of sunshine cut through the dappled light.

"Those are the photosynthetic panels," he said. "They create all the energy the estate needs—and then some. I'm actually feeding electricity into the grid."

"Wow." She was impressed. The implications were astounding.

"The water used on the gardens is all dirty water collected from moisture traps underneath the estate. This place doesn't use a drop of extra water from aquifers. It's self-sustaining."

"Moisture traps?"

"Yup. Ever seen the movie Dune?"

"I remember something with the singer, Sting, in it, wearing a skimpy leather thong, and big worm things," she replied, teasing his geeky question.

"That's where I got the idea."

"Sting's leather thong?" She liked to make him laugh just to hear the sound.

"See? You've just interviewed me, and you didn't even realize it. Your search is over, Miss Price. Journalist it is."

Chapter 11

SOMETIMES THE TRUTH HURTS

T he next morning, Anna set off to work early, finding the commute a tedious drag in comparison to the revelations of the previous day. It'd been a magical afternoon with Corey talking about her writing ambitions and his quest to revolutionize energy on Earth. His passion had been infectious, but never selfish, as he'd moved the conversation back to Anna and her dreams for the future. Time flowed while they'd talked, and somehow the blue of the desert sky had given way to a spectacular view of the constellations. She recalled with a guilty glow of pleasure the disappointment on Corey's face at the prospect of her departure.

She drove through the bustle of the Phoenix suburbs while her intuition warned of an approaching dilemma. Things had been great with Jim Peterson, but they'd reached the stage at which their relationship either needed to move to the next level, or come to an end. To complicate matters further, now there was Corey. Again, a thrill of nervous excitement deep inside Anna greeted his name.

Oh, dear, she thought, worried by the desire conjured from the simple mention of a word.

The man she'd believed to be a shy, retiring college professor had turned out to be anything but. In fact, after getting home last night, she'd spent another hour researching him on the web.

Corey T. Young had been born to humble roots, just as he'd said. Unlike his vague mention of wealth, however, he'd become the richest man in Arizona and one of the wealthiest people in the United States. In fact, Forbes magazine estimated that his personal wealth now approached eight billion dollars. The scientific community had been blown away by his discovery of the artificial photosynthetic cell, which was now under serious consideration for several awards, including a Nobel prize.

His private life story read like a tragic mystery. Both of his parents had died in a car accident while he'd still been a student at university. This had left him in the appalling circumstance of being alone in the world at nineteen years old. A wave of sympathy and kinship washed through her on learning of such a cruel fate—her own experience of losing both parents to cancer was a testament to that. Many would have crumbled under such ill luck, but he'd obviously used the tragedy to spur himself onward to the dizziest of heights.

Her findings had not uncovered any mention of him having a wife or partner, though—a fact she'd tried and failed to ignore.

What about Jim?

She felt helpless and filled with anxiety. Events had moved so fast over the past few days that there'd been little opportunity to share these complex feelings with Julia.

As usual, she arrived early at the office and began her daily routine in a vain attempt to distract herself from other pressing concerns.

Most of Bill Moyer's appointments had been cancelled today—a situation that had become the norm, of late. Even his ridiculous commercials had dried up, recently, and she'd often found herself alone all day. When he did decide to grace the business with his disheveled presence, he would bury himself away in the paper-strewn pit that had become his office, presumably getting high and neglecting his duties. It was becoming painfully obvious that the once-proud lawyer had lost any semblance of control.

Anna felt certain that a complete crash would follow soon, leaving her jobless and, in the unladylike words of her gran, "without a pot to piss in." In truth, she cared less about that depressing conclusion than the poor unfortunates who relied on her useless employer—especially, the legal case raised by the Tonto National Forest trust. As Jim feared, there seemed scant evidence of a strong case being mounted against the Vaudrillion Corporation in the case files. The implications for the natural wilderness couldn't be greater:

if the trust lost, no obstacles would remain to prevent large-scale fracking.

As a child, Anna visited the beautiful Tonto with her parents and Julia. She still had vague memories of a tranquil ponderosa pine forest with a stuffed picnic basket and the sweet sounds of laughter. The idea that such a wonderful place could be violated was an appalling thought made worse because a hopeless junkie named Bill Moyer had been entrusted to stop it from happening. Of course, she'd continued to report to Jim, as promised, but his tricky political position had resulted in no firm action. With her frustration rising, she knew something needed to be done.

By two PM, Bill still hadn't arrived, and she considered closing the office early, since there was little point in staying. As she reached for the keys, the lawyer stumbled through the door, only to fall face-first onto the faded, green carpet in the lobby.

"Help me up, will ya?" He slurred, helplessly rolling around.

Anger exploded in Anna, job be damned. "You need rehab," she shouted, ignoring his call for aid.

"Fuck you!" He moaned. "Give me a damn hand, woman!" His portly cheeks blew beet red.

Although his tone sounded harsh, she felt sorry for this poor excuse for a human being. Against her better judgement, she approached him and offered a hand. "You need to sort this out, Bill," she insisted, while helping the grunting man to his feet. Without a word of thanks, he shuffled through his office door.

On impulse, Anna followed and watched from the doorway as he fell into the leather recliner. Without noticing her presence, he swiped the papers on his desk aside and produced the glass pipe she'd seen before, clutching it like a holy relic.

He bunged a white crystal into the small bowl and flicked at a grimy lighter, only to grunt in frustration at the uncooperative flint.

"What the hell happened to you?" She asked.

Bill paused his frantic motions and faced her. "None of your fucking business, that's what," he replied. "Don't forget I'm still in charge here, girl. What I do in my office has nothing to do with you!"

"It is my business when I lose my job because my employer is a fucking tweaker!" She shouted, her frustration finally spilling out.

"What do you care? Hmm? A pretty little ass like yours will open most doors, right?" He replied, sneering.

"What about your clients? Don't you care that they're depending on you?"

A flash of guilty recognition passed over his face. "I do my best," he protested, running a shaking hand through his wispy hair.

"You're doing your best in the forest trust case?"

"Those tree-fucking hippies!" The outburst betrayed his sensitivity toward the subject.

"Bill, it's important. You know it is!" She protested. "Why don't you resign from the case before it's too late?"

"I can't!" He retorted.

She found the note of sincere despair in his voice puzzling. "I'm not going to let you ruin the case. It needs someone who is… well, in a fit state to take it on." Anna said, amazed at how calm her voice sounded.

Bill's expression twisted into a grimace. "And what are you going to do? Hmm? You're just a fucking woman!" He spat the words like an insult.

She hesitated, flushing at the contempt in his tone. "I'll tell James Peterson," she said finally, certain that he feared the young congressman.

The threat didn't have the effect she expected. For a moment, he looked confused then burst into an unpleasant hacking laugh.

"James Peterson! So, he's the one diddling ya, hey, girly?" Anna blushed while the horrid chuckle continued. "What did he tell you? Hmm?" Bill dug deeper, sensing her weakness. "Oh, I'm so concerned about the lovely forests and all the cute, fluffy animals living there? And, by the way, why not check out the leather at the back of my limo?" He said, slamming the pipe down on his desk and stroking the arms of his chair in a leery gesture.

"It wasn't like that…" she began, the tremble in her voice betraying her growing disquiet.

"Oh, I'm sure it wasn't." His sneer deepened. Tell me, Miss Price, you stupid, blonde bimbo, did you even bother to check his voting record in Congress? Or who actually funded lover boy's last election campaign?"

"James wouldn't lie…" she replied, knowing how gullible it sounded.

"Jim is a fucking politician, you dumb bitch: of course he lies! The whole Congress is a pit of vipers, and he's the king cobra."

Against her will, the facts fell into place. Yet, her heart still clung to a forlorn hope. "But why?" She whispered, fearing that she already knew the answer.

"You want me to spell it out? Congressman Big Dick is blackmailing me. He wants the trust case to fail."

The truth was stark, making her feel utterly ashamed for being so foolish. "How did he blackmail you?" She asked, slumping against the door frame in shocked resignation.

He picked up the glass pipe and threw it at her feet. The fragile glass shattered on impact, showering Anna's polished, red stilettos with its burned filth.

Her lingering doubts vanished in that final, pitiable action. Every awful thing he'd just said was so obvious, in hindsight. It left her feeling sick with embarrassment at the thought that she'd almost slept with the corrupt scumbag.

Now that his outburst had run its course; Moyer sat hunched in his chair, looking every inch the defeated, old man. They remained silent for a few moments, with Anna lost in her own sea of guilt and sense of stinging betrayal. Refusing to bow to the shame, she wrestled her mind onto dealing with the situation, however painful its resolution.

She'd vowed before never to allow another man to use her, and this would not be the time to break that promise.

"I quit," she said, her voice low. He stared back blankly, his hands twitching. "Oh, and you can tell Jim—his game is finished," she added, the words sounding surprisingly firm.

He seemed to focus again at the comment, and a shadow of apprehension passed over his watery gaze. "What do you mean?"

"I think it's perfect for my first article."

"Article?" His mocking tone was gone.

"I'm studying to be a journalist. Did I not mention that, Mr. Moyer?" Despite the light delivery of the statement, inside she brimmed with outrage. A satisfying expression of panic appeared on the lawyer's face. "Goodbye, Bill. I hope your business gets all the success it deserves." She said before striding out.

"Anna!" He called.

She ignored his alarmed appeal and continued marching to the reception desk. Reaching down to collect her car keys, she also, on a whim, picked up a USB stick from the desk drawer and plugged it into the desktop PC. She copied a file marked "Forest trust v Vaudrillion" and then left her job at the law firm for good.

Chapter 12

THE MASK SLIPS

Anna sat in the gaudy college cafeteria, staring at a freshly-brewed Americano, and pondering what to do. Now that the heat of the moment had passed, the implications of her forthright decision-making began to sink in. Not only had she just kissed her paycheck goodbye, but she'd also made a powerful enemy: a congressman of the United States of America, no less.

Welcome to the city of FUBAR, Population: one stupid dumbass called Anna Price, she thought with a sense of rising dread.

Following the confrontation with Bill Moyer, she'd gone back to Julia's and confirmed everything he'd said. There was no doubting James Peterson's public record. He'd always sided with big business when voting on legislation, even going so far as to over-turn old public health laws. And it didn't take a genius to work out why: his twenty ten election campaign had received millions of dollars from none other than Vaudrillion Corp. The system had become so corrupt that he'd not bothered to disguise the obvious conflict of interest. Worse still, as the chair of the congressional energy committee, he had enough influence to sway the process in favor of his paymasters.

She hadn't spoken to James since the revelation at the office, for her sense of betrayal remained too great. *What is there to say?* She thought. *You betrayed me. You almost seduced me.*

No, she intended to make actions speak louder than words. Lost in thought, Anna barely registered the cafeteria emptying, as her fellow students went to class. She sighed, placing the plastic lid onto the cardboard cup, before heading to the start of her English lesson.

Anna took her seat in the auditorium, still oblivious to her surroundings. She prepped her laptop, considering whether her sudden lack of enthusiasm for education had something to do with the absence of Corey. And with regret, she wished she'd spent more time trying to change his mind during their afternoon together.

"Holy shit. Looks like the oompa loompa has done another tag-team with retard boy," the acid tone of the class jester announced. The words made Anna's breath quicken. She looked toward the front of the lecture room, where Corey stood, scrawling a topic in neat, clear letters on the giant white board.

"Rule number one: a writer always writes," it said.

Again, she found herself struck by the strength of joy generated by seeing him again.

After completing the task, the professor turned his attention to the class. Anna noticed a renewed sense of confidence about him, while he surveyed the waiting audience. Briefly, his gaze fell on her, and a definite smile played across his otherwise serious expression.

"Morning, all," he announced as the room settled down. "Before you ask," he stated, "Yes, I'm back, and no, I'm not telling you what was wrong."

He seemed a different man than the awkward, stuttering individual who'd greeted them before. But she noted with concern, that the offensive class asshole had already raised a pudgy hand to gain the attention of their professor. She had no doubt that the intention was to humiliate Corey. To her surprise, however, he didn't hesitate to invite the malicious kid to speak.

"Yes, the lady with her hand raised." Corey indicated politely without any sign of mischief.

Sniggering broke out across the classroom while the curly-haired youth reddened at the apparent blunder. It was true: the curve of the kids face and his soft hair gave him a feminine appearance—a perception not helped by the grubby, pink shirt he always wore.

"I'm a guy," the boy declared indignantly. More tittering greeted his obvious sensitivity at the subject.

"Oh, I'm sorry," Corey replied. "I didn't realize," he added without any obvious guile. A smirk grew on Anna's face, as her suspicions grew at the unfortunate "mistake." "What's your question?" Corey asked.

The expression of the youth sharpened again at the prospect of upsetting the mild-mannered teacher.

"What does: 'a writer always write' mean?" He scoffed. "Sounds a bit retarded, to me." A wall of silence followed the offensive observation. The kid looked rattled.

Corey grinned in response. "Interesting question—sorry I forgot your name?"

"Ryan," came the sulky reply.

"Oh, of course. I remember your essay Ryan. Hmm, now what was it called?" Corey looked like he was enjoying himself. He placed a finger on his chin, as if attempting to recall. "Oh, of course: 'I Want to Write Stories About Me.'" The sniggering continued at the visibly crestfallen kid. "So, I suppose, considering your main motivation, you need to consider how to find constant inspiration from oneself." The tittering became open laughter.

Corey had them, now, and he quieted the room with a few waves of his hand, before launching into an explanation of the importance of consistently producing prose. Anna couldn't be prouder—it must have been difficult to return with such wit and grace under the cloud of former failures.

Despite enjoying the lecture, Anna couldn't help but wish away the minutes until they could be alone again. *Just to encourage him,* she thought.

As the lesson ended, she did her best to look natural,

wasting time filing away papers, or pretending to be engrossed with her smart phone, while the other students filed out of the auditorium. But with a mixture of pride and a small measure of jealousy, she noticed a group had gathered around Corey, asking various questions. Her internal green-eyed monster observed that the majority of his new fans were female. She dismissed the selfish thought until a particularly attractive brunette with huge breasts giggled at one of his jests.

After several eye-rolling moments of listening to the well-endowed girl flirt with Corey, the room finally cleared, leaving them alone together.

"Well, Miss Price," he greeted her with that grin. "Fancy meeting you here."

"Professor Young," she replied, finding his smile infectious, "It seems you are full of surprises."

He performed a florid bow, which made them both laugh, and then he bounded up the stairs toward her. His muscular thighs flexed as they propelled him up the wooden steps.

"Well?" He pressed with boyish enthusiasm after reaching her side.

"Well what?" Her face was a vision of innocence.

"What did you think?"

"Meh," she replied, finding the urge to tease him irresistible. But she swapped her neutral expression to a matching grin, finding his disappointed expression unbearable. "I'm tugging your chain, Corey. It was great!"

His youthful smile returned immediately, prompting an amusing mental image of a puppy dog wagging its tail. "Woo hoo!" He exclaimed, followed by a spontaneous, silly dance. She couldn't help but chuckle at the ridiculous spectacle. Oh, I nearly forgot," he said, producing a small parcel wrapped in silver paper from his pocket, "To say thank you."

Touched, she took the neatly wrapped item. "Thanks for what?"

"For helping me realize I was being a big pussy and to stop feeling sorry for myself."

Lost for a suitable reply, she removed the silver wrapping to reveal a polished, red gift box made from a heavy material—not the cheap plastic she'd become accustomed to. A handwritten note accompanied it, simply stating, "Anna". She lifted the lid to find a black, leather notebook. A single word embossed the soft material: "Truth." Beside the notebook lay a sleek, silver fountain pen. Its hallmarked nib looked like the solid, expensive kind.

"I don't know what to say," she replied. "But we didn't talk about why you left the class."

"Didn't have to," he said with a shrug. "Before you turned up on my doorstep—"

"Some doorstep," she interrupted.

His mouth twitched with supressed humor, but he became serious, once more. "I felt like a hopeless teacher. You made me feel, well, different."

Without thinking, Anna stood and kissed him on his cheek, her lips lingering a moment longer than

intended. She felt her cheeks blushing at the spontaneous show of emotion. The sentiment he'd expressed
was simple, yet beyond anything she'd received from any
man before.

Awkward silence followed, while her thoughts raced to
the rhythm of her pounding chest.

"Listen, I hope I'm not being too forward, but would you
like to do something tonight?" He asked finally.

"Sure," Anna replied instantly.

"Cool. Listen, I just need to grab a few things from my
office and meet with the head of my faculty to sign off my
return. Then, I'm all yours," he said, reddening at the inappropriate choice of words.

"No problem. How about we meet in the cafete-
ria in twenty minutes?" She suggested, secretly enjoying the
minor indiscretion.

She left the lecture hall feeling light-headed. There
seemed to be a definite spark between them—something
new, and so intense that she needed a moment to breathe
before diving back into his company. Anna headed straight
to the cafeteria.

Unable to face another cup of coffee, she, instead, took
the opportunity to reign in her tumultuous emotions.
Everything had moved so fast—even Julia remained
unaware of just how complicated things had become. As if
to emphasize the point, her phone pinged to announce an
incoming text.

"Hey, Little B. Your favorite congressman came to the

house. He looked v keen! I told him you're at college. Hope that was okay? Love ya."

"Shit!" Anna exclaimed, not believing the awful timing.

She did want to express her disgust to James at the way he'd treated her. But she didn't want to do it with Corey around to witness the end of her relationship with the manipulative pig. Looking at her wristwatch, she could see it'd been a little over five minutes since leaving the lecture hall. Julia's house was only a few minutes away, so there would be enough time to head off James when he arrived and send him packing.

Anna headed toward the main entrance around the corner from the cafeteria. As soon as she reached the aircraft-themed area, James came through the swinging glass doors ahead and spotted her. He looked agitated, and his handsome face held none of the warmth of their previous meetings—the mask had slipped. Obviously, Bill Moyer had relayed news of the previous day, because Jim strode straight toward her. His expensive suit and tinted sunglasses made him look every inch the congressman. She mentally prepared for the confrontation, relieved that he'd, at least, come without his hired thug.

"We need to talk," he said, taking her arm roughly to lead her to one side.

"Take your hand off me," Anna responded, shrugging off his grip.

The heated display gained the attention of a pony-tailed girl passing by and James let go, a flash of surprise passing over his features. Obviously, this was a man unused to others resisting his controlling behavior. He smiled toward the girl and then Anna to allay the tension. His grey eyes, however, continued to glint icily. Seeing that the situation had seemed to ease, the youth continued on her way.

As soon as they were alone again, the reassuring smile dropped with an effortlessness Anna found disconcerting. The real Jim Peterson now stood before her, and she didn't like what lay underneath the shallow, slick exterior—not one bit.

"Stay out of my business," he stated, after checking that they were out of earshot.

"What business would that be, James?" She asked, folding her arms. "The business of perverting the course of justice, by any chance?"

Again, his shocked look conveyed a misplaced expectation.

"Listen, Anna, you don't understand. It's not as simple as you think." His tone was persuasive. "This country isn't run in the magical land of fucking Narnia. Decisions have to be made for the good of all. Sometimes that means breaking a few eggs."

"That's some fucking omelette, James," she retorted. "Sabotaging a court case, so your buddies can destroy a National Forest."

His expression became incredulous.

"You don't buy all that left wing bullshit about fracking, do you?"

"What if I do? How many acres of forest will your little endeavour destroy, hmm? What about anyone living nearby? Do you think they'll be oh, so grateful to the mighty congressman in his infinite wisdom for poisoning their drinking water?"

Adopted a look of naked aggression. "Do you think the opinion of a fucking dumb blonde matters?" He said, his attractive features marred by a contemptuous sneer. To her further dismay, something about the sheer venom in his expression reminded her of Tony—an implied threat that spoke for itself. "You think that anyone will take you seriously, woman? A fucking part-time secretary who dreams of being a reporter. You're still in college, for God's sake, you stupid bitch!" He continued with venom. His sudden, alien change of character horrified her so much, that she didn't know what to say. "Even if you did write your 'story,' tell me, how will you afford to defend the monumental fucking lawsuit I'm gonna stick up your cute, little ass?" He leered down at her body as he spoke, obviously encouraged by regaining the upper hand.

"Who's gonna stump up the cash to protect you?" He added, removing his sunglasses and staring at her, like a cat toying with a mouse.

"I will," a male voice said from behind Anna.

The spell had been broken. Anna turned to find Corey standing there, outrage written all over his face. At once, feelings of relief washed over her. He laid a hand on her shoulder in a clear gesture of support.

For a moment, Anna thought she saw a wave of envy pass over the face of the congressman, as he digested the significance of the action. "Oh, I see," James said, his tone insinuating. "Well, let me tell you, Teach, this bit of fluff isn't worth the trouble. She's nothing but a cock tease —trust me."

Corey flushed at the leering comment, but continued to grip Anna's shoulder regardless. "I don't know who you are, but you should leave," he replied.

James Peterson eyed the couple menacingly, but with a renewed hint of uncertainty. He looked at Corey as if trying to recall his face. "Well, Prof, I hope you've got a big pension fund, because, by the time I'm done with her, you're gonna wish you'd never clamped eyes on this dumb whore."

The next moments seemed like a blur. Anna felt Corey's arm leave her shoulder, and within a split second he'd punched the sneering congressman in the jaw, sending him flying onto his back in the middle of the passageway. He started forward toward his prone adversary a second time, but Anna laid a restraining hand on his arm.

Jim sat up after a few stunned moments and then wiped away a single trickle of blood running down his chin from the corner of his mouth. He appeared wary, now, like a cornered rat ready to defend itself.

"I think my pension fund would surprise you," Corey said ominously. "Ready when you are, Anna," he added, offering his hand. Without comment she took it, and they left.

"Do you want to take my car or yours?" Corey asked, as they walked into the huge, adjoining parking lot. He seemed unconcerned by what'd just transpired.

"We'd be lucky to get to the end of drive in mine. Better take yours," she replied, embarrassed by the thought of her sad station wagon featuring in their first date together. *Shit,* she thought, *A date.*

"No problem. I just need to remember where I parked," he said brightly.

Corey led them through rows of parked vehicles, apparently more concerned about where he'd left his car than anything else. While they searched, she found a new wave of affection toward him. He'd not hesitated for a second before choosing to defend her, proving the true metal beneath his shy facade. Although the assault on James would be considered downright Neanderthal by some, she felt thrilled that he felt strongly enough to intervene. No man had ever done anything that brave for her—certainly not Tony in the years they'd been together.

They stopped in front of a black sports car, where Corey tapped the key button. Anna headed to the polished door on the passenger's side. But she quickly realized that the answering beep had actually come from a modest hatchback behind its grander neighbor.

"Sorry. It's not quite what I expected," she observed, stepping away from the expensive automobile. "I assumed you'd have one of those supercars I passed on the way to Clear Water."

"It's not very dramatic, is it?" Corey agreed, opening the passenger's door invitingly. "Trust me, though, I've met plenty of guys driving V8 monsters, and they're always boring assholes trying to compensate for the size of their dicks," he quipped. "Plus, it makes me a little less 'look at me, kids, I'm really a billionaire playboy.'"

"Playboy? Really?" She teased.

"Well, maybe more of a playman."

"Playman? That's a new one for me. What do playmen do differently from playboys?"

"Our dicks are big enough not to need a huge car." He paused and winced, realizing the implication of his joking response. "You get the idea."

"Yeah, I get the idea: you've got a big dick."

Corey grinned before sitting in the driver's seat and pulling his seatbelt over toward its socket. As he did so, he let out a sharp intake of breath, while clutching the same hand he'd hit James Peterson with.

"Not used to socking people in the jaw, huh?" She asked with sympathy, and then took the seat next to him.

"It's been a while since I was angry enough to hit someone," he confessed, rubbing his bruised knuckles.

"How long?"

"Nineteen ninety seven," he confessed. "A kid called Billy Bright stole my G.I. Joe."

"You didn't have to," Anna replied, watching the way the smooth skin of his brow furrowed in pain.

"What's the point in having friends, if they don't stick up for you?" He shrugged. Corey started the engine of the little car, and they quickly left the college behind, only to hit rush hour traffic. "I don't want to intrude on your business Anna, but considering I've just thumped a guy in the face, it might not be a bad idea to tell me why—other than he is clearly a prick, of course."

And he talked like my lover, she thought the unspoken point for him.

Sensing the importance of being honest, she told him everything about her job and the blackmail Jim had orchestrated against Moyer. As she relayed the details, it became obvious that Corey was already familiar with the ongoing battle between the energy sector and environmental interests.

"You're telling me Mr. Butthole is the Jim Peterson?" He asked, recognition dawning. "Wow. If I'd known that, I would have smacked him twice."

"You've met him?"

"I know of him," Corey explained. "My pals at Greenpeace call him Congressman Frack. He's got his tongue so far up the ass crack of Vaudrillion Corp that you can't tell where he finishes and they start."

"Aren't you worried because he's a congressman?" Anna asked, articulating her own concern.

"Hey, he's not the only one with friends in high places,"

Corey glanced over and winked. His lack of fear gave her a reassuring sense of safety. "Seriously, though, Anna, wow. You said uncovering truth is your thing, but I'd expected maybe you'd start with a few sharply-worded food reviews, not skip straight to busting corruption at the heart of government," he said with undisguised admiration.

"It's not like I set out to," she protested.

"Listen, what you're doing is great—seriously. I'm just glad I found out, so I can help. Those Washington parasites can be slippery fuckers. Trust me: I learned from bitter experience." She believed him. "Have you got any proof that he's blackmailing Moyer?"

"I'm not sure," she replied. "I copied computer files from the office, but I haven't checked them, yet. They could show that Bill had no intention of defending the trust."

"We need to warn them," he concluded.

"Corey, you don't have to be involved..."

"No," he disagreed, "We're in this together, now." He gave her another reassuring glance.

Anna's sense of relief was palpable. Here was an ally who was more than a match for James Peterson.

Chapter 13

INTO THE NIGHT

L eaving the suburbs of Phoenix behind, the car sped onto the interstate and into the gathering dusk. A gloriously crimson sun hung low in the sky as the world darkened around them. It occurred to Anna that they weren't headed in the direction of the Clear Water Estate, as she'd expected.

"Where are we going?" She asked, her racing thoughts finally allowing her to focus.

"It's a surprise."

Intrigued, she did her best to find out their secret destination, but, after another thirty minutes of travel, he'd refused to spill the beans. Although the sensible part of her grew frustrated with the game, it felt thrilling to drive into the night with the promise of unknown pleasures to come.

She didn't have to wait long before part of the mystery

unravelled. Corey exited the interstate and headed toward a sign marked "Coolridge Municipal Airfield."

"We're headed toward an airport?" She asked.

"Airfield," he corrected. "It's privately owned."

Hold on a cotton-pickin' minute. "We're flying?" She exclaimed. "Corey, I've never flown!"

"Perfect! You'll love it," he replied, seemingly oblivious to the note of terror in her voice.

She was quickly learning that her new companion had a spirit of adventure so natural that he seemed to assume everyone else was made of the same stuff. Pushing aside her fears, Anna willed herself to embrace the daunting prospect of stepping into a metal can before being propelled into the air at the speed of sound.

Soon enough, twinkling, red lights appeared in the distance to denote aircraft taking off. As they drew closer to the illuminated complex, she could hear the unmistakable sound of prop engines roaring into the air. A second later, the entire scene rolled into view.

A single control tower sat at the center of the hub, its tall body covered in satellite receivers and blinking indicators. A variety of craft could be seen on show, from single engines Cessna's to the sleek jets of the super-rich.

They carried on past the bustling spectacle, and then approached a large hangar at the extreme north end of the facility. It stood apart, surrounded by a tight ring of security fences. Several armed guards patrolled the exterior. Corey pulled the hatchback in front of a gate, which gave access to the mysterious building, before winding down his window opposite a muscled professional manning the checkpoint. His uniform sported a green leaf motif accompanied by the name "Green Gen."

"Good evening, Mr. Young," he greeted them.

"Hey, Jed," Corey replied. "How are things?"

"Quiet one, sir: we've only gunned down three terrorists today," Jed replied, obviously comfortable enough to jest with his boss.

"Only three? I need to pay you fellas less."

"I'm not sure that's possible, sir."

Corey laughed, clearly used to the cheeky banter. "Have you seen the latest weather reports?" He asked, his tone more serious.

"Looking fair, sir," Jed replied. "I reckon you're good to go."

"Excellent. Looks like my friend, here, will get to fly for the first time, after all," Corey remarked, introducing Anna.

"Hello, ma'am," the guard said, touching a hand to his black cap. "You're in for a treat—the Mark II is one hell of a machine."

She smiled politely while quivering with fear inside. *What the hell is a Mark II?* She thought in near panic.

The entrance gate parted, and with a final wave to Bill they passed through before parking opposite the ominous, black hangar. Corey exited the car and walked around to the passenger's side, opening the door for Anna.

"Would Madam care to see her transportation arrangements?" He asked theatrically.

"Madam would," she replied with forced enthusiasm.

He took her hand and led them to a brightly lit control panel on the front of the building. Its digital display read "Authorization." Anna had expected to see some kind of numerical number pad, but instead, a mirror-like interface greeted them.

"Ever seen a thumb scanner?" Corey asked.

"Yeah, sure—I've got one on my laptop," she said, finding his nerdy questions irritating in the face of the monumental task ahead. *A bunch of flowers and a movie would have done, but I got Buck Rogers,* she thought.

"Check this out," he declared.

Corey moved his face in front of the panel, and as he did so a spread of red laser light scanned his chiselled features. Within a split moment, a composite image had formed into an exact likeness of his face on the display. The representation looked so detailed that it replicated the cute scar above his eye. With the scan complete, Corey's name appeared on screen in green letters.

"What do you think? Cool, huh?" He asked, grinning at her with that puppy dog look again.

"Wow," she replied, with what she hoped sounded like a suitable amount of enthusiasm. Inwardly, she rolled her eyes, noting that boys really did love their toys.

A second later, the front of the hangar parted to reveal a shadowed interior. Anna could only make out the silhouette of something large and smooth in the gloom. When the opening sequence had completed its automated routine, a bank of flood lights washed the interior with intense, electric illumination. For a second, Anna's vision became dazzled by the sudden contrast, but her eyes soon adjusted.

The plane looked pitch-black, and its polished surface reflected the surrounding environment perfectly. At a first glance, the machine seemed like the other business jets she'd seen dotted around the airfield. On closer inspection, however, there were subtle differences: its wings appeared to be much longer than its conventional counterparts, and the fuselage had fluid-rounded edges.

"Say hello to HELA," Corey announced.

"Wow!" This time, she really meant it. "Why's it called HELA?"

"It stands for High Efficiency Light Aircraft."

With that, Corey strode over to the barely-discernible outline of a door on the side of the plane and activated another device identical to the one on the outside of the hangar. This time, the access request prompted the fuselage door to open with a whoosh of compressed air, followed by a set of retractable, chrome stairs, which unfolded to the concrete floor.

"Your carriage awaits, milady," Corey said, gesturing toward the interior.

Anna gulped and approached the waiting plane, while supressing the terrified screech threatening to escape her throat. She had the sudden urge to run into the desert, like some crazed banshee, never to be seen again.

The inside of the craft seemed reassuringly luxurious: ebony-colored panels and chrome surfaces dominated the décor. Everything appeared polished to the same high standard as the exterior. Molded against the curvature of the inner shell was a stylish, black couch, surrounded by all the creature comforts one would expect for a wealthy traveller, including an intricate, silver drinks cabinet. Subdued, blue lighting gave the furnishings a mellow glow.

"It's amazing!" She exclaimed, running her hand over the soft cushions of a recliner.

"No expense spared," he agreed jovially. "She's only just passed her final test flights, and you've given me an excuse to give her a proper spin."

"Glad to be of help," Anna replied, wishing he hadn't used the phrase "test flights."

"Don't we need a pilot?" She asked, pointing toward the empty cockpit.

"He's already here, and the best pilot on Earth, in my humble opinion," he replied, with a smirk playing across his mouth.

"Oh. But, I don't see…" she looked puzzled.

Corey seemed not to hear her and proceeded to seal the outer doors behind them, before heading to the cockpit nestled in the oval-shaped nose of the plane. Anna followed, looking around them for the elusive pilot.

Jesus, is this guy tiny, or something? She wondered. *Maybe it's another robot?* She didn't relish the idea of being flown by bunch of circuits.

Anna stared in bafflement at myriad technicolored instruments and data displays.

"Take a seat," Corey said, tapping the chair she assumed belonged to the co-pilot.

"Oh, I don't think I'm supposed to…"

"It's fine—trust me," he reassured, his mischievous twinkle remaining.

She sat, and then buckled herself into the seat with haste.

"Seriously, though, Corey, where's the pilot?"

In response, he made a point of plonking himself into the pilot's seat, his cheesy, infectious grin returning. "You're looking at him," he replied. "Like I said, I'm the best pilot I know."

At first, she thought it a poor joke, until she realized he sounded completely serious. "No fucking way! You can fly?" He didn't reply and just gave a bigger grin. "Oh, hell," she blurted.

"Captain Corey Young at your service! Pilot number five-four-three-six-nine," he said, giving a salute from his imaginary cap.

I trust him, she thought, surprised by the certainty of the feeling. "Let's do it!" She said, unable to resist his relentless eagerness.

"Excellent! Secret destination, here we come!"

"You're not telling me where we're going?"

"Nope, sorry, but I don't do spoilers."

"Argh! You're an ass, Corey!" She replied with mock exasperation, her anxiety levels increasing with each passing moment.

"Better hope I don't fly like one," he said, but the light-hearted comment didn't help her one bit. He proceeded to place a wireless headset over his head before flicking a bewildering array of bright buttons and dials. "We're good to go, Jed," he spoke into the headset after several minutes of calibrating instruments, which appeared lifeless to Anna.

She heard a brief, muffled reply, and then the sound of a mechanism rotating. Her expectation had been that the hangar entrance would open and allow the aircraft to taxi out, but, to her surprise, the roof began to fold away above them until the Milky Way shone in all its glory through the cockpit window. Dumbfounded, she watched as the process of unveiling continued. It didn't stop at the roof—the walls also disappeared like a giant, folding garage door surrounding them.

"You're kidding me! What the hell is this thing, Corey?" She asked, her adrenaline levels off the chart.

"Would you mind pressing that, please?" He replied, ignoring her strained question and pointing to an ominous, red button.

"What does it do?"

"Press it and find out," he replied with infuriating calmness.

OMG! A red button!

Taking a firm grip on her swirling emotions, she reached out a trembling hand and pressed it. Immediately, the previously blank panel leaped into life with a thousand LEDs blinking at her from every direction. Rising above the other instruments, a holographic representation of the plane formed the center piece of the display. It'd been divided into dozens of segments, each one colored a healthy shade of green.

"All systems optimal," Corey spoke into the headset. "Roger," he added in response to an instruction she couldn't hear.

Although Anna knew next to nothing about aircraft, she couldn't help but notice that it all looked very different than anything she'd seen on TV. Corey became focused, pressing controls and performing what looked like a series of preflight checks. Eventually, he stopped and turned back to her.

"Are you ready?" He asked.

The thought of letting him down overrode her instinct to chicken out. She nodded. In response, Corey pressed a small, black switch to his right. As he did so the sound of liquid pouring through pipes surrounded them.

"Primary fuel cells deployed," he confirmed to the listening ground team. With that done, he wiggled his fingers, before taking hold of a flight stick in front of him. "Say hello to my little friend, called vector thrust!" He said, looking over at Anna and obviously loving the moment.

He proceeded to flip open a plastic cover in the middle

of the instrument panel to reveal another red button marked "purge."

Purge! Holy fucking spiders!

He pressed it and the mother of all roaring noises rose from beneath them. Anna sent up a silent prayer as she gripped the sides of her seat for dear life. She could feel a definite lifting sensation as the machine rose gracefully upward. The mighty power of its engines drowned out any other noise. This continued for a few minutes while Corey did little more than inspect various data feeds. Suddenly the upward motion stopped, leaving them hovering several hundred feet above the ground.

"Launch sequence complete—proceeding with flight plan," he relayed, seemingly relaxed about their current status. Corey pulled on the stick, and incredibly the vehicle's nose tilted up at an angle. "Here we go!" He said.

The HELA Mark II thrust into the night sky, like a giant bat carrying one jubilant billionaire pilot and one ex-waitress who wondered, and not in a good way, if she would need a clean pair of under garments before the evening concluded.

THE PLANE MOVED at an incredible rate after having levelled again, and the initial deafening cacophony had subsided. Anna relaxed enough to un-dig her fingernails from the arms of the co-pilot's chair.

"Deploying props," Corey stated, and then pulled a lever next to the disturbing "purge" button.

Now what? She thought, alarm rising again.

This time, she heard the rotation of gears spring into action. In response, the holographic representation of the plane changed to show twin prop engines on its virtual wings. Shortly after, the gentle hum of turbines replaced the sound of roaring jets.

Trying to distract her mind from the nerve-racking situation, she tried to think of things to ask. "You said it did well in testing?" Her voice quivered.

"Sure did! The Mark II is our most advanced prototype, yet," he said, as if it were the most normal thing in the world.

"You mean this is a test plane?"

"Yep. Don't worry, though—we haven't had any serious issues since the Mark I." His attempt at reassurance didn't have its intended effect. "The same solar cells you saw at the Estate power the props," he added. "It's far superior to the previous gen of solar planes. Actually, you're sitting in the world's first hybrid jet. Basically, once it's reached altitude, it can switch to electric flight."

"But it's night. Cells won't charge in the dark," she replied, puzzled.

"High capacity batteries," he replied, as if it were obvious. "They charge during the day. That's only part of it, though: the cells on this baby are so delicate that they can draw power from the moonlight. It's not enough to power the engines alone, but it keeps the juice flowing way beyond anything that came before."

Anna's apprehension quickly turned to wonder, as her gaze drank in the stunning panorama surrounding them. Thousands of feet below, lunar light bathed the rolling hills of the Badlands. In the distance, she could make out the neon, yellow streak of the interstate winding through the wilderness like a great, electric snake. Contrasting with the man-made illumination, the lights of the stars twinkled with an intensity she'd never seen before, framing a full moon that shone like a beacon guiding the HELA to its destination.

"Am I allowed to know where we are headed, yet?" She asked.

"A little place I've got in mind," he said enigmatically.

"Corey, I can't cope with any more surprises today. If you don't tell me where we're going right now, I'm gonna kick your ass!"

"Las Vegas," he answered quickly, seeming to get the message loud and clear.

"Las Vegas!" She exclaimed. "But I'm still in my day clothes!"

"It's taken care of. Take a look in the rear, next to the sofa," Corey replied, looking pleased with himself.

Anna cautiously unclipped her belt and moved to the interior of the plane. Just as Corey indicated, a plain, black box sat next to the sofa. She opened the lid and moved aside protective tissue paper before lifting out a folded square of soft, black material. It unravelled to the floor, revealing a stunning, cut-out dress. The design shimmered, even under the low light of the cabin, while she turned it round under the soft glow, admiring its finely interwoven stretch fabric and asymmetric neckline. A solid-looking gold zip on the back completed an elegant look. She found more inside: a pair of gold stilettoes, a delicate, fringed drop necklace, and a selection of outrageously expensive looking, makeup accessories.

"I'll be," she murmured.

"I hope you don't mind—I took the liberty of picking up a few things," Corey said from the front with a note of anxiety. "Size ten is a guess. It would have kind of killed the surprise, otherwise. What do you think?"

Size ten—perfect. The guy buys me a dress worth more than my car and he says sorry, she thought.

"They're great," she replied, refraining from mouthing the word, "wow," yet again.

"Anywhere I can change?" She called back, deciding to go with it.

"Sure. One second," Corey replied, sounding more relieved than the moment they'd launched into the stratosphere without exploding into thousands of pieces. She heard him flick a switch, and shortly after a tinted, metallic screen folded down between the living compartment and the cockpit. "Just tell me when you're done," he added.

The compartment seal closed, leaving her alone with overwhelmed senses and soaring expectations. She took the opportunity to let out an explosive breath and tried to sort her racing thoughts into some semblance of order. Unfortunately, this process ended in an image of Corey's strong features and a corresponding girly reaction in her stomach.

Can't I just fall for a normal guy, for a change? She thought in protest to her own reaction. *Tummy says no...*

After changing, she checked the result via a floor-length mirror, which filled the entirety of a cabin panel. The transformation looked gratifying: she appeared the very picture of a wealthy, socialite beauty. Nothing like the care-worn creature who'd stared into a greasy kitchen mirror back in Kingman. Her features remained familiar, yet somehow different. She had the same blue eyes and soft, rounded jaw, but they were now framed by the sparkling drop earrings. Her fuller lips and skin glowed with energy. She felt good —real good.

Am I the same woman, anymore? She wondered.

After a time of contemplating her change in fortune, she finally built up the courage to tap on the divide between her and her date. It obediently folded into a recess in the aircraft ceiling, and Corey pressed a button marked "Auto Pilot" before letting go of the flight stick and turning to face her. Although appreciating his full attention, Anna couldn't help but feel a little disconcerted by his abandonment of the controls.

"You look like a million bucks!" He said, and then reddened at his own overt enthusiasm.

"Just a million? That's small change to you, fella," she teased.

"A billion, then," he responded.

"That's more like it."

"Want to see something else cool?" He asked. Anna groaned.

"Look," Corey said, pointing toward the window.

Below them, the dazzling outline of the Las Vegas strip approached, like the extended finger of a neon giant flipping the bird to mother-nature in the inky darkness. It lay before them in all its glory, a mighty collection of bustling casinos and fluorescent billboards. In contrast, the sound of rushing wind combined with the stunning view added to the surreal quality of the experience. It felt like holding hands while flying through the sky in splendid solitude.

Without thinking, Anna reached out and gripped his arm.

Chapter 14

VIVA...

They landed at McCarran Airport and found a bright, red helicopter already waiting for them.

"These things scare the crap out of me," Corey confessed.

"You're kidding me," she replied, taking her seat beside him.

"It just doesn't seem natural. The HELA is far safer."

"You're a strange man, Corey Young."

"I'd take strange over boring any day," he winked.

"You mean kinky stuff? Women with three breasts, and such?" Her expression became a picture of wicked ignorance.

Hook... she thought naughtily.

"God no!" He reddened. "I meant life in general."

Line...

She adopted a phony look of extreme offense, as she

glanced down at her chest. He glanced over and looked instantly horrified.

And sinker!

"Anna, I'm so sorry—I didn't realize you meant yourself."

She laughed, touching his shoulder. "That's for strapping me to a rocket, you asshole!"

He appeared gratifyingly relieved.

The ride in the chopper felt markedly less comfortable than the smooth plane ride. Anna held on for dear life amidst the turbulence, as it buffeted through the air. Only the thought of puking all over the expensive dress was enough to steel her against the unfortunate possibility. They swooped toward a massive, pyramid-shaped structure at the center of the strip. Explosive jets of theatrical fire shot from its sides in a sporadic visual effect that she found mesmerizing, despite their choppy approach. A monumental billboard on its golden, sloping roof read, "The Grand" in thirty-foot high letters. The less-than-tranquil journey ended after a buttock-clenching landing on a private helipad far above the main building.

Anna marveled at the sights surrounding her as they strolled arm in arm underneath a rose-covered trellis, leading away from the landing platform and onto a gravel path, which continued through a roof garden. At its center stood a golden fountain with gilded cherubs cheekily urinating into the pool.

"Feeling lucky?" He asked, while she enjoyed the fresh air and solid ground beneath her feet.

Upon first realizing that their final destination was a casino, she'd been surprised and excited by the prospect of the guilty pleasure ahead. "But I don't have any cash on me," she replied. He shot back a look conveying exactly what he thought of such trivial considerations.

A male attendant wearing a red blazer with a pyramid logo on the breast pocket greeted them. He stood beside a set of metallic elevator doors built into the main structure at the end of the path. "Mr. Young, it's been far too long," he said with a warm smile.

"Luis, how's it going?" Corey replied, taking the man's hand and shaking it. "I've not had any willing victims to corrupt for a while, but I may have found one."

The man laughed and then turned to Anna. "May I enquire who sir's enchanting companion is?" He asked.

"Miss Price," Corey answered.

"Welcome, Miss Price. May I say how beautiful you look." He gave a slight bow. The compliment went so beyond the norm that all Anna could do was smile.

"Please follow me." He pressed a discreet button. The silver doors opened to reveal a mirrored elevator car.

During the short descent, Luis chatted with Corey like they were old buddies. They emerged into a plain lobby, with every surface and wall colored a dazzling, unadorned white. A single female staff member sat opposite in a small booth, flanked on either side by two men wearing traditional, black tuxedoes. Discreet ear pieces emerged from their crisp lapels, betraying the real purpose of their presence.

"Good evening, Mr. Young. Would you care to purchase some chips on your account?" She asked.

"Yes, please. Two hundred each should be plenty to get us started."

"Certainly, sir."

The woman entered a code into a keyboard on the white desk before her, and a cube-shaped object rose from its inner workings. She proceeded to press her thumb into the square surface. In response, a small hatch popped opened to reveal stacked multi-colored tokens inside.

"Are chips worth ten okay, sir?" She enquired.

"Perfect," Corey replied, giving Anna another happy glance.

Inwardly, she felt a little disappointed that all the showy build up led to a rather miserly four hundred dollars.

Oh, well, she thought. *It's how these guys get rich. Watch the pennies and the dollars, take care of—*

"There you go, sir: four hundred thousand dollars. On behalf of the Grand, may I wish you both the best of luck," the attendant said with a smile, pushing the chips over.

Anna stifled a cough. *Four hundred thousand!* She stared in amazement at the twenty little plastic tokens repre-senting more than her entire earnings for the past decade.

IT SEEMED to Anna that an entire floor had been dedicated to a small number of elite guests. She observed no more than a dozen other couples strolling among the many Poker tables, Blackjack boards, and other high-stake games of the extravagant gambling plaza. The décor gave off an aura of supreme wealth: crystal chandeliers twinkled above the opulent, gold trim of blood-red carpets and polished, hardwood surfaces. Sounds of laughter greeted their arrival, mixed with an occasional well-mannered curse. The sense of exclusivity was further emphasized by a discreet team of house staff who doled out free drinks to their pampered guests.

"So, what's your poison?" Corey asked, gesturing at the games surrounding them.

Anna pondered the question while observing an ancient man wearing an oversized toupee, rub a pair of dice against the pouting lips of his young, lady companion. Following the bizarre ceremony, he rolled the newly-blessed objects onto the green Craps table.

"How about Poker?" Corey suggested.

"I haven't got a clue of how to play," she confessed.

"Me neither."

Anna laughed, causing the elderly gent to shoot them a flat stare— presumably for interrupting his pervy ritual.

"Blackjack?" Corey ventured.

She recalled playing once as a child with her parents. "Sure, I'm an expert at the ol' Blacky Jacky."

"You just made that up."

"Yup."

They took their seat at a large table where a bow-tied dealer greeted them. Following Corey's lead, she laid one of the red chips in the betting box. It seemed obscene to be laying down ten thousand dollars on a silly card game. If the money were hers, she would have scoffed at such insanity. This wasn't her cash, though, and there was an alluring aspect to the idea of risking such huge sums on a whim. Beside her and Corey, two other players stood at the table, watching the dealer intently. The first was a grey-haired elderly woman in a flower-print dress, looking like she would be more at home in the local garden center. The second, a serious-looking Asian man in a pinstripe suit, sipped half-heartedly at a glass of whiskey while staring at the main deck, as if his life depended on it.

The dealer began to whip out cards in a blur from the shuffling machine in rapid succession from left to right, before also leaving one in front of himself. Anna wished she'd paid more attention to the rules as a youngster, fearing looking a fool. She turned her card over to reveal a three of clubs. The dealer had turned over a ten of diamonds.

I'm supposed to stick on a number higher than him, without going bust at twenty-one. She thought, dredging up vague memories.

"Hit," Corey stated. She replicated the command, and the others followed.

After the third pass, she'd been left with a total of fifteen.

"Hit," she said. The grinning face of a jack landed in front of her, making her bust.

By ten PM, lady luck had not been kind to Anna. After a series of losses, she'd won a few hands—enough to regain the twenty chips she'd started with. But even that small victory eroded as they hit the Roulette table. She appeared to possess the rather dubious gift of unfailingly selecting the opposite color of where the little white ball landed. Despite her cursed efforts, however, she enjoyed the thrill immensely—particularly after drinking liberal amounts of the excellent fruity wine on offer.

Corey chatted with her between games. "Yowzer! Did you break a mirror today?" He observed, after an especially eye-watering loss.

"Yeah—I looked into it."

"Now you're just fishing for compliments, naughty woman." He slurred his words, clearly also worse for wear.

"I am shameless."

"Shameless and looking great, as far as I'm concerned."

Anna stuck her tongue out.

They strolled arm in arm, talking about trivial matters and enjoying the atmosphere. There'd been one awkward moment when she'd had to skirt around the subject of her previous relationships. She refused to risk soiling a wonderful experience with the mere mention of Tony. So, after vaguely alluding to a split months ago, she'd turned the subject onto his past loves. Surprisingly, Corey had never been serious with anyone—his work proved to be an all-consuming mistress, it seemed.

Maybe until today, she reflected with a smile.

By midnight, she'd whittled her multi-colored booty down to one last, lonely token while Corey had increased his winnings.

"Oh, well, maybe next time," he sympathized. "You win some, you lose some."

"Easy for you to say, cheeky swine," Anna exclaimed, the irony of the situation not lost on her.

"I just don't know what to do with all this cash," he agreed with a mocking sigh. "But, I suppose it's always handy to have a few grand lying around, in case the Estate gets chilly during winter and we run out of fuel for the wood burner." Anna punched him playfully on the shoulder. "Ouch! That hurt!"

"Big girl," Anna said. Her state of being tipsy had long since given way to outright drunkenness, not that she cared in the slightest.

They unsteadily strolled toward a huge slot machine in the shape of a pyramid surmounted by a squatting sphinx. "The Grand - Million Dollar Drop!" The words flashed across the body of the mythical beast. She noticed the machine accepted the chips issued by the house, rather than the usual cash.

"What do you think?" She asked Corey, holding up her last, red token. "I can't possibly do any worse."

"Do you feel lucky, punk?" He replied, attempting a terrible impression of Clint Eastwood.

She drained her glass in one long swig. "As my late father used to say, when the chips are down, Anna, don't take no shit." With that, she plopped the token into the machine and pulled the old-fashioned brass lever beside it. A small trumpet sounded, and three large reels began to rotate. She watched with a pleasantly floating sensation, as symbols continued to whirl for what seemed an age.

Hurry and lose, you stupid thing. I need to go pee, she thought

The first reel stopped on a pyramid. "Cool." She murmured, crossing her legs slightly to ease her uncomfortable bladder.

The second reel halted on another pyramid. "Interesting," she observed, feeling less distracted by her urgent issue.

The third reel landed on a pyramid, as well. *Hmm. What does three pyramids mean? I'm going to have to tell Corey I need the bathroom...*

A deafening alarm sounded from the mouth the sphinx, followed by multi-colored lights racing in rapid succession around the edges of the machine. For one horrible moment, she expected that the two imposing guards they'd encountered in the token room earlier would come bounding around the corner before wrestling her to the floor, at which point she would most definitely wet herself.

"Congratulations, oh, mighty pharaoh! You've won one million dollars!"

"Holy shit on a stick!" She cried in a most unladylike fashion.

SHE REMEMBERED CHAMPAGNE, polite clapping, and laughter —so much laughter that it seemed the earth had turned on its axis and transformed into a world in which bad things never happened. Now, they stood outside her room, gazing at each other. She knew the time for uncertainty had passed, leaving a simple choice: should she bet on love one last time?

Corey's eyes looked dark and unreadable, echoing the same hunger in her.

She reached across and pulled his lips onto hers, while strong arms enclosed her waist. Her body shivered in anticipation, as a feeling akin to liquid fire ran down her spine. His tongue entered her mouth tentatively, becoming more urgent as the need between them grew.

Reluctantly breaking off the physical interaction for a moment, Anna turned and pressed the electronic key against the interface next to her door. It clicked and, without speaking another word, she took him by the hand and led them into the unknown.

She caught a brief glimpse of luxurious surroundings, but the awareness was vague, for they clung to each other, grasping and touching. Faces pressed together with an intensity that caught her breath and left her panting for more. Her hand slipped downward around his firm buttock —a gesture that seemed to give him the courage to do the same. She revelled in the feeling of moving his taught flesh beneath her fingers. After several moments of the delightful exploration, Corey stepped back and gazed at her in the half-light with the look of a hungry animal. He began to unbutton his shirt. She instinctively unzipped her dress, allowing it to fall, leaving only underwear between her vulnerability and the sultry air.

Corey revealed a muscular torso. It called to be touched, so she did just that, running her palm across his strong ribs and over a small birthmark next to his navel. Without thinking, she kneeled and kissed him there. Tantalizingly, she left the urge to keep moving her lips southward. But, before the temptation became too great, a gentle hand stroked her cheek, until he joined her on the floor for more kissing.

This time, his mouth continued to move down her neck, and then further. Guessing where the exploration wished to go, she slipped one hand behind her back and released her bra. Corey must have noticed this, because he moaned in anticipation. His soft touch moved across her chest, removing the last remnants of clothing from her upper body and making her nipples swell. She blushed at such sensations of exposure. Her awkwardness faded quickly, though, for his sensual lips had settled around her right breast. He sucked, causing a wonderful tingling to grow.

Not able to stand it any longer, Anna returned him to her waiting mouth, and then reached down and unbuckled his belt.

"Wait," he said suddenly. Surprised, she gazed at him, fearing a cruel change of heart. "Move to the bed."

Her disappointment turned to soaring pleasure at the words.

They rose together, hand in hand, stepping over a dyed sheep skin rug, before reaching a dimly-lit, canopied bed. She fell back onto the soft sheets, willing Corey to follow, but, oddly, he remained standing. Anna rested on her elbows, staring at him, with longing coursing through her veins.

"Are you ready?" He asked.

Puzzled, she gave him a quizzical look. *What do you think? Jesus, fella...* she thought impatiently.

Without waiting for an answer, Corey reached into his pockets and removed two bulky objects.

What the...? He's into some serious contraception.

Corey raised his arms above his head and threw the two objects toward her. Instinctively, she closed her eyes against the mysterious items cast into the air. But without any noticeable impact, she cautiously opened an eyelid only to widen it in amazement. Surrounding her, a thousand twenty dollar bills fluttered onto the bed.

"Welcome to the millionaire's club, Anna," he said, laughing. "Sorry—I've always wanted to do that."

"Asshole!" She said, unable to prevent a smile. "Now, come here!"

Corey didn't need the command a second time. He moved to the end of the bed and then toward her on hands and knees, his motion sensual, like a panther heading for prey. Unable to prevent her carnal intentions from taking over, her legs parted, allowing him to come within her most intimate space. Pausing between her thighs, he continued to caress her legs before drawing closer to his ultimate goal. Her breathing became labored, while a wonderful tension built between them, like the calm before the fury of a thunderstorm.

A single finger hooked the top of her panties and slid them down her legs with infinite ease. There was a pause, and before she had time to think, he'd placed his face against her groin. It was glorious. He began to explore with his tongue, and something primal developed inside her— something uncontrollable and growing. The gentle probing became more vigorous, proceeding in its quest, while hitting her spot with an unfailing precision.

"Oh, I... I..." She started to mouth a final protest to halt the inevitable, before touching the side of his head with the vague intention of trying to remove him. Instead, she clutched his hair. The exquisite tension built unbearably, until, in a climatic explosion, she unleashed her ecstasy.

It took some time for her senses to re-enter the world

once more, only to be gripped again, this time by the sight of Corey removing his boxer shorts to display his manhood. The need in her that'd been temporarily sated returned with even greater demand. She grasped his member and pulled it toward her without hesitation. He entered her and she felt so beautifully full that her orgasm built with a speed neither of them seemed able to inhibit. He rose and then fell, all the time deep within her, pushing on and on. Ecstasy then burst like a dam within, leaving her enslaved to lust.

So great were the passions they'd awoken that the two lovers clung together, repeating the act many times into the early hours. Anna's consciousness passed from dream to dream, all the time with the closeness of another nearby, offering a taste of paradise she'd not thought possible —until now.

Chapter 15

REUNION

Julia had been more than a little intrigued by the mysterious text message she'd received the previous evening, indicating that Anna might not return home that night.

"The congressman might finally pass his bill through the house!" She'd replied, assuming he'd finally managed to win her over.

"Not with Jim—long story. Will talk soon."

She wasn't sure what to make of the enigmatic answer, but it was unquestionably a shocker. "Damn, girl—you've got another fella on the go?" She wondered out loud. *But who?*

She feared that this might mean some kind of reconciliation with Tony. Was it possible that they'd found a way to patch things up—even after the appalling way he'd treated her?

Maybe she's too embarrassed to admit it? Julia shuddered at the implications.

A large part of her doubted it, though—the part that placed trust in the young, confident woman her sister was becoming. Anna had been traumatized by her experience, expressing nothing but regret about a past spent with a bullying scumbag. Surely it hadn't all been a show?

"She wouldn't do that to me," Julia muttered, taking a sip of warm coffee.

So, what possibilities does it leave? If not Jim or Tony, who? Big Bird pondered. *What about the rich professor guy she came home in a tiz about? Cozy late night study sessions, no doubt.*

Could just be studying...

"It's not the fucking dark ages, Julia," she agreed aloud, challenging her old-fashioned thinking.

But when it came to Anna, her inner curiosity refused to be silenced. She'd spent too long worrying for that. Inevitably, these thoughts led to her contemplating how she could extract the truth on her return.

"Lemon cheesecake," she declared to no one, plopping the mug down and spilling brown liquid over her clean table.

Julia mentally ticked off the stages of her dastardly mission, and then put the plan into action. She opened the pantry and brought out her favorite Momma cake tin, named after the special lady who'd spent many a happy hour teaching her to bake. She smiled, because it was a sunny Saturday morning—the kind that washed away black thoughts, leaving a clear path to the future. Perfect for making the ultimate, badass cake.

She removed heavy cream from the fridge, and then dug out the extra large mixing bowl from the pantry, not wishing to stint on the effort. This would be all out food war and she would take no prisoners. To emphasize the point, she opened the lid off of the cream and dipped a finger into the surface before taking an indulgent taste.

"Yum."

It brought back memories of doing the same with her ever present co-conspirator. It was a habit they'd started in their teens on the day she'd found Anna sobbing in the bathroom, because of another long forgotten asshole boyfriend. Without saying a word, she'd led her to the kitchen, where they'd baked chocolate rice crispy treats together. Julia still recalled her feelings of growing close-ness as they'd sat and munched the still-hot, mushy treats. When finally stuffed beyond sensible limits, they'd laughed hysterically at their chocolate-smeared faces. It'd been the first time she'd felt a proper bond of trust. And it was the beginning of them both understanding the importance of their relationship together. Since then, they'd stuck to the same ritual: Julia would cook and listen, and Anna would talk. For years, the sisters had repeated the same unspoken rule, knowing instinctively that this was their special thing.

The time passed pleasantly, and she listened to old eighties songs while squeezing fresh lemons. She worked methodically with the kind of quiet competence that only someone who'd honed their craft for years could do with ease.

Creating the perfect cheesecake was all about finding the perfect balance between bitter and sweet—a trick she'd mastered long ago. The real challenge came from Anna having a sweeter tooth than her own.

I'll go with sweet, she thought, hoping for a speedy and preferably lurid confession.

She turned the radio up, recognizing one of her all-time favorite tunes. The music began to pipe loudly into the fragrant room. In her element, Julia sang along to the chorus, dancing on the spot, while slicing a vanilla pod with a practiced hand.

The sound of the front door slamming suddenly broke her pleasant reverie. With a soaring heart, she realized that Anna must have returned home earlier than expected.

Even better, she thought.

Footsteps approached from behind. "Hey, kiddo. Guess what's on the menu?" She shouted above the pumping chorus. There was no reply. Undeterred, Julia pressed on. "Who's the dirty stop out, then, hmm?" She teased, giving another impromptu jig to the music.

"Hello, Julia," a man's voice said, causing the morning sun to drain from the room.

JUST AS ANNA thought the station wagon would give up its struggle for good, the white, picket fence surrounding her sister's little house rolled into view. Normally, a wave of anxiety would greet the familiar sound of the sputtering engine, while she contemplated the prospect of a future without transport. Now, the jerking contortions only brought a smile to her face, because a check for one million dollars lay inside her bag.

"One million dollars," she tried the words on again for size. "One miiiillion dollars," she repeated, this time doing a poor Doctor Evil impression.

Her day had started with the sensation of silk sheets lightly touching her skin, followed by sheer bliss. As her mind had risen further from the veil of sleep, she'd actually blushed when the details of the previous night flooded back. She felt no regret at those images, though—only joy. Suddenly, her future felt like an open road, rather than a dead end. Best of all, she'd found an incredible companion to start that journey with.

Anna wearily parked opposite the old cactus in the yard. Despite being bone-tired, her mind still raced with images from the previous night, thrilling her to the point of wondering if it would be possible to sleep again.

It wasn't a dream, she reminded herself.

Parting company in the mundane setting of the college parking lot had seemed surreal. Where, less than twenty-four hours before, the adventure of her life had begun. Fearing discovery, they'd not dared to share a final kiss, and she'd been forced to stop her hand from reaching out to him, although her body craved for one last touch.

Corey had invited her to visit the Estate the next day, but she'd insisted that he come to Julia's for Sunday lunch, instead. Instinctively, she knew that Big Bird would love Corey, and it felt important to seek approval from the one person whose opinion mattered most. She reflected with a note of guilt that her scandalous text hinting at spending the night with someone other than Jim would be driving Julia crazy with curiosity. And, she had no doubt that her sis would also be furious to learn how the congressman had turned out to be a manipulative dick. She also needed Big Bird to understand that Corey wasn't a knee-jerk reaction to that disappointment: he was special. The sooner they met, the quicker she could prove it, and it would only take five minutes with her kind, gently-spoken man to settle any doubts.

"My man," she said, loving the way she already thought of him as such.

She watched as a young boy rolled past on a pair of orange skates, grinning from ear to ear as he swished the boots to create momentum.

Bet you'd love the HELA, kid, Anna thought, feeling a kinship toward the carefree joy of the motion.

She turned the ignition key off, and the car made a sound like an audible groan, before it fell silent. Anna flung the creaking door open and gazed over at the house, expecting Julia to be at the window, peering through the curtains—especially because the station wagon sounded so embarrassingly loud. There was no tell-tale twitch today, though. Anna frowned.

"Please be home, Big Bird," she murmured, stepping onto the curb.

The prospect of not sharing her incredible news immediately was almost too much to bear. She did recall, however, Julia saying that she'd be home all day and would in all likely-hood, be rustling up something tasty already. A sympathetic pang of hunger greeted the thought.

On the spur of the moment, Anna turned back to the old car and patted it affectionately, realizing that it would probably be the last time she would need to depend on its dubious mechanics. "I can buy a new car!" She exclaimed aloud, the enormity hitting her once again. "Shit, why not buy two?"

She contemplated the fun shopping trips ahead, while her hand remained on her soon to be ex-faithful friend. The sound of the swishing roller skates stopped, and Anna turned to see that the boy had stopped to watch her at the end of the street. He must've seen her wistful moment with the car, because he stared her way with an expression clearly reserved for crazies. She gave the kid a quick salute, and then headed toward the familiar, red door of the place she'd come to think of as home.

Halfway along the garden path, Anna stumbled, prompting her to take more care. Particularly because, on a whim, she'd earlier decided to throw on the gorgeous stilettoes from the previous evening, knowing they'd make a great way to mischievously grab her sister's attention before unleashing both barrels of her super fantabulous gossip.

Anna paused in front of the door and took a deep breath, the anticipation threatening to turn her into a giggling girl. *Play it coolio, kiddo,* she thought, planning to reveal her cards with a slow relish.

She suspected that Julia may already be plotting to deploy every trick in the book to garner a juicy confession. Of course, she would oblige—but only after stringing out the special treatment for as long as possible. It would be wrong not to.

Wait until she sees the cheque... She reached out for the front door handle. It turned easily and swung inward, unlocked.

Julia's home!

The air felt cool against her bare arms as she entered the tidy little porch. The door clicked behind her, and she took a moment to bend and sniff the comforting aroma coming from the vase of fresh pansies that Big Bird always kept there to greet visitors. She noted with affection, that they'd not once been allowed to wither for a single day since her arrival.

Anna's attention turned to the loud music drifting from the kitchen. Just as she'd hoped, the golden oldie radio station boomed out a former hit. It was a sure sign that another culinary masterpiece was underway. In truth, she'd never had the heart to tell Julia that she was a little too young to remember most of the tracks they'd jigged along to over the years. Not that it mattered.

What's on the menu today, Miss Price? She wondered, tossing her keys onto the battered, old ashtray sitting on the hallway trestle table. Despite its shabby appearance, the heirloom represented a bygone time, making it unthinkable to part with.

She strode toward the source of the music, brimming with excitement. "Hi, Big…"

The kitchen stood empty. But strangely, she saw clear evidence of recent activity: Julia's favorite mixing bowl had made a welcome appearance on the linoleum counter surface, surrounded by tasty-looking ingredients. Peering over its rim, she observed a mixture of broken biscuit and butter. The half-dozen squeezed lemons on a plate nearby provided the final evidence to be certain what the end result of the endeavor would be.

"Wow, you are playing dirty," she grinned, taking a piece of the biscuit and munching away in the knowledge that the pilfered morsel would've earned a slapped wrist, if big sis had been present.

"Muhaha," she added theatrically. "Guard your treasure more closely, my dear."

The sound of crunching came from underfoot. Broken glass, she realized.

She hadn't noticed it upon entering, but there it was, scattered over the normally-spotless dark, wooden floor. Puzzlement soon turned into a rising sense of foreboding when she took a closer look at her surroundings. Something appeared amiss with the usually-ordered state of Julia's private kingdom. Utensils were scattered across the draining board, and several eggs had joined the glass on the floor by the sink.

"Hello?" She called out, a small tremor betraying her inner worry. *Maybe she's cut?*

Anna darted back into the hall, toward the bedrooms, this time noticing that the sheepskin running down the center of the passage was askew. Something else caught her eye: a deep gouge running the length of the flower wallpaper, just above the rug.

What the...? It almost looks like someone has raked... "Julia!" She shouted this time, her voice sounding shrill in her own head.

Only the sound of a bored DJ blasting from the radio replied. "This one is for all you love birds—we are going all the way back to nineteen fifty nine..." There was a pause then the sound of a needle running along vinyl.

She followed the path of the disturbance, eyes tracing the undulating pattern of the ugly indent, until it ended outside the doorway to Julia's bedroom door. Suddenly her limbs felt like lead, making the few dozen steps needed to cover the ground akin to walking through tar. At the rear of her mind, an urgent warning screamed at her to turn and leave.

Do not stop and collect two hundred dollars, Anna, just leave. LEAVE NOW.

But her instinct to help overwhelmed any sense of self-preservation. She wouldn't abandon Julia—not for one second. Committed, her view fixed onto the doorframe, where a red thumbprint had been pressed against the white gloss.

It's fine, it's fine. Just a nick of the thumb, her mind protested, refusing to think the worst.

Ice-cold shards of fear stabbed down her spine while she examined every detail of the stain. It appeared to have been pushed hard onto the frame and then smeared. Time slowed while she tried to reason through a set of events leading to the grim signpost that didn't involve tragedy.

Only one way to know for sure, Little Bird... Please, I don't want to...

You must.

She reached out with a shaking hand and turned the knob, unable to pull her gaze away from the sight of the print.

She'll be fine, you wait and s...

The door opened onto a vision from hell. There was blood, most of it drenching soft, linen bed sheets where a pale, naked figure lay still.

Then came the sound of screaming—a detached part of her noted that the sound came from her own lungs. The wailing rose and mixed with the sounds of the playing love song while her heart broke into a thousand shards. How she wanted to join that separate part of her mind and soar away from the horror. A primeval force coming from within refused to release her.

YOU ARE IN DANGER! It cried, and although impossible, the voice sounded like Julia's.

But it was already too late. The presence of another person looming to her left touched the periphery of her vision. She turned just in time to see a fist heading directly at her. *Way too late, sweetie.*

A bloom of pain struck her forehead, followed by a bright wave of stars flooding her consciousness. Anna flew. At first it came as a blessed relief because it meant that the fight had been mercifully brief. No more fear. *No more.*

Her ribs struck the wooden floor, forcing air to whoosh from her body and leaving her gasping for breath. The ensuing panic tore away the dream state, and the sunny hallway swam into view once more with unforgiving clarity. She felt compelled to face her attacker, even while writhing against the polished slats like a fish ripped from the water and then tossed onto the bank to die.

Seeing just how old Tony looked shocked her almost as much as her desperate fight for oxygen. His face had a grey pallor, clinging to a skeletal frame so thin that he appeared like a wraith sent from the underworld. A red-rimmed gaze burned into her with an intensity she would have scarcely thought possible. His hair had been shaven to reveal a tightened skull framing a widened mouth, filled with yellow teeth. He grimaced in devilish triumph. Nothing remained of the man she had once loved, only a creature of death bent on ending her and anything else she cared for.

He continued to stare at her, seeming to relish the moment. The brief respite finally allowed her to take two shuddering breaths. Tony closed his eyes for a second and swayed while the crooning tune still played.

"Perfect," he mouthed the words.

Silence followed, while they watched each other—he with hands slick with blood. *Julia's blood,* she wailed inside, before the stone wall of her own predicament descended, cutting off another path to madness.

Reality stilled, while every atom of her being flooded her senses with adrenaline-pumped detail: the wetness on her forehead, the sound of her heaving lungs, and, the thumping rush of her pulse coursing through her arteries. She raised a shaking hand to her head and looked down at the red mark on her hand.

"She's not dead, yet, Anna," he said in rasping whisper. "I wanted to save such pleasures for you." The rictus grin broadened.

Still alive... the words rolled over her like thunder.

Despair turned to hope and then fury. "No," she murmured. *After all I've been through, it comes to this? Letting him take away my hope again? No... I must be strong. I must help.*

"No!" She screamed, rising unsteadily, and then plunging toward the kitchen.

From the corner of her eye, she saw him move with a terrifying fluidity. Anna tried to fling herself through the open door frame, but a vice-like grip wrapped around her throat from behind, while a second arm pinned her body to his chest. Hot, fetid breath washed over her cheek as the hand became ever tighter, constricting her airway with a deadly resolve. She responded with a vain attempt to claw his arm. But the choke-hold only strengthened, forcing the pressure against her wind pipe to build further. Little black dots formed at the corner of her vision, gathering together. She knew that allowing them to coalesce into a total darkness would seal her fate.

Her frantic gaze darted around the kitchen, searching for something, anything. She railed against the inexorable surge with all her being, but even her rage ebbed away under the relentless crush. Flashing lights began to dart among the black dots. Anna tried to harness the last vestiges of her will power, grasping for elusive wisps of a plan to halt the inevitable.

Julia! The name rallied her. Her own death paled at the thought of failing to help the one person who'd always been there for her.

The squeezing grew tighter.

What about Corey? She thought while images from the past weeks swam before her fleeting mind. She would never know what their future together would hold. *That's sad,* she decided, as a tear rolled down her cheek.

The pain receded into a dull cloud. She reflected on her adventure the previous night, soaring in the night sky, wearing the most expensive dress money could buy.

Was it a dream? She wondered. *No, it was real, Anna. Hell, I'm still wearing the shoes to prove it.* She found this fact comforting at the end.

The stilettos.

The last word repeated in a soundless scream, echoing over and over.

In one final, lucid moment, she raised her right leg and brought the heel of the gold shoe down onto the bridge of Tony's foot with the force of the damned. The long, slender point plunged into fleshy cartilage. Now it was his turn to scream. Immediately, she felt pressure lift from her neck, and blessed oxygen flooded back to her.

Anna's system rebounded, lifting the veil of shadows. The kitchen snapped into focus and she plunged through the doorway, as if finding an exit from hell. She tumbled onto the floor among the remains of shattered glass. A thick shard pierced her elbow, making her yelp in agony. Perversely, the wound drove away the last shred of lethargy, and she scrambled to regain her footing. Still deprived of energy her legs gave way on the first attempt and, as she began to rise again, a heavy weight landed between her shoulder blades, squashing her frame against the floor, leaving her right arm trapped underneath. A calloused palm reached around her throat, once again.

She struggled, but without her strongest limb to add leverage, the effort proved futile. Her actions became more desperate.

This is Last Chance Saloon! All passengers wishing to exit, please do so. Next stop: Town Oblivion.

Anna's fingers brushed against the sharp edge of another glass sliver. Instinctively, she grasped the shard, before turning it upward and jabbing it above her left shoulder. Tony howled like a dog, and then rolled off. Once again, the exhilarating thrill of freedom greeted her like an old friend. Clinging to the opportunity with all her being, she pushed against the floor and launched backward into a squatting position. He faced her, writhing among the debris, clutching at an eye socket dripping with blood.

What now? Think! There's a phone in here...

She looked toward the landline caddy next to the cooker, seeking the familiar form of the handset. It was missing.

Fearing that the onslaught could resume at any second, she risked another panicked survey of her surroundings. Julia's handbag rested in its habitual spot beside the drainer. But seeing her sister's possession only served to reinforce the overwhelming image of the pale, lifeless body. The world swam.

No! Not lifeless. He said so.

The sound of fresh movement disrupted her chain of thought. She turned to find Tony rising, with one hand pressed against his ruined eye and the other bloodied claw pointing at her.

"Why don't you leave us alone?" She sobbed.

"Annaaaaaa," the creature she'd once loved replied, beginning a deliberate, awful shuffle toward her.

She ran for the bag and then reached inside, hoping to find Julia's cell phone. Her hand grasped something solid. She removed the object.

"You are..." Tony rasped. Anna turned, pointing the black barrel of the Glock toward him. "Mine," he finished, before she pulled the trigger.

The first bullet took him in the shoulder with such force that he spun like a rag doll. The second speared into his right hip, finally turning him into a crumpled, broken thing. His arms splayed impossibly, as if in a moment of unholy personal rapture. A single, glassy, blue eye continued to stare at her with sightless hatred.

Anna dropped the smoking gun and ran from the kitchen to help her Big Bird.

EPILOGUE

With blue and red lights flashing the ambulance raced down the interstate.

They'd already pulled over three times to successfully defibrillate their lucky passenger.

"Be advised, base: ETA three minutes," the driver called into his radio. "Patient bagged and remains unstable."

As a professional with over twenty years' experience patching up the worst humanity could throw his way, he'd developed an instinct to recognize those who refused to leave this world behind, whether through love or sheer stubbornness.

This one sure is a fighter, he thought, pushing on the gas pedal.

THE AIR AMBULANCE raced through the darkening Arizona sky line, the technician raising his hands after finally giving up on a futile effort to save their patient.

"Shit," he murmured.

The recipient of his treatment had suffered multiple wounds across the body and head. Considering the violent trauma suffered, it was a miracle they'd lasted this long.

"You had spirit, that's for sure. Most people would have given up by now," he said, wiping the sweat from his brow before checking his wrist watch. "Time of death: six thirty-seven," he called to the pilot. "Inform Stanford that the patient will be DOA."

LITTLE BIRD

ANNA SERIES BOOK 2

Chapter 1

ALIVE

Anna strolled along a sun-dappled path, enjoying the early afternoon sunshine. Tall, ancient look-ing trees lined the walkway on each side, obscuring the view beyond. When she looked up, she could see a blue sky punctuated by fluffy clouds undulating across the horizon. It was a glorious day. A gentle, warm breeze brushed through her blonde hair, carrying with it the sound of children laughing, reminding her of days long gone, when she and Julia had run through the school yard together.

Julia. The name jarred her. *Something important about Julia.* Golden sunrays ticked her skin, causing the distracting thought to fade like a wisp. She stopped once more to enjoy the simple tranquillity of her surroundings and inhaled. The simple pleasure made her wince, as a brief, yet sharp pain in her lungs contrasted with the perfection of the day. A shadow passed over her contented expression.

Maybe it's time for a rest, she thought, rubbing her breast bone. *I've been walking for such a long time... What was it I set out for?* The question troubled her. She turned and looked back in the hope of getting an idea, but the path trailed into the distance, exactly the same as the road ahead. No, it seemed that the only thing to do was to carry on until she reached her destination—wherever that was. *Maybe I should stay here a little longer? Maybe a lot longer.*

Facing forward again, she became aware of a circular, turfed clearing ahead, bordered by pretty, white lilies. In the center of the clearing, a female figure sat on a knitted blanket. A picnic basket lay next to her, along with an array of tasty-looking dishes. Anna felt oddly reluctant to approach the stranger, but she experienced the overriding compulsion to do so.

Julia. Her sister's dark hair was tied in a ponytail—a youthful style she'd not seen Big Bird try for years. She wore a dazzling summer dress that reminded her of the type Mother had used to love.

"Hey, Little B," Julia greeted her before making a patting motion next to her. "Take a seat." Anna needed no encouragement. Her sibling's picnics were legendary, but even by those impressive standards, this was a veritable feast with rows of salads, pastries, cakes, and dainty, butter-brushed pies—the kind they'd used to bake together. *Used to...*

"Wow, you've been busy," she exclaimed, scooping up a

particularly tasty-looking cream-covered scone. She took a big bite and it melted in her mouth. The soft, doughy interior burst with a generous dollop of raspberry jam, while the cream was indulgent and fresh. She approved. "These are the best you've ever made."

Julia smiled and winked, looking beautiful. Her brown-eyed gaze radiated love. "We need to talk, kiddo," she said after a moment. They both watched a small, emerald-green butterfly land between them.

"I know," Anna nodded, already finishing off the scone and moving onto one of the pastries. "I haven't told you about Corey, yet—he's amazing!" she said as she nibbled at the crusty treat. "–Oh—OMG, Julia! The casino!"

"Anna." Julia's tone held a stern, yet reluctant note. The hard edge to her voice, snapped Anna's attention back to her sister's serious expression. "Something's happened," Julia said with a sad look in her eye.

Don't ask her. Don't you dare ask! "What?" she asked in a small, childlike voice.

"Something bad." The words sent a chill down Anna's spine. A dark, angry-looking cloud drifted over them, and the breeze became much cooler.

"Listen, hon, I need you to know that I will always be here for you." A tear ran down Julia's cheek as she spoke. "I won't let him break you, do you understand? No matter what." *Tony.* The name came unbidden, as if her consciousness had overturned a rock, only to discover the ugliest spider underneath. "You need to be strong for both of us now, Little B," Julia said. She reached out and set her hand on Anna's chest. "It's time to grow up, kiddo."

The wind grew ever colder, becoming a freezing torrent. It blew through the carefully-arranged spread, scattering its contents across the now frost-covered lawn. "Oh no!" Anna voiced her alarm, looking to Julia for guidance. "The lovely cakes."

A downpour started, and great thudding droplets soaked them both, ruining Julia's beautiful dress. "I love you," Julia said, pressing her fingers against her breastbone. Immediately, the discomfort returned, infinitely more intense than before. A rising scream caught in Anna's throat, unable to get out.

COREY FELT HEARTBROKEN as he gazed down at Anna's sleeping face. The bastard had brutally split her soft, full lips —the same ones that, only three nights ago, he'd caressed. An ugly, black bruise sprawled across her otherwise unblemished cheek and, to complete the outrage, the vicious scumbag had left her with a cracked breast bone and a bad concussion. The doctors said she was lucky to be alive.

No, he thought with fierce pride, *luck had nothing to do with it.* He'd discovered the true extent of Anna's dire situation after calling her cell. A burly-sounding voice had answered as Arizona State P.D., before demanding to know who he was. A cold tendril of fear had shot through his core upon hearing this, but it had been replaced by hope when he learned that she was alive.

Shortly after, they'd questioned him at the hospital and the police had confirmed the terrible truth. Although they'd stated they weren't certain that Anna was the victim not the perpetrator, he could tell from their sympathetic manner that there was little doubt. After establishing his own solid alibi, they'd grilled him for what little information he possessed. Following that, he'd faced the challenge of persuading the hospital staff to allow him access to her, and he'd eventually convinced them to call the college to confirm his identity. To his surprise, he'd learned there were no other family members present, and as far as the medical team knew, she had no next of kin to call upon, other than a sister, who was probably the other victim.

The medical team had assured him that Anna would regain consciousness in her own time, advising that it was far better to allow her body to achieve this naturally, rather than risk extra distress to her already-battered psyche. He'd agreed, despite his burning desire to uncover how this tragedy had occurred. He was terrified of losing her—the first person he'd ever loved. Although they were still at the beginning of their relationship, the bond between them already felt like fate.

Their time in Las Vegas had been the most fulfilling experience of his life: a joyous night of fun-filled laughter. The love-making that followed had been most profound, going beyond simple lust. It had been a meeting of two soul-mates—the kind of shared understanding that one rarely, if ever, experienced in life.

Could he give himself over to this gentle, kind woman who'd come into his carefully-structured life and turned it inside out? *Yes.* The answer was firm. *What do I really know about her, though?* They'd spent so little time together, in fact, that every effort he'd made to uncover the truth about that fateful night had quickly descended into futile speculation. The police still hadn't confirmed the identity of the assailant found at the scene, and what, if any, his relation-ship had been with the sisters.

He knew she'd been involved with two other men before. The first was Congressman Jim Peterson, a repul-sive, self-serving cockroach. Was it possible he'd orches-trated some kind of terrible revenge and maybe paid a local junkie to do the deed? Despite the spiteful comments the guy had directed at Anna during their brief but violent confrontation at the college, Corey felt fairly certain he wasn't behind the horrific attack. James Peterson was many things, including corrupt, but the jealous mastermind of an unspeakable crime? After several inquiries amongst his own network of friends and colleagues—some with first-hand experience with Congressman Frack—it seemed unlikely that such a self-serving prick would hatch a plan so recklessly brutal. It just didn't fit his M.O., and based on what Anna had said, his secret intention had been to use her. No, he wouldn't possess any of the genuine hate-fuelled emotion needed to carry out such a wicked act.

For the thousandth time since starting his bedside vigil, he tried to recall anything else of value to explain such a tragedy. His mind turned to the ex-boyfriend again—the guy she'd mentioned leaving prior to moving to Phoenix. They'd only briefly discussed the subject, but he remembered an unusual note of sadness in her voice and perhaps even fear when she'd spoken of him.

The flapping sound of the ward doors interrupted his tortured deliberations. "Excuse me, sir," said a low male voice. Corey turned to face a middle-aged African American wearing a beige mac and sporting an impressive mustache. He maintained a respectful distance while chewing a piece of gum and gazing at them both with alert curiosity. "Lieutenant Raymond," he introduced himself and produced his badge. "Homicide Unit." Corey laid Anna's hand on the bed and nodded in greeting.

"I'm here to investigate the incident."

"Anything you need from me, you've got it," he replied, hoping to gain a few insights, himself.

"Mind if I take notes?" The Lieutenant asked as he strolled to the bedside.

"Sure, but I probably know less than you," Corey answered honestly. "Two beat cops—sorry, I mean officers —already asked me a bunch of questions."

"Indulge me." The other man fixed him with a gaze that

Corey recognized from the boardroom. This guy expected answers. *Good. We need him on our side.* "Your name, please?"

"Corey Young."

"May I ask what your relationship is with Miss Price?"

He felt his cheeks redden. "I'm her college tutor."

"Her tutor?" he raised an eyebrow.

"Well, actually, I'm more than that, now," Corey admitted, seeing little point in holding back.

"I see," the Lieutenant said, rolling the gum around his mouth while seeming to consider his next question. "Have you been together long? Assuming that's what you mean by 'more'?"

"It is. Only a few days, actually."

The gum rolled again. "Can you explain your whereabouts between the hours of two PM and seven PM on Saturday, the first of March?"

Corey nodded. "Travelling to a business conference in LA. I stayed the night there. I tried to call her Sunday morning." He suppressed his annoyance at answering the same questions again.

"Did you see her Saturday?"

"Yes. We'd spent Friday night together in Vegas. I last spoke to Anna around one-thirty at the parking lot of Scottsdale Community College."

The gum stopped rolling. "Did you often meet in the college parking lot?"

"No," Corey stated firmly, irritated by the lurid suggestion. "She'd left her car there."

"I'm afraid I need to get to the bottom of this, sir, and the quickest way to do that is to be direct."

"I know," Corey agreed, rubbing his crooked neck. "Sorry, Detective. It's been a long few days. Listen..."

Lieutenant Raymond raised a finger, cutting him off mid-sentence. "Can you give me some names to verify your whereabouts that day?"

"Erm, yeah, sure." He proceeded to give him the details of half a dozen people he'd come into contact with at the airstrip and the energy conference.

The Detective scribbled the names in a pocket book he'd produced from one of the trench coat's cavernous pockets. "You're a wealthy guy, huh? Some kind of millionaire?"

Corey had to resist the temptation to say, "Billionaire, actually." Instead, he replied, "Yes."

Again, the response was a shrug. "Do you know Anna's sister, Julia Price?" There was a pointed edge to the question.

The Officer's brusque manner made his stomach sink. "No, we haven't had chance to meet, yet," Corey answered.

The flat stare of the burly cop offered no comfort, either. "Do you recognise this man?" The detective continued, producing a single Polaroid picture from another huge pocket.

"Jesus." Corey winced, staring at the badly-injured and gaunt appearance of the man in the picture. One of his eyes had been covered by thick gauze, and his sandy, blonde hair was streaked with blood.

"No, I've never seen him before," Corey admitted, trying to place the face without success. "Is he dead?"

"Annnnnnaaaaaa," the voice called from far away.

"Anna." This time, it was much clearer.

"She's waking," said a female voice she didn't recognize. "Her vital signs are elevated: she's in pain."

"Can't you give her something?" asked a familiar man's voice. *Corey.*

"We'll make her more comfortable," the woman said.

Anna tried to open her eyes, only to shut them again when a searing, white light flooded her vision.

"Hey, honey. Welcome back to the world," the female voice said. "Open them gradually—it's easier."

She tried again slowly this time, and the world swam into focus. The figure before her wore the medical fatigues of a nurse. "Where?" Anna croaked though a throat that felt like it'd been sand-papered.

"You're in Saint Joseph's, hon, and you're safe."

Anna did her best to process the words, but they popped like bubbles in her mind. She attempted to adjust her position, but the movement caused a sharp pain to balloon in her chest.

"Try not to move, honey," the nurse urged. "You've cracked your breast bone."

"Corey," she mouthed.

"I'm right here," he replied, heavy with relief. She felt a comforting hand cup hers.

"What kind of a date do you call this?" she asked haltingly. Her attempt at levity didn't end with the laughter she'd hoped for, though.

Chapter 2

LEGACY

ulia's dead. After almost a week, the mantra continued to run round her mind like an alien concept that her entire being rejected, no matter how much reason dictated it must be true. The part of her already bereaved of two parents said, *Fuck logic, fuck reason. My beloved Big Bird must be alive.*

At first, she'd tried to lose herself in the numbing arms of medicine, demanding ever higher doses of morphine. Corey and the medical team soon started to suspect her true motivations, though, and refused to allow her to board the despair train. Worse still, her memories had started to return: images of him, the bastard.

She dared not think his name any longer, so strong were her feelings of disgust. Unfortunately, that hadn't stopped his evil sneer from playing on hard rotation in her memory, along with the events that had occurred after she'd entered Julia's house that day. Since awakening, Anna had developed the unwelcome ability to pause the horror with an inner remote control. Mercifully, the moment she'd opened the bedroom door remained a blank spot, sparing her from the ultimate agony. Her only cold comfort came from the memory of pumping two lead slugs into the creature she'd once lived with.

That's where any sense of justice ended, though. Unbelievably, the bastard still drew breath. Corey had attempted to console her with the certainty that a crime as heinous as his would only mean a death sentence, but she found his continued presence on planet Earth an affront to her grief regardless.

Anna sighed and then stared across the sparsely-furnished hospital room and through the open window, wishing she could fly away. Corey remained the one person preventing her from doing just that. She glanced over at his slumbering form in the visitor's chair next to her bed and found herself smiling at the cute scar above his left eyebrow.

He'd stayed by her side the entire time, of course. When she awoke from a particularly bad dream, clutching at her chest and soaked in sweat, he would always be there to provide comfort. It gave her hope to see him reading one of his geeky sci-fi novels, or sleeping in the same clothes he'd worn the previous day. It was hard to believe they had been together for only such a short time. Most men would have run for the hills when confronted by such a damaged and distressed partner, but not her man. Her silent deliberations broke at the sound of the door opening.

Lieutenant Raymond entered with a look of regret on his face. As always, he wore the same worn mac. She greeted him and then nudged her slumbering guardian angel. He came round with bleary-eyed confusion, before focusing on their visitor and raising a hand of welcome.

"How are you feeling today?" Raymond asked her.

"Less like I spent a month in a meat grinder," she replied. Only sudden movements caused her pain, now, rather the ever-present agony of the previous days. He nodded, obviously impatient to cut to the chase. "What can I do for you, Lieutenant?" Anna asked, opting to put him out of his misery.

"We've charged him."

The information came as a relief. Just to know that Tony would stay off the streets felt like a lead weight being lifted from her shoulders. "Good," was all that she could manage to say through a wave of emotion. Corey stood beside her and then placed a comforting hand around her shoulder.

"There's more," Raymond added. With a sinking feeling, she guessed the reason for the Lieutenant's air of concern would soon be explained. "We're investigating other murders," he looked uncomfortable, "and well, we think he's responsible."

The words sliced between them like a knife. The implication was too awful. Unbidden, a single tear ran down her cheek. She wiped it away, determined not to let this latest revelation break her. "How many?"

Chapter 3

GOODBYE

"This is Phoenix Today - with Marty Dean and Kirsten Leicester." The anchor's voice rang out after a long and dramatic news theme tune.

The TV camera panned from the station logo, then focused on the immaculately dressed Marty, who grinned through bright white teeth.

"Good evening Phoenix - the news at the top of the hour." He relayed the practiced phrase before adopting a more somber tone.

"There's speculation tonight that the police may have finally captured the infamous Phoenix strangler." Marty paused a moment to allow his viewers to digest the information. "Over to our crime correspondent - Ron Whitmore."

The TV image switched from the news room to a balding reporter in a patterned shirt, clutching a microphone. He stood outside the colonnaded front of the police HQ.

"Thanks, Marty," Ron replied without the polish of his desk-bound colleague. "We're seeing dramatic developments in the Phoenix Strangler case, this evening. Police have charged a thirty-two year-old, male named Tony Eckerman with the brutal murder of Darleen Maxwell, a local sex worker found dead a month ago."

The screen split, bringing the anchor back into view alongside the reporter. Putting the two men side by side served to highlight the stark differences in their appearances.

"So, why the connection to the strangler case, Ron?" Marty asked, as if the audience hadn't already worked out the obvious. To the veteran's credit, the redness rising on his neck gave the only outward sign of his annoyance at the unnecessary intervention.

"Interesting question, Marty. Police sources talk of strong evidence linking the suspect to the murders of five other women in the last decade."

"Hence the speculation that he may be the Phoenix Strangler?" Marty interjected once more.

"That's right, Marty." Ron replied.

The anchor raised his right hand to his temple, as if receiving instruction from a higher being. "Are all the other victims sex workers, like Miss Maxwell?" He asked finally. If the reporter held any distaste for the salacious angle to the question, he hid it well.

"No, Marty. Unusually, for these kinds of cases, the strangler targeted victims of different backgrounds. This made tracking the killer particularly difficult for investigators."

"Do we have any more information about these other victims, Ron?"

"Details are patchy, Marty, but viewers may recall the three-week search for eighteen-year-old student, Marie-Ann Dewer. I'm told that she may well have been one of the unfortunate women to have fallen prey to the notorious killer."

Satisfied that they'd dished up a suitable dose of doom and gloom to the audience, the anchor wrapped up the interview. He moved onto a story about an elderly church-goer discovering an image of Madonna on a giant cookie.

A LINE of black-clothed mourners gathered in the pouring rain, watching the solid, wooden casket lowering into a waiting grave. Anna stared at the thick droplets of water bouncing off its polished surface. Above her, skittering clouds raced against an ominous grey canvas. The swirling gloom matched her mood.

She found little comfort in her fellow mourners. All that remained of her once-extensive family was a distant great aunt who she barely knew. Her dark thoughts turned to her dead parents. *Perhaps it's for the best that they're gone. This would have broken them,* she thought.

The funeral directors had offered to postpone the service until the worst of the monsoon season passed, but Anna insisted they push ahead. She needed to grieve, and that process couldn't begin until this dark day ended.

One of her late sister's work colleagues had suggested the "celebrate her life" approach to the service, but she'd refused. Nothing good could come from this tragedy. Julia had been cut down in her prime by a vicious animal who should never have entered her happy life.

The animal you introduced. She stood in the leaden downpour, defeated by constant anguish and tortured by feelings of guilt. Her mind raced to recall memories of their time together. *Why can't I picture her face?* A sob escaped her.

Her tortured search could only provide one thought: her vivid dream on that first day after she'd awoken in the hospital. "What had she said?" Anna murmured, trying to recall Julia's parting words. The intensity of the downpour increased and droplets drummed on the disappearing casket. *"You have to be strong for the both of us, now."*

I don't know if I can be.

Chapter 4

TIL DAWN

Anna gazed over the moon-bathed oasis, drinking in the sounds of the night. The Clear Water Estate appeared as a sea of green peppered with dazzling flower beds during the day, but now it looked like a silver dream. She paused on her usual midnight stroll to examine an intricate flower. It was pale, but beautiful under the lunar shine.

She'd been staying at Corey's home for three months. The place resonated with such vibrant life that it became almost impossible for her to dwell on death here. Indeed, its tranquil setting had proven the perfect tonic to her crushing misery. The guilt remained immense, though. First, there'd been her natural tendency to blame herself for putting Julia in harm's way, and then came the revelation of the other victims. For a while, that knowledge had set her back to the point of not caring about recovery. Instead, she'd obsessed over every memory of her time with Tony, searching for any clue that would point to his secret life of evil. Each time she'd travelled down that particular rabbit hole of pain, though, she'd drawn a blank. Oddly, it gave her a small measure of comfort. No matter how hard she tried, though, there was no smoking gun. There was no moment he'd returned home with blood-stained clothes and no mysterious disappearances in the middle of the night. Only his inner rage had given any real sign of his true nature.

If her self-accusations hadn't been enough, the lies printed in the gutter media made matters even worse. It seemed that every screaming loon and woman-hating misogynist south of Vegas had sent her messages of ill will, or worse. It wasn't the half-baked theories about her being an accomplice that bothered her the most, because she knew them to be wrong. But articles entitled, "How Didn't She Know?" only added to her well of regret. His guilt had yet to be proven in court, but Anna knew it was him. The monster who'd done that to Julia must have been capable of doing it to others.

She pulled her light cardigan tighter around her flowing, night dress to keep out the chill. The hypnotic figure of a bat fluttered past; its shadowy beauty was another one of the wonders that made this such a special place.

The decision to come here had been the easiest one of her life. The day before they'd discharged her, Corey had finally plucked up the courage to invite her to live with him. Of course, she'd thrown her arms around him and accepted, but only after pointing out his official status as a complete asshole for making her wait until the last minute.

While she smiled at the happy thought, Anna suddenly felt cool hands slip around her shoulders. For a moment, the unexpected contact made her tense. She soon recognized the familiar touch of her lover, though, and his soft lips kissed her neck.

"Looks like I found the intruder." He spoke in a low voice. She smiled, touching his fingers in response. "I'm going to have to start calling you Moon Maiden," he teased.

"You really are a hippie, Corey."

"Hippie? Moi?" he replied in mock protest.

"Well, let me see: you live in your green flower palace and now you want to call me Moon Maiden. I rest my case. Go hug a tree, flower boy."

"I'd rather hug you," he countered, circling his arms around her waist. "Did you get much sleep?" The question had become a daily ritual since her arrival.

"A whole three hours. Lucky me." She frowned with fatigue. Her inability to switch off had become a real issue—the same frustrating problem that'd led to her midnight strolls through the Estate. Although his question had been mundane, she sensed tension in his voice. "What's wrong, Corey?"

He didn't speak, but turned her to face him. The moon highlighted the upper half of his handsome features, whilst the lower remained in shadow. "Anna," he said, kneeling before her.

What the... she thought, missing the significance of the gesture.

From the gloom beneath her, a ring fashioned in the shape of a daisy emerged. Looking closer, she could see that the petals were, in fact, gleaming pearls. At its center was a circular, green emerald. She held her breath as the gesture hung before them.

"Anna Price," he said, "since my parents died, I'd lost hope of finding love." He halted, seeming to struggle to find the words. "I was wrong." Anna's heart began to thud in her chest. "I can't stand the thought of being without you." There was one more pause before the plunge. "Will you be my wife?"

The moon flower ring lay between them, waiting. She reached out and ran a finger down its intricate petals. "Yes," she said. "I will marry you." She couldn't imagine life without this man before her. At the same time, she felt terrified by the certainty that, whatever the future may bring, one day, fate would part them.

Corey rose, and the light of the moon shimmered around them, as if the night goddess, herself, had reached down to bless the union between them. Anna reached out her hand, offering her wedding finger. He placed the ring there, and the metal felt cool against her skin. He took her by the hand again before kissing her tenderly on the symbol of their commitment. As he did so, Anna noticed another silver flash in his left hand. Bringing it up into the light between them, he revealed a necklace identical to the ring.

"Now you're just showing off," she laughed, before turning and lifting her hair to allow him to clasp it around her neck. The tiny links tingled as he clasped it, but the sensation didn't end there: tendrils of pleasure travelled downward through her body and into her groin. She turned and kissed him fiercely. His breath tasted of the sweet tea he liked to drink before bed.

Corey ran a practiced hand down her spine before returning her embrace. He pressed his lips against hers more urgently, and Anna moaned with desire. She reached down to her waist and pulled her shift and cardigan over her head until she stood naked before him. He did the same, and they were free to admire each other's physiques in the glorious half-light. He'd been working out of late, and a toned, masculine frame presented itself for her caress.

Anna pushed against his body, noticing how hard he'd become. Corey lifted her by the buttocks, leaving her to wrap her legs around him. He entered, finding her ready. She began to rise and fall against him, and their movements became ever more passionate until they climaxed together.

THEY LAY in the canopied bedroom of the penthouse suite a hundred feet above ground level. From beneath silk sheets, Anna gazed at the sun rising above the desert horizon, like a fierce, golden colossus.

As usual, on the stroke of six-thirty AM, George politely

knocked on the door. He entered with the tell-tale swooshing of his robotic limbs, and Anna smiled at the sound. She found the way he entered their room immediately after knocking, regardless of their state of undress, amusing. It made the whole low-key entrance thing a bit of a farce, but a welcome one nonetheless.

"Good morning, campers," the robot declared.

"Piss off, George," Corey groaned in response, pulling the sheet over his head. He'd clearly not recovered from the previous night's activities.

"Early bird catches the worm," George chirped on before presenting Anna with a glass of water on a silver tray. "And what were you two up to last night?" the mechanical waiter asked in his odd, synthetic tone. "My sensors detected you both remained in the dome from two-thirty-seven AM until four AM this morning."

"Fucking in the flower beds," Corey replied grumpily. The snarky outburst prompted Anna to laugh out loud and spill cold water over her exposed breasts.

"How lovely," George responded. "May I join you next time and learn more about this fucking process, to which you refer?" he asked innocently. Anna laughed even harder.

"Perv." Corey quipped.

"What is Perv?"

"Never mind, George!"

"There is mail for madam, this morning," George announced, presenting Anna with a white letter marked for her attention.

Curious, Anna accepted the expensive-looking envelope. She'd never received correspondence at her new address before, and the unusual nature of the event made Corey emerge from his quilted man cave to glance at the subject of her interest.

"Could be a nut job," he cautioned.

Ignoring his sage advice, she opened the envelope and started to read. Immediately, her cheeks flushed with annoyance. The originating address was her former employers' law firm: Howard and Moyer, Attorneys at Law. The contents looked less than friendly:

....................Cease and Desist Notice..................

Re: False and defamatory statements made by Anna Price to William Moyer, esq. Attorney at Law.

Dear Miss Price:

We represent William Moyer in connection with the above-referenced matter. The afore-mentioned persons are hereby warned and notified to CEASE AND DESIST making false and defamatory statements.

It has come to our attention that false statements were made with regard to William Moyer's competence.

The statements made regarding William Moyer are false, defamatory, and constitute tortious interference with business, and as such, are actionable under Arizona law. If our client is forced to commence a lawsuit against you in order to stop continued false and defamatory statements, be advised that we will seek recovery of all attorney fees and costs incurred herein as a result. While we hope this is not necessary, we will pursue whatever avenues are necessary on behalf of our client to stop the continued false and defamatory statements. Furthermore, we instruct the former employee, Anna Price, to return all company property immediately, including and not limited to proprietary data, electronic devices, and written material owned exclusively by Howard and Moyer, Attorneys at Law. Sincerely,

William Moyer, esq. Attorney at Law

"Son of a bitch!" Anna exclaimed after re-reading the contents.

"Good news, then?" Corey asked, pushing away the last pretence of trying to sleep. In response, Anna threw the envelope toward him, while continuing to mutter her frustration. He picked up the paper and read the offending content as he yawned. "Ouch," he said.

"Those bastards must know everything I've been through, yet they still send this crap."

"What do you wanna do?" he asked, his tone suggesting he'd already formed his own conclusion.

"If those wankers think they're going to intimidate me, they've got another thing coming!" she replied angrily.

"Wankers? Wow. That's a new one, hon."

"I overhead your British CEO use that one. It sums them up: Jim Wankerface Peterson and his fat, wanker stooge."

"It does have a double meaning, dear." She could tell he was doing his best not to laugh.

"Don't care. That's what they are."

"Agreed. So, what are we gonna do?"

In truth, because of the chaos of previous weeks, she hadn't even thought about the pending environmental case to defend the forest trust. She'd uncovered a plot between her former employer and Congressman James Peterson—the same James Peterson who'd come far too close to seducing her into spying on the hopeless drug addict, Moyer. It had all been in an effort to ensure he upheld his part in sabotaging the defence of his own client, the forest trust. The ultimate goal would have allowed a giant energy corporation to frack in the Tonto National Forest, and Anna had vowed to stop that from happening.

She'd learned the disturbing truth from the mouth of the corrupt attorney, himself—a fact later confirmed by James Peterson's own aggressive response upon learning of her threat to write an exposé highlighting his efforts to pervert the law. She hadn't even thought to carry out the threat until now.

"Do you know what happened to the court case?" she asked suddenly, fearing it would already be too late.

"Postponed at the request of the forestry commission," he replied with a certainty she found odd. "On the grounds of new evidence coming to light."

"What's that?" she asked, confused by the turn of events.

"I heard talk of some hot-shot journalist taking an interest in the case," he said, giving her a wink. "Apparently she promised to produce killer proof of dodgy deals."

"But how do you know?" Anna didn't finish the sentence before the penny dropped. "What have you done, Corey?" She felt both a combination of alarm and elation. His corresponding grin may as well have been a signed confession.

"Looks like you're gonna need a sugar daddy with deep pockets to pay those legal bills, kiddo," he remarked, stretching. "If you do find said amaze-balls guy, I'd be considering what you can do to keep him happy," he commented with a salacious intonation. This earned him a well-deserved slap on the chest from Anna.

"Thank you," she said, after her initial shock had passed.

"Don't thank me, hon. This is my fight as much as it is yours. Cheating scumbags like Peterson could ruin my business," he said before throwing off the bed cover. "Tis my solemn duty to help you kick his mother-fuckin' ass!"

"Mind your language!" She glanced at his prominent display of skin.

"The dear lady doth peruse my wiener. Does she like what she sees?" Anna could see that he'd awoken with more fun in mind.

"What is wiener?" asked George. They both ignored the question.

Anna tapped the notice against her chin, pondering her next step. "What are you thinking?" Corey asked, sounding disappointed that she had other business in mind.

"George, could you call the office of Congressman James Peterson, please?"

"No problemo." George's eyes went dark as it hooked up to the internet to start the call.

"Do you think that's a good idea?" Corey asked with a note of concern in his voice. She raised her finger to signal her intention to see the action through. This particular insult required a direct response.

The sound of the phone ringing followed the dial tone. "Good morning, Congressman Peterson's office. How may I help you?" an officious female voice answered.

"Hello. May I speak with the Congressman, please?"

"I'm afraid the Congressman's busy at the moment, but I'd be happy to take a message for you." The voice took on a guarded tone obviously reserved for cranks calling to alert the government about the impending Martian invasion of Earth.

"He will speak to me. Could you tell him that Tracey called to discuss, well, things," Anna said with a hint of suggestion. "We met at the party last week."

"What?" Her voice trailed for a second, clearly not missing the implication. The level of concern Anna detected in the other woman's tone went beyond the natural curiosity of a work colleague. She began to think that Jim's PA did a lot more than her contract demanded. "Hold," the woman said curtly, adding further weight to Anna's suspicions.

"Er, should I be feeling a little jealous, at this point?" Corey whispered.

"Trust me," she mouthed silently. Corey huffed before retreating back into his man cave. The pause on the other line lasted for an unduly long time before the gruff voice of Jim Peterson greeted her.

"Listen, Miss, I think you may have called the wrong number." The statement was a projected one, seemingly for the benefit of his personal assistant.

Jesus, is there anyone this guy doesn't try to screw? Anna thought as cold fury grew inside her. "Jim, listen to me, you sack of shit."

"Anna?"

"Yeah, remember me, the woman you tried to snare in your sick games? I'm not as stupid as you thought. I'm gonna nail you to the wall, buddy boy. Do you hear me?"

His reply lacked the oily smoothness she remembered: he was rattled. "Look, all that legal business can go away, if you—"

"Did you know what happened to my sister?" She cut him off.

"Yes. It was all over the papers, but I don't see what it has to do—"

"Therein lies the problem, Jim: you're a selfish, little

prick. Didn't it occur to you that I have bigger issues to deal than your pathetic schemes?" She spoke with a steely calm that surprised even her. "Oh, but guess what? The note from your lap dog just reminded me of unfinished business. I'm writing the article. Sue me, if you dare." With that, she clapped her hands twice in quick succession: the signal for George to hang up the call. The line went dead.

"Wow. Remind me never to piss you off," Corey said.

Chapter 5

TRIAL

Tony stared at jury member number four and knew he was screwed. The ugly bitch looked like she would puke over her shiny, white stilettos every time the prosecutor detailed more of his handy work. No, that particular self-righteous skirt wanted him to fry. She would also persuade the dickless men on the jury that death was exactly what he deserved. *Cowards,* he thought, knowing they must secretly wish for the same power he wielded.

Tony turned his efforts back to sketching on the legal pad before him. He enjoyed the sense of unease it caused the great and the good gathered within the cramped confines of the court room to watch his public flogging. It also helped him ignore the monotonous whine of the prosecutor's voice, while she delivered yet more tedious details about fingerprints, DNA, blood splatter trajectory, yada yada, yada.

He yawned, and the action mercifully cut out the incessant drone for a second. Annoyed, he continued to outline the picture of the woman with huge breasts hanging by her neck.

"This shows the defendant had a premeditated intention to lure the victim..." Scribble, scribble. *If only it was as much fun hearing about it as doing it,* he thought.

The memories brought a smile to his usually-passive appearance, but the momentary display of emotion caused the wound in his eye to protest. It thudded with a persistent itch he'd never quite become accustomed to. Although insignificant in comparison with the white-hot fire he'd experienced in the early days, it still remained a distraction.

His hand rose instinctively to scratch the irritation, only to stop half way. As always, it would prove physically impossible to reach the source deep within his now-empty eye socket without causing a wave of agony. At the beginning of the trial, he'd arrived each day without bothering with the eye patch. After several horrified glances from observers, however, the judge ordered him to cover it. *It's important to meet expectations, old boy,* he thought. Remembering felt good—so, so good. He loved to visualize his favorites. The jury heard the technical terms, but he could see the real flesh of it. They couldn't possibly understand the control one felt from taking the life of another. Maybe if they were real lucky, he would teach them—especially juror number four.

The itch interrupted his wonderful reminiscences once again, bringing less pleasant memories of a gun being raised toward him while fear snaked down his spine. He saw the gleam of the barrel before she pulled the trigger. He hadn't died, though. Even the doctors had seemed curious about his surprising powers of survival. As one cop had uttered before spitting straight in his face, he was a "tough fucking cockroach."

He liked to imagine Anna as the figure swinging from the paper gallows he drew, with her blonde hair matted with gore. Tony smiled at the encouraging image and looked up at White Shoes again. She returned him another scowl of repulsion, and he gave her a slow, deliberate wink in reply. *Go right ahead, sweet cheeks, barf on those lovely tootsies.*

Despite such small victories, though, even his most desperate hopes had failed. He'd eagerly waited for the moment Anna came to court. Perhaps it would give him the opportunity to lunge from his seat and snap her neck right in front of that pompous, old judge. He could almost feel her soft hair beneath his fingertips while he wrenched. She hadn't come, though—not once. *What's the point of a circus if the lion has no one to maul?*

Before the trial started, he'd so looked forward to scrutinizing her expression, especially while they described the finer details of his final masterpiece: Julia. Alas, there'd been no opportunity for one last dalliance with his beloved. *Such a shame. The pain would have been... exquisite.* Now he understood why she hadn't come. Not wishing to pass on the chance to inflict petty torments, the court guards had one day thrown him a magazine during one of the many long recesses.

"I hope they're happy while your carcass rots," had been the accompanying sentiment.

He'd read the title: "Arizona's Richest Man Finds Love Amidst Tragedy." After that came the kicker: a picture of Anna and some other fuck emerging, hand-in-hand, from an upmarket eatery. He'd only read the first paragraph before losing his shit and rewarding the young court officer with a broken jaw. The resulting fracas had left him with a Taser burn to add to his list of mementos. She was no longer his. Another had claimed her—a fucking billionaire, no less. Tony ripped the paper from the pad then crushed it into a tight ball. The outburst drew the attention of the court, including the prosecutor, who paused mid-flow and then gave the jury a look that said, "See what I mean?" "The man before you has a pathological hatred of females. Furthermore, I believe the state has proved beyond any reasonable doubt that the defendant is guilty on all counts," she said, resuming her tedious rant.

She paused to allow the entire jury to stare at him in unison—a ridiculous sight that caused him to laugh out loud. In all their righteous indignation, they reminded him of the nodding porcelain dogs Mother used to keep. This prompted the fat, red-faced judge to bang his gavel. *Nodding dogs and a toy monkey bashing his drum.*

The judge droned on—something about contempt of court. Of course, Tony did his best to appear ashamed, stifling the grin that threatened to spread across his face. Another contempt of court ruling would only delay matters further, and he wanted this over and done with. He had a plan now that required him to exit the main stage—for a little while, at least.

I'll be a good circus beast while they parade me around the ring. I won't even snarl when they poke me. Must be patient. He faced the front of the court, waiting for the inevitable verdict. The peacocks had completed their intricate dances, the media had their juicy meat thrown to them, and all was ready to condemn the bogey man. Soon, it would be time to serve a good, old fashioned slice of star spangled, apple pie justice.

"The court will recess for one hour," said the fat monkey, bashing his drum once more.

Tony stood with the others while renewing his internal vow: no matter how long he waited, he would find a way to get to her. Even if just for a fleeting moment, she would be his once again. Once he did have her, he would take her down to that dark place where his soul lived. Down to the stone. There, he would feed on her light forever.

ANNA LOOKED out at the court room from under the thick, black wig. The heavy disguise added discomfort to her already-unbearable anxiety. She'd positioned herself at the back of the gathered spectators behind a tall man who could be used to block the view from the front, if necessary.

It'd been difficult to decide if she should attend the verdict. As for the rest of the trial, the judge had deemed the circumstances extreme enough to allow her to give testimony via video. The prosecutor had agreed, due to the mountain of extra evidence against him. At the time, this small mercy had been a massive relief, because she knew her presence would have fed his perverse mind. But the cross examination could hardly have been more testing if she'd been there in person.

The crux of the defence had been one of insanity, painting her as the cold, distant partner who'd pushed away his repeated pleas for help. The timing of her relationship with Corey formed the backbone of that spurious crap. They'd tried to claim the "affair" had contributed to Tony's fragile mental state. This line of attack had clearly failed, however, when she'd responded to the question, "Do you have anyone who can support that story, Miss Price?" Her reply was, "My sister, but unfortunately, she can't be here today." Her reply had received cries of support from the families of the other victims and had visibly shaken the defence. After that, the overwhelming procession of evidence seemed to crush any remaining doubts.

Despite her previous avoidance of proceedings, she

needed to see him receive justice for Julia and those other poor women. Finally, they could rest in peace. The decision hadn't been an easy one, though. Telling Corey had caused their first serious row, ending in several days of miserable silence between them. But she couldn't blame him for worrying. The media had already been in a frenzy over the so-called Phoenix Strangler case, and it hadn't taken long for them to connect the dots between that and their relationship. Shortly after, the first scandalous headlines had appeared. One particularly vicious web blog read, "Arizona's most eligible bachelor linked to Mrs. Strangler."

The resulting press interest reached a fever pitch, testing even Corey's considerable resources. The security team at the Estate had to be tripled, and she hadn't been left alone for five minutes without some towering ex-service type nearby. The whole thing had become so oppressive that Anna had threatened to leave. Only then had Corey agreed to relax some of the more extreme measures. "All rise." The command from the clerk made her heart beat faster. Dread mixed with anticipation within her.

There he was: Tony appeared smaller than the hellish version of himself filling her darkest nightmares. He shuffled passively behind three burly guards, seeming uninterested by his surroundings. The events of the past year had taken a toll on him not only because of his visible injuries, but also his leaner frame. He reminded her of a wiry, old panther pacing its cell and biding its time. There was nothing frail or defeated in that look, though. Instead, he oozed brooding tension.

AS IF PICKING up on her morbid interest, his gaze roved across the public surrounding him with one bright, penetrating eye. The gesture held such a deliberate quality that she guessed its purpose immediately: he searched for her. Determined not to give him the satisfaction, she ducked behind her unwitting protector. The different protagonists took their seats, ready for the drama to unfold. The atmosphere buzzed, and it took several gavel knocks to quiet the loud speculation. Occasional sobs from broken relatives punctuated the charged air. "The court may rise." The creaking sound of bodies rising from wooden benches followed, and then there was complete silence.

"In the matter of the State of Arizona versus Tony Eckerman," the judge paused to shuffle some papers around, "Madam foreperson, have you reached a verdict on all counts?" A thin woman with bags under her eyes, wearing a flower print dress, rose with a notepad in her hand.

"We have, your Honor."

"Verdict form count one, Stacey Williams," he pressed.

"We, the jury, find the defendant guilty of murder in the first degree," she croaked, clearly intimidated by the situation.

"And the second count, Marie Hernandez?"

Little Bird

"We, the jury, find the defendant guilty of murder in the first degree."

An audible groan went up from the family of the eighteen-year-old college student.

"Verdict count three, Darleen Maxwell?"

"We, the jury, find the defendant guilty of manslaughter in the first degree." Anna recalled that the prosecution had failed to find enough supporting DNA evidence to push for murder, but they had established Tony's presence at the scene of the prostitute's murder.

"Verdict count four, Patricia Smith?"

"Not guilty," the chair-woman confirmed. The note of regret in her voice was not entirely disguised.

"Please keep to the formal procedure, Madam foreperson."

"Verdict count five, Connie Ramirez?"

"Guilty. Sorry. I mean, we, the jury, find the defendant guilty of murder in the first degree."

A woman began to shout in Spanish. The judge banged furiously in response. "I will have order!" If the tragic litany of death didn't seem to move the old public servant, a breach of court room protocol did.

"Verdict count six, Mary Gentle?" he continued with a steely edge. Mary was believed to have been his earliest victim. She came from the same trailer park where he'd been raised. The poor thing had been his first girlfriend, and he'd beaten her to death in a drunken rage. How dreadfully familiar that tale sounded to Anna, now. The case had lain cold for years, after the original investigators were unable to find the mysterious boyfriend several witnesses had alluded to. They found him guilty.

Here it comes, Anna thought, knowing the final victim was her own beloved. She couldn't help but look toward Tony, hoping to see something approaching the pain and regret she'd experienced these past months. He seemed oblivious, though. Instead, he continued to doodle on a pad before him.

"Verdict count seven, Julia Price?"

Anna had cried so much that she'd thought it wouldn't be possible to shed further tears. They did come, though, thick and fast.

"We, the jury, find the defendant guilty of murder in the first degree." She closed her eyes and wept.

Chapter 6

A FRIEND

Anna sat at her usual spot in the auditorium, feeling like she'd just emerged from a dream. Their time together over the past weeks during her recovery and since the trial had been wonderful. There remained a part of her, however, that was in need of grounding away from the constant stimulation of Clear Water. *And wow, what a lot of stimulation I've had,* she mused, a flush rising in her cheeks.

Asking to resume her writing studies had come from a need to return to reality. Corey agreed, albeit with a slight pout to his bottom lip—a sure sign that he disagreed, but wished to avoid an argument. Today, though, he was in fine form, running through the many techniques a writer could use to improve their craft. Most involved a good dose of constant practice. Anna noticed that his workman-like ethos didn't always sit well with her fellow audience members. In particular, his frequent calls to "just write" were often greeted with audible sighs.

At present, he was busy scribbling some of the principles he'd just described on the white board. She couldn't resist watching his butt move under his tweed trousers, whilst he remained lost in his own enthusiasm. She contemplated getting her hands on those cute cakes later, and her cheeks reddened once more. *Concentrate, you stupid woman. You're here for a reason, and it's not to daydream about Corey's ass!*

Despite her fiancé's current good mood and her own contentedness lately, she'd also noticed a change in the mood of her classmates. More than once, she'd seen curious glances in her direction accompanied by whispered comments. At first, she'd put these disconcerting observations down to her own sense of heightened paranoia, but the obvious scrutiny had continued until she'd concluded that their poorly-hidden secret was out, as well as, in all likelihood, every other juicy detail of her story. They were the same things she wanted to replace with something approaching a normal life. *How long did you think that would last, kiddo, with your face all over the media? Ex- lover of a convicted serial killer and now betrothed to a billionaire.*

"Jesus, she's humping that?" The familiar high-pitched voice of the class wise-ass interrupted her attempts to focus.

Because the vindictive comment coincided with her own inner angst, she turned to look in the direction of the spotty, red-haired youth. With a sinking feeling, she realized he was staring straight at her, whilst a freckled blonde girl whispered in his ear.

"No fucking way!" He exclaimed further. The blonde nodded in response, as if to say. "And I'm not even joking."

Anna felt a well of sadness, rather than anger. Of course, they'd discussed if it was the right thing for her re-join the class. It'd taken much persuasion on his part to convince the college administration team to allow the return of such an infamous figure. They'd expressed serious concerns about the effect it would have on her classmates. He'd gotten his way, in the end, but Anna suspected it'd more to do with Corey being a major donor to the institution than his power of persuasion.

"Jesus, she's like the Black Widow, or somethin'!" The spotty kid blurted. This time, he drew the attention of the entire class.

Anna felt her cheeks burning. In response, the blonde gave an altogether unpleasant smirk. Her ginger conspirator had also noticed her discomfort and grinned. His brace-filled mouth opened for the follow up.

"Shut up, you geeky little dweeb." The insult came from an attractive, dark-haired woman in her mid-thirties, wearing a faded, chequered shirt. She tapped her pencil in annoyance, while glaring at the two teenagers. Anna didn't recognize her and assumed she must be a newcomer.

"Yeah, but..."

"You know nothin' bout nothin', you irritating little shit," the woman said with a dismissive tone. "Now shut your flappin' trap." Her accent sounded unusual—more mid-west than southern.

The youth folded his arms in a childlike gesture and looked to the gossiping girl to back him up, but she'd already slunk away, seeming not to want a confrontation with the older woman. The other students nearby had suddenly become engrossed with the lesson again. Anna noted with annoyance that Corey seemed oblivious to the minor crisis unfolding in the room.

The kid made a last attempt to gather support around him, before averting his gaze to the front of the class. Anna turned to the dark-haired newbie, and on an impulse, mouthed a silent thank you. The woman responded in kind with a warm, "You're welcome." She followed this up by pointing an imaginary pistol at the disruptive kid. Anna couldn't help but laugh at the movement. Although extreme, it perfectly reflected her own sentiment toward the little creep.

The rest of the lesson passed slowly, and Anna found herself unable to concentrate. In a state verging on panic, she brooded over what other rumors and lies must have been floating around campus.

When Corey drew proceedings to a close, she had to stop her urge to hurry to him. To do so in front of the class would only encourage gossip. Instead, she chose to hang around the entrance to the auditorium, while feigning interest in the various posters along the hallway. Occasionally, she'd pop her head through the doorway, only to see Corey answering queries from her classmates. For a moment, she feared they were quizzing him on his personal life, but his relaxed manner soon made it clear that the conversation was about their studies. Bursting with impatience, she continued to wait.

"Catchin' up on the latest health and safety news?" The question came from behind her.

Anna turned to find the woman who'd intervened on her behalf in the auditorium. A grey-eyed gaze regarded her with curiosity. Although not unattractive, they gave the newcomer an unusual, otherworldly look.

"Is it that obvious I'm waiting?" she replied, deciding to be honest with the thoughtful stranger.

"Just slightly."

Anna smiled, with the awkwardness of people greeting a potential friend for the first time. "Say, listen. Let me buy you a coffee." Anna said on an impulse, not wishing to pass on the opportunity to thank the woman. "Trust me, you'd be doing me a favor."

A guarded smile greeted her offer. "Sure, why not? I never say no to free coffee."

While they strolled toward the cafeteria, her new acquaintance introduced herself as Claire. They were soon chatting in a way she found refreshingly natural—so much so that she almost forgot Corey wouldn't have a clue where she'd gone, so she dropped him a quick text upon reaching the NASCAR-themed eatery in the college.

Anna indulged in a large, full-milk latte. The stressful

confrontation earlier made her in dire need of a pleasant distraction. Claire opted for a green tea.

"Hey, if you think you're gonna sip tea while I drink this monster, like a fat cow, you can think again!" she joked, guessing her new companion would be open to gentle ribbing. Claire laughed as she'd hoped, and then opted to change her order to coffee topped with whipped cream. "That's more like it." Anna approved.

After watching the barista perform the usual juggling act with various frothing pipes and clinking cups, they settled down into one the racing car booths, sipping their naughty treats.

"So, you're new, right?" Anna asked after a moment of shared cream Heaven.

"Yep. Moved from Wichita last month with my little monster. Fresh start."

"Wow, that's a big move from Kansas for a family," Anna commented, her mind already trying to read between the lines. "How old's your kid?"

"He's five. Still a baby, really. Well, at least in my eyes," Claire replied, taking a big scoop of creamy froth of the top of her drink with a straw and dropping it in her mouth. "So, is it true that you're together? With Mr. Young, I mean."

Anna blushed at the other woman's directness. "Do we make it so obvious?"

"You guys can't keep your eyes off each other." Anna couldn't help but sense a moment of distaste pass over

Claire's face as she spoke, before dismissing the feeling as her own paranoia.

"Oh boy. I knew it would be a bad idea to come to class," she sighed.

Claire stared at her for a moment with that disconcerting gaze. Anna suspected this thoughtful woman knew more than she expressed. "Who gives a shit what those kids think? They have no right to judge," she said, her tone clipped. Anna got the impression that she wanted to say more, but chose not to.

"Thanks. It's kind of you to say, but..."

"No buts. He's a pimply little twonk and doesn't have the right."

Anna smiled. "Twonk? That's new for me." She felt an overwhelming need to find out exactly what rumors had circulated. It occurred to her that this frank woman could be the perfect person to ask. "How much do they know?" she asked, deciding to place a little more trust in her. At the back of her mind flickered the warnings from Corey's security team. In truth, however, she was desperate for female company in her life.

Claire pursed her lips, playing with the straw. "That you're together, and that Corey isn't just their teacher."

No wonder he's Mr. Popular all of a sudden, Anna thought, immediately regretting the unkind sentiment. She no longer felt like drinking the coffee and pushed it away. The potential implications for his voluntary role at the college made her feel depressed.

"Do they know what happened to me?"

"Yes." The abruptness of the reply didn't leave any room for doubt.

"What are they saying about... what happened?" Anna asked, unable to resist the temptation to lift each stone and see what crawled out.

"Depends who you ask," Claire's answer was hesitant. Anna sensed that she was not the only one being wary about how forthcoming to be. "It's just dumb gossip." The other woman shrugged. "They're kids."

"Please. I need to know."

Claire pondered for a time, stirring the sweet mixture in front of her, with unreadable grey eyes. "Like I said, they're kids," she said eventually. "A tragedy for you is a Facebook feed to them. The closest most of these little runts get to danger is getting tangled in their sheets. They don't understand what it must feel like to be afraid every day, or the lengths a woman will go to protect her man." The final point seemed deliberate.

"I didn't know what he did," Anna said. "I swear it."

Claire didn't react straight away, but continued to stir the contents of her cup. Anna began to wonder if she'd made a mistake by confiding in this straight-talking person. She half-expected Claire to rise and throw the contents of her cup across the table in disgust. *Maybe she'll throw in a few of the beauts you've been asking yourself lately, kiddo—the real humdingers. How could you not have known? Did you choose to ignore the signs? Even if you didn't, what kind of a woman misses something so wrong with her man?* Anna braced her hands against the table, ready to leave when the time came. Claire blinked and then wiped the corner of her eye. *Are those tears?*

"I've been around men like that," Claire said.

Men like that?

"Maybe not in the same way as you," she continued, "but violent men—dangerous men."

"Oh," Anna said in a half-whisper. "Is that why you moved to Phoenix?"

Claire nodded, wiping away a forming tear again. She seemed pensive, now—lost in her own demons, for a second. Anna noticed how she fingered a small, silver crucifix around her neck with a quiet desperation. She wondered what this poor woman had endured. Across the woman's slim features, she could see a similar guilt to her own.

Just as she was about to offer Claire a comforting hand, Corey bounced around the corner with a cheesy grin on his handsome features. He looked energized, full of enthusiasm, and pretty much the opposite of what would be appropriate right then. Anna's irritation grew. When he shot her a grin of recognition, she returned with a dark glare. He took the hint and suddenly became fascinated by the drinks dispenser.

"Oh, well. Some of them are just dopey, rather than dangerous." She said, trying to excuse her lover's ill-timed entrance. Claire didn't respond with anything approaching warmth, though. If anything, her grip on the silver religious trinket tightened.

Wow. Some guy has really hurt this one, Anna reflected, regretting her poor attempt at humor. "Look, I know we've only just met, but I'd like to thank you properly for your help today."

"Hey, I ain't after any charity here, lady. I meant every word I said, period." Claire crossed her arms in a gesture of mild offense.

"No. I don't mean anything like that," Anna assured her. "It's just—I'm having such a bad time of it lately, and I could do with someone to have a few drinks with. What do you say?"

Claire's mood visibly changed and a tentative smile returned to her lips. "Sounds good," she agreed. "I don't know anyone in this town."

"Cool, it's a date," Anna said, pulling a notebook from her handbag and asking the other woman for her phone number. The smile Claire gave her looked strained, as she read out the digits. "Will call soon," Anna said, pointing at the note with a gesture emphasising her intention. "Time to put Iurkio out of his misery."

Resisting the temptation to plant a reassuring kiss on the other woman's cheek, she strolled back toward the corridor with a sheepish-looking Corey at her heels.

"Wasn't it a great session today? Did you see how many questions I got at the end?" he asked, after catching up with her. "Gotta be a record."

"Corey..."

"Who was that?" he asked. "Isn't she one of the new starters?"

"Why are you asking me? You're supposed to be her teacher, right?" The curtness of her reply must have started to ring a few alarm bells, because he adopted a more careful tone.

"Hey, honey. What's wrong? Did I piss you off?" He placed a hand on her shoulder in a bid to slow down her march.

She stopped and turned to him. The hurt expression on his face made it difficult to stay mad, but Anna felt determined to make her point, regardless. "Sometimes, you walk around in a world of your own, Corey! You big dope," she said, half-heartedly slapping him on the shoulder. "Do you know that?"

His expression turned to confusion. Anna became more exasperated than ever—particularly as she felt a strong twinge of guilt at how she was treating him. Knocking the natural exuberance out of Corey held no pleasure for her.

A group of first-year students passed, giving them curious glances. Anna stepped back and clutched her bag to her breast in a poor attempt to look casual. *Great! We're giving them more to talk about!* After the group had passed out through the aircraft hangar-themed doors, the couple resumed their tiff. Corey spread his arms wide in the universal sign for "what the fuck did I do?"

"Corey, didn't you notice all the whispering in class?" she asked, doing her best to restrain her frustration.

"About what?"

"About us, you dip shit!" she said between clenched teeth.

"Oh." Finally, the penny had dropped.

"They know everything," she said. "About us, about you, about what happened. Everything."

"Are you sure?"

Anna clutched the bag tighter still. "You asked me who that complete stranger was in the cafeteria."

"Yes."

"She defended me against that little ginger asshole." Her voice rose, "A stranger stuck up for us while you were playing teacher." Immediately she regretted the harshness of her tone. Worse, the color rising in Corey's neck showed that this particular barb had hit its mark.

"I'm sorry. I didn't know." He looked crestfallen.

She placed a reassuring hand against his shoulder. "I shouldn't take it out on you," she said, her anger draining. "I'm upset because it means we can't be together here."

Corey grasped the hand she'd offered. "Why should it change anything?" he asked. "We knew this was bound to happen sooner or later. I'm amazed we got away with it for this long."

"Yes, but it means I can't stay here."

"Why?" His blue eyes were serious, determined.

"Well, because..." she struggled to answer. "What if they keep...?"

"What if they do? We've got as much right as anyone to be happy. Who cares what the gimpy little shit thinks?" he said with a serious expression. "Besides, you've never been forced to read his stories. They're about as mature as holding a cream-eating contest in a strip bar. Trust me, he's the worst kind of lonely dweeb." His gaze became fierce. "You really want to give in to that? After everything you've been through?"

He's right, kiddo.

She gripped his hand. An old saying of her father's came to mind. "You're right: fuck 'em."

"Amen to that, sister."

Chapter 7
A FAN

The tap dripped into the chrome bowl. At first, it was a quiet sound, but in the confined, dank air of the cell, it'd grown louder and louder until it became a wall of sound in his mind. It totally blocked his access to the many wonderful memories, his sole outlet of pleasure.

The soft feel of clean-smelling hair as I squeeze.

Drip.

The blue panties.

DRIP.

The soft throat.

D R I P.

He threw the plastic tray of rancid food at the opposite wall, and the unidentifiable brown matter slapped against the black and white tiles with an audible thwack. He tried to laugh at the action, but couldn't

258

find any respite from the tortuous sensations surrounding him.

One of the strip lights had begun to flicker a week ago. At first, it'd offered some welcome variety to the soul-sucking drip, but now they formed a double act straight from the bowels of Hell. The dripping tap felt like a worm burrowing through the soft flesh of his ear drum, while the flickering light became a switch between the over-bright cell and a darker world.

"Drip, drip," he repeated the sound, unable to remain silent any longer. *That was a mistake, old boy.*

Sure enough, a high-pierced screech rang out from his neighbor's cell. He'd woken Teddy. "Is it time, Motha?" the older man called out his usual line.

"Shut the fuck up, you fucking loon!" Tony couldn't help but take the bait.

The response was the same, as always. "You knows I done it for you, Motha. You knows that, don't you?"

"I'm not your pissed-riddled, scabby whore of a mother, you twisted freak!"

"I done it for you, Motha."

Tony slunk onto the hard cot, forcing himself to stay calm. He'd become better at doing that, lately. The first month without booze had been torture, making his present situation seem like a stroll in the park. Going cold turkey had forced him to appreciate the value of patience.

"Patience is a virtue, old boy," he said.

"Motha?" Teddy answered.

In the early weeks, Tony had puzzled over why such a crazy fool would be kept in the max wing. That was, until he'd overheard the guards referring to the old goat as Uncle Teddy Bear. It turned out that he'd been notorious in the seventies for luring toddlers into his car with promises of a free teddy bear. The police were still finding body parts to this day.

He'd been curious to know how such a nut job could've kept his shit together and give the cops the slip for a decade. After a while locked up here, though, the depressing truth came to him: this place had fried Ted's brain like an egg on a hot plate. *Your future...*

Not that he cared about the old freak. He thought child killers deserved everything they got. Sure, he'd done that pretty college kid, but she'd been eighteen, going on thirty-five. Besides, he hadn't even needed to speak to her to work out that she was a whore.

Her hair smelled of cheap perfume, he recalled. Once again, he tried to find that special zone in which he could reminisce.

Drip. Flicker.

"Fuck!" He roared. *There must be a way I can get to her again!* he thought, the sudden outburst unleashing his biggest mind fuck.

Drip.

His work could never be complete until he'd dealt with her. She'd make the ultimate trophy to add to his gallery of souls. *You came so close—so very fucking close.* He could almost taste her. *No prizes for second place, old boy.*

"There must be a way!" He pressed himself for the thousandth time, but no answer came.

Tony wondered if it was possible to gather the right materials to fashion a noose and hang himself from the light fitting. *No more chances to tickle her fancy... time to die.*

The sound of booted footsteps thudding along the corridor broke his internal deliberations. The timing of the unannounced visit was unusual, because the regime of the prison demanded a strict routine. It was long past the mid-day feed.

The trudging drew closer until, to Tony's surprise, the overripe presence of Officer Plum-Dike stopped outside his cell. Just like his namesake, the sweating, fat man was the shape of a plum and gave off an odor akin to rotten fruit. There was no doubt his other colleagues had nominated him for this isolated position in order to spare their sense of smell. It also served to inflict one more torture on the institution's special residents.

"Afternoon, Officer," Tony greeted the guard standing before him with hands on hips. Plum-Dike's narrowed gaze weighed him with a look of undisguised contempt.

Tony had learned early on that it was a mistake to show any kind of discomfort—or, God forbid, emotion—to the sadistic asshole. Plum-Dike did so enjoy his petty torments. At the beginning of his sentence, he'd made a naïve request for the dripping basin to be fixed. The response of Officer Dick Face had been to take his heavy mag light and whack the faulty tap. His helpful intervention had increased the rate of the leak.

The guard rocked on his heels, prolonging the act of wafting his rancid body smell in Tony's direction. After several moments of sharing, his gaze landed on the flickering strip light. "You wanna report the faulty light, boy?" He asked, black service shoes creaking as he continued to sway.

"Didn't notice no broken light, sir," Tony replied, maintaining his respectful tone while wishing the bars separating them would disappear.

Plum-Dike hooked his fingers into his belt, pondering the answer. With each thrust of the man's crotch, Tony endured a fresh wave of his delightful body perfume. He restrained his urge to gag and considered how good it would feel to spend the rest of the afternoon chopping the fat prick into handy, washing machine-sized pieces.

Plum-Dike appeared to become bored by his inability to provoke a reaction. Just as Tony thought he would leave, the guard removed an envelope from his brown service trousers before crushing it into a tight ball. He flung it through the bars. "Looks like you got fan mail, boy," he said. "Fucking prisoner rights, my ass!" he added to no one in particular.

Tony looked at the letter as if seeing a visitor from Venus.

"Don't wet yer knickers just yet—it's already been

checked," Plum-Dike said. "And don't you so much as breathe in the wrong direction, you hear me? You sick little puke. Drugs, porn, any of that filthy shit, and I guarantee you will be the sorriest mother chucker who set foot behind these walls." Tony wondered what a mother chucker looked like. "I mean it, boy. We've learned every sneaky trick in the book. If you try it, we'll find out. Got that? I guaran-fuck-ing-tee a world of pain will follow. Do not fuck with me."

"Yes, sir," Tony replied, wishing to rid himself of the guard and be alone with his unexpected prize.

The truth was that he hadn't spoken to anyone other than haters or fruit loops, since the trial. This could prove an interesting curiosity, indeed. He hoped the sender was a family member of one of his girls—a mother would be ideal. Maybe she wanted to know details of how her precious died. *Oh yes, wouldn't that be a treat!* Of course, he'd be more than happy to oblige. He would drag it out—maybe for years. *Sweet. Collect all three-hundred pieces and build your very own Spanish galleon!*

Plum-Dike gave a final disapproving sniff and marched back down the corridor. Elated, Tony reached out, but then he stayed his hand halfway to the paper.

"Could be a trick," he muttered. *No way. Too elaborate for him, old boy.*

Unable to resist, he paced over to the crumpled envelope and lifted it. Still not trusting its contents, he lifted it to his face and inhaled. This time, he did gag. It smelled heady with Plum-Dike's odor. The nausea soon passed, when he realized there was another, more subtle scent underneath: something female.

He looked down at the envelope and unfolded the creases. The handwriting was plain enough, with his name and the address of the prison—nothing special.

He traced his thumb across the seal, where he guessed a soft pink tongue had passed down its length. He spent some time imagining different pretty faces performing the intimate act, especially his special girls. For good measure, he added jury member number four into the mix: good old White Shoes. In his mind's-eye, she had that same look of fear he recalled while she licked the envelope. She licked it with a longing to be punished. Afraid for sure, but still unable to resist the temptation not to flirt with her favorite killer.

Examining the seal further, he noticed the existing thin tear down its length: the prison team had already examined its contents. Ignoring his irritation, he removed the single sheaf of paper inside. The first thing he noticed was more of the perfume. It was strong—too strong to have been a coincidence. Most women would avoid sending someone like him such a provocative signal. *Hell, even that sour-faced bitch paid to defend you didn't wear makeup during our rushed interviews together. Interesting.*

He spent several moments inhaling and savoring every detail. He then tried and failed to match a face he recognized to the scent. No, he needed more to unlock this puzzle.

The paper was good quality and textured—definitely not the kind used for bureaucratic tediousness. This was personal. He unfolded it to reveal a handwritten page. Some of its contents had ugly black blocks running through it, where Arizona's finest had removed personal details. He noticed with disappointment that this included the address of the sender. There still remained a wealth of delights for him to feast upon, though.

REDACTED

Dear Mr. Eckerman,

My name is Kate ***. I felt the need to write and express my shock at the lack of justice you received at your recent trail. Your innocence was clear for all to see, and I could hardly believe how poorly you've been treated before the eyes of our Lord. It makes me wonder how those evil people can sleep at night, knowing their souls are in peril from such wicked lies. Tell me, kind sir, how have you coped during your long fight? Have you been born again, as I?

You looked so calm during the sentencing. How? It reminded me of the story of Saint Ignatius, when faced by wild beasts and the ungodly cheers of the Romans, while they tore away his blessed flesh.

These so-called women that your accusers have so shamefully defended were obviously ***. It is an abomination in the eyes of God, when such *** are defended by the earthly courts. Does the Holy Book not make it clear that Eve should not tempt Adam?

God-fearing women need not worry about the passions of men. The light of our savior envelops us and removes impure thoughts from the eyes of the beholder. Such women of virtue are held high in the Lord's esteem. Only on our wedding day do we give ourselves over to the miracle of creating new life. Is it not an abomination that a good man such as you has been brought low and chained, like a beast, because of the wanton lusts of Eve?

I pray you take comfort from the fact that there are at least some clean women left in the world—those of us who repent the wickedness of Eve; those who vow not to profane the purity of Adam by exposing our flesh, or seek to raise ourselves above the divinely appointed status of our sex.

Be assured, I would never seek the apple.

Please, I must know. Have you also been saved?

Yours, with grace,

Kate

Chapter 8

BIG BIRD

Anna stared down at the blank page of her laptop screen feeling like a fool. She'd felt fired up to write the exposé after receiving the cease and desist order, but now that it came to it, she didn't know where to start. Not only that, but the stakes were so high that there was a real risk she would write a libellous disaster, damaging the very cause she'd vowed to aid. The Tonto National Forest was a beautiful, unspoiled landscape facing ruin all because of the scheming blackmail perpetrated by James Peterson. This article could be the only thing standing between him and a likely victory.

Corey had already been in touch with the forestry commission to warn them. They'd been shocked by the allegation, but agreed that Moyer's efforts fell way below their expectations. In fact, they'd already considered ditching him as their lawyer. With the court date fast approaching, though, Corey advised them to stick with the useless fool while his top journalist worked on springing the trap that would destroy the corporation's chances for good. *No pressure, then, kiddo!* she thought, tapping the desk in frustration.

She decided to go over the facts again, but her memories from before Julia's passing had become dim. It was as if her damaged psyche tried to resist any recollection around the time of Big Bird's murder. *Get a grip. You can do this.* She delved back, forcing herself to remember anything beyond hearsay.

"The data stick!" she said after a moment. On her last day, she'd copied the entire case file onto a USB drive. *Not so fast, smartass. Where is it now?*

Anna rose and paced the brightly-lit bedroom at Clear Water, racking her brain. She'd definitely thrown it into her old purse at the office the last time she'd seen it. With this in mind, she strode over to the Japanese-style walk-in closet and slid the doors aside. As she did so, the interior became bathed in natural light from the translucent tubes funnelling daylight directly from the roof. It was another one of Corey's genius touches to their amazing home.

A small house could fit inside the under-used interior of the store they'd come to refer to as Narnia. Corey had little time for fashion, keeping few clothes in a facility that many would give their left leg for. Of course, she'd done her best to remedy this embarrassing situation by filling her own corner. Although she'd added several dainty numbers to the collection since her arrival, it still looked like the room that fashion had forgotten. When she'd pointed out this sorry state of affairs to Corey, he'd agreed that it was a waste and proposed turning it into an office. She'd sulked mercilessly at this evil plan until finally making him get the hint. His next question had been to ask if she could fill it. Her reply had been, "Of course I can, dumbass!"

Adding to their growing clothing collection had been one of the things keeping her mind off the murder. But today, she sought her belongings from that dark time— something she hadn't been strong enough to do, yet. Anna forced herself to approach the pile of plastic bags marked "evidence" which'd been returned after the trial.

She looked down at the piled collection of a past life, surprised by how little they amounted to. Some contained Julia's things, and that was definitely not a place she wanted to go—the task before her required focus, not a blubbering wreck. She began to move aside the packages with her foot, as if booby-trapped.

Anna reached down after building enough courage and began to sort by hand. It didn't take long before she felt the distinctive shape of her old handbag amongst the clutter. Ripping open the plastic, she grasped the black clutch bag and removed it. In doing so, something else dropped onto the polished, hardwood floor, causing her to glance at the glint of metal. Her heart began to hammer, and the grinning face of Sesame Street's Big Bird stared up at her from the scuffed broach. "Big Bird says you can do it, kiddo!" said the speech bubble emerging from his beak.

Anna was seven years old, painted bright green, and sobbing. She'd fled her class's second grade production of The Wind in the Willows to hide backstage amongst the props. Lumbered with the part of Toad, her teacher had painted her bright green before dressing her in a smelly, old tweed jacket. The large pillow stuffed over her thick jumper only added to her monstrous appearance. She felt convinced that the result made her look like a fat alien. Worse, she was sure the ugly outfit would provide her friends with many laughs at her expense.

A sudden rustling amongst the costumes behind brought Anna's crying to a halt. Relieved, she turned to find the freckled face of Julia. At nearly ten years old, her big sis towered above her. To Anna, her sister also looked much prettier than her.

"I don't want to be a stupid toad! I look so ugly and there are so many people!" she said without waiting for Julia to speak. "Please don't tell them I'm here, Ju Ju!"

Julia didn't say a word. Instead, she'd put her arms out in a gesture that made Anna run straight over. They clung together while the youngest continued to weep. "You can do this," Julia said.

"I can't," Anna insisted. "There are too many people, Julia!"

"So? What's the worst that can happen?"

"They'll laugh at me." Her initial hysterics had reduced to an occasional snotty shudder.

"They're supposed to laugh at you. You're Toad of Toad Hall, remember?"

"I suppose so."

"Here, listen, if you play the stupid toad, I'll give you this." Julia reached in her pocket and brought out the cheap badge. Anna's crying stopped instantly, and she wiped her nose on the sleeve of the stinky jacket. She then gazed down at the happy, smiling character.

"Big Bird says you can do this, kiddo!" she read the words aloud, smiling. Julia buttoned the happy charm onto her sister's coat. "Thank you, Big Bird," she said to Julia, instead of the badge, as intended.

"You're welcome, Little Bird," Julia smiled. "Now, I think we need to find some green paint, or it will look like Mr. Toad's face got run over!"

They laughed.

THE TEARS CAME hot and thick as Anna held the badge in trembling fingers. "You can do it, kiddo," she murmured, before pinning the badge to her soft, white dressing gown.

She found the data stick and took it to the bedroom

where her laptop sat waiting. The flashing cursor blinked, daring her to type. Placing the stick in the USB port, she waited a moment while the file loaded. After opening it, she started to scan the contents. Three sub folders sat underneath the root: Billing, Case Content, and Correspondence. She opened the Billing folder first. It soon became obvious that Moyer's lack of effort on his clients' behalf hadn't stopped him from billing them heavily. *Talk about adding insult to injury,* she thought as she read through the eye-watering figures.

She clicked on the Case Content folder and found it far less populated. There were some half-hearted notes in a dozen documents, but nothing of substance. She browsed through them without seeing anything of particular interest, before going through the Correspondence. This seemed to be a better maintained set of records, including rows of scanned paper docs and some emails. She recalled that it was one of Blanche's jobs to open the post and support Moyer's non-existent computer skills.

"Miserable old bag," Anna muttered, voicing her dislike for her unpleasant former colleague.

Some of the scanned documents had been labelled "Law for Schools." Anna pursed her lips, trying to place the odd phrase. *Why are they in this case folder?* She thought. Curious, she opened one of the PDF documents bearing the strange title. A blue rotating ring appeared for a second, and then the scanned words appeared.

"Bingo!" she said after skimming the content. "Thank you, Blanche, you dumb bitch!"

The seal of Congressman James Peterson headed the brief letter. It thanked the offices of Howard and Moyer for making the Congressman aware of the voluntary work it did with the local school districts. It seemed that Bill Moyer had been teaching underprivileged kids the importance of the justice system. In fact, the Congressman had been so impressed with the law firm's philanthropic efforts that he wanted to personally donate ten-thousand dollars toward the worthy cause. The whole idea of Moyer volunteering for anything was laughable. There was no doubt the greedy junkie had smoked his way through the concealed bribe.

She went over more of the correspondence, but couldn't find anything of interest. Peterson was slicker than a greased pig trying to outrun an amorous hillbilly. Moyer, though, was the weak point in the chain. His lack of diligence combined with the super anal filing habits of Blanche had already exposed them. Anna felt certain that a smoking gun must be in here, somewhere, but she needed one more nail in this coffin. *This dumb blonde is gonna call your bluff, fuckers.*

There were maybe a dozen more letters between the pair, which didn't take long to scan through. Most of them looked like made up progress reports, presumably to make the cover story appear more authentic. Even this, Moyer had failed to do with competence. Often, they read as single line phrases to show all was well, and the lazy bastard had even repeated the same expressions on three separate occasions. Although interesting, it didn't deliver the killer blow she sought.

Anna flicked through sub-folders, trying to guess the most likely place to find more dirt. Her gaze fell upon one entitled Monthly Deletion. *People put their crap in the trash, kiddo.* She found only one untitled email chain inside. The original communication came from Bill Moyer to a personal address.

SUBJECT: (BLANK)
Jim, Where have you been? I've tried to call a thousand times, and your PA is ignoring the office email.
I NEED MORE MONEY. I'm sick of putting my fucking career on the line to do your stupid bullshit. Wire it to the usual account TODAY. If you don't, then I will blow the lid on this shit.
Don't forget: YOU CAME TO ME. SEND ME ANOTHER $30K, AT LEAST.

. . . .

The reply:
SUBJECT: (BLANK)

Where did you get this address, you stupid, fat fuck? Never ever contact me at this address again. Delete this email chain. I'm wiring another $10k. No more.

Ask me for cash one more time, you walking corpse, and I'll make sure you are buried with a hundred dollar bill lodged in your windpipe.
P.S. I know I came to you. I was looking for the biggest waste of oxygen still able to practice law, and you certainly didn't disappoint. Your fucktard approach to security proves it. P.P.S. Scrap the hundred bill—you're not worth it. I'll just ram that glass cock you love to suck on down your fat gullet. DELETE THIS EMAIL CHAIN, OR I SWEAR THE ABOVE THREAT WILL BECOME A PROMISE.

....

FINALLY:

SUBJECT: (BLANK)

Blanche. Could you make sure you delete this chain? I'm not used to this email crap. I keep dragging it over to the trash can on my desktop, like you said, and nothing happens! Bill

A<small>NNA STARED AT</small> <small>THE SCREEN</small>, not believing her luck. Blanche had placed the message chain into the delete folder just a few days before the monthly data purge. She sent up a silent prayer for the staggering incompetence of Moyer and his staff. Why the lawyer would trust anyone with such a damning piece of evidence remained a mystery. *Maybe they were lovers?*

It didn't matter now. Writing the article remained the only important thing. Anna was so elated that she felt the need to share her news without delay, so she gave George the command to call Corey. He'd been at a conference in LA for the past few days, leaving her to carry out her writing mission in the splendid solitude of Clear Water.

"Hey, sugar buns. How's my favorite concubine doing?" Corey answered after the second ring. She could tell he had male company, because of the borderline sexist greeting. Although annoying, she didn't have the heart to squash the boyish game.

"Hey, asshole, I thought you were my concubine?" She was in a good mood, so she played ball. "Biiiatch!"

Corey laughed. "What's up, hon?"

"I've found it—the evidence!" She went on to explain how she'd found the data stick.

"Fantastic, I knew you would," he replied without sounding the least bit surprised.

"How did you know I would?" she asked, still sulking that he'd made a promise to the forest trust on her behalf.

"You're a truth-seeker, remember?" he answered. "After the evil shit you've beaten, this is a walk in the park. I didn't doubt it for a second." She glowed at the words.

"Look, you'll be home tomorrow, so why don't we celebrate?" she asked.

"Oh, shit. Sorry, babe. I forgot to say that they've extended the conference for another day. We're on the verge of doing a deal with the Japanese that could halve our cell costs. They'll expect me to sign the deal in person."

"Oh, poo," she sulked. "I was looking forward to seeing you again."

"I miss you, too." His voice was lower, now, "I wouldn't stay longer, if I had a choice."

"I know."

"Why don't you hook up with your new friend? You both seemed to get on."

Anna mulled the idea for a moment. Claire had been a breath of fresh air, and they'd already promised to meet up. Also, she missed female conversation—particularly about the wedding. "I might do just that," she said. "Catch you later, sweetie. Love you. I've got some writing to do!"

The article flowed after the call, and a few thousand words later, she felt certain the plans of Peterson were finished. "Put that in your pipe and smoke it, asshole," she said, pressing the final period key of the text.

After emailing the finished piece to Corey, she gave the

Big Bird badge a quick rub of gratitude, and then contemplated what to do with the rest of her evening. Although she wanted to contact the kind and friendly Claire, she found herself hesitating. *Maybe you're not ready for friendship, yet?* "There's only one way to find out, kiddo." She said aloud.

Anna dug out the crumpled piece of paper with the other woman's number scribbled on it and then instructed George to dial.

"Hello, this is 492-111. How may I help you?" a sweet child's voice answered in a slow, practiced tone. Anna found the immature formality impossibly cute. *Might be her kid?* She thought.

"Hello, could I speak to Claire, please?"

There was a pause, as if the listener were wrestling with an unfamiliar term. "Would you like to speak to Momma?" the kid asked.

"Er, I think so. I mean, yes, please," Anna replied, hoping she hadn't punched in the wrong number.

"You certainly may!" A series of ear-shattering thuds and bangs followed, presumably while the child transported the handset to his mother.

"Hold on, please, Momma is sleeping. I need to wake her."

"Oh no, sweetie, it's okay, you don't have to..." Her intervention came too late, though. More banging followed before she heard the boy call his mother.

"Wake up, Momma! There's a lady on the phone asking for you." An adult voice asked a muffled question.

"Who is speak—" the kid's voice cut off as Anna heard another inaudible instruction. "May I ask who is speaking?" he repeated, this time with extra politeness. Anna smiled, hoping that one day she would get the chance to guide her own children in the same way.

"You certainly may," she answered. "Could you tell your momma that it's Anna, the lady she met at college."

"Mom, the lady is called Anna and says you met at col... col... at school."

"Pass it here, Hermie," Anna heard. "Hi, Anna," the voice was Claire's, sounding friendly, but tired.

"Oh, hi, Claire. I'm so sorry, I didn't mean to disturb you," she answered, embarrassed by the intrusion.

"Hey, no problem at all. This little critter made me sit through a marathon session of Barney until two AM. My brain is shot."

A brief moment of silence followed before Anna realized Claire was being too polite to ask why she'd called. "So, I called to arrange that drink," she said, trying not to sound desperate. There was a pause, and she expected some kind of half-hearted apology. *I wouldn't blame you, considering my track record,* she thought. *Stay clear, world, toxic jinx approaching!*

"That's the best offer I've had in months," Claire replied, putting a stop to her paranoia. "The problem is that finding a decent babysitter for my man, here, is like searching for hen's teeth."

Anna smiled when she heard the boy ask if hens really did have had teeth. She tried to think of a solution to Claire's child care issue, but all she could come up with involved a comical vision of leaving the kid in the care of one over-enthusiastic house robot.

"Bring him with us," she said. "I'm sure we can have a good time with... sorry, was it Hermie?"

"Hermie by name, Hermie by nature," Claire replied, prompting them both to laugh. "Say hello properly to Hermon."

Anna heard the phone switch again, followed by the heavier breathing of the child. "Hello, Hermon. I'm Anna. Would you like to go out with your mom and me?"

"Where to?" he asked, his tone immediately perked up.

"I'm not sure, yet, hon. Put your mom back on and we can decide," she replied.

"Can we go to Krispy Dough?" he asked expectantly. The sound of a groan coming from the background indicated that his mom wasn't so keen on the idea.

"Why don't we ask your mom, honey?" Anna suggested. The phone switched again.

"He's obsessed with the Star Wars toys you get there," Claire explained. "We've been twice already this week, and he doesn't care if he turns his poor mother into a fat, penniless blimp to get it."

"Typical male," Anna agreed.

"What can you do? It's the natural order of things," Claire answered. Anna took this to mean mothers being hauled from pillar to post by their kids.

"Hey, not a problem. He's more than welcome, and it's been so long since I've been around a little one that it'd be a novelty for me."

"Wish I could say the same," Claire added. "Tell you what: buy me a coffee and you get the company of one Hermon Pike."

"Deal."

Chapter 9

PLANS

A nna's brand new Toyota drew more than a few curious glances as she drove along the run-down neighbourhood in Tolleson. Ironically, her old station wagon would have left her feeling less vulnerable. She passed the assorted dollar stores and pawn brokers, feeling grateful that these places didn't feature in her world, anymore. Poverty had become a distant memory for her, and the idea of having to sell one's most cherished items just to be able to put food on the table was unthinkable for her, now. A street not dissimilar to this one, however, had been her reality for years. She didn't miss it; there was nothing noble about living day to day not knowing if you'd be able to pay the next rent. No, she felt no nostalgic desire to be here, and she pitied Claire for not having a choice in the matter.

The GPS directed her to pull up outside a house still

with the For Rent sign stuck into a small patch of turf beyond the front porch. Anna recalled Claire saying she'd moved to Phoenix recently and guessed from the dilapidated dwelling that the move had been a rushed one. Even someone with a moderate income wouldn't have chosen this place, especially not someone with a young child. It made her feel more than a little uncomfortable to think about the vast luxury she and Corey enjoyed by comparison. She couldn't help but check the street for dodgy characters before exiting the car. Reassuringly, the only person around appeared to be an elderly bum pushing a squeaky-wheeled shopping cart full of plastic bottles in the direction of the convenience stores. Stepping out, she pressed the key fob twice to double lock the car, despite her willingness to think the best of her fellow man.

"You're turning into a snob," she muttered as she approached a flaking green door.

Anna pressed the discolored doorbell hanging from the rotten frame. Nothing happened, so she rapped three times. The door opened immediately and Claire stood before her. The dark smudges underneath her deep, grey eyes spoke of her lack of sleep. Little Hermon stood beside her, and one look at his angelic face made Anna's heart sail. He had the same colored gaze as his mother, but instead of giving him a mysterious appearance, it added to his innocent charm. He'd been well-dressed in a light coat with matching Star Wars-themed boots. By contrast, Claire's coat looked worn and ill fitting, like it came from a second hand store. Behind the two lay a bare hallway littered with cardboard boxes and other items associated with a new resident. "Hi, there!" Anna said in an enthusiastic tone for the benefit of her young audience. She had to resist the urge to laugh at the happy grin on the young boy's face, which contrasted with his mother's resigned smile.

"Are you the lady I spoke to on the phone?" he asked.

"I certainly am, kiddo."

"Wowee! Krispy Dough, here we come!" he declared, tugging his mom toward the street. "I'd let you in, but it looks like a bomb hit it." Claire apologized while being marched past Anna. The poor woman barely had time to reach behind her and pull the door shut.

"Yowzer! Is this your car?" Hermon asked, pointing at the white Toyota. "It's totally sick!"

"You need to call the lady Anna—and where did you learn that word?" Claire asked, clearly not liking the youngster's lingo.

"Sick is good, Momma, didn't you know?"

Claire rolled her eyes. "Can't you say 'cool,' instead? The other word doesn't sound nice."

"Okay, Momma," he replied, although Anna suspected he had no intention of keeping the promise. "Which Krispy Dough are we going to?" Anna asked, opening up the car and inviting them in. Claire took a seat next to her son in the back and buckled him up. "Can we go to the one with the slide, Momma? Can we? Can we? Please?" Hermon asked, turning up the charm to the max. This prompted another groan from his parent. "It's the big one in the City Center," Claire said.

"Okilly dokilly," Anna replied, mentally wincing at the dated Simpson's reference.

"I haven't heard that for a while!" Claire said.

"Sorry, it's been a long time since I've been around kids."

They drove to the huge downtown mall and parked in a ten-story parking garage. It was the kind the old Anna would've avoided because of the eye-watering fees. They browsed the stores dotted throughout the main plaza, which, this close to Christmas, featured more than one gigantic inflatable Santa. The mall owners had even brought in a group of real reindeer, which looked more than a little uncomfortable in the Arizona climate.

The retailers had tried their best to outdo each other to create a more extravagant, festive theme than their competition. Hermon, of course, was having a great time. He ran from one gaudy display to another, taking in everything with infectious wonder. Claire seemed to disapprove of the consumerist eye-candy, though, and she often tutted and made comments about these places detracting from the real meaning of the holiday. Anna suspected that if she hadn't been with them, Claire would have taken a stronger line with the boy. While his mother was being forced to be more tolerant, however, Hermon appeared to drink in his surroundings with glee.

Even Claire laughed when they came to a special educational display put on by the city. It featured the many different yuletide traditions observed around the world. The specific cause of their hilarity stemmed from a Spanish tradition featuring Tió de Nadal, the magical Christmas log. The bizarre ritual involved drawing a happy face onto one end of said log and then fixing a long cloth bag at the other. Leading up to the big day, children would feed Tió by placing various foody treats into his tummy bag. On Christmas Eve, the log would have magically digested the food. The kids would then proceed to beat the log until it pooed various presents.

"It poops presents?" asked Hermon after Anna relayed this for his benefit. "I want a magic pooping log, too, Momma!"

"No, sir." Claire chuckled.

"Krispy Dough!" Hermon shouted, dropping his request on sight of the original reason for their visit.

A crowd of stressed-looking families packed the large donut store, where dozens of children lined up to access its indoor playground. Judging by the tense look on the faces of their parents, Anna guessed Krispy Dough wasn't proving to be the well-earned break they'd hoped for. Hermon wasted no time in flinging off his coat before throwing it to his mother.

"Can I go on the playground, Momma? Can I?" He could barely get the words out, such was his level of excitement. As soon as he heard the word, "okay," he sped off toward the other children, even while Claire was still uttering the word, "but."

"He looks like a happy boy," Anna said as they watched him wait in line with the others.

"Hermie is officially amaze-balls," Claire replied, as they strolled to the second line of customers snaking up to the service counter.

"He's coped with the move better than me."

"Children are strong, like that," Anna said, trying to sound supportive.

"Strong's not the word," Claire replied, her face reflective. "The poor kid's been through Hell. Now, with the move on top, I'm amazed he doesn't think I'm the worst mom in the world."

"It's obvious that he thinks the world of you."

"Hm." Claire frowned. "Not that I deserve it. Half of his presents are gonna come from the dollar store this year. What kind of a great mother allows that?"

"Money's not everything," Anna replied, instantly regretting how patronizing it must have sounded.

Claire seemed to ignore the point. "Do you want kids?" she asked.

"Is it so obvious that I don't have any?"

"You don't have the thousand-yard stare," Claire pointed at her own drawn features, "which is a better way to put it than my nasty-ass gran used to."

"How was that?"

LEE ALAN

"'Your nips better still be pink, young'un.'" she said in a crotchety, old voice.

The vulgar outburst caused the well-dressed woman in front of them to turn and give them a disapproving frown. Claire ignored this at first, but after their prudish neighbour turned back, she made an exaggerated cross-eyed expression. Anna couldn't help but laugh at the bold cheek of it.

Although the line stretched to the entrance door, they'd soon retrieved their order of indulgent treats. They'd also succeeded in securing the all-important children's meal, but only after Claire made the harried staff rummage through a collection of small, plastic characters until they found one that Hermon didn't already own.

They reached the cramped seating area just as a young Asian couple dragged a screaming, red-faced toddler away. He'd clearly enjoyed a little too much sugar and excitement. After removing the sticky remains of the kid's tantrum, they sat and spent a few minutes sipping coffee while watching Hermon make friends with a girl sporting fake Princess Leia buns.

"Welcome to my world," Claire said. "If I hear one more thing about that movie, I'm gonna personally visit George," she waved her hand, "whatever his name is, with one of those killer light sticks."

"Light saber" Anna corrected her. Claire gave her a look that said, "please don't tell me you're a fan."

"Corey loves it," she explained and received another one of those looks.

"So, you guys are serious?" Claire asked, tucking into a chocolate special with sprinkles on top.

"I hope so. We're getting married."

"No shit!" Claire said, although she didn't look surprised.

"I'm afraid the shit is real."

"You got a bun in the oven?"

"Nope. Well, at least, I don't think so." Anna blushed, expecting something sounding more like congratulations for the upcoming wedding.

It also struck her that she couldn't answer the question with complete certainty, and she made a mental note to take a pregnancy test. Her thoughts turned to what Corey's reaction might be to such news, and this caused her stomach to flip. The truth was that they hadn't even discussed their lack of care about such things.

"Sorry," Claire said. "In my neck of the woods, it's the usual culprit."

"Was it a rough place?" Anna asked, curious. "Where you grew up, I mean?"

"Strict is more the word," Claire said a little too quickly. "How about you?"

"My parents were lovely," Anna said. "The best."

"Were?"

"Both passed away," Anna answered, fighting the usual emotions the statement stirred in her.

"Sorry to hear that."

"Yours?"

"In heaven, I hope," Claire said, stirring the coffee. She seemed lost in thought for a moment. "I pray for their souls every day."

"Is that why you moved here?" Anna pressed gently before regretting the direct question. "Sorry. It's none of my business."

"It's complicated," Anna noticed moisture welling in Claire's eye, but the other woman wiped it away before it could form into a tear. She decided to change the subject, not wishing to push the sensitive subject.

"Hermon is such a cute name," she said, looking back to the little boy playing. "Where did you get it from?"

"Guess what his middle name is?" Claire asked, ignoring the question.

"Tell me," Anna replied, noticing Claire's demeanor had visibly lightened.

"Shmermonson."

Anna blinked. "Wow. Really? Hermon Shmermonson. I mean, is it like Swedish, or something?"

Claire blinked, her face deadpan. She then burst out laughing in a rich, warm tone. A second later, Anna realized how gullible she'd sounded and joined the other woman's chuckles.

"Swedish? Really?" Claire asked, placing her coffee on the table to stop it from shaking. "Actually, it's from the book of Enoch," she said more seriously. "Well, the Hermon part, anyhow."

"The Bible?" The question drew another one of those grey-eyed "well, duh" looks.

"It's a mountain, I think—the place where angels gathered on Earth."

"Wow. Sounds pretty deep," Anna commented. "What made you pick that particular passage?"

"I didn't. My pa did." Claire returned to stirring her coffee, and intense emotions seemed to simmer beneath her outer calm.

"Yowzer," Anna said.

"Told you he was strict."

"No kidding." A dozen questions flew through Anna's mind, along with a swell of sympathy for her damaged, new friend. "I still love the name, though." she added, again not wishing to risk being the cause of more upset.

"Yeah. It's hard not to like everything about Hermie."

"Things are going to be tough, then? For Christmas, I mean?" Anna asked, not sure if she'd just traded one difficult subject for another.

"We'll be fine—I was just bitchin', earlier. It would just be nice to have a pot to piss in, for a change." She sighed. "Oh well, at least he's allowed gifts this year." Anna opened her mouth to make a suggestion, but Claire headed her off by waving a half-eaten donut in her direction. "Don't you dare say what I think you're about to say," Claire interrupted her. "This isn't about me beggin' for money. You dig?" Her tone sounded deadly serious. "It's important to me that you don't offer, Anna."

"But..."

"No buts, lady. I mean it. Me and Hermie will be fine. He needs to understand that life doesn't involve filching off others. Understood?"

"Understood," Anna relented, although she felt terrible. It would be so easy to help this young family without any real cost to herself, but she had to admire Claire's determination to instil her child with principles. She also found it refreshing to find someone interested in her, rather than her money, which had become a familiar issue lately.

"The next donuts are on me, by the way," Claire added, obviously wanting to emphasize the point.

"Okay, okay, you win." Anna held her hands in surrender. "I just want you both to be happy."

"What's happiness got to do with anything? That's for the next life." Claire looked serious. "The Almighty provides. That's all we need to count on."

"Got it," Anna replied. Even as she spoke, though, another idea came to her—one that could give an excuse to treat this lovely family and which may also fit with Claire's strict moral compass.

"Claire," she began, trying to frame the question in her mind.

"Anna," she responded lightly after the pause lasted a second too long.

"This might sound a bit crazy, but how would you like to be my bridesmaid?" she asked, cringing at how needy it sounded. Claire's body language conveyed a mixture of elation and guarded curiosity.

"You're shitting me?" she asked. "If this is getting me back for the Shmermonson thing, you've beat me, hands down."

"I shit you not."

"Why me? I appreciate that you're grateful and all, but this trip out is more than enough, thanks."

"It's not about that," Anna disagreed. "You're the first person I feel I can trust after, well... since everything happened."

"You don't know that, and what about your other friends?" Claire asked. "Surely there's someone you can rely on. A family member?" Despite the words, Anna could sense her interest.

"Trust me, there's no one. Not since Julia... not for a long time. It's hard to explain, but for years I had no choice in my life, including choosing friends. Now, it's like I'm starting from scratch, but with only Corey to share it with." She said this with welling passion, "I know that must sound crazy, but it's the truth. Nothing creepy—I just want another person to share all this with."

Claire stared back, her feelings a mystery to Anna. "You mean you want someone to shop with?" she asked after a moment, lips twitching with amusement. Anna enjoyed the pleasant connection passing between them.

"So, when's the big day?"

"February."

Claire looked like she would choke on the last morsel of her treat. "In two months? You are pulling my chain!"

"February," Anna repeated, grinning at the shock she'd caused.

"Where?"

"London."

"Why the hell do you want to get married in Ohio?"

"No. London, England."

Claire looked puzzled for a second, but then her eyes widened as the full realization struck. "Holy cow!"

"Indeed," Anna answered, rewarding herself with a bite of the gigantic cookie she hadn't touched until now.

"What about Hermie?"

"Leave him here."

"What?"

Anna smiled. "Now, that was for pulling my leg before," she said, her eyes twinkling with fun. "Bring him with you."

Claire mulled it over. "Looks like I'll be needing a passport."

Chapter 10

AGENT ORANGE

Officer Plum-Dike loved toilet time. A small part of him argued that he shouldn't get any pleasure from reading the prisoner's correspondence while taking a dump, but he couldn't help but get off on the crazy shit that came from learning about the lives of his loving flock.

He'd come to understand the three types of deluded fools writing to the inmates. The first and most sensible kind were those who dumped their prisoner spouse shortly after lover boy was safely locked away. They usually went for someone a tad less stabby. Plum-Dike considered delivering the sad news to these rejected inmates as another perk of the job.

The type he found more puzzling were those long-suffering fools who chose to stay in touch with their former lovers for years. Sometimes it was even after hearing in graphic detail how Mr. Perfect had strangled a kid to death while wearing his dead granny's tights. Last were the ghouls —he despised these sick fucks with a passion. These certi-fied, bat-shit crazy, prison wife wannabes, were attracted to serial killers like flies to dog shit. Hell, even Teddy Bear—as sick and twisted as it could get—had his fan mail.

Plum-Dike stared at the most recent letter between Tony Eckerman, the Phoenix Strangler, and some religious nut-job. "Disappointing," he said, holding the envelope upside down to see if any dirty pictures dropped out. No such luck today.

"Hey, is that what yer old lady says when she clamps her eyes on yer shrivelled old pecker, Plum-Dike?" the voice was Finnan's, coming from the stall next to his.

"Fuck you, Finnan. Why don't you jerk off in your sister's panties some more?"

A mocking snort replied.

Jesus, I hate that fucking Mick prick. Oh well, I won't be strangling the snake today, he thought, turning his atten-tion back to the letter.

He took several squares of paper from the roll attached to the door and considered giving up on his afternoon entertainment. While he waited for inspiration, Plum-Dike inspected the toilet paper, wondering how it was possible to invent a material which actually repelled mois-ture, instead of absorbing it. *Typical—all they care about is saving pennies, these days, even if it means making a hard-working fella wipe his ass on this chicken shit tracing paper.*

He decided to switch to plan B and read the letter to search for something worth knocking one out for. Unfortunately, it turned out to be the same crazy Bible shit she'd spouted in her first communication: something about the coming of the end of days for the wicked. He almost felt sorry for the Strangler that he'd gotten himself lumbered with such a fucking prude. With a sigh, he finally decided to give up, and he raised the letter to return it to the envelope. In doing so, he noticed an odd citrus smell.

Wow, did they finally get around to cleaning these toilets? Concluding that such a rare event was beyond the realms of reason, he searched for another source to explain the fruity aroma.

Orange, he decided.

He hated the smell. As a child, his mother would force him to eat at least one a day after reading that fruit was the miracle cure to all illnesses. In his case, the ailment was a skin condition giving him an unfortunate body odour problem—the same problem that'd led his classmates to give him the knick-name Rotten Plums. After several tearful complaints to his parent, the daily dose of what he'd come to call 'agent orange' had followed. Of course, it'd made didly shit difference to his skin condition, but it had left him with a lifelong dislike of the stench.

He looked around for the source of the smell, but couldn't see anything obvious lying around on the dirty bathroom floor. Curious, he breathed in again.

"Definitely orange," he said.

Laughter followed from next door. "I'd get the doc to look at that, if I were you, Plum boy!"

"Shut it, Finnan!"

Inwardly cursing his neighbor once more, he shifted his considerable bulk around on the toilet seat to get a better view of his surroundings. In doing so, he happened to bring Eckerman's letter closer to his face. The pungent, fruity smell became much stronger. He sniffed the paper and wrinkled his nose.

Maybe Bible freaks use it for perfume?

His twenty years of experience as a prison guard disagreed, though. The Strangler was a slippery customer who'd not been in here long enough to be broken. It was possible that he could be trying to hatch some mischief with the Bible nut. She was his only known contact on the outside, so if he was going to do something, it would probably be through her.

Plum-Dike made a mental note to send the letter to the forensics team based in C-wing.

November 23rd,

Dearest Kate,

What can I say? How can I express the feelings of joy passing through my spirit as I read your words? You ask if I have been saved. Do I understand the passion of our Lord?

The truth, I swear, is that until I saw the light of wisdom through your gentle encouragement, I'd been a lost sinner without being reborn.

I have something to tell you, dear Kate. One of the few free-doms we have in this God-forsaken place is to seek out our true saviour. Dearest Kate, I did it! Even now, I can feel the water kiss my forehead. It was like the touch of the sun on a warm summer's day.

Kate, I imagined you next to me during my deliverance. You held my hand, but I could not see your face. In the moment of my rebirth, I knew the Lord was sending me a message to seek out the woman responsible for saving my soul.

Does that offend you, Kate? I pray this is not so, for I couldn't bear it. I need to see your face. I'm not sure if they will allow it, but I beg you, please send me a picture.

Since my baptism, I've passed my time by learning the sacred way and have read many things about my brother martyrs—they, who experienced the same persecutions I do.

My Kate, we are not the only ones to have corresponded during the depths of injustice. In the old country, England, holy men would be imprisoned in the dreaded Tower of London.

In those dark times, even a simple piece of fruit—an orange— sent from their loved ones, would be enough to keep them from falling into despair. Did you know that such a simple thing as an orange could be this important, Kate? I would urge you to also learn of these amazing men.

Please read my words carefully and write back soon. Although I am no longer wretched, I still need your light to give me hope. Please, send me a picture.

Thank you is not enough,
Tony

DECEMBER 1ST,

Tony,

I knew you were the one. I could feel it, even as I watched the tragedy of your trial unfold. Now, I am more certain than ever.

It's hard to express the joy in my heart to hear you are saved.

I have enclosed a picture, as you ask, but fear that you will not like my appearance. Does it please you?

I have done as you asked and read of the martyrs. Please be assured that I will be inspired to follow humbly in their footsteps. I hope my efforts are of some comfort to you.

Please say I can visit. Is it allowed? When can we meet, my darling? If God is merciful, then let this be soon. I pray for this happy day to arrive.

Write to me soon, my love,
Kate

TONY HAD RISKED one of Plum-Dike's secretly-delivered beatings by smuggling the lighter into his cell. His costly prize felt like it would rupture his anus as he strode back from the tiny exercise yard. He concluded that the forty-minute daily ritual was a treat best enjoyed without a gas-filled plastic oblong container shoved up one's ass.

After completing the delicate operation of removal, he sat alone in his cell, staring at the letter from the woman calling herself Kate. The anticipation was almost too much. If she'd missed the real message, his cause was screwed. *Please, you crazy bitch!* He feared the worse. High intelligence had never featured in his estimation of religious types. *Only one way to find out, old boy.*

Tony raised the paper above the lighter close enough to provide heat, but not so close that the paper would set alight. He flicked the ignition and watched as a low, blue flame appeared under Kate's neat handwriting. At first, nothing happened and his hopes sank, but a few seconds later, darkened words appeared below the visible ink.

My Darling,

You are so clever. The orange idea must have been divine inspiration. It fills my heart with joy to speak to you without the eyes of the heathen upon us.

It doesn't surprise me to know that your previous state of spiritual darkness came from the evil ways of Eve. To think such a creature would steal your heart and then forsake you for a man of greed—a wizard of Babylon, no less.

My answer is yes, with all my heart. I will help you bring the Lord's judgement upon them. But how?

Oh, my dearest Tony, you have no idea how happy this makes me. I put my trust in the will of our Lord, and he brought us together.

For too long, the doubting Thomases of this Earthly realm have tried to persuade me that my beliefs are a sickness of the mind. You have proven them wrong, my love. Only you had the grace to have faith in me. I beg you, my master, allow me to return your trust.

Pray for me,

Kate

"Hallelujah!" Tony grinned, allowing the accompanying photo to fall back into the envelope without bothering to inspect it.

This fishy didn't float his boat. He couldn't care less if she had the face of a supermodel and the body of a Brazilian hooker—he was already surrounded by crazies, and having another in his life was not part of the plan. She would come in useful, though, oh, yes. He would use this little fishy as bait to hook a better prize.

Chapter 11

KATLIN

The first time Katlin Macintosh entered the Clear Water Estate, she thought she'd wandered onto the set of a sci-fi movie, complete with giant UFO mother ship at its center. Sitting behind the wheel of the company van, she half-expected the branching structure of the dome to rise into the air. *Amazing,* she thought, as she parked in front of what seemed to be a deserted reception area.

She stepped out and pulled aside the sliding van doors. Despite her feelings of intimidation in the face of such a grand sight, she continued to remove her cleaning kit, while mentally going through her plan for the hundredth time. *You need to gain their trust, but how?*

She let up a small prayer for guidance while pressing her hand to the small crucifix under her starched, white uniform. *Forgive me, Lord. I know that what I'm about to do is a sin, but it's for the love of Him.*

She resisted the urge to pull out her cigs and take a few drags before entering, but she could feel eyes on her, and she knew cleaners had been fired for smoking on the grounds of a client.

"Forgive me," she murmured, as the blonde-haired woman emerged from the entrance.

ANNA STROLLED out from the main reception to greet the new cleaner, feeling awkward about the whole concept of bringing in hired help. It didn't sit well with her blue-collar background but, for months, she'd fought a losing battle against dirt in the living quarters. Although an army of staff kept the main grounds of the estate in immaculate condition, the smaller private area had no such provision. There was still a huge space to clean between her and Corey, and unsurprisingly, Corey was far too busy for such mundane considerations. He was so caught up in the business that he probably wouldn't have noticed if a plague of locusts descended on them.

They'd allowed the situation to drag on for far too long. In truth, Anna found it so hard to trust anyone that she'd put off making the necessary arrangements. Knowing her reservations, Corey had tried to teach George the complex actions needed. Although he'd proven an excellent duster, they'd soon found the limits of his physical abilities. Several costly lessons later, including a broken toilet bowl, they'd agreed to consider extra help.

Anna had suggested that one of the grounds staff members could be reassigned to keeping their love nest from becoming a pig sty. Much to her irritation, however, Corey had laughed at the suggestion. It would seem that the people she'd regarded as well-spoken gardeners were, in fact, senior research academics. Asking them to divert their valuable time into picking up their employer's dirty undies would likely earn Corey a reputation as the new Howard Hughes.

As luck would have it, an agency had contacted her to offer their services. Tiring of the constant warnings by the security team not to accept unsolicited services from anyone, she'd agreed to give them a try.

The woman before her looked the part, dressed in a smart, pressed, white uniform emblazoned with the company logo. "I was kinda expectin' a little green man to come out," the woman greeted Anna in a gravelly tone. It reminded her of her grandmother's rasping, no-nonsense voice. The cleaner's face had a weather-worn, hardworking cast to it—the kind that came through years of toil.

"It's a bit other-worldly, isn't it?" Anna smiled, enjoying the woman's direct manner. "Don't worry, though, it hasn't flown anywhere, yet."

"Impressive, though," the cleaner said. "If you don't mind me saying so, Mrs.—."

"Price," added Anna. "It's Miss, actually. For now, anyway." she added, feeling color rise in her cheeks. Something about the older woman made her feel self-conscious. Maybe it was the way her lips pursed, as if in judgement at the comment.

"If you don't mind me saying so, Miss Price, I don't think one cleaner will be enough."

"Oh no, it's not the whole thing we need looking after," Anna reassured her. "Just mine and my fiancé's living quarters."

"Fiancé, ya say?"

"That's right," Anna replied, feeling strangely defensive.

The cleaner introduced herself as Katlin Spence, Senior Hygienist Practitioner. Anna offered her hand to shake while hiding her amusement at the grand title. Katlin looked down at Anna's arm, seeming to hesitate before accepting it. Her lips remained pursed, accentuating the deep creases around her mouth.

Although the woman's odd behaviour bothered Anna a little, she also found her refreshingly different. She'd experienced too many people behaving in a deferential way toward her because of her newfound status. To find someone, other than Claire, who wore their heart on their sleeve appealed to her. She needed these kind of grounded people in her life.

"Best get down to it, then," Katlin said in a business-like manner before retrieving a serious-looking mop and bucket from the van.

"Great. Let me give you the tour, first," Anna replied, leading her through the gleaming, white arch of the main entrance.

"Holy mother of God," Katlin said when they entered the double doors to reveal the splendor of the interior.

Anna turned to find the cleaner stopped in her tracks, her expression slack-jawed.

"It catches out most people, at first," Anna said to fill the awkward silence.

"It's wonderful," Katlin remarked in stunned amazement. She turned around on the spot with her neck cocked backward, and her plain sneakers squeaked on the inlaid marble floor. "It's like paradise."

The mechanical sound of George approaching them broke the moment. As soon as Katlin set eyes on the robot, she froze in shock and dropped the bucket on the ground with a loud clang, before proceeding to present the mop in front of her, as if about to engage in single combat.

"Greetings, visitor!" George announced, striding toward the terrified woman.

"Back off, tin can!" Katlin shouted, brandishing the mop.

Anna did her best to stifle the laugh welling in her, even as she stepped forward to calm the misunderstanding. *Yep, I definitely need this in my life,* she thought.

Chapter 12
JOURNEY

Anna had never been outside the US. Now, however, she sat beside Corey while the rolling green hills of Ireland flashed beneath them some twenty-thousand feet below. The landscape looked so unreal from this height, like a model constructed for her benefit. The sea appeared like tin foil, and when they'd passed over the white peaks of a mountain range, they'd looked like tiny, iced cakes. The irrational part of her expected the stunning visual effects to be an elaborate fake, and after landing, the fuselage door would open to reveal that they were still in Arizona.

What a set of wonders she'd seen during their journey to Europe. No matter how long she lived, no experience could match cruising into a crimson sunset above the sparkling waves of the Atlantic. During that magical hour, Corey had brought the altitude of the Mark 2 well below the norm with electrifying results. The tinfoil waves had transformed into reality, and the desolate beauty of the ocean had unveiled itself.

It'd been Corey's idea to travel to Europe to get hitched, and the concept had appealed to her. It was so grand of a gesture, and he'd conveyed it with such natural enthusiasm, that she'd found it impossible to resist. She also hoped the unfamiliar environment would distract her from the void of Julia and her parents.

"We are over the Irish sea," Corey said, sounding weary from the long flight. He'd been in the saddle for over twenty-four hours and was clearly overdue a rest. She ran her hand over his back to show empathy.

"Next thing you'll see is Wales," he added, giving her a tired-looking grin.

"I know they're big fish, but I'm not sure we'll see them from up here," she teased. Despite his intelligence, Corey had a gullible streak that she loved to bait.

"Not whales, W-A-L-E-S," he corrected her. "It's a country next to England," he added, before turning to see the mischievous smile playing on her lips.

"I make it ten times," she declared with a chortle, and then tweaked his nose. Corey rolled his eyes.

She'd invented the Corey fishing game during one of the more tedious parts of their flight. The rather cruel sport involved exploiting his natural tendency to slip into teacher mode, given half an opportunity. Much to her amusement, Anna had found that this pompous trait could be exploited.

"Where are we landing?" she asked.

"London City Airport in about…" he looked down at the glowing dials, "thirty minutes." Anna's sense of excitement grew.

IN TOTAL CONTRAST TO ARIZONA, England was a lush country. The very air itself was alive with moisture. She lost count of all the lakes and rivers they passed over. As they descended through the cloud clover, it became clear just how varied the climate was. They'd passed through at least three rain showers interspersed with sunny patches. The outside air temperature was a cool, yet not unpleasant fifty degrees Fahrenheit.

As they approached their destination, she could see that it was far more populated than she'd expected. The great, green belt of land dominating much of the landscape was often interspersed with major urban areas.

"London," he said, pointing. Ahead of them loomed the largest city she'd ever seen—far bigger than Phoenix.

"Buckle up," Corey added. "It's time to land this baby."

Another thrill passed through Anna. Because they were moving so fast in the final moments before landing, she could barely make out the sights below. She did, however, catch a glimpse of a giant, white wheel beside the bank of a mighty river lined with skyscrapers and older buildings.

"What's with the big wheel?" she asked, trying to calm her nerves during the approach.

"The London Eye," he replied. The opportunity for him to elaborate passed, because the sprawl of the airport soon drifted into view.

"London Airport's cool," he declared. "It's built into the center of the river, so when you're landing, it feels like you're going to roll right off the end and into the water!" he said happily, directing a grin at her worried expression. "It's perfectly safe." he added, obviously detecting the scared look in her eye.

Corey nudged the sleek, black nose of the plane lower still and pressed an intercom button above his head.

"Be advised, London Control, this is yankee foxtrot twenty-nine seeking permission to land." A staccato buzz answered, followed by a voice in a thick accent she hadn't heard before. "Yankee foxtrot twenty-nine, permission to land granted. Welcome to the UK, Mr. Young."

"Cool, I got the VIP greeting," Corey approved, directing another toothy smile her way.

The Mark 2 drifted toward the earth, far lighter and quieter than a more conventional plane. It glided downward with only minimal power needed from its twin solar-powered prop engines. Just as it seemed they would skim the tops of the tallest building, Corey flicked a switch marked Landing Gear. Anna heard the reassuring sound of the mechanism responding, and shortly after, she started to feel the nausea in her tummy associated with a steeper descent. After several more tense seconds, Corey guided the sun-powered winged missile toward a concrete floor at a hundred miles per hour.

"Why is the airport in the middle of the city?" Anna asked, clutching her stomach.

"It's not the main airport," he replied, turning the aircraft in a wide arch—presumably to align them better. The maneuver made Anna feel queasy. "They specialize in business traffic. Plus, London Airport is closest to our hotel, and I'm a VIP, don't you know?" he finished in a mock posh accent.

"Do we have to turn so fast?" she asked, resisting the urge to bring up her breakfast.

"'Fraid so, hon. It's either turn or land on the grounds of Buckingham Palace, and I'm pretty sure the Queen can have us beheaded for messing up her lawn."

"Smartass." The following laugh made her want to give him a slap.

Anna liked the hints of special treatment to come, though. They were both close to exhaustion, and the thought of a soak in a warm bath followed by a long sleep in a soft bed sounded like Heaven, right then. They'd spent so long in the air that she feared her legs would have forgotten how to walk on solid ground.

Corey's insistence that she wear special flight socks the

whole journey had made her feel even more uncomfortable. At first, she'd thought he was joking when he presented her with what could only be described as a pair of ugly-ass tights. She'd refused to wear them, of course, pointing out that they would make her look like an extra in a seventies cop show. He responded with a lecture about exploding veins, so, after much sulking, she'd agreed, but on one condition: he spare her from more nerd talk.

The runway appeared as a single, white line in the middle of the River Thames. As they got lower still, the length of the landing strip looked too short, while the fast-approaching surface of the river raced beneath them.

"Corey..." she began, unable to hide the concern from her voice.

"It's an optical effect, dear," he replied, without bothering to ask what the matter was.

After several nerve-shredding moments, the Mark 2 touched the earth with a barely-perceptible bump. As soon as the wheels kissed the tarmac, she heard the power of the engines audibly reduce. Corey followed the deft manuever by slowing the plane's speed. This proved enough to allow Anna to unplug her fingernails from the co-pilots chair.

Unlike the larger airports, London Airport only had a single runway with a modest complex of buildings surrounding it. A giant, white dome dominated the view ahead, and further to the left, a collection of colossal skyscrapers stood out against the grey London skyline. The plane speed had reduced now, while Corey taxied them toward a collection of private jets.

"What's with the dome?" Anna asked, trying to contain her excitement.

"It's the O2 Arena," Corey replied, flicking various switches and steering toward a space amongst the other aircraft. "The Brits built it to celebrate the year 2000."

"Why do you know some much about London?" she asked, always curious to learn more about her future husband.

"The UK has some of the best engineers in the world. I go where the talent is," he said as he slid their remarkable vehicle between two business jets. "It's not just that, though: I kinda fell in love with the place and the people. The British are pretty reserved, but when they learn to trust you, they're great." He turned more glowing dials. "London happens to be a beautiful city—you'll see." he added for the tenth time since they'd set off.

When the Mark 2 trundled to a gentle stop, a luxurious-looking navy-blue car with tinted windows emerged from the squat terminal building. As it drew closer, Anna could see a motif in the form of a shapely winged female sitting on its solid grill. Below the iconic symbol, on a polished plate, two interlocking, embossed R's gave away the vehicle's unmistakable identity.

"Cool - they sent the Rolls." Corey observed the car as he turned off the engines and removed his flight headpiece. "Phew!" He threw the headset onto the dashboard and then rolled his shoulders to remove the kink from his neck. "Not sure about you, honey, but I'm ready for the three 'S's," he said.

Anna remembered her father using the same rather vulgar phrase on a few occasions when he'd returned from a long day at work. "Shower, shit, and shave?" she asked.

Corey laughed. "Speak for yourself, love. Actually, I was thinking: shower, sausages, and sex."

Anna blushed before punching him on the shoulder playfully. "You should be so lucky."

"What do ya reckon, ready to see London?"

"Meh."

He laughed again before taking her by the hand and leading them through the cabin and out into the cold, afternoon air. The colors and sights seemed super vivid outside the confines of the small cockpit.

A driver exited the passenger's side of the car, wearing a long, footman's navy-blue overcoat and cap. Another group of airport staff joined him and removed baggage from the plane's hold before loading it into the shiny trunk of the Rolls Royce. Anna noticed with a thrill that the steering wheel was on the opposite side of the car from cars in the US. *Wow, I really am in another country,* she thought, finally convincing her subconscious that it was all real.

Corey held her hand while he escorted her down the chrome steps of the Mark 2. The supportive gesture wasn't just for show: she'd made the decision to greet Europe in style, wearing an elegant, emerald dress with matching high heels. Anna wanted to make an impression as his future wife, rather than the waitress with a tragic past who'd gotten lucky.

The driver strolled over to the passenger side of the car and removed a large bouquet of red orchids.

"Your carriage awaits, m'lady." Corey indicated the waiting passenger seat.

"Good afternoon, Mr. Young and Miss Price. On behalf of the Nightingale-Carlton, welcome to the United Kingdom." the driver said, handing Anna the bouquet.

Their escort opened the back passenger door, allowing them to sink into a brown, leather interior. Anna caught the image of a wealthy couple reflected in the surface of the polished, chestnut wood surrounding them. *That's me.*

"Did he just say the Nightingale?" she asked Corey while the driver moved to the front of the car.

"He did."

"As in THE Nightingale Hotel?" Even in the US, the name was famous for its luxurious standards.

"Did ya think I'd dump me bootiful Mrs. in any old flop haas?" he replied in a terrible English accent that made him sound more like Dick Van Dike than any real English person.

"We need to make a short stop to take you through customs, sir," the driver informed them as he pulled the limo toward the main terminal building. "My apologies, but it shouldn't take long. We have a special arrangement for our Platinum Suite customers."

They drove straight past arrivals before pulling up outside a discreet, unmarked doorway. The red carpet running from its opening spoke of its real purpose.

Anna felt like she was visiting royalty during the following formalities. She found it hard to believe she'd been the same Phoenix girl who, until recently, had scrubbed pans to make ends meet. The courteous team greeting them seemed unaware of her previous status or the nightmare she'd endured. Anna realized that, to them, she and Corey must look like the same happy couple she'd seen reflected in the shiny surface of the car: a successful man and his elegant partner. The sense of liberation was amazing. For the first time since the trial, she dared to believe in a future free from notoriety and suspicion.

They were soon done with customs, and the final leg of their journey began. They passed a bustling mix of yachts while cruising through the dockland area next to the airport. The functional tugs used to keep the busy operation running sat side by side with the play-things of the rich. The surrounding quay heaved with crowds of tourists, and giant cranes dotted the water line, presumably for unloading the larger vessels. It was hard to tell whether they were a figment of London's past or still in operation.

They continued toward the white dome of the O2, but as they drew closer, even this huge construction was dwarfed by the surrounding buildings. The names of the corporate sponsors occupying them emblazoned the silent towers: banks, for the most part, she noticed.

"Canary Wharf, the finance district," Corey explained, with a note of contempt in his voice. "Bunch of tight-fisted parasites."

One of Corey's favorite gripes involved the big finance houses' inability to invest in new ideas. Ignoring his comment, Anna cocked her head upward to stare at one glimmering tower of steel and glass topped by a pyramid-like roof. "The buildings are beautiful, though," she said.

"Sorry, hon—I keep forgetting this is your first time here. You're right; I just wish someone more worthy occupied them."

"Someone a bit more like you?" she asked, turning to look at him with one eyebrow raised.

"Well, er, not necessarily." His face reddened.

She laughed and turned back to discover the city in which they would wed. Ever present to their left ran the mighty River Thames. It snaked through the city, like the pulsing artery of some giant creature. The contrast from the arid barrenness of Arizona couldn't have been greater—this place was alive with water. Unlike the dock, tourist river boats dominated this section, and they passed a bright yellow truck labelled the River Duck. She watched as it ambled to the edge of the river before plunging into it. Anna nearly called out in alarm, but instead of sinking, it bobbed about and then powered into the current, much to the delight of its passengers.

A grand, Victorian-age bridge came into view ahead, spanning the length of the river with awesome arrogance. Two decorated towers stood at either end, tied together at the upper level by two horizontal walkways.

"Is that the London Bridge?" she asked.

"A lot of people assume so," Corey replied. "It's actually called the Tower Bridge. London Bridge is further upstream." He followed this up in a whisper, "The new London Bridge actually looks a bit dull."

"Oh."

"Guess where the original is?"

Anna rolled her eyes, feeling too tired for more lectures. "Tell me."

"Lake Havasu City."

"What? Arizona?"

"Yup. They sold it to us evil Yanks. Put that in yer learnin' pipe and smoke it, lady."

"You really are a smartass, Corey."

As they rolled closer to Tower Bridge, she noticed the traffic had stopped at each end. The reason soon became clear when the central span rose into the air. With a small thrill, Anna watched as a high-rigged sailing boat passed underneath the mighty construction. The whole process took about twenty minutes to complete. When both ends had lowered into place, the winding backlog of traffic flowed once again.

. . .

WHILE THEY PASSED over the now-solid bridge, her attention turned to the ancient walls of a castle on the bank of the river. It wasn't some Disney fairy tale castle, but a grim-looking fortress topped by interlocking walls. At its center stood a white tower thrusting into the cloudy sky, and a dim memory from high school came back to her.

"It's the Tower of London!"

"It certainly is," Corey agreed. "It's hard to believe now, but it used to be Hell for some poor souls."

She remembered something about a king of England who had six wives; he'd executed two of them at the tower. A cold shiver of sympathy ran down Anna's spine, and suddenly the battlements took on a sinister aura. Even here, surrounded by one of the world's great cities, stood a lasting reminder of the power men could exercise over women.

She shuddered and focused her attention on the road ahead. They'd turned left onto a major thoroughfare running parallel to the river. On the opposite bank, she saw a colossal building dwarfing even those they'd passed at Canary Wharf. It looked like an enormous icicle rising into the sky, with a green light winking on its pinnacle to ward off low-flying air traffic.

"What's that?" she asked, pointing.

"The Shard," Corey said with a hint of pride in his voice. "The tallest building in Europe. Guess who's got an office there?"

Anna sensed the opportunity to bring him down a peg or two. "Someone compensating for a small dick?"

Corey roared with laughter and gave her an exploratory tickle, which also sent her off. To their embarrassed surprise, a suppressed guffaw drifted from the driver. She'd assumed the divider separating them would prevent such awkward moments. Corey adopted his "doh" expression and mouthed the word "intercom" to her.

"I know now, dumbass," she whispered.

A blur of sights followed over the next twenty minutes. The sensory input became almost overwhelming for the tired bride to-be.

And there is the small matter of the wedding, kiddo. She thought. The weight of this heavy realization made her mentally pause and consider the implications. *Am I ready to commit?* Her inner paranoia piped up, *It won't work out, in the long run. He'll become distant—wrapped up in his work—and you? Do you honestly think you're good enough for him? A waitress? You should stop this madness.*

Fuck that, came her reply. *I've earned his love.*

"Did you hear from Claire?" Corey interrupted her thoughts, perhaps sensing her changing mood.

"Yep. She dropped a text to say they've landed at Heathrow."

"What I'd give to be a kid flying for the first time, again," Corey said with a wistful cast to his eye.

The limo turned away from the Thames and drove past the length of what she recognized as the British Parliament building. Shortly after, they glided along a wide, tree-lined avenue with a park on either side. Ahead, a grand palace came into view. Its grounds had been ringed by imposing, black gates topped with gold paint. Outside the main gates and directly in their path sat a marble monument topped by a beautiful, winged messenger painted in gold.

"Is that the Nightingale Hotel?" she asked, her feelings of awe rising to new heights. "No," Corey chuckled. "Buckingham Palace, remember? - where the Queen lives."

"Oh, wow. I wonder what she's like."

"I met her at a dinner once. Very polite—a tad formal, though. Of course, you'd kinda expect that from royalty."

She turned to face him, eyebrow raised. "You're showing off again." "Sorry. It's annoying," he apologized. "I'm just happy to share all of this with you." "I know, honey," she said, patting him on the leg before pointing out a red-coated soldier, wearing a large, uncomfortable-looking fur helmet, marching behind the gates surrounding the palace. A large group of sight-seers photographed him as he stomped by.

They drove around the monument at the center of the road before leaving the Queen's residence behind. After passing through the Palace gardens, they stopped outside an impressive, colonnaded building. The words "Nightingale Hotel" could be seen displayed against the royal blue canopy above its high, arched entrance. Short stone steps led up to its polished wooden doors, which stood invitingly open. A uniformed doorman standing on the threshold tipped his hat toward them as they arrived. The opulent display spoke of a venue beyond the standards of any ordinary hotel.

"Welcome to the Nightingale," the driver said. "The footman will escort you from here."

With practiced efficiency, the waiting attendant opened the car door and invited her to step onto yet another red carpet running up the stone stairway. Anna took his offered hand and stepped out while her heart skipped a beat.

Upon entering, Anna felt as if she'd been transported to another age. Light dazzled off a thousand crystal fittings, while a polished, marble floor led through gilded archways. Beyond those lay the large, brightly lit plaza of the main lobby. Immaculate art nouveau décor ran throughout to a level of grandeur she'd only ever seen in movies, like Titanic. It captured the pre-war style of the last century on a scale that took her breath away.

Two smiling bell hops wearing traditional, brimless hats stood on either side of the arch. At the other end of the plaza, a suited reception manager stood behind a hardwood desk. The pleasant aroma of flowers permeated through the air from the orchids surrounding them.

It was almost more than Anna could take: first the flight, the city, and now this. She began to wonder if Corey's attempts to impress his bride would have the unintended consequence of giving her a stroke.

"Welcome to the Nightingale, Mr. Young and Miss Price," the mustached reception desk clerk greeted them. His tailored appearance spoke of old world taste. "My name is Lionel Torrance, and it's my job to ensure your every comfort." His accent was the height of English posh. "May I be the first to congratulate you on choosing one of our Platinum rooms, sir—they really are something special—and welcome to you, madam. If you don't mind me saying so, you look stunning in that wonderful dress."

"Thank you, Lionel. It's good to be here," Corey replied with a chirpiness she didn't share. It was all she could do not to collapse into the well-dressed man's arms and beg for sleep. Despite her bone tiredness, she beamed at him. It was a nice compliment, after all.

"Please, allow me to escort you to the King George suite," he said, indicating for them to follow him. Anna wondered if she would be able to go anywhere in this country without being escorted.

Perhaps sensing his guest's fatigue, and much to Anna's relief, Mr. Torrance didn't provide a grand tour. Instead, he pointed out the many beautiful facilities in passing. After what felt like a stroll through the set of an Agatha Christie novel, they came to a stop outside another set of elaborate, gilded doors.

"Originally built in 1770 as an informal residence for his majesty, King George III, may I present," Lionel began, before pushing both doors inward, "the King suite."

What lay before her was a staggering display of an older, even grander style. The walls were high and covered from floor to ceiling with superb frescoes featuring scenes from mythology. Anna stared in wonder as winged soldiers stormed across a clouded landscape in chariots, beside a muscled figure hurling a thunderbolt from a golden throne. Three sashed windows overlooked a view of the Green Park, ending with Buckingham Palace in the distance. Anna found herself speechless. "Is it to your liking, madam?" the manager asked with a note of worry in his tone.

"I..." the sentence froze in her throat. Instead of answering, she turned and threw her arms around Corey. She clung to him, overwhelmed with gratitude and fatigue. When her future husband had first offered to help organize their special day, she'd rejected the idea, having always imagined it to be her role. Corey agreed, not wishing to overshadow her wishes. When she'd begun to investigate, however, she'd soon found herself lost in the scale of it, particularly due to the long distance nature of the preparations.

The first problem had been the revelation that Corey wanted to invite two hundred or so "intimate" guests—only a few of which were relatives. Most came from the politics surrounding his expanding business interests.

The responsibility had brought her close to being ill. She simply didn't have the experience to organize such a prestigious event. Finally, the situation had reached a crisis point when, with less than a month to go, Corey had found her crying over Claire's shoulder. The ironic icing on the situation had followed a failed search for a cake definitely not containing nuts. Corey had tactfully asked if she would like some help.

"Go fuck yourself!" had been her equally polite response.

After the stormy bridezilla moment had passed—not for the first time in recent weeks—she'd finally conceded to the logic of his offer. "I get final say on everything. Got that, smartass?" had been her final verdict, delivered with an apologetic kiss on the cheek.

From that point forward, the decisions had come thick and fast, but not so much the promise to consult with her. In typical Corey style, the sneaky shit had used his position in the driving seat to somehow keep half the arrangements a complete secret from her. It was no doubt another well-intentioned, yet frustrating effort to surprise her. The result had been one freaked out Anna. But what her man didn't know, was that she had an even bigger secret of her own. "Ahem," the manager politely interrupted her prolonged handling of the groom. She stepped away, blushing. A seemingly never-ending procession of cases and wrapped garments were paraded into the waiting room by a small army of bell boys—all done under the eagle-eyed direction of a portly gentleman whose sole job seemed to be overseeing the arrangement of baggage. With typical British precision, they'd soon placed the collection throughout the palatial suite. After completing their task, and with a final bow from the baggage master, the huge doors of the apartment closed together with a click, and they were alone.

Corey went to the doors, produced an ornate key from his shirt pocket, and locked them before turning to face Anna. The mischievous look on his face told its own story.

"About those three 'S's," he said.

"Oh, you got a bad tummy, hon?" she teased.

"I was about to say you're definitely in need of a shave," he countered.

"Do you need a shower?" she asked.

"Do you need a sausage?" his grin widened.

"How 'bout a bit of both?"

THE SHOWER ROOM turned out to be more of a washroom annex complete with swimming pool and a silver bath big enough to accommodate a small football team. Like the main apartment, a fresco dominated the décor in the circular-domed water world. The theme, this time, was of ancient sea gods. In the center of his underwater realm stood the mighty figure of Neptune holding a trident in his life-like, blue hands. The god stared on with an inappropriately serious expression at the naked couple beneath him as they clung together in the pool. "I feel like he's watching us," Anna said as she arched back while Corey kissed her neck.

"He's just jealous," he murmured, moving further down.

"Hope you can hold your breath, fella," she breathed.

He replied by lifting her from the warm water and carrying her to the pool's edge. She lifted her arms and placed them on his cheeks, and he responded by gripping her under the buttocks while squeezing and pulling up at the same time. A second later, he was inside, his lust giving him a vigor that soon transferred to her. She gripped the back of Corey's head while he sucked and kissed her wet, steaming breasts. They climaxed together with a passion that left her uncaring of what some crusty old sea monster thought.

Chapter 13

QUEEN

Detective Raymond received the call just as he was about to break an eight-month vow not to smoke. He'd even cleared his schedule for the afternoon just so he could savor the moment of surrender. Sure, the operation to remove a malignant tumour from his armpit had been a success, but after a year from Hell, his resolve had eroded to the point that a little good old-fashioned self-destruction was overdue—preferably away from the prying eyes of his wife and colleagues, who would suck the fun out of his foolish mission.

After twenty years of service, man's capacity to inflict cruelty on others still never failed to shock him. Since summer, he'd been on the scene of no less than two mass shootings. Both had been tragedies perpetrated by seemingly upstanding citizens. In reality, each man had been just a rifle away from unleashing their lurking demons.

He'd gone through the motions of providing reassurance, of course, but inside he felt just as helpless as the average Joe in the face of such pointless slaughter. What could the law do when a psycho could buy an assault rifle in a city awash with illegal firearms and then stroll over to a preschool to kill a dozen toddlers? What could anyone do when a whole country became gripped by homicidal madness?

The persistent ringing from his cell phone refused to go away. It was the kind that said, "If you don't pick me up, you're gonna regret it." The unlit cigarette sat in his mouth, tantalizing his tongue. He could almost feel the creamy smoke filling his lungs. The match remained poised. All he needed to do was ignore the call and bring the flame a few more inches toward the end of the blessed cancer stick.

The cell phone continued to ring. "You total mother f…" he muttered as he flicked the match out and threw it across the darkened room of his tiny city apartment. He refused to rush his movements, as he strolled over to the still-buzzing phone, already resenting the son of a bitch who'd just stopped him from making one of the stupidest mistakes of his life.

"Raymond," he said, answering the call from a number he didn't recognize.

The voice on the other end spoke for almost five minutes while his expression became concerned. After the urgent conversation concluded, he agreed to investigate. His thoughts turned to the Price case and the frail, blonde woman he'd interviewed all those months ago.

"Poor kid's been through enough already," he said, determined to head off whatever sick mischief Eckerman had conjured.

ANNA WOKE to soft morning light streaming through the beautiful sashed windows. Tiny dust motes danced before her in the air as she left the dark recesses of sleep behind to return to a reality even better than her dreams. She felt a momentary sense of weightlessness, as if floating on a cloud.

"GOOD MORNING, MADAM," Corey said, already awake. She smiled and arched her back, while pushing her arms out across the cream silk sheets of the canopied bed.

You're getting married today, by the way, kiddo. The implication lanced through her mind like fire, cutting off the lazy yawn. "Holy fuck, Corey, we need to get up!" She threw the sheets off them both, exposing herself. "What time is it? Did we oversleep?"

"Relax, it's only six AM. The transport isn't here until three. We have plenty of time." "Plenty of time my ass! Get up!" She nudged him harder than intended.

His use of the phrase "transport" had also triggered more stress-inducing uncertainty. "What do you mean by transport?" Corey made a locking gesture with his thumb and forefinger over his lips before throwing away the invisible key. Huffing, she decided to switch tactics, and Anna pushed her breasts out toward him before giving her most alluring "come get me" eyes.

"Please, Mr. Young?" she said, giving them a firm jiggle. Corey's grin grew at the display. "Your evil Devil's dumplings will not succeed in making me spill my secrets, foul temptress!" he cried, tickling her. "And in His Majesty's bed! Shame on you, wanton hussy!" She screamed with laughter at the unexpected onslaught and threw her head back onto the pillow. "Foul temptress? Devil's dumplings? How dare you, sir!" "Fouler than the foulest hag, madam!" He continued the tickling. "Stop it! I'm going to pee the bed!" "Never!" "Quit!" Her tone became firmer.

Having the good sense to do just that, Corey let go, leaving her panting with sudden exertion. "I've got an early wedding present for you," he said, the smile returning. Anna forgot about the manhandling. "Show me! Please, Corey, pretty please." The bouncy boobs were back. To her surprise, he placed a newspaper in front of her: the Arizona Herald. After reading the bold headline, her initial disappointment at the sight of such an ordinary item faded. "Fracking case collapses amidst claims of corruption."

The more she read, the more elated she felt. Vaudrillion Corporation had withdrawn their application to exploit the

Tonto Forest, due to "procedural irregularities." That was just the official line; the paper went on to lay out the damning case against Peterson and Moyer, referencing her article. The Herald also quoted several extra sources of their own, including the Attorney General's office. A full investigation was now in progress.

"You did it, honey! You beat those fucking assholes," Corey said after she dropped the paper onto the bed in stunned amazement. "So, the Tonto National Forest is safe?" she asked. "They couldn't even pick flowers, and it's all because of you." "Woohoo!" she yelled, bringing his lips to hers.

As they made love once more in the glorious sunshine, she thought about the gift she'd brought with her: the one that would change both of their lives forever. But however tempted she felt to tell him right then, though, she'd promised herself to wait until the moment of their marriage. *I'm going to make you so happy, my man. Just you wait.*

After finishing their unplanned activities, they showered together, and then changed into matching dressing gowns each bearing their own embroidered initials. She noticed with a thrill that her own read AY, rather than AP.

At eight AM sharp, the real business of the day began with a loud knock on the door.

"Here we go," Corey said, taking a deep breath before answering the persistent rapping.

A man dressed in a red velvet suit with frilled-lace

sleeves stood before Corey. Behind him stretched a long line of staff. He remained in the doorway, ignoring the groom. Instead, he gazed intently past Corey's shoulder toward Anna. After what seemed an age, the stranger waved Corey aside like a bothersome child and strode into the grand apartment with feminine black hair bouncing around his shoulders.

"My dear, this brute would only allow a mere four hours to complete your transformation!" he declared.

"Four hours is..." Corey started to object, his cheeks reddening.

"Shame on you!" the black haired man interrupted him. "What would you know? You're a man!" he said before turning his attention to Anna.

"Anna, this is—" Corey started, until the flamboyant man raised a single finger to silence him.

"My darling, I am Lawrence Mcloughlin, and my quest is to make you a princess," he said with a bow.

At a loss for words, she could only manage a simple, "Hello."

"Hello, indeed," he replied with a smile, before placing a finger of contemplation on his chin. He gazed at her with pursed lips.

After an awkward second, Lawrence clicked his fingers, and the troupe followed him into the room before gathering around Anna. Each member of the team stared at her as one might a challenge. She gave them a self-conscious wave while considering calling Corey for help.

"My apologies for the abrupt introductions, my dear, but we simply don't have a second to waste," Lawrence said before gazing around the room. This brought a frown to his otherwise smooth features. "Where is the head bridesmaid?" he drew the words out in his rich, English accent.

"Oh, er, Claire is staying in another room," Corey said, sounding like a naughty school boy. "We've not had chance to catch up with her, yet." A stab of guilt shot through Anna as she realized they'd neglected her friend in all the excitement of the previous day.

"Well, man, bring her on! For goodness' sake, this is a wedding, not a shin dig at a barbecue pit!"

Anna couldn't help but smirk at her fiancés discomfort when dealing with the overbearing stylist. "I'll go," Corey said before scurrying off to fetch Claire and Hermon.

"Be quick about it!" Lawrence shouted after his retreating billionaire client. "I'll wager he wanted to keep you in his clutches as long as possible," Lawrence said. "Men are such pigs!"

This is going to be a long morning, Anna thought, giving him a wan smile.

Ten minutes later, Corey returned with an overwhelmed-looking mother and son. Anna managed a passing greeting before they were also whisked away by the makeover team. With that, Lawrence gave the now-sulking groom a lecture about bad luck and then ordered him to prepare elsewhere. Corey stalked off after being allowed to give her only the briefest of parting kisses.

ANNA DIDN'T RECOGNIZE the woman gazing back at her from the regency mirror. Lawrence had said he would transform her into a princess, but now she could see he'd meant it literally. The dress was a vision of ageless, flowing beauty. Cut in a traditional style, the design would've been familiar to the original residents of the room she stood in. The neckline was low, giving her cleavage an ample aspect that accentuated the healthy weight she'd put on in recent weeks. For good measure, Lawrence had painted a beauty spot on the left; on the right, he'd placed a small, red heart.

In addition to the precious stones lining the seams of the stunning dress, the accompanying necklace and earrings were of the finest natural pearl. They glistened against her skin, like the tears of a moon goddess. Small ribbons and gemstones adorned the loose locks of Anna's hair. The pale foundation applied to her cheeks had been lightly rouged, and her eyelashes were dark, giving her eyes a deep quality, like an ocean in which a man could drown. Her veil shimmered in the light, delicate and ephemeral.

"What do you think?" Lawrence asked with obvious concern as he inspected his work with the rest of his team. Evidently, he worried more about the standard of his work than insulting the man paying his fee. The following silence made his staff shuffle in anticipation.

"I don't look like a princess," Anna said at last, and

Lawrence's shoulders dropped like a man defeated for the first time, "I look like a queen."

Lawrence stared up at her, his green eyes filled with hope once more. "Is that good?" he asked, the fussy comic tone gone.

"Princesses are for kids, but I'm a woman." She paused as a single tear running down her cheek. "Thank you, Lawrence. Thank you for making me feel special." Anna could see from the way he dabbed at his eye that she wasn't the only one touched by the moment.

"Don't thank me, thank your fiancé," he said.

"He's a good man," she agreed while he applied a tissue to her mascara to stop it from running.

"Trust me, my dear, any man who pays a fee as high as mine really does love his bride."

The sound of tiny running feet interrupted them. "Wowee - Look at you, Anna!" Hermon shouted with excitement. He'd been dressed in a blue drummer boy jacket, inlaid with gold thread and silver, embossed buttons. A little white wig sat above his delighted expression, and his costume left no room for doubt that this was to be a themed wedding. "Look at me, I'm a pirate!"

Anna laughed, not having the heart to tell the kid that he looked more like a soldier.

"Shiver me timbers!" she replied, much to his further joy.

"You look far too elegant for pirate talk," Lawrence observed.

Claire followed shortly after Hermon in a gown almost

as stunning as the bride's. Her black curls were hidden under another elaborate wig, and again, her gown looked designed to accentuate her cleavage and hips. Even under the makeup, though, Anna could see that she looked tired and perhaps also angry. She wondered if it'd been too much to ask of her new friend, who was clearly unused to such pampered decadence.

"You look amazing," Anna said, hoping to trigger a conversation. She felt terrible for spending so little time with them since their arrival. She'd assumed Claire would understand under the circumstances, but perhaps that'd been a mistake.

Before Claire could respond, though, another polite knock at the door interrupted her. One of Lawrence's team members opened it, and a bell boy stood there with his cap removed in a gesture of respect. "Madam, your carriage awaits."

Surprised, Anna looked at the oak grandfather clock beside the fireplace. Her tummy flipped to see that it was exactly three PM.

"Are you ready?" Lawrence asked. She took a deep breath and then nodded.

Dazzling flower arrangements ran along the corridors of the Nightingale as the entourage passed. She lost count of the different types of species on display: blood-red roses, blue spotted orchids, and white chrysanthemums.

They approached the entrance to find a golden banner

raised before them. It read "Mr. and Mrs. Young." She'd expected to find the Rolls waiting outside, bedecked for the occasion, but instead, a sleek, open-topped carriage greeted them. A pair of kissing silver doves etched on its side, provided the only decoration upon its mirror-like surface. The driver, dressed as a uniformed servant, waited for his passengers.

A stunning pure-white stallion stood in front of the carriage. His strong haunches shone in the crisp winter morning. Anna noted with delight that the ribbons woven into his braided mane matched those in her own hair.

"Woohoo!" Hermon exclaimed. "I'm Lord Hermie of Arizona!" Claire had to restrain her son before he could run through the hotel entrance and to the carriage ahead of the bride. A crowd that'd gathered outside to witness the spectacle laughed to see the boy's antics.

Anna stepped through the doorway with as much grace as possible, despite feeling like her legs belonged to someone else. A gasp emerged from the waiting crowd as she emerged and descended the stairs to the street. The driver tipped his hat toward Anna before hopping down from the bench, ready to assist her, Claire, and Hermon into the carriage. Just then, Anna heard hurried footsteps approaching.

She turned to see the red-jacketed figure of Lawrence hurrying to her side, before thrusting a simple bouquet into Anna's hands.

"We nearly forgot!" he said, as if speaking of a crime. "Could you imagine your wedding photos without the bouquet? My reputation would be ruined!"

Anna rested a reassuring hand on his shoulder. "I don't care how much he's paid you—it's not enough."

Lawrence beamed at the high praise.

Getting in proved a daunting prospect, considering the elaborate dress, but the driver provided a discreet lift into the cushioned interior. The tourists applauded on completion of the tricky move, and more than a few pulled out phones to capture the moment when the mysterious, yet beautiful bride set off on her journey. Claire and Hermon followed her lead shortly after, prompting more than a few comments about how cute he looked.

Feeling obligated to show her appreciation, Anna waved at the onlookers, who rewarded her with even warmer clapping. Some shouted out words of encouragement while one comic called out, "Don't do it!" The latter caller received several disapproving looks from the female members of the group as a result.

With much pomp, the carriage set off with a pleasant clip-clopping. The following journey was much shorter than expected. Instead of heading into the city, they rolled through the Green Park toward the river bank. Soon, they passed under the mighty clock face of Big Ben.

"Hey, Hermie!" Anna called to the kid, who stared around him in wonder while clutching his mother's hand.

"Hey, Anna!" he shouted back.

"Guess what?"

"What?"

"That's Big Ben." She pointed up at the iconic tower.

The boy gave a disbelieving snort. "A clock called Ben? No way, that's silly!" He laughed.

Not long before, Anna had seen a huge cathedral on their right and wondered if it was their destination. The carriage, however, continued toward a signpost labelled Westminster Pier'

They approached a section of the river bank where a host of people gathered, and it soon became obvious why, for as the wharf came into view, so did the wedding barge. The contoured white hull of the vessel stood out in stark contrast to the black carriage. A silver bird with outstretched wings sat upon its prow above the name *The Royal Swan*. A burly line of professional-looking oarsmen in red jackets manned both sides of the boat. The rowing team had raised the oars on the port side to allow access for the shore party to embark.

"Is that my pirate ship, Momma?" Hermon asked, hopping up and down with excitement. "Is it? Is it? Momma?" He tugged his unresponsive mother's dress for an answer.

"It sure is, Captain Hermster!" Anna replied when Claire didn't.

Why is she so off? Anna thought, speculating that perhaps

Claire had been married before. *Is it a jealousy thing?* Her growing concern had to wait, though, because the carriage pulled alongside an ornate boarding ramp. A group of wedding guests already mingled on board, sipping champagne and making merry. Like her, they'd dressed in the high fashion of the 18th century.

After being helped down again, a second retainer in a blue uniform greeted them at the wide ramp.

"It's a good thing this baby has a rail, 'cause I'd sink like a brick in this dress!" she said to Claire while they boarded in an attempt to lighten the woman's mood.

"Aha."

We fly your ass on a free holiday and all I get is "aha," Anna fumed inside. She suppressed the ugly emotion, though, reminding herself of what a jarring experience this must be for the young mother.

They'd spent a great deal of time together over the previous month since their first outing, and there was no doubt that she'd developed an affection for the damaged woman, despite her reservations. In truth, she had to admit that Claire and her adorable son had started to fill the void in her life since the death of Julia.

She had proven to be the kind of friend she'd been looking for since her loss: kind, loyal, and uninterested in her wealth. Even so, she'd learned little about her new companion. Claire had clammed up whenever Anna had asked about her past. One day, at the Estate while Claire had briefly left them alone, Anna had asked Hermon a few discreet questions about his family. After noting his horrified reaction, though, she'd changed the subject, fearing her friend would take offense at such obvious snooping.

A cool breeze and the approaching sound of laughter made her focus again. As she did so, the attention of those on the wedding barge switched to her. A polite applause broke out, and ladies she didn't recognize curtsied while giggling at the novelty of the situation. More than a few gazed at her with envy, while gentlemen seemingly from a bygone age toasted her with crystal glasses. Guessing that they must be some of Corey's many business friends, she looked for a familiar face, but gave up after a moment, without success.

Her escort led Anna to the stern, where a heart-shaped throne carved from pure-white wood stood before her. On its surface were hers and Corey's intertwined married initials. *Holy shit. He hasn't actually made me the Queen of England, has he?* she joked to herself.

She smiled and nodded at the guests, doing her best to get into the moment, despite her crushing nerves. After being seated on the cushioned dais, though, she realized her groom was missing from the happy picture. Anna scanned the surrounding guests for his handsome features before turning to the footmen who'd shadowed her since they'd embarked. "Erm, excuse me, where is Co—Mr. Young?"

He smiled and gave her a mysterious wink. "I'm afraid I'm not at liberty to say."

"Does that mean we're not getting married on the barge?"

"No, madam."

Holy shit

A group of overdressed servants unlashed the barge from its mooring and pushed it into the current. A minute later, the rowers lowered their oars into the river and rhythmically propelled them downstream.

They proceeded with majestic pomp toward Tower Bridge and the intimidating Tower of London. All along the river bank, large crowds began to gather to point at the passing spectacle. The guests continued to mingle as if this was the most normal thing in the world.

As they glided past the intimidating battlements of the Tower, she noticed an ancient water gate built into it walls. The gloomy portal was bricked shut now, but she realized it must've once provided direct access to the river. The barge drew opposite to reveal a name above the disused entrance: Traitor's Gate.

"Protect my son, Holy Father." The words came from Claire. Anna turned to see her friend beside her, gazing at the same spot with a lost expression on her face while fingering the small, silver cross at her neck.

"Are you okay, hon?" Anna asked, laying a worried hand upon her shoulder.

Claire faced her, eyes brimming with tears. "I'm sorry," she mouthed.

"Hey, you've got nothing to be sorry about. I'm about to freak, myself," she said, managing a wan smile to hide her concern. "You just stick with me and we'll get through this together. What do ya say?"

Claire gave half a nod and then turned back to staring at the old fortress of death. Her dark hair blew in the breeze, as a gull cried its lonely call high above them.

They continued for another twenty minutes before their ultimate destination became clear. On the south bank, what looked like another palace slid into view. Identical colonnaded wings formed the two halves of the imposing building, and each twin section had an exquisite clock tower surmounting it. The theme was of perfect symmetry on a grand scale. This elegant place was the polar opposite of the grim Tower of London. Unlike its older cousin, the aim seemed to be to elevate beauty and elegance above the projection of power. A white stone path led from the water side, through the grounds, and toward the stunning main building.

Yet another group of guests had gathered on the vast green lawn before the magnificent edifice. Again, all wore the same wonderful period dress as the barge party. A picnic fit for a king had been laid out on white-clothed tables, and serving staff frequented the milling crowd, offering drinks and other treats on silver trays. Anna's stomach gave a small protest at the sight of the piled platters —she hadn't eaten since the previous evening.

Music drifted toward her from under a huge marquee sporting the same kissing dove motif she'd seen on the carriage. Of course, Corey had commissioned a full orchestra to greet his bride to-be. *Perfect*, she thought, smiling at the prospect of seeing him shortly—although she wasn't quite certain if she would marry him or slap him, for the nerve-shredding experience she'd been through.

The wedding barge slid to a smooth halt opposite the land celebrations. The attention of the guests turned her way, once again, and more clapping followed, interspersed with the odd cheer. Anna stepped onto the solid stone of the quay side with hidden relief and gave a little wave to the throng surrounding her. Two little girls wearing pink frocks hurried over to scatter rose petals before her as she strolled amongst her admirers. Some wore high, white wigs, while others wafted themselves with antique bone hand fans. The orchestra continued to produce soft tunes she didn't recognize, yet which fit her emotion with perfection. The overall effect gave her the oddest, most profound sensation, like passing through a painting. With every step she took, it seemed she revived the former glories of this incredible place. The feeling was unique, and if Corey's aim had been to give her something special, then he'd succeeded beyond her wildest dreams.

The same footman who'd spoken to her on the barge appeared by her side a moment later, drawing her back into reality. "Welcome to Greenwich. If madam approves, would you care to mingle with the guests? We are a little early for the ceremony."

"Certainly, but may I ask," she began, before fighting off a wave of flowery language, "where's Corey?"

"Inside, madam. Don't worry—he'll be ready when you are."

Anna nodded, and then with a sudden idea, looked around for Claire. "Claire!" she called, spotting her pale-looking bridesmaid stepping off *The Royal Swan*. Claire paced to Anna's side, seeming to ignore the happy scenes around her.

"You sure you're okay?" Anna asked again.

"Fine." The accompanying smile didn't reach her eyes.

"Listen, can you do me a favor?"

"Sure."

"Can you find Corey and tell him we're here?" Anna paused. "And that I thought it was wonderful." There was a long pause, so she filled the gap. "He can get so anxious, and I don't want him getting stressed out before the ceremony." She secretly hoped the task would provide her clearly flagging friend with something practical to focus on.

"What about Hermon?"

"I'll keep an eye on him."

"Do you promise? No matter what?"

"Of course—goes without saying," she replied, unsure of why her friend labored such an obvious point.

The reassurance appeared to work, because Claire responded by kissing her on the cheek before bending down to Hermon. She whispered something into his ear and then hugged him fiercely. He seemed reluctant to let his mother go, but after a long second, Claire gently pushed him away before hurrying off toward the main building as fast as her ponderous dress would allow. Anna felt a rush of relief upon seeing her rise to the occasion.

Chapter 14

FOR HIM

Lieutenant Raymond burst through the swinging doors of the palliative care department with a uniformed officer by his side. Two doctors in the middle of discussing a patient's chart turned to face the determined duo as they strode straight toward them.

Raymond frowned at the familiar scent of illness and feces that always seemed to pervade hospitals. It gave an unwelcome reminder of his own all too recent treatment. This ward, in particular, brought feelings of dread into his usually well-ordered mind; people came here with a one-way ticket.

The two youthful clinicians stared at him with curiosity. They looked barely old enough to drive, let alone save lives. "I confess, officer," said one of the unshaven young men with a tarnished stethoscope hanging around his neck. "This place is stuffed with drugs."

His companion chuckled, although he eyed the grim-faced arrivals warily. The Lieutenant put on his best "I'm not here to dick around" expression.

"Raymond, Homicide Unit. We're looking for a person of interest," he said while displaying his badge. "Really?" asked the same doc before sharing a puzzled glance with his colleague. "Sorry to disappoint, Lieutenant, but most of our patients don't even know what year it is—and that's if they're conscious at all."

"Not a patient, a visitor. We need to see her now," he emphasized the last word.

"Who?" Raymond showed them the photo provided by the cleaning company. "Mrs. Macintosh?" The doctor asked after glancing at the head shot of the middle-aged woman. His look of confusion turned to shock. "Is she here?" "Well, yes, but are you sure? That lady has more than enough problems to deal with."

Raymond eyed the unkempt doc with an expression conveying what he thought of the question. The kid held up his hands and then indicated for the officers to follow him. He led them down one of the long, white-washed corridors, further into the ward.

Raymond gave a silent thanks to the gods of luck for allowing him to identify a suspect so soon after reading the prison lab report. The strict vetting processes put in place by Corey Young's own security team had aided the process; few people were allowed access to the reclusive couple, so it'd been a simple matter to find out who'd recently started working at the Estate.

On the surface, Katlin Macintosh passed muster with flying colors. She had no previous record, no known affiliation to political groups, and was a long-term employee of a reputable company. His interest in the woman had sparked, however, when a call to her manager uncovered the fact that she'd sought business with Anna Price, herself. The action wouldn't have normally been unusual, except that the firm had its own sales team. Not only this, but she also shared a similar first name to the mysterious Kate in the secret messages sent to Eckerman.

"Wait a minute," the doctor paused mid-stride. "Aren't you supposed to have a warrant or something?"

"We just want to talk to her."

The kid seemed to ponder this before nodding and continuing to escort them.

Kids are far too accepting of authority, these days, Raymond thought, aware of how many procedural rules he'd just ignored. He also sensed that this matter was too pressing to respect the finer points of protocol. The last chilling instruction sent from the strangler to his sick fan rang through his head: "You must do this before they wed."

The doctor led them through three identical wards before they stopped beside a small cubicle after spending several depressing minutes passing the last vestiges of life. The Lieutenant recognized Katlin inside, standing over the prone form of an unconscious younger male. She washed his pale face gently while humming a soothing tune. His only response to her soft crooning came from the mechanical whirring of the respirator inflating his lungs.

At the sound of their approach, she turned to face them, her features looking older and far more worn than those from her work ID. Upon seeing who interrupted her lonely vigil, her expression registered pure panic. She dropped the cloth into the small bowl and swooned. Reacting quickly, the doctor rushed to support her before she fell. This woman clearly didn't welcome a visit from the police. "Damn it!" the doc muttered as he caught her. "It's okay, Katlin. They only want to ask a few questions. Isn't that right, Lieutenant?" he added, giving the agents of the law a dark glance. "That's right." Even while he mouthed reassurance, however, Raymond knew something was amiss. He didn't see any calculation in her fearful expression; this vision of a troubled caretaker didn't tally with the crazed fanatic he hunted.

The beat officer helped the physician to escort the trembling woman to a nearby rest area. Raymond followed, his mind grasping at possibilities. While the two other men sat her in one of the plastic seats lining the empty room, he strode over to the water cooler against the back wall and poured her a cup. She took it as if he were offering poison, and again, her look of worried guilt didn't add up. "You know why we are here, don't you?" he asked, deciding it was best to give it to her straight. This cookie would crumble without effort, which bothered him more than it gave comfort. Katlin took a deep sip of the water, blinking at him through a gaze brimming with tears. "This is serious, Mrs. Macintosh," he said, certain Katlin would break. She looked at the other men gathered around her, as if searching for understanding.

"I did it for him," she said finally in a quivering voice after the others offered no objection.

"I know," Raymond replied, trying to reel her in gently. *Maybe it is her, after all,* he thought with a small measure of hope. "Do you love him?" he added, wanting to bring out the relationship between her and Eckerman.

She gave him a look of both confusion and anger. "Of course, I love him: he's my son."

His sense of unease grew. "Your son?" He'd read up on Eckerman before the trial and recalled learning that the killer's mother had died years ago.

Her tone became defiant, "Tell me, Lieutenant, what would you do to save your son's life?"

"Why do you think we're here?" he asked bluntly, sensing that he didn't have much time to unravel this mess. The question hung between them while an internal struggle played across the woman's face. "He asked me to find out anything I could about Corey and Anna," she said. Her shoulders slumped in resignation. "What kinds of things?" "Are they on drugs? Is one of them having an affair? Bad stuff. You must know that already, though, or you wouldn't be here, right?" Katlin took another sip of water. She looked calmer, now, like a great burden had been lifted from her shoulders. The Lieutenant pieced this together in his mind, but it made no sense. Why would a psycho like Eckerman want to blackmail his ex-partner? The answer was simple: he wouldn't. The realization hit Raymond like a fist.

"Katlin, this is important. Have you ever spoken with or written to Tony Eckerman?"

There was more confusion, along with undisguised revulsion, this time. "That filthy animal? No!" she said, her eyes searching the Lieutenant's face for answers. All his twenty years on the force told him she was telling the truth.

"You said you did it for him, though."

"I meant for John, my son," she said, pointing an impassioned finger toward the unconscious man in the nearby bed. "He needs a liver transplant, but there've been no donors." She stared at the floor in total despair. "The doctors talk about new drugs to buy him more time, but my insurance..."

Raymond blinked, understanding finally descending upon him. "Let me get this straight: you were paid to spy on the couple. That's all?" "What do you mean 'is that all?' Isn't it bad enough for you people?" He could see anger flare in her once more. "I've betrayed them, lost my job, and John..." she sobbed the final word. The grizzled Lieutenant exchanged a look with the uniformed officer as his mind raced ahead of the conversation. "She's not the one," he declared. "What do you mean?" Katlin asked, her face a mixture of relief and worry.

The Lieutenant pressed a hand to his temple, trying to

process the possibilities. First, he had to remove Eckerman from the picture. "Did you have any contact with the person who asked you to watch Corey and Anna?" Katlin gazed at him. Demons played out on her exhausted face. *She's weighing the risks of telling me.* "Katlin, I don't think you understand how serious this is. I'm a homicide detective." Her hands flung to her mouth in shock. "Has someone been killed?" she asked. "No, but I think Anna Price is in danger, and I need your help to stop the threat. That's why I need to find out who asked you to spy on them." She nodded with wide eyes. "Yes. Yes, of course. It was my lawyer," she said.

"Your lawyer?" "Bill Moyer, the bastard." The name rang a bell with him. "The guy from TV? The cowboy?"

She nodded again as she took a tissue from her white cardigan sleeve and blew her nose. "I'd taken him on to build a claim against the insurance company to get money for John," she said, dabbing her eyes. "I heard nothing from the useless, fat pig for months, until one day he called me and said the claim wasn't going well."

"So he made you an offer?" the Lieutenant pressed.

She nodded again. "He said one of his clients had serious legal issues with some rich celebrity couple, and then he promised me ten grand if I kept an eye on them. That's all he asked, at first." "But he wanted more?" "Yes. When I started telling him what they did and where they went, he got angry. He started pushing for dirt." She shook her head with clear regret. "Please believe me: I would never have done such a thing if I'd known what good people they are." Her face screwed up with supressed rage. "The snake never paid me a friggin' penny. I swear it on John's life." Raymond knew it was time to put this poor woman out of her misery. The thought that he'd willed this kind, abused woman to be an accomplice to a creature like Eckerman left a bitter taste in his mouth. Options drifted through his head and the next step became obvious: he needed to warn the couple's security team. He cursed himself for not doing so, already.

"Where are Anna and Corey now?" "Getting married," she replied, "in London." "London, England?" "Yes. Look." Katlin removed a small phone from underneath her plastic hospital apron and passed it to the detective. "See?"

The picture was of a smiling Anna, wearing an astounding wedding dress. She'd put on a healthy amount of weight since their last meeting. The happy bride had been joined by a pretty, dark-haired bridesmaid with grey eyes and a young page boy.

Raymond sighed with relief. While out of the US, she would be safe from whichever loon Eckerman had brainwashed. He almost handed the phone back when he suddenly felt the need to look again. He stared at the woman beside Anna. "Who's that?" he asked the red-eyed Katlin, pointing at Anna's bridesmaid. "Oh, that's Claire, Anna's new friend. The little boy is Hermon, her son." Katlin smiled for the first time since they'd met. "He's such a cutie pie—just like my Johnny, at his age."

The Detective stared into Claire's disconcerting gaze.

There was something deep in her eyes—something sad. *Something familiar.* "How long have they known each other?" His heart started to beat faster. "Not long, I think. I've maybe only seen her a couple of times at the Estate over the past month, but heck, it's not like I'm part of the furniture, myself."

Raymond ignored the reply as something stabbed for his attention from his memory. It was something he'd seen in the newspapers. His hand strayed to his temple. He knew her face.

"When did Anna send you the picture?"

"About an hour ago."

He barely registered the answer, because he'd worked out who stared back at him. "Sweet Jesus," he murmured, already starting to dial numbers on the cell phone.

Chapter 15

EYE FOR AN EYE

Corey sat before the mirror having a full-blown panic attack. He'd wimped out and hid himself in a changing room, rather than face the hundreds of guests waiting to witness the biggest day of his life.

The fact that his every exaggerated emotion played out on the mirror didn't help matters in the slightest. He groaned on further inspection of his red, puffing cheeks and wide, blinking eyes. Such was his state of meltdown that he'd sent a concerned-looking steward to retrieve a paper bag to give him something to blow into. That'd been twenty minutes ago.

To top it all off, the one person who could make him feel better was currently being landed on the river bank like a fish, and in all probability, in the foulest of moods, due to the ridiculous surprise he'd foisted upon her. "What was I thinking?" he said aloud for the third time, not believing his own stupidity. "She'll never forgive me."

Corey heard the creaking hinges of the door behind him, and he silently sent up a prayer of thanks. He'd suffered from panic attacks since the death of his parents, and the bag trick had proven to be one of the few things to control his breathing when experiencing the worst episodes.

He could see a dainty hand curl around the heavy, antique frame and push it further inward. Corey didn't recognize the woman in the spectacular dress, at first, until he registered the visitor as Claire. Although she'd spent a lot of time with Anna over the past few months, she'd treated him with something approaching disdain. With that in mind, as well as the fact that Anna so obviously needed female company, he'd learned to avoid her. So it was with some surprise that he greeted her now. She appeared drawn, even under her heavy makeup.

"How is she?" he asked, the collar of his starched shirt feeling like a noose around his neck. "Does she like the day, so far?" "She likes the boat." Claire's expression didn't match the sentiment.

"Oh, thanks, I was so worried she'd freak about," he waved a frilled sleeve around at the grand venue, "all this." For some reason, Corey didn't feel the relief he'd just indicated.

Claire stepped into the room and glided toward him, lifting the heavy dress as she did so.

"She asked if you are okay."

Corey held his head in response. "I'm just so nervous," he said. "I wanted to make this the best day for her, but now that it's come to it, I wish I'd just booked a suite in Vegas without all the..." he waved his hand again.

"Wicked self-indulgence?"

"Well, sorta, but... was it too much to expect that arrogant, overpaid ass, Lawrence, to at least give me a God damn hair cut?" he said, picking up the steel scissors that, a few minutes before, he'd considered using to give himself a trim. He tossed them back onto the table to emphasize his frustration.

"Don't insult the Lord's name."

"What? Oh, sorry," he mumbled, embarrassed by his outburst. "I know its Anna's big day, and I wouldn't change that for the world, but I look like a sack of shit!" he added, trying to explain in more reasonable terms.

There was a pause. "I can cut hair."

"Really?" "I used to be hair dresser." The offer sounded genuine, but he just wished it had been made with a little more warmth.

"Claire, thank you so much. I'd really appreciate it." He felt happier, already. "I don't want to get married looking like a scarecrow in a suit." The joke only gained fleeting movement from her lips.

Without speaking, she lifted the dress once more before moving to stand behind him. Only then did he notice the sea-grey gaze contemplating him. He hadn't been this close to her until now, and he made a mental note to be a little kinder to Claire. They hadn't gotten off on the right foot, but this was a favor he planned to return.

She picked up a nearby towel and placed it around his shoulders before grasping the scissors. The heavy metal of the sharp blades grated against the ancient, dark wood dresser as she brought them behind his head. He found the slow, deliberate action strangely disconcerting. *Is her hand trembling?*

He could see her inspecting the lethal, yet mundane implements, and then came the sensation of the cold steel sliding against his neck. She took a single snip of hair while resting her other hand on his left shoulder.

"Thanks so much, again. Do you think we have enough time?" he asked, finding the silence uncomfortable.

"If the Lord wills it." His gaze flicked back to her. Above her cleavage, a small, silver cross hung around her neck. "That's a pretty necklace," he said, determined to distract himself from the events ahead.

"My father gave it to me."

There was another snip as the steel started to warm against his skin. "That's nice." "Not really." Snip. More silence. Corey didn't trust himself to speak further. "Do you really know her?" she asked.

"Anna? I'd like to think so." He laughed uncomfortably.

"Then she must have told you she was engaged to another."

"Yes, but we don't talk about it." His face flushed in anger at the inappropriate question.

"God sees a betrothal as a contract, you pathetic fornicator!" Claire spat the words. "She already belongs to him!" The hand on his shoulder became a clamp, and Corey turned to face her, shocked. "We both belong to him—to Tony," she said, as the raging torrent beneath the calm surface rose to the fore. "An eye for an eye, my love."

The scissors glittered in the afternoon sunshine as she raised them above his stunned face. The point plunged downward and time slowed. Something primal took over in Corey, and he felt himself thrusting his body to the left and knocking her arm aside.

He continued his desperate bid for life, even as he knew his efforts would be too late. A searing lance of agony erupted in his collar bone, sending pulsing aftershocks down his right arm like a rolling sheet of molten lead. He tumbled to the floor, his skull cracking painfully against the edge of the table as he went.

Corey scrambled while his mind tried to respond to the alarm bells ringing through his body. Clawing back some semblance of rational thought, he realized that he lay face down against the flags. He tried to push himself upward, but the effort made him scream as a fresh wave of jarring, hot fire coursed down his injured right shoulder. The dark stones swam before his vision as he felt himself passing out. *At which point, you are dead, and Anna will be left to pick up the pieces.*

"No!" he cried, pressing down with his left hand and flipping himself onto his back, like a stranded turtle. He found her bending toward him with blood dripping from the end of the scissor blades. Any semblance of sanity had left her face, only to be replaced by a hate-filled sneer.

"Heretic filth!" she screeched, going in for the kill. "You led her from the righteous path, away from the family of our lord. I will bring her back to the light, back to our betrothed."

The heavy dress slowed her enough to give his battered senses time to come up with one last roll of the dice. He pushed himself further onto his good shoulder, straining with effort, until he lay panting on his side. As Claire approached, he swept his leg around and connected with her ankles. She tumbled to the ground beside him, thudding against the hard floor, causing the air to rush from her jolted lungs with a gasp.

He tried to clamber on top of her and wrestle away the vicious weapon still clutched in her fist, but the problem became clear with brutal speed. With his good arm pinned beneath him, this left only his damaged right to try to grab the blade from her. He tried a feeble snatch at the pincers while she remained stunned, but the metal was slick with blood, making a firm grip impossible.

Claire blinked, like a corpse revived, before turning her head toward him, her gaze fixing on his once more. The blow to her head must've hurt, because one of her pupils had blown, causing a red ring to form around her grey iris. The once-mysterious sea of hers now ran red with blood.

Corey could feel her body tense before she whipped the scissors over her head at his exposed face again. He caught her wrist halfway, though, and she roared in frustration, redoubling her efforts to push against the resistance. At the same time, she turned her frame to lever more force.

He could feel himself losing the battle; the agony was unbearable, and he was getting weaker as his life force ebbed from the bleeding wound she'd inflicted. Sweat broke out on his forehead while the deadly struggle continued. Inexorably, his vision filled with the blade point moving ever closer to its soft destination.

Corey's soul filled with horror, but overriding this was the knowledge that the woman he loved would be destitute, yet again. She didn't deserve that. The thought sustained him beyond endurance to withstand the agony, but willpower alone would not be enough. The blade loomed, and at any second, his tortured muscle would give way.

Please, let her get through this and be happy, he sent up a final prayer before the inevitable.

The sound of a crashing slam interrupted their death struggle, and then the pressure lifted. At first, he thought the battle had gone against him and what he now experienced was the cocoon of oblivion before the final curtain descended. He closed his eyes, sending up thanks for not feeling further pain.

"Mr. Young? Sir! Are you okay?" The gravelly, low voice belonged to Matt Smith, the head of his security team.

Corey's eyes flicked open. The final proof that he remained with the living came from the fresh protests of agony coming from his body. Under normal circumstances,

Matt wouldn't be considered a good-looking man by any stretch, but right then, he appeared like an angel.

"Sir, we've got her," he went on. "Jesus, you're injured! Johnson, get me an ambulance!"

"Get me up," Corey said through lips which suddenly felt parched.

"No way! You can't be moved," he replied. "I can't believe it! We got a call from the US to warn us. Jesus! That was way too close, damn it!" Corey heard the ripping sound of cloth and then pressure being applied to his collar, causing him to cry out in pain.

"Sorry, sir, but I need to stop the bleeding."

"I said get me up!" Corey demanded.

"But—"

"Just do it!"

He feared that the burly ex-marine would refuse his request at first, but after a pause, Corey could feel strong arms move him into a sitting position. For a second, his vision swam before settling enough to allow him to focus on the bloody scene around him. Claire still lay beside him, pressed face-down on the floor underneath two members of the security team. She didn't struggle against the plastic cuffs binding her wrists, but continued to radiate a look of pure venom toward him.

"I stopped it!" she hissed. "I stopped the wedding, just as he asked of me. Praise the vengeance of the Lord!"

Corey hadn't had time to grasp the full nature of what the attack had meant through the turmoil of the past minute. While he stared into her wild, blood-shot eyes, though, the words she'd spoken hit him with a terrible force. *She said, "Tony..." he realized, "We both belong to Tony."*

A deep rage filled him. She served the creature who'd brought such anguish to the person he loved most. Somehow, the bastard Eckerman had managed to slink into their lives again. The specter of evil had returned to haunt them.

She cackled. "Lost for words, eh, fornicator?"

The urge to kick her took him over, and with a sudden burst of anger propelling him through the pain, he rose to his feet.

"Sir, please, wait for the ambulance!"

Corey shuffled over to Claire. If she was scared by the gesture, she didn't show it. "Go ahead, strike me. I am but a daughter of Eve—we deserve to be punished for tempting Adam! We are but the rib!"

Cool understanding washed through Corey. He knew how to defy the beast and this pathetic excuse for a woman. "Fetch me my jacket," he said to a fourth member of the security team standing in the open doorway.

"But the ambulance?" Matt sounded confused. "You can't..."

"I said: fetch me my jacket. My hair will have to do," Corey said, looking into the mirror at the glassy-eyed figure before him. He grabbed a packet of wet wipes off the dresser with a trembling hand before cleaning the red flecks from his face. Matt followed his movement, pressing the rapidly-soaking cloth against him.

"What are you doing?" Claire asked with a note of apprehension in her voice.

"Matt, wrap my shoulder," Corey said, ignoring her.

"I really don't think that's a good idea, sir."

"Just do it." "You're the boss," Matt said reluctantly, taking his make-shift bandage and binding his employer's wound. No sooner had he begun to adjust the position of the dressing than Corey went light-headed. He swayed until Matt clamped him between two vice-like hands.

"Where are you going?" Claire asked, her voice rising.

"To get married." With that, he turned and began to limp down the hallway.

"No, stop!" she screamed as he reached the exit and leaned against it.

He paused to take a breath. "You're not fit to be called a woman." He pointed in the direction of the great hall. "She belongs to herself and no one else."

ANNA DIDN'T FEEL the least bit surprised that Claire hadn't returned. In fact, she felt relieved, because her friend had clearly been wilting under the pressure. She hoped Corey had spotted her obvious distress and told her to take some time out. Hermon, however, remained a concern.

As promised, the boy had followed her closely since his mother's departure. Anna gave him the occasional glance to check that he was okay, and whenever she looked, the little man beamed, seeming happy to tag along in such grand surroundings.

She made slow progress toward the wide, stone steps leading to the ornate building dominating the view from the lawn. So many guests passed ahead of her into what the staff called the painted hall that her throat ached from returning their compliments. By the time she came to stand before the surprisingly modest, rectangular, stone entrance, she felt like a marathon runner with one last milestone before reaching the finish line.

The columns lining the entire face of the structure on either side of the doorway dared her to wonder what might be on the other side. Two uniformed footmen opened the wood-panelled doors and beckoned her to enter. Only she and Hermon remained outside, and he took her hand.

"Here goes," she said, squeezing the posies for luck before stepping forward. On the threshold, she paused and looked down at Hermon. "Hermie?"

"Yes, Auntie A?" He'd never called her that before.

"Will you give me away?" The question caught in her throat. She'd agreed with Corey, considering her family situation, that they'd be bold and do without the tradition. Now, however, as she stood on the verge of the most important moment of her life, she missed her daddy.

"Give you away?" Hermon cried. "I can't give you away! You're worth, like, a million-billion dollars!"

Just a million or so, kid, she thought, smiling. "Just to Corey, kiddo."

"Oh well, that's fine, then. I like him."

She let out a long breath, puffed away the wisp of hair falling into her eyes, and then stepped in. At first, Anna could only see a checkered marble floor. As she gazed beyond a short flight of stairs leading up, however, her jaw dropped open. The most vivid, life-like frescoes covered every inch of the walls and ceiling of the massive hall. High above her, within a halo-like, golden border, a couple wearing crowns sat upon a cloud surrounded by cherubs. It was a vision of Heaven. To her right and left, the guests had gathered upon rows of silver chairs, and all looked to her. Light blazed through high, wide windows, illuminating her path to the altar. The two figures standing at the far end made her heart leap with Joy. *Corey.* The traditional sound of the Bridal March burst through the hall, making her swell with expectation. *It's all for me,* Anna marvelled.

She stepped carefully up the short set of stairs leading onto the main plaza and became entranced by the spectacle. Every column plinth had been painted a radiant gold and each windowsill appeared embossed with silver roses.

Corey hadn't looked back, yet. He gazed ahead at the most stunning of all the images in the painted hall, which depicted more angels upon their celestial thrones. The whole elaborate scene gave the illusion of real depth, though, as if Corey and the green-robed priest stood before the gates of paradise, waiting for someone to join them before crossing over.

The music surged, and she stepped down the sun-dappled length of the checkered floor with Hermon in hand. Everyone fixed their attention upon her and the boy, and she continued through the fairytale scene, until stopping beside her groom. Only then did he turn to face her. Corey looked very pale, but he still managed a wan, genuine smile. She took his left hand and squeezed his palm.

"Thank you," she mouthed.

His smile widened, but not with his usual puppy-like enthusiasm. He looked deeply weary, and beads of sweat ran down his brow. And as he took her hand in his, she could feel a slight tremble in his clammy palm. It appeared that this day had tested even his boundless energy. The song ended, and she could hear the guests shuffling and whispering in anticipation.

"We are gathered here today to witness one of life's greatest moments—to bring together man and woman under the union of marriage." The red-cheeked priest greeted them all. "Marriage is a sacred promise to be made between two people that, once made, shall forever unite you both until death." He paused to stare at them from under metal-rimmed spectacles, as if to emphasize the point.

Anna realized this would be a good time to inform the cleric of her decision about Hermon. "He is giving me away," she whispered to him while nodding toward the boy. The rotund man of God gave a solemn nod and then winked at Hermon.

"Before I continue, may I ask who is giving this woman away?"

"Lord Hermon of Arizona!" Hermie declared, puffing up his chest with importance. The congregation chuckled at the grand announcement.

"Very well, Lord Hermon of Arizona. You may join the other guests, now," the priest said. An usher stepped in to lead the boy aside, leaving both of them to complete their vows.

"Corey Young, will you take Anna Price to be your wife? Will you love her, comfort her, honor and protect her, and, forsaking all others, be faithful to her as long as you both shall live?"

"I will." Corey's voice sounded strained, and Anna wondered if the emotion had gotten the better of him.

Oh dear, I hope he doesn't faint.

She noticed that Matt, the head of Corey's security team, stood close by. He had an unusual look of anxiety on his rugged features, causing a small measure of worry to mix with her excitement.

"Anna Price, will you take Corey Young to be your husband? Will you love him, comfort him, honor and protect him, and, forsaking all others, be faithful to him as long as you both shall live?"

"I will," she replied, with all her heart.

"Corey and Anna, I now invite you to join hands and make your vows in the presence of God and his people."

She took his hand once again. It felt cold, though, and the tremble seemed far more pronounced than a second before.

"Are you okay?" she mouthed. His nod barely registered.

After the priest read out the vows, Corey followed haltingly:

"I, Corey Young, take you, Anna Price..." he hesitated, "to be my wife; to have and to hold from this day forward; for better, for worse, for richer, for poorer, in sickness, and in health; to love and to cherish 'til death," he paused again, swaying on his feet "do us part." A murmur went up from the crowd as his discomfort became visible to all.

"Would you like to take a break, Mr. Young?" the clergyman asked, clearly concerned.

"No."

The kind-faced man turned to Anna in a gesture seeming to ask her agreement. Anna nodded hesitantly, unsure. Upon the sight of her groom's pasty-white complexion, she repeated her vows with as much meaning as her growing alarm would allow. They were so close—so very close.

"Corey and Anna will now exchange rings as a symbol of their love for each other," prompted the priest.

With all the slow care of a man moving a mountain, Corey reached into his pocket. Anna retrieved her own band of gold—the one she'd kept since the death of her father. It lay in a specially-made concealed pocket in her dress.

On his first attempt, Corey clutched at her fingers before seeming to steady himself. With huge effort, he slid the ring previously belonging to his mother onto her slender digit. "Anna, I give you this ring as a sign of our marriage. With my body, I honor you. All that I am, I give to you, and all that I have, I share with you within the love of the Father, Son and Holy Spirit." he repeated after the priest, his words a whisper.

As Anna reached down, lifted his arm, and then placed her own ring on his finger, a smudge of red on the underside of his shirt cuff caught her eye. She repeated her own vows, transfixed by the ominous stain. Her mind swam, torn between growing dread and the need to complete the act that meant so much to them both.

"In the presence of God, and before this congregation, Corey and Anna have given their consent and made their marriage vows to each other."

She looked across at Corey's right hand and her heart stopped. A single line of blood ran down the length of his wedding finger, pooled around the newly-placed band, and dripped off the end and onto the bright, white marble below. Anna put a hand over her mouth in shock. Even now, she didn't dare break the final moment of the ceremony—something about his determination forbade it.

"They have declared their marriage by the joining of hands and by the giving and receiving of rings. I, therefore, proclaim that they are husband and wife."

He fell with an audible thud against the hard floor, even as the priest spoke the last word. Gasps rang out amongst the guests, and it took Anna a second to register the dark red stain revealed when the flap on his jacket opened. She'd only seen such a sight twice before in her life.

"Corey!" she screamed, falling beside him.

Dimly, Anna became aware of thudding footsteps reaching their side. She looked up to see two paramedics racing to reach them with Matt beside them. "Let us help him, sweetheart," said a pony-tailed medic kneeling beside Anna. She opened his jacket further to reveal the extent of his injury.

"She attacked him before the ceremony," Matt said, laying a restraining hand on Anna's shoulder.

"What?"

"He insisted we go through with it, Anna. I'm so sorry—I should have made him..."

Anna didn't hear, though. She stared down into a faltering gaze, willing the return of the bright, keen look that she'd come to love. "I'm not going to lose you, do you hear me?" she wept. Corey's gaze dimmed. "No! Don't you dare!" she yelled with a passion welling from her soul. She laid his head on the marble floor before reaching under her dress to retrieve the wedding gift she'd been saving under her garter. "Do you see, Corey Young? Do you see that I need you?" She lifted the pregnancy kit toward him, the blue line challenging his growing stillness.

Anna thought she saw a flicker of recognition.

EPILOGUE

Detective Raymond let out an explosive breath and then replaced the receiver after hearing the update from the Clear Water estate security manager. It seemed the British doctors were still fighting to save the life of Corey Young.

Raymond couldn't help but feel a sliver of sympathy for the security manager. The guy on the other end of the line had sounded hoarse with exhaustion and concern. To lose your job was one thing, but losing the life of the person you'd been sworn to protect must be a bitter prospect to face. He pinched the bridge of his nose with thumb and fore finger, while sending up a silent prayer that he'd at least given the fella a fighting chance. Something bugged him though: why Corey and not Anna? Surely, Eckerman would have used his accomplice to murder Anna Price rather than her fiancé?

Maybe the sicko still thinks they can get back together? He speculated. But that wouldn't explain why Claire would target Corey Young rather than the person she must surely see as her love rival.

"I hate this fucking job," he muttered, suspecting that his brush with the big C had more to do with the stress caused by this kind of shit, rather than the cigs.

He pushed his wheeled office chair across the length of his work desk, which often doubled as a place to lay his head during all nighters, such as this.

After glancing around to check that he was alone, Raymond reached into the third drawer down, and felt toward the back, until his hand settled on the familiar shape of the whiskey bottle. He kept the secret treat there for occasions just like this, when life demanded liquor. Realizing that he didn't have a shot glass to hand, he instead finished off the last dregs of stone cold coffee in his stained white mug, before pouring the amber liquid into it. He took a long swig of the concoction, still tinged by the taste of its former contents, and then saluted the security camera at the end of the office. "I'm on my time now you sons of bitches. If I want a god damn drink, I will." He said to the blind mechanical eye that he knew to be broken. Like most things round here, it'd stopped working some time ago.

He logged onto his PC, then completed a web search for the same reports that had triggered his recognition of Claire in the wedding picture. After a few moments, he'd found the unsettling story and accompanying image once again.

The last time he'd seen the article was on the cover of the Hays tribune, while spending several days in Kansas at the home of his mother. She'd become frail of late and had taken a nasty fall in the kitchen, while cooking breakfast pancakes for his even frailer father. The precinct captain had allowed him a whole two days compassionate leave.

Raymond felt surprised by the same feelings of pity that came to him, on seeing Claire and the kid again. Just as he remembered, she looked wide eyed and terrified by the full force of the state gathered to rescue them, the kid even more so.

The paps had snapped them emerging from a white washed farm house, dressed like they were attending church circa 1840, between two uniformed officers. It struck him that the home looked like the safe kind you saw on a T.V series like the Waltons. An old time place, owned by the kind of folks who'd leave the door unlocked at night and where kids spoke respectfully to their elders. In reality, it'd been a house of horrors.

Tom Pike, Claire's father, had decided that he alone was the mouth piece of the almighty after being shown the light by a talking tree, no less. What followed had been a tale of one man's descent into madness, while dragging his own family with him.

Over a six-month period, he seemed to have converted a handful of locals. If the neighbor's statements had been anything to go by, his new disciples' mental health issues were almost as serious as his own. After whipping them all in to a holy frenzy, both metaphorically and literally, he'd declared that the lord in his infinite wisdom had decided that the women in the group should become his wives. Including his own biological daughters.

The Pike farm was a remote place, where people 'kept themselves to themselves,' abusive puke or no. The sorry affair had gone on for three years before one of Claire's sisters had run away and blew the whistle. In addition to the news clippings, Raymond had checked the police report into the raid on the house.

After receiving a tip from a local, like any good, all seeing messiah would, the father hung himself in the barn, before the cops had a chance to get him. The mother had slit her own throat under his swinging corpse. It was telling that some of the group had stayed at the property, after the deaths, for almost two days before the law arrived on scene. Clearly, not all of them had appreciated their liberation.

He'd found the interview tapes with Claire and the boy. It was clear the kid knew nothing of just how fucked up his family had become, and was mercifully oblivious to the full wickedness of his grandfather. Claire though, had refused to co-operate for the most part. But he'd found one telling response to the question: "How do you feel about your sister?" The chilling transcript of her answer gave him the closest he would get to a motive: "We are of eve—of the rib.

Adam guides us. Adam—who begot Cain and begot Able. My sister will come back to the fold. She will reject Satan and embrace the lord and his seed once more."

Maybe she saw Eckerman as a replacement for her father?

Raymond finished off the glass, feeling the burning liquid run down his throat. The article, dated a year ago, concluded that the escaped sister had been admitted into a private clinic. This left him curious to know who funded the treatment. The fate of Claire and the boy since the incident, however, was uncertain.

The paper skirted around the subject of incest, seeming to err on the side of caution, by saying that the parentage of the boy in the photo was 'unclear.' But the inference was clear.

Raymond could only imagine the kind of confusion experienced by the vulnerable duo after being thrust back into the world. To go from a freakish vision of Victorian life, to the land of 24/7 porn and all you can eat pizza, must have been a huge shock. And he'd seen first-hand what passed for social care these days: food stamps and a bag of sugar put in your kids School milk allowance.

No, despite the wicked nature of her actions, his pity remained. Pity for a woman who'd never been taught to respect herself, and let down by a society that valued butt cheek implants over the wellbeing of each other. It all amounted to a perfect breeding ground for predators like Eckerman to find a damaged, deluded, fool to exploit.

Raymond poured himself another.

BIRD OF PREY

ANNA SERIES BOOK 3

Chapter 1

THE DEEP

Corey banked the Mark 2 into the slipstream, feeling the hum of the amazing craft pulse beneath his feet. The black, elegant body of the plane barely buffeted as he adjusted the angle of approach to drift into the air current with ease. It was a practiced move that never failed to send a thrill down his spine. He looked over to the co-pilot's chair, ready to fire a grin at Anna, but the half-formed smile froze on his lips when he saw she wasn't by his side.

That's a shame, he thought. *If only she could see how well this baby is handling today.*

He scanned the horizon, marvelling at the sea of blue surrounding him on all sides. Far below, the ocean surface called to him like a hypnotic beacon demanding his attention. Despite his great height, he could see the white tips of waves rolling in a never-ending cycle, hiding a dark world beneath.

Corey pushed on the stick, plunging him toward the depths like a bird of prey diving at its target. He guided the HELA with instinctive mastery, knowing exactly how to test her limits without pushing beyond what she could take. Laughing at the sensation in the pit of his stomach, he felt one with the machine for one glorious minute before leveling her out the moment she started to shudder in protest.

The late afternoon sun created a stunning optical effect on the fluffy clouds, giving them a vibrant pink tinge framed against an electric blue heaven.

I wish my wife could see this...

"Am I married?" He asked himself aloud, unable to answer.

A dark cloud appeared against the azure horizon, interrupting his confused train of thought. It was strange to see the black spot expand so fast against the incredible backdrop, like cancer spreading in healthy tissue. The ominous ball of swirling gloom continued to grow until its bulk dominated the entire western half of his vision.

He'd heard of such spontaneous weather events, but had yet to face one so ugly. The question of turning back played on his mind, but despite his unease, he felt an overwhelming urge to throw caution to the wind and head straight into the heart of the beast. He checked the instruments once more and was reassured to see that every indicator remained a healthy shade of green. Strapping himself in, he prepared to grapple with nature's awesome power.

Corey switched the engine from solar to the far more potent twin jet thrusters, deciding he would need every ounce of power the HELA could spare for the flight ahead. The delicate prop turbines retracted without issue, soon followed by the gurgling sound of fuel pouring into the rear jets. In the split second before ignition, his stomach lurched as the plane became a billion-dollar rock falling from the sky. With reliable efficiency, however, the thruster kicked in, and raw G-force pressed him back into the pilot's seat.

Darkness filled the cockpit window now, and sheet lightning crashed within the approaching maelstrom like the artillery fire of the gods. All that stood between him and oblivion was a few inches of steel and the powerful beating heart of this remarkable machine. Chunks of ice thudded against the fuselage, causing him to wince at the expensive damage.

The flight stick proved almost impossible to wrestle into position as colossal forces tossed the plane around like a doll in the jaws of a raging bear. A hailstone the size of a human fist smashed against the toughened glass of the cockpit, leaving a spidery crack.

He plunged on, increasing the power to maximum, hoping to ride the chaos through the belly of the monster. The jets roared at his command, and the Mark 2 surged like a bat in the mouth of hell. Corey roared in fear and pain at the thunder assaulting his eardrums as an image of a blue line flickered into his consciousness.

I must survive for them.

The torrent gained more power, though, dwarfing the valiant efforts of the HELA. She couldn't take much more. Still, he tried to maintain a futile grip on the controls, even as warning lights flared around him.

The MK 2 plummeted from the sky, and inside, Corey could only watch as the abyss approached. As the end neared, he thought the sea resembled a gray, hate-filled gaze that burned into his soul. He closed his eyes and waited.

Nothing followed, other than sudden silence. After a moment, he forced himself to look, only to find that his nightmare had changed from one vast world to another below the surface of the ocean.

The cracking glass continued its journey before his horrified gaze. Water sprayed through the ever-widening fissure, until icy liquid fingers crept up his legs and enveloped his torso. Corey gasped in shock, thrashing his legs against the chilling grip of the water. Panic set in, and he wrenched at the seatbelt mechanism, trying to free himself. But unlike the simple action of release he'd come to expect, the clip refused to budge, seemingly stuck fast by an inexorable force.

The creeping death ran over his shoulders now, and the freezing cold made him shout in pain. He pounded his feet against the dashboard with all the waning strength he could muster. His efforts were in vain, though; just as the water began to lap under his nose, the crack in the windshield spread further, until finally, it exploded inward. Water poured in and sealed his fate. Corey wept for the life he could've had, knowing he would be entombed in this terrible, dark place forever, kept away from her love.

Chapter 2

HOPE?

The nurse opened the curtains, allowing bright light to flood into the private room. As usual, the morning ritual illuminated the dozens of cards, flowers, and well-intentioned sentiments lining the white interior walls.

Anna lifted her head from the couch that'd become her bed for the past week and smiled at the woman she now regarded as a friend. Once again, she felt a wave of gratitude for the fantastic staff here.

"You're eating this morning, Misses," Nurse Jessie said in the same no-nonsense tone that'd kept Anna from losing her wits on several occasions since their arrival. "How about a full English breakfast, hmm? You promised me you'd try again today, honey," she added before turning to a frizzy-haired Anna, clearly expecting a positive reply.

"It's not just me I'm eating for now—I know—you don't

have to give me another lecture, Jessie," Anna replied, then yawned and stretched her arms. She glanced to where Hermon still slept in a bed they'd brought in for him. His blonde curls remained buried deep in his pillow, a sign that he hadn't woken yet. "I'm not eating any of that blood pudding crap, though," she added, continuing their ongoing joke about the strange foods the British considered a treat. Jessie had an easy manner that made such banter a welcome distraction.

"Black pudding," the nurse corrected her. "How about some kippers, then?"

"What the hell are those?"

"Smoked fish."

"What? You've got to be..." Anna said, suddenly feeling ill. Jessie retrieved a bedpan from her trolley and presented it to Anna with a practiced hand just before she began to retch.

"That'd be morning sickness," the nurse observed.

"Oh my God." Anna spat. "How long will this last?"

"Only another ten weeks," came the happy reply.

"Ten weeks! I feel like death," she spluttered after emptying the contents of her stomach. Jessie patted her back, seemingly immune to the sight of puke. "Sorry," she added, embarrassed.

"Don't apologize, hon. It's not easy, especially with your first," Jessie said.

"You okay, Auntie A?" the worried question came from Hermon, woken by her urgent call of nature.

She gave him a wan smile and a shaky thumbs-up in reply. Despite her own situation, Anna had insisted the authorities allow him to remain with her since the attack and his mother's arrest. Now, a week later, he'd become her rock and another reason to hope. "I'm fine, Hermie—just a poorly tummy is all," she said, trying to ignore a fresh wave of nausea.

"Oh, okay," he replied with a note of caution. "You sure?"

Poor kid's terrified that everyone he cares about will disappear, Anna thought, cursing the woman who'd betrayed her. In a sense, Claire had also betrayed her son—perhaps more than anyone. *If she could see the mess she's left him in...*

"Anna's fine, sweetheart," Jessie said. "Everyone gets a bad tum, sometimes."

"Would you like me to get you some water?" he asked in his usual eager-to-please way.

"Oh, yes please, Hermie, that would make me feel much better," Anna replied, suppressing the sickness. That seemed to be enough to reassure him, because he hopped out of bed before skipping to the water cooler. The two women shared a brief smile at his consistently sweet nature.

"How's Corey?" Anna asked the inevitable question that'd become another daily ritual.

"The same," Jessie replied, as always. "Could be a day..."

"Could be a year," Anna finished.

"Hey, I've met coma survivors, hon. Corey is young and fit—we've got every reason to think he might pull through."

Might.

"I know, I know. I just wish..."

"You wish you were sunbathing on a beach in the Caribbean together and not stuck here."

"Something like that," Anna sighed. "If it weren't..." she cut off her next bitter sentence just as Hermon returned with her drink. Jessie covered the bedpan and replaced it under her trolley.

Hermon sat in Anna's lap and began to tell her about the funny dream he'd experienced in the night. She pushed aside any dark thoughts and focused on the boy's story, instead. Seeing this as a good moment to leave, Jessie gave her a supportive squeeze on the arm before trundling off to do the rest of her rounds.

WITH HER MORNING SICKNESS GONE, Anna kept her promise to Jessie by ordering eggs and bacon in the hospital cafeteria, while Hermon tucked into his usual pancakes with syrup. She knew a healthier start to his day would have to start soon, but she hadn't had the heart to deny him anything after all he'd been through. Although he'd borne the terrible situation with remarkable bravery, his deep hurt and confusion was plain to see. As an adult, she was at least able to understand the reasons for their current situation. The poor kid, however, had no idea why he'd suddenly been taken from his mother.

But what could she have said, without messing with his

head even more? She'd considered being completely honest with him, but no matter how carefully she practiced the discussion in her head, it always seemed to amount to, "Hey, kid, your mother tried to knife my husband, and now she's going to rot in prison for years."

In the days following the wedding, she'd suppressed the temptation to tell him the truth as a way to get some kind of revenge on Claire. It was a dark feeling that she regretted, but maybe that was the difference between good people and bad people. The bad gave in to hatred, while good people put it aside for the well-being of others. As it stood, she still hadn't built the courage to tell him the full story, other than to say his mom had gone away because she'd done a bad thing. It wasn't enough—God knew she understood that— but what else could she do without destroying him?

She'd used the same argument to stop the social services team from taking him away, and it'd only been with a super-human effort by Corey's legal team that she'd managed to gain temporary custody of the boy.

"So, can we go on the London Eye today, Auntie A?" he asked, staring at a string of syrup as it drizzled off his fork.

"Well..." She hadn't been able to face going outside, yet. The thought of leaving Corey alone, even for an hour, seemed disloyal. She also knew it was unfair to keep Hermon cooped up for much longer. Despite what happened, life needed to go on. The hospital had offered her childcare while she adjusted to her strange new reality, but she'd refused, fearing the boy would panic. "Sure, why not?"

The unexpected sound of Anna's ringing cell phone interrupted his excited approval. They'd been in a protective bubble of officialdom since the incident, so whoever was calling must have been on the list of approved people, vetted by Corey's security team. She exchanged a puzzled glance with Hermon, who looked at her with clear concern, his mouth half-closed around his fork.

"Hey, Anna. How you doin'?" the voice of Lieutenant Raymond greeted her.

"Lieutenant! Oh my gosh, I haven't called to thank you."

"Don't thank me," he said, warm, but sober. "I should've worked it out sooner."

"No. You saved his life," she said, feeling grateful beyond words for the efforts of the hard-bitten cop. His timely intervention had given Corey a fighting chance of survival, at least. "I'd be a widow now if it weren't for you."

He grunted in a manner that sounded like embarrassment. "My pleasure." There was a moment of pause. "Listen, can you talk right now?"

"Hermie, hon, I just need to take this call. You finish your breakfast. I'll be right over there," she said, pointing to the corner of the cafeteria.

"But..." He looked worried.

"Look," she said, taking the phone, pacing out of earshot, and waving back to him. Hermon frowned a little, as if contemplating how concerned he should be, before becoming distracted again by the tasty treat in front of him.

"It must be late over there," she said, relieved the boy would give them a little time, at least.

"It's early, actually," he said. Anna thought she could hear him stifle a yawn. "I'm what you might call a night person."

"Me too, lately," she agreed, knowing neither of them had to explain why.

"If you don't mind me asking, who's Hermie? I didn't think you guys had kids."

She paused, feeling oddly embarrassed by what she was about to say. "Hermon, her son."

"Her son?"

"Claire," she replied, covering her mouth with her hand, in case the boy was trying to follow what she was saying.

"You mean the attacker? Jesus, Anna, you'd shouldn't be expected to—"

"No, it's not like that," she cut him off. "He's a good kid, and right now, he's all I've got."

"Still, maybe—"

"Trust me, it's fine," she said with finality. Although she didn't want a disagreement with the man she respected, the thorny topic remained a red line for her.

"Well, okay, as long as you're sure," he said, not sounding convinced. "Wow, that's gonna' make this conversation even more difficult." There was another pause and Anna's heart sank. "I called because I thought you'd want to be the first to hear about Claire."

"I'm listening."

Raymond sighed in response. "Damn it. Where to start?"

He seemed to be directing the question at himself. "Her father abused her."

"That doesn't excuse—"

"I know, but it's more than that. He had a cult thing going on. It was, well, bad."

"She tried to kill Corey," Anna countered, refusing to hear anything that would give Claire a human quality. *Fuck that. I've suffered too much at the hands of people like her.* "I say let her rot."

"I know, I know," Raymond replied. He sounded hesitant, like he wasn't sure whether to go on.

"Just tell me, Lieutenant."

"She's dead." The words dangled between them while a roller coaster of emotions hit Anna—feelings that she couldn't visibly express under the boy's continued scrutiny.

"How?" she asked, her voice trembling.

"In the prison earlier. Hung herself."

Anna wanted to say, "Good," and although her inner sense of justice demanded it, an overriding sense of sorrow on behalf of the curly-haired little boy made it feel like a cruel reaction.

There was a pause. "There's something else."

"What?" Anna had to turn and wipe the tears forming at the corners of her eyes.

"She didn't act alone."

She nearly dropped the phone in shock and a flutter of fear hit the pit of her stomach. "I didn't see her with anyone else. Surely you don't mean Hermon?" The flutter became a stab.

"No, no, the boy had nothing to do with any of this, and her family members are either dead or in an institution, including her father." Relief washed through her, only to be crushed again a second later. "Anna, she'd been corresponding with Tony Eckerman."

"What?" Her voice sounded distant in her own head.

"I'm so sorry, Anna. I've seen the letters, myself; he put her up to it. Looks like she was trying to find someone to replace that God damn monster of a father."

"Why would she want to, after what she'd been through?"

"Who the hell knows? I'm no psychiatrist, but trust me, there are some messed up people out there, Anna."

She wiped away more tears. "I need to tell Hermon," she said after another long pause, her mind racing with implications and familiar feelings of self-blame.

"He needs to know," Raymond agreed. "What will you say?" The man's usual gruff tone had softened.

"I don't know. Not the truth, that's for sure." Anna gripped the phone. "Lieutenant?"

"Yes?"

"Will they punish him—Tony?"

"Oh, yes. What he did makes the prison look bad, and believe me, they're gonna' make him count every second of every minute of every hour until he gets sent to hell."

"Good," Anna said, touching her hand to her belly.

Chapter 3

DARKNESS

Tony grinned in the darkness. He liked the inky blackness surrounding him—it felt like home, the place where he belonged.

Time didn't have any meaning in this dark realm, and he'd lost count of the days they'd left him to hang here. The hours washed over him like the stench from Plumdike when he came to administer a beating accompanied by a sudden blinding light. No doubt these friendly visits were the freaky little sadist's personal revenge for the letters. Tony drew some comfort from that, despite the efforts of the vindictive little prick. More recently, the guard would only observe from the doorway, his body odor the only thing giving away his presence. Tony wondered if this was a new tactic designed to break him. It would fail, as all the others had.

He was close to breaking, though—not because of the

petty torments of the prison, but from the realization that the bitch had failed. There was no reconciling the fact that Anna and her new plaything still lived. Now he'd been left to pay the price for her incompetence. Tony cursed his luck for being forced to trust another whore—he wouldn't make that mistake again.

Your own motha' failed you. Why did you think the crazy bitch wouldn't? The thought made him shriek into the gloom because he'd just sounded like old Teddy, asking for his motha'. Four decades of rotting in this place had roasted his brain in its own memories until the old man had been reduced to a screaming husk of the mighty predator he'd once been, and Tony had come to understand that his fate would be the same as Teddy's. He would dangle on this rope, going insane, while Anna thrived outside, far away from his final embrace.

He twisted his arms, trying to relieve some of the pressure. The agonizing sensation that followed went from the land of pain and into the realm of nightmares.

"I'm a nightmare inside a nightmare," he giggled to himself through clenched teeth. His efforts to adjust the bonds, however, had only served to make him rotate like a chicken in some dark corner of hell's kitchen.

Ten green bottles standing on the wall... the ear worm began again. He regretted his attempt to pass the time with old rhymes, as they continuously repeated between his ears, becoming another torment.

"And if one green bottle should accidentally fall," he sang, forcing the slow turning to become a twirl. He imagined himself riding a carousel. She was beside him, of course. "Nine green bottles, standing on the wall..."

Anna smiled at him with those come-get-me eyes—the ones she'd used to hide from him and had now given to another. She tossed her head back and laughed, singing along with him. He slid off the back of his gently rising horse and stood beside her. Anna gave him a wink as he raised his hands to the soft contours of her throat.

A sudden blaze of light filled the dank room, along with the waft of his favorite law enforcement official. This time, however, another scent came with it: cheap cologne. Tony winced at the glare, but he could make out two silhouettes against the doorway.

"Jesus H Christ. Plum-dike, I thought I said no more than three days in the hole!" The voice was one he seldom heard, Deputy Warden Rich, Tony concluded after a moment.

He'd heard the long-timers refer to him as Tricky Dicky, because of his resemblance to Nixon. Along with Plum-dike, he shared a reputation for loose standards when it came to the care of his wards.

"Why, what an unexpected pleasure, sir," Tony croaked at his visitor. "I'm gratified to know you're taking a personal interest in my every comfort." He emphasized his welcome by urinating loudly onto the filthy flags below. "As you can see, I'm overwhelmed with gratitude." His pretense of playing nice with the staff had ended the same day the attack on lover boy failed.

"Shut the fuck up, you twisted puke. You wanna feel more of my tickle stick, huh?" Plum-dike asked. The sound of his booted feet followed, splashing through the puddle of piss, and then came the cool sensation of a nightstick rubbing against ribs still raw from the last beating. "Please continue, inmate. Make my fuckin' day." Tony braced himself for the blow.

"Enough!" It was the voice of Tricky. "I don't want this inmate dead. I won't cover your ass again, Plum-dike—not after Chapman. Do you hear me?"

"Sir," Plum-dike spoke with sullen contempt.

"There's a good boy," Tony added. A searing jab in his guts followed, causing him to gasp. While he struggled to regain his breath, he heard more footsteps, these seeming to skirt around his recent bladder offering. The cologne smell got stronger, mixing with the fishy reek of the guard.

"You think this is the worst we can do to you, boy?" Rich asked in a low voice. "We've been breaking sickos like you for years. You think you're something special?"

Tony tried to shrug in reply, but found it caused a tearing stab of molten pain to run through his shoulder blade.

"We've got years to wear you down." He felt something small poke him, maybe a pen, punctuating each word.

Silence followed. Tony considered answering back, but in truth, he'd become tired of this game. He wanted to get back to his meditation. Already his mind craved the memories of the former glories it fed upon. Although nothing like the feast of the real thing, it was enough to sustain him.

"Take him down, clean him up, and put him on half rations," Rich said after Tony offered no comeback.

"Sir," came more grudging compliance.

"Don't forget what I said, Plum-dike: this cockroach turns up on the slab and so will your career."

There was no reply—just sounds of steps retreating, along with the cologne smell. Only the stench of Plum-dike remained. Even as his consciousness sank away to avoid the thrashing he was about to receive, Tony sent up a silent prayer for him to be granted one last dalliance—one last chance to be free and to find her. In return for his freedom, he vowed to take Anna down to the stone and lay her soft neck against the altar.

Chapter 4

THE NEW BOSS

Corey's pale complexion was the only outward sign that he wasn't just having a peaceful night's sleep. That outer tranquility was a deception; after three months without any sign of change, Anna feared the worst. She stared at his handsome face, trying to force his eyes to open through sheer willpower alone, but she had no such luck today.

"I know you said we'd spend our honeymoon in bed, but I don't think this is quite what you had in mind, hon," she whispered at his unresponsive face, then kissed him on the cheek.

As usual, Hermon had curled up on the visitor's chair beside them before nodding off in his pajamas. She smiled at the way he'd tucked his new teddy bear under his chin. He'd acquired the cute companion while on their recent trip to visit the Tower of London and now refused to be apart from the toy dressed in the red jacket of a tower guard. She noticed that the furry ear of Mr. Boo already looked worn from frequent embraces, although it had only been purchased a few weeks ago. Anna winced at the thought of how Hermon would react if his friend disintegrated in the washing machine.

The boy had reacted to the news of Claire's death in a heartbreaking display of despair, but more recently, had shown the first signs that his natural curiosity was returning, while the number of worrying periods of silent reflection had grown fewer. It'd been a huge relief to see him start the slow healing process. She knew all too well how difficult that could be.

Anna gave him a grateful touch on the arm and smiled. Any other kid would've become bored with this daily vigil over her husband, but not her kind, gentle, little Hermon.

She wondered how Corey would react to the news that she'd volunteered him to be an adopted father, as well as a biological one. Her decision to begin formal proceedings to keep the boy had come after learning that the church to which Hermon's family belonged had started a legal petition to get the boy back. Most alarming of all, they wanted him returned to the States and placed in the care of his aunt, who they claimed had now recovered following her escape from the clutches of her evil father, Hermon's grandfather.

Panicked by the prospect of losing the boy, she'd turned to Corey's legal team for advice. Much to her surprise, it seemed her husband had made a will prior to the wedding, instructing that, in the event of his death or his incapacitation, she would get control of everything. Luckily, those huge resources could be used to aid her custody fight.

Far less convenient had been the clear instruction that Corey wanted Anna to become acting CEO of Green Gen in his absence. The fact that he'd put such total trust in her was both gratifying and terrifying at the same time—so much so that she'd questioned if it was even legally possible. The answer had been a simple yes. Not only that, but the whole estate came as one package. She either accepted or rejected the entire thing, corporation and all.

Hoping to avoid such crushing responsibilities under the circumstances, she'd tried to untangle the million-dollar win at the casino acquired all those months ago. She and Corey hadn't been apart since, however, so she hadn't bothered to create a separate account for her money. In effect, the cash was his, and on paper, at least, she didn't have a pot to piss in. The simple fact was that she needed Green Gen's lawyers to fight the case and keep Hermon by her side.

Serious doubts remained, though. She'd asked herself many times if fighting for him was the right thing to do. After all, this aunt had shown the strength to leave their sicko parents, and if the reports were right, this brave act was something Claire had never tried or wanted. What if her own selfish needs were dictating the adoption bid, though, rather than what was best for the boy? What if her inner demons were right to suggest that her swirling maternal hormones had twisted her thinking? Surely it would be reasonable to at least check out the aunt and find out if she was different from Claire?

No. Fuck reason—the kid's been through enough.

Anna had nothing against their close ties with a religious community, having known many kind, decent, and devout people, herself. But she couldn't help but feel horrified by the prospect of sending him back to a place his mother had been so violated, and it was clear the family had been congregation members of the same organization now seeking to take Hermon back. She needed to know more about this Church of the Serene Martyrs. Was it a legitimate, well-meaning group, or something more sinister?

With this in mind, she'd visited their website to try to gain a measure of reassurance about their motives. Instead of images of Jesus and charitable work though, she'd found page after page of rattling Old Testament fury, threatening non-believers with hell and spouting theories about original sin, a concept she'd always found particularly repulsive. As far as she was concerned, the last thing the kid needed was to be told he was born evil. So, after a two-day running argument with Corey's legal team, she'd made them file the papers.

"Big day tomorrow, kiddo," she whispered at Hermon's sleeping form. He squirmed, making Mr. Boo fall from his makeshift perch and onto the chair. Anna reached down and rescued the wayward toy before placing him back under the boy's nodding chin.

THE BOARDROOM at Green Gen's London HQ projected a display of raw corporate power. The single white desk running the length of the Spartan room on the twentieth floor made a dramatic contrast to the imposing backdrop of the London skyline behind it. The company logo, a vibrant green leaf, embossed into the desk's gleaming surface, gave the only visible decoration in the spacious suite. Natural light flooded the room, emphasizing the stunning view around them on every side. It wasn't unknown for visitors to leave, complaining of sudden onsets of vertigo, such was the sense of height here.

She hadn't been convinced that such opulence would be the most appropriate setting for the video conference, but her legal team advised the formal location for the session with the court in Arizona, arguing that it projected wealth and, by extension, the kind of stability she had to offer Hermon.

A huge monitor hung on the far wall. Half of the display showed the courtroom in Phoenix and the other half, a meeting room so gaudily decorated with clouds and Bible quotes that it made its occupants look like they'd already passed through the pearly gates of heaven and dropped into the session direct from the afterlife. The angelic scene featured a banner raised behind its grim-faced attendees. Along its length read the intimidating phrase "Embrace the light, or it will embrace you."

Anna wrestled with the vaguely threatening connotation in her head before pushing her glasses back onto her nose. Although only reading specs, she'd once heard Julia say they made her look like a no-nonsense kind of gal, so on a whim, she'd popped them on. Now, however, she felt self-conscious and even a little silly. In comparison, though, she must have looked mundane to the odd cast of characters greeting her on-screen. At the center sat a man dressed in all black and wearing a tell-tale padre hat. He was the thinnest person Anna had ever set eyes on, and he grinned with ultra-white dentures protruding from his veiny jaw as he surveyed the room with a lizard-like gaze. On either side of him sat two women dressed like stunt extras for the Whistler's Mother painting.

The older woman on the right was plump and motherly-looking, while the lady on the left held a remarkable resemblance to Claire, leaving no doubt that this was Emma, Hermon's aunt. She looked younger than her sister, but she had dark bags beneath her gray eyes, the same color as her nephew and sibling. The weird coif covering on her head only served to emphasize her pale, exhausted appearance.

A middle-aged, auburn-haired woman wearing the robes of a judge dominated the view from the court. A note-taker sat by her side with fingers poised above a touch-type recorder. The backdrop of the taxpayer-funded room looked drab in contrast to the divine scene of the church and the corporate grandeur of the Green Gen office. Anna got the uncomfortable feeling that the image of humility on show by her opponents was a deliberate attempt to present her as the greedy capitalist.

"Good afternoon, everyone, and thank you for attending today. I realize it's a logistical challenge for us all," the judge greeted them with a slight sound lag.

Anna gave a polite smile and nodded in acknowledgment, while inside, her stomach churned with nerves at the prospect of what was at stake.

"It's a small sacrifice for doin' the Lord's work, Yar Honor," the skeletal man said in a thick New England accent that sounded almost British to Anna's ear.

The judge ignored the comment and placed a pair of glasses on the bridge of her nose. She glanced down at a sheet of paper before her. "I understand we are here to make preliminary statements by both parties in relation to the non-parental petition by Mrs. Young for the custody of Hermon Pike, age eight, son of the late Claire Pike, originally from the state of Kansas," she said, followed by a pause. "My condolences, Miss Pike," the judge gave Emma a sympathetic look.

A pang of anguish passed across the young woman's face in response. It was a very human reaction that Anna found disconcerting enough to trigger more feelings of doubt about her current course of action.

"Furthermore, because there is no existing custody agreement in favor of either plaintiff, this hearing falls under US law," the judge added.

"It is as the Lord wishes," the preacher interjected in a

sage tone that made Anna want to roll her eyes. If he insisted on mentioning the Lord in response to every point, this would be a long meeting.

The judge frowned. "May I ask who you are, sir? What is your relationship with Emma?"

"I'm her spiritual healer, Yar Honor. Clarence Riley at yar service," he replied, doffing the big black hat.

"That's all very good, Mr. Riley, but who is the legal representative of your..." she paused again, as if trying to come up with the correct term, "your ward?"

"I'm also her legal counsel, as in all matters of the Church," he replied, his grin unflinching. "The Almighty granted my passing of the bar in the great state of Kansas in the year of our Lord 1986."

The judge pursed her lips, as if sucking on a lemon rind. "I will need documented proof of that, Mr. Riley," she added ominously. His cheeks reddened before he nodded.

She turned to Emma. "Is that correct, Miss Pike? Have you appointed Mr. Riley as your legal representative in this case? Please think carefully before answering."

Clarence swiveled his head toward his young ward—an odd gesture that reminded Anna of an owl spinning its head to spot its prey. "That is so," Emma replied, not making eye contact with the man beside her. The tremble in her voice gave away her nervousness.

"Yar Honor," Clarence added for her.

"Your Honor," she followed in a tiny voice.

This act of condescension made Anna wonder what kind

of situation this woman had found herself in, and the possibilities made her blood run cold. The preacher's tone suggested this poor creature was being punished, instead of praised for exposing her father's wickedness.

The judge stifled a sigh, then nodded in the direction of Howard Baines, Anna's lawyer. "You would be Mrs. Young's legal counsel?"

"Howard Baines of Smith and Coburg, Your Honor. I'd be happy to have my PA send over a copy of my bar papers, if you'd like," he replied in his usual smooth tone.

The twitch of a smile at the corner of the judge's mouth gave Anna hope of a positive start. "That won't be necessary, thank you, Mr. Baines—I'm familiar with your law firm." Howard nodded politely. A quick glance at the preacher, however, revealed another dark look on his thin features. "Mr. Baines, could you make your opening statement, please?"

"Certainly," he replied. "The view of my client and several eminent child psychologists is that Hermon has developed a close bond with Mrs. Young in the absence of his natural mother. Furthermore, returning to his old home could be very harmful to an already-traumatized boy. What Hermon needs right now is a safe, stable environment, and we have a wealth of evidence to show that my client is giving him just that."

Anna was starting to see why Corey had placed trust in his chief legal advisor. There was no complicated legal waffle, just straight facts delivered in a sincere manner. He'd also been consistently supportive of her, even when advising against making the petition. Although sympathetic, he'd made it clear that he thought their chances of success were slim, because Anna wasn't a blood relative of the child. The aunt, though, had known Hermon from birth, and in the eyes of many, she was a hero for exposing the truth about her father. Despite his reservations, Howard was a clever guy, and smart was what she needed right now.

"I hope you are not trying to suggest my organization is in any way implicated with the actions of a wayward member of its flock," the preacher said, shaking his head as if the mere suggestion was an outrage.

Wayward, that's one way of putting it, Anna thought, feeling her hackles rise.

"Not at all," Baines said, dismissing the righteous indignation. "My client is concerned for the welfare of the child because he's already been through a difficult time and has only just begun to experience a normal—"

"A life devoid of spiritual guidance is no life at all, sir!" Clarence said, his jaw shaking with sudden anger. Anna wondered if his dentures would drop out, such was his fury. "God is in his holy temple and little Hermon must be brought under his roof!" The older woman next to him nodded solemnly, as if the Almighty, himself, had just spoken.

"Is that not right, sister Emma?" he added. She responded by nodding like an invisible puppeteer had just tugged a piece of string stuck to her forehead. Clarence nodded in unison, his expression taking on a reasonable veneer again.

"While we pray for the soul of your fiancé, following the unfortunate incident," he began again.

"Husband," Anna corrected him. "He managed to make it to the altar after your wayward brethren stabbed him." Howard laid a comforting hand on her arm in a polite warning to keep her emotions under control.

The churchman spread his hands in supplication. "Congratulations on your divine contract. I will pray you serve your husband well, child," he said with an effortless drawl. Anna blinked, unable to trust herself to reply. "It is true that our Claire was a very troubled soul filled with lust and demons. Dear, sweet Emma, however, has returned to the loving folds of her church and repented her incestuous ways." He smiled the smile of the benevolent. "Surely our little angel should be allowed to return and repent his sins with his aunt."

"Repent his sins?" Anna burst out. "He's eight years old!" Baines' grip became firmer.

"Why, we all sin, child. Even a boy can sin," the preacher purred. Anna started to suspect he was goading her.

Some sin more than others, she thought, wanting to push her fist through the screen and send those teeth flying down his throat.

"Mr. Baines, please inform your client that she should refrain from such outbursts," the judge said, although her tone was more sympathetic than her words.

"My apologies, Your Honor. My client has been through a very difficult time, herself, and as you may already be aware, not for the first time in recent years." The judge nodded, this time with concern.

"I understand that," she said before sighing. "Mr. Riley," she began, looking at the preacher as if dreading the question.

"If I may be so bold, I prefer the title 'Reverend'," he interjected again while nodding piously.

"Reverend Riley, could you summarize your statement for us, please?"

"That would be my divine pleasure," he began. Anna thought she saw a flicker of annoyance on the judge's sober features. "The law is very clear on this matter: the biological kin of a lost innocent should have preference. Our Emma is ready to resume her duties after slaying her demons—with the help of her beloved church, of course."

"Preference does not mean automatic right," Baines objected. The judge raised her hand to stop them both.

"This is a preliminary hearing only, gentlemen. As you know, I will also be listening to the assessment of a court-appointed social worker." The preacher scoffed at her last comment. "Do you object, Reverend?" the judge asked with more than a hint of steel in her voice.

His sanguine smile returned immediately. "Not at all, your Honor. If the Lord," he paused briefly.

If the Lord is mentioned one more time, I might pay someone to move you closer to him! Anna thought darkly.

"If the Lord permits Earthly courts, 'tis the duty of us Godly folk to follow their wisdom."

"Hmm." The judge almost seemed disappointed that he'd chosen not to challenge her. She turned to address Howard. "Mr. Baines, I take it you've already instructed your client on the legal difficulties she faces with this petition." Although spoken in a sympathetic tone, the words still stuck Anna with dread. Howard had, indeed, pointed out the likelihood of failure.

"I have, Your Honor, but she feels strongly that Hermon's interests are best served in her care."

Anna thought she saw a flash of triumph pass over the face of the preacher. The appalling prospect of losing Hermon to this questionable group was all too real. She racked her brain, trying to think of some way to level the odds. One glance at the resentful, forlorn look on Emma's face gave her an idea, and she quickly pulled over a legal pad and scribbled a note, then pushed it to Howard.

"I think that concludes our business for now," the judge said. "Unless anyone has anything to add?"

Baines hesitated, seemingly puzzled by Anna's proposal. "Your Honor, my client would like to invite Miss Pike to visit her nephew here in London. She feels it would benefit them both and potentially help us all reach an amicable arrangement for Hermon."

Clarence rose from his divine perch, clearly appalled at the prospect, before regaining his composure. Back came the raptor grin. No doubt the judge's raised eyebrow had made him moderate his body language. "Whilst that is a generous offer, our organization is but a humble group, without the means to support such a—"

"I'd be happy to fund the visit," Anna glared at the old goat, "and I'm sure you'd have no objection to Emma checking on her nephew."

The preacher took his hat off and proceeded to pull a handkerchief from the breast pocket of his jacket, then mopped his brow. "It's not just the cost. Our dear, sweet sister is a vulnerable member of our congregation, and I fear a long journey in her delicate condition may cause her a great deal of harm."

Anna crossed her fingers under the table while the judge pondered. Her instinct told her that removing Emma from the dubious influence of her self-appointed guru would prove critical.

"Reverend, your patient was discharged from the clinic..." her secretary shuffled through more papers and then presented them to her senior colleague, "some months ago. Are you saying she is still unwell? If so, I will have to take this into consideration with my ruling."

There was more frantic brow mopping. "No, no, Yar Honor. Emma has been freed from her inner demons. Still..."

The judge raised her hand and cut him off. "Miss Pike, do you feel well enough to travel?" she asked Emma. In turn, Clarence swiveled two beady eyes toward Emma again— this time with a barely-disguised threat.

Anna felt herself burn with frustration at the obvious intimidation on display. To her surprise, however, Emma gave an almost imperceptible nod. "Yes," she added.

Clarence suddenly appeared to have swallowed something large and unpleasant. He seemed lost for words, and the throbbing vein on the side of his wispy temple looked to be in danger of blowing.

"Very well, that's decided. Miss Pike will visit Hermon while the state considers the pleas of both parties," the judge said. Anna noticed a twinkle in her eye as she spoke.

"For poor Emma's sake, could Sister Gray and I be permitted to escort her on her journey into the depths of Babylon?" Clarence asked, his tone a mixture of wheedling and exasperation.

"That is entirely up to Mrs. Young, who's funding the trip," the judge replied, turning her gaze over to Anna.

"Unfortunately, with the legal costs and all, I'm afraid I could only fund one ticket," Anna lied. She even managed a regretful manner as she spoke. "Oh, and we're not in Babylon, Reverend. I think you'll find that's in the Middle East. London is in Europe," she couldn't resist adding.

The preacher grew red with fury. "Little Emma must have her spiritual guide with her in such a wicked place! I find it hard to believe that a man such as your husband—a suckler from the teat of the money men, no less—cannot afford extra tickets!"

This son of a bitch has nerve.

"I can assure you, Reverend, that my husband does not

suckle on anyone's teat, as you put it." *That's a lie,* she thought, thinking of their last night together. "One ticket, that's all."

"Then the church will have to dig deep into our meager coffers and..."

"Miss Pike, would you like your legal counsel to travel to London with you?" the judge asked Emma, ignoring him. "It's your right to decide."

Anna detected a tremor in her pretty face as Emma shook her head. There was naked fear in the gesture, but also resolve.

"Emma!" The reverend's eyes bulged from their sockets.

"Excellent. The court notes the amicable way in which both parties have approached these proceedings," the judge dismissed him again. "The next hearing will be three months from today." Before Clarence could object further, the view of the courtroom winked out. He gave them a look filled with righteous thunder, then reached forward and flicking his screen off.

Left alone in the boardroom, Anna let out the breath she'd been holding before tossing her false glasses onto the desk.

"Well, that was interesting," Howard commented in his clipped English accent.

"That's one way of putting it," Anna replied, turning her head to loosen the knot in her shoulders. "I can't believe that poor woman is staying with that creepy, old freak—and after everything she's been through..." she shook her head in disbelief.

The lawyer was too well-trained to disagree with a point that had no legal relevance. Although she hadn't told him, Anna appreciated the way he indulged her hormone-fuelled outbursts with quiet stoicism. She suspected he'd learned this approach from her husband, who relayed a dozen new ideas every hour. Coping with such inexhaustible exuberance required patience.

"Can't the judge see that she's being manipulated?"

"I bet she can, but that makes no difference, Anna. This is about family law." He paused, seeming to consider what he was about to say. "Listen, I kind of get where you are going with this idea of bringing the aunt over, but don't you think it's a little risky?" The same doubt already played through her mind, but she didn't have an answer other than telling a trained lawyer she was going with her gut. "How do you know she's not like her sister?" he added. "To be blunt, Anna, you guys have been through enough already, and while I think trying to take the kid on is an amazing gesture—"

"You saw the look on her face, Howard; that woman was terrified. Anyone who has the courage to run from a monster like her father deserves respect."

"Still, she's back with the church," he argued.

"That's not by choice—anyone can see that. The poor thing is probably so confused, she doesn't understand what the hell's going on. It's the best chance I have of keeping him." Anna couldn't help but reflect on how her own circumstance could have ended in a similar way. What if she'd gone straight back to the apartment that night and called an ambulance? What if Tony had apologized and they'd made another go of things? The thought made her shudder. This woman had shown strength before, and maybe Anna could bring that out in her and turn this doomed case into a moot point.

Howard held up his hands in defeat. "Okay, okay. It's a plan, I agree. Her state of mind isn't the only problem, though. What if the boy likes her so much that she wins him over and takes him back to Reverend Fire and Brimstone?"

Maybe he's right.

"I don't think so. We need to get her away from those parasites."

"Are you sure the boy will be safe with her?"

"If she's anything like Claire, then I'll know and you can bet your ass she won't get Hermon. Only over my dead body."

Howard sighed. "Let's do it. One thing I don't understand, though, is why this church is so hell-bent on keeping her and getting the boy back. All this time and expense, just for two members of the congregation. It seems odd."

The question hadn't occurred to her before. Why did one boy and a woman add up to a big deal for them? If today's performance was any indication, the idea that it was out of genuine concern seemed suspect. This organization had done nothing while one of its members abused his own family, and considering the close ties between them, Anna didn't believe they'd had no idea about the horrors unfolding at the Pike farm. She'd grown up in one of those small towns, too, and everybody knew each other's business.

"Maybe they're afraid," Anna suggested.

"Of what?"

"That, if they let Emma and Hermie leave, others will follow."

Howard frowned. "Did you see the panic on his face when Emma agreed to come here?"

"Yes," Anna pursed her lips. "I'm gonna' do some digging."

"We've got people who can do that." Howard seemed surprised by her sudden declaration.

"No, thank you. Trust me, I'll get to the truth."

I also need something to take my mind off Corey, she thought.

"I understand, but you know where we are, if you need us," Howard replied, too polite to suggest she wasn't the best person for the job.

"Don't worry, I'll ask for help if I get out of my depth. This is too important."

Chapter 5

STORM

"This is Phoenix Today with Marty Dean and Kirsten Leicester," the off-screen announcer declared after the dramatic theme song of the news station faded. The camera panned to focus on Arizona's most trusted presenters, smiling through pearly white teeth.

"Good evening, Phoenix. The weather event of the century is nearly upon us. Storm Vlad, now officially a category five hurricane, is already wreaking havoc across northern Mexico. Here's Ron Whitmore with a special report," Marty greeted the audience in his most serious tone.

The screen cut to a shaky, wind-strewn hotel balcony with a grim-faced reporter clutching a handrail. Even Ron's famously unmovable hairpiece looked like it may disappear into the night like a flying squirrel. In the reporter's long career, he'd survived a roadside bombing in Iraq and a brush with a great white shark, so the sight of old "Iron Head" looking rattled could only spell trouble for the good people of Arizona.

"Good evening, Marty," he shouted into the camera. "Tonight, I'm live from the devastated city of Hermosillo on the tail end of Vlad." A sudden gust forced Ron to cling to the railing before he could continue. "As you can see, it's living up to its nickname, Vlad the Impaler, by stabbing deep into the mainland."

The camera returned to the studio. "Wow, it's really looking dangerous out there, Bill. I hope you are in a safe location?" Kirsten asked with maternal concern. Her face held an overly-taut quality under the studio lights.

"We're fine, thanks, Kirsten. Unfortunately, that's not the case for the people of Sonara. I'm hearing reports of multiple casualties from state officials. One source told me the current death toll sits at twenty and is set to climb."

"And Vlad is headed our way, Bill?" she asked the obligatory, I'm-a-scared-woman question. She'd performed the same function on many occasions before on topics including the chances of being shot by Islamic terrorists on the streets of Phoenix to the likelihood of being kidnapped by a Mexican drug cartel.

"I'm afraid so," Ron replied while a fresh gust pummelled him. "The National Weather Service has confirmed Vlad will be crossing the state line during the early afternoon and into northern Arizona during sundown.

"Thanks, Ron. You get yourself inside—it doesn't look too great out there."

"I was just thinking the same thing," the reporter shared a brief laugh with the two anchors, as if the whole stunt hadn't been set up for less than a minute's worth of network share-grabbing.

With Ron dispatched to find safety, a stoic-faced Marty ended the piece. "State and federal agencies have advised citizens to remain indoors until tomorrow and not to travel under any circumstances."

TONY CONTINUED to dig while the first drops of rain spattered the back of his shaved head. It felt good to feel the earth under his feet again, away from the unending fluorescent torture inside the prison. The cemetery was one of the few places an inmate could feel human, even if the experience came with an unpleasant reminder of where his final destination would be. Ironically, the resting place for so many rapists and killers was a beautiful one, located next to the penitentiary on a slight rise overlooking the Colorado River. Of course, they'd surrounded it with a chain link fence, complete with a guard tower manned especially for his benefit today. How gratifying.

They could've brought the usual group of three men to form the burial party, of course, but they'd chosen to make him do all the digging—another treat for the institution's favorite inmate.

Teddy Bear, his wonderful cellmate, was dead. No more appeals remained and no more last minute reprieves. After over four decades, they'd finally found the balls to put the fucker down by injecting a lethal cocktail of poison into his body. Not wishing to pass the opportunity to torment Tony, Plum-dike dutifully reported how the old man had screamed for his mother one last time before soiling himself.

Still, looking on the bright side, peace had reigned on the cellblock since. He wondered if the sick puke had found "Motha" at the end. Tony had learned something amazing about the real identity of the creature Teddy had called to over and over. Motha wasn't the scabby, old bitch who'd shat Ted into the world. No, Motha was something more magnificent: an all-powerful god of darkness. He stopped digging and gazed up at the growing gloom just as a sudden gust rose, causing the cheap wooden cross to tilt.

Is that you, Motha? Have you come to claim your son? I wouldn't claim him. He failed you, wasting away in this place, instead of offering you flesh. Will you reward me if I serve you?

"Stop slackin', Eckerman, ya' sack a' shit," Plum-dike said. "You want me to pokerize you again?"

Tony glanced at the scowling, fat guard. Heavy rain droplets beat on the man's wide fedora and wax jacket, which was two sizes too small for him. At that moment, as the darkness gathered around them, Tony knew how to gain the attention of his new master.

Great Motha, I give you sacrifice, he thought, scooping another clod of dirt and tossing it onto the plywood coffin lid inside the hole. The now-sodden soil thudded against the wood like a drum, summoning the spirit he sought. Bending to get another shovelful, Tony scanned the wide courtyard. The gathering gloom had obscured the view of the watchtower, and the downpour thickened while the wind rose to a howl. He was alone with Plum-dike.

"Call it a day now, fuck face. We need to get inside before Vlad hits," Plum-dike said above the noise. He emphasized the point by spitting out a lump of chewing tobacco onto the coffin. "Sick fuck has the rest of eternity to burn in hell, anyhow."

Tony rested against the handle, enjoying the sensation of the gathering storm.

Great Motha, if you free me from here, I vow to give you fresh souls. Do you hear me, Motha? A swirling eye appeared in the sky—an inky, black hole of infinite darkness. It was the place his savior waited with a gaping maw. He smiled.

Yes, my son, do my work. Kill them. Start with the pig—give me his scalp.

Tony turned to face Plum-dike and grinned.

"What you looking at?" He could no longer see the whites of the other man's eyes, but he could detect a note of caution. The staccato sound of the guard's radio trilled.

He's trying to contact the watch tower.

Unlike the usual response, a hiss followed. He could hear Plum-dike repeating the action, but there was only more hissing.

"Motha says no," Tony purred.

"What the fuck did you say?" Plum-dike's tone had become a high squeak.

"What do you think? By the hairs of your chinny chin chin?" Tony asked and then screamed his triumph. Plum-dike began to back off, but he was far too late. Tony spun the shovel around in his fist and then swung it deep into Plum-dike's neck. The first blow severed his aorta, spraying its precious contents into the grave. Stunned by the blow, he staggered with wide, unbelieving eyes. Tony laughed as the guard tried to cry out, but only managed to produce a gurgling rasp before falling to his knees.

"Sorry, old boy, I didn't quite catch that. Come again?" Plum-dike squealed, his beetroot complexion draining to the pallor of death. "I must say, it's refreshing to get the right tools for the job!" Tony said, then hefted the spade at the other man's exposed wound again. This time, he felt the spine give, and the head flew from his shoulders before falling at Tony's feet. For a fleeting second, he thought he saw the tiny, malicious eyes stare at him one last time before blinking out.

With the deed done, Tony waited for the boom of gunfire that was sure to follow. Nothing came, though. The eye of Motha opened above him, as if accepting the rancid soul of Plum-dike. Tony lifted his arms and gave praise.

"Release me, Motha!" he cried into the torrent. "Release me, and I will bring you such wonders!"

He promised to become an instrument of pain—the cleaver in Motha's right hand, the poleaxe falling onto the flesh of the innocent. He stood at the edge of the grave and waited for his reward. It came in the form of a swirling twister, moving through the treeline outside the fence, wrenching aside trunks and foliage like playthings before tearing up the chain link fence like tissue paper. It continued its inexorable path toward the guard tower.

The sound of the storm hitting the wooden structure of the watch post came like a thunderclap, and debris flew past Tony's head. He wasn't afraid, though, because now he was under the protection of his god. Nothing could touch him— he'd become a dancer entwined with the reaper.

The finger of destruction continued not more than sixty feet away, wrenching up tombstones and flinging them into the jaws of Motha. Tony stood in awe, feeling as safe as a babe in the arms of a deadly father. He felt Motha sucking at his body, reminding him what would happen if he failed to keep his promise.

"I won't fail you, I swear it!" he said in ecstasy, clasping his hands in front of him.

Go, my son. Do my bidding, he thought the beast whispered in his ear. *Bring me life.*

The storm demon dissipated back into the void, and great swathes of sheet lightning followed from the west like a beacon guiding his way.

Before leaving, he dragged the blood-spattered corpse of Plum-dike into the open pit. As an afterthought, he strolled to the head of the guard, lifted the grim trophy by its greasy hair, and lowered it face down into the grave onto the crotch of the corpse.

"Enjoy, sir," he said.

Invigorated, he put his back into the task of shovelling a thin shroud of dirt over the remains. Although he knew the body would soon be found, he hoped it would give him enough time to provide a head start.

Chapter 6

EMMA

Anna nearly overlooked Emma as she emerged from the departure lounge wearing modern clothing, instead of the Victorian garb she'd expected. Although her sweater and jeans looked dated, they were at least from the right century. The young woman's remarkable resemblance to her sibling was the only thing that caught Anna's attention. After the two women saw each other, Emma lowered her gaze in a clear sign of submission.

"You're not gonna' fool me, lady," Anna muttered under her breath, before putting on a smile and striding toward her guest.

Anna noticed those striking gray eyes again as she approached. Emma looked so similar to Claire in fact, that her bleach blonde hair was the only obvious difference.

Without the dye, they'd look almost identical, which wasn't an encouraging thought.

"Wow, you look different!" she said to fill the awkward silence.

Emma blushed. "Please don't tell him," she said like a naughty school kid. "I was on the plane and, well, I thought I'd change."

Anna touched her arm gently. "Hey, you can do what you like, kiddo." She looked her straight in the eye and was shocked to see surprise register in the other woman's expression.

"C'mon, I'm buying you a coffee, and then we can see your nephew," Anna suggested.

THE EXPERIENCE in the coffee shop was a surreal one, as memories of the first time she'd met Claire came to mind. Emma's own apparent shyness and obvious discomfort, however, proved a reassuring contrast to the more forth-right character of her sister.

"Thank you for coming here," she said after buying them both a large drink. "I know it was a lot to ask under the circumstances. Emma toyed with the milkshake straw in front of her, seemingly uncertain with how to respond. "Speak, please. I can tell you want to."

"It's just that…" Emma hesitated.

"Go ahead."

"The reverend said you'd punish me for what Claire did."

Emma seemed genuinely disturbed by the flash of anger passing over Anna's face upon hearing such nonsense. Anna shook her head. "I'm not angry at you. I'm angry at him for saying that," she said in an effort to reassure the girl.

"You must be mad after what Claire did." There was more nervous toying with the straw.

"With her, not you."

"But we're still kin. How do you know I'm not the same?"

"Are you?" Anna asked bluntly. As much as she wanted to like this kid, she refused to compromise the safety of her family again.

Emma gave her a wide-eyed shake of the head that seemed devoid of guile. "I don't understand why she did it," she added, her confusion plain. "Claire was always kind to me, and especially Hermon. She always stopped Dad from..."

Anna had built a wall against such compassionate thoughts for Claire, but the tragic admission chipped at her anger. To paint a monster was easy, but to hear of the reasons for it forced her to reconsider the hatred she'd nurtured against her former friend, even in death.

"Do you miss her?" Anna asked, feeling sympathetic despite her reservations.

Emma nodded, wiping away tears with the frayed sleeves of her sweater.

"Listen to me, Emma. I'm gonna' be really honest with

you now, and I want you to be honest back. Can you do that for me?"

"Yes."

"One day, I might be able to forgive your sister, but I'm not ready for that yet. She hurt my family. Do you understand?"

"Yes," she nodded in agreement. "I know Claire did a bad thing, but I believe it was because of bad men. I don't think she would have tried to... if those bad things hadn't been done to her," Emma added with sudden strength.

The simple truth of it cut through Anna's defenses. It was her turn to nod. Perhaps it was time to direct her hate toward the two bastards who were ultimately to blame for such evil. "I want you to promise me one thing."

"Okay."

"Promise me you'll never hurt my family, and I promise you can stay as long as you need to." A look of dawning real-ization came over Emma's soft features. "And if I think Hermon will be happier with you than with me, I'll let him go." Anna added, even though it pained her.

Emma removed a silver cross identical to her sister's from under the sweater and held it before them. "I swear."

ANNA WAS in a foul mood-like really super pissed and ready to kick ass. Her ankles hurt, she needed to pee every five friggin' minutes, and as she stared into the bedroom mirror, she thought her normally slender frame now resembled that of a person who'd wandered into an all-you-can-eat pizza place and forgot where the exit was. She also felt certain that the people who designed maternity clothes were the kind of parents who dressed the same as their kids.

"Bring on the comfortable shoes," she said, huffing at the portly figure before her.

The grumpy pregnant lady part of her considered asking Corey's medical team to remove the organ from her husband that'd been the cause of her present condition.

Nah, he should be awake when I tell him I'm gonna chop his dick off! The mean-spirited thought only brought fresh tears, though, as the image of him still lying there often did.

Her present foul temper wasn't entirely down to her personal circumstances, though. There was also the matter of the invitation from Corey's executive board to attend the quarterly meeting at Green Gen's London HQ. When she'd asked what possible purpose her attendance would serve, she'd received the rather disturbing answer: "Well, technically, you're in charge."

It seemed that her ever-trusting husband's crazy instruction that she should become defacto CEO in the event of his death or incapacitation was being taken seriously. She had a vague recollection of him sticking an official document under her nose about a month before the wedding and asking her to sign while using the enigmatic phrase, "just in case," but she'd been so drowned in planning for the big day that its significance had slipped by her.

Why me? she thought, unable to understand why he wouldn't have appointed someone else. "Why not you?" she could hear him say in reply.

"Asshole!" she growled, applying dark, almost black, lipstick onto her pursed lips.

There was a knock on the bedroom door, then Greta's ponytailed head ducked through. "The car is here," she said in her infuriatingly professional tone. Although she'd barely met Corey's PA before the wedding, they'd become firm friends since, at first through necessity, but now because she found the ever-calm presence of the pretty brunette indispensable.

"Fine," Anna said, sighing heavily before putting on her no-nonsense glasses. Her efforts at severity seemed totally undermined by her bump. "Why can't men have babies, Greta, hmm? Most of them don't care what they look like, anyhow."

"I think you look great," Greta countered, used to her employer's hormone-induced outbursts.

"What the hell do they want from me, Greta? I'm a friggin' waitress from Arizona. I know nothing about all this business stuff. Surely they can get by until, well, until Corey is... back on his feet again?"

"He seems to think you're the best person for the job," Greta said, laying a comforting hand on her shoulder.

"They won't take me seriously. How can they with this?" Anna pointed to her obvious protrusion.

"Hey, unless you're the first woman to have a baby in history, I think they'll understand."

"It must be like taking orders from a weeble," Anna replied with a sigh. "I won't understand what the hell they're talking about."

"You read the brief, right?"

"Yes, but half of that was technobabble to me and the rest had numbers so big, I had to Google the number of digits, for fuck's sake!"

Greta laughed.

"I'm glad you find it funny."

"I'm laughing because you think most CEOs understand even half the stuff they're being told."

"Well, don't they?"

"Like hell they do. Trust me, I've worked for several before moving to Green Gen." Greta nodded, full of sympathy. "The one thing these big, scary boss-types have in common is knowing how to handle other people. They don't manage the details—they manage the people who manage the details."

"I still need them to respect me, though, and respect is earned."

"True, but they respect Corey's judgment. If he says you're a good egg, they'll at least give you a chance." She smiled.

"Which is good, because I literally look like an egg." They both laughed this time, just as Anna felt a prodding sensation in her belly. It wasn't unpleasant, just unusual. "Oh," she said.

"What's wrong?" Greta asked with sudden concern. Rather than answering, however, Anna took her hand and placed it on her bump.

"Do you feel that?" she asked as the sensation hit once more.

"Wow! The little fella has got some kick!"

"Hell, yeah. It feels like the little mite just slam-dunked one of my kidneys."

"First time?"

"Yup." Although her reply was flippant, she felt another well of emotion, which caused her eyes to brim. She wiped away the tears, refusing to have to do her mascara again. "He should be here," she added, voice low.

"I know."

"I keep thinking about what he would say to me," Anna said, staring at them both in the mirror, the other woman's hand still in place. "Probably some really bad sci-fi joke about an alien inside me."

"I saw that movie. An alien bursting from your chest would certainly get the board's attention."

"I'm not sure that's the kind of leadership they're looking for."

"Do you want me to postpone it?" Greta asked more seriously.

"The alien baby? Yes, please," Anna said before smiling at the other woman's warm laugh.

"No, the meeting."

Anna sighed. "Nope, let's get it out of the way. I'm in the mood to kick some ass, anyhow."

They called in on Hermon and Emma on their way out of the swish Mayfair apartment that had become their temporary home while staying in London. They found the pair in Hermon's room, engaged in an animated video game, which involved wearing a weird headset attached to a console.

"Argh! It's chasing me again!" Hermon howled with delight while turning his head, as if looking around a corner.

"Run, Hermie!" Emma called, laughing at his virtual predicament.

Anna hadn't played the stupid game, herself, because of an irrational fear of harming the baby. So, with a small stab of jealousy, she watched them with a happy expression from the doorway. Underneath, she remained nervous about the other woman's intentions regarding the case, especially because of the obvious closeness between them. On the positive side, Emma seemed to have fallen in love with their home and showed no sign of wanting to take the boy away. Without having built up the courage to ask the question directly, though, Anna felt uncertain about the outcome of her gamble.

Since Emma's arrival a month ago, she'd appeared to thrive here, free from the crushing oppression of the cult leader. It was as if she were experiencing a second childhood. Anna soon realized her guest must have been eight years or more younger than her sibling—hardly much older than a teenager, really. So it came as no surprise that she'd blossomed in a safe environment.

"Hey guys, I'm off to a work meeting, now. Be back in a few hours," she called to them both.

"Okay, see you later, Anna." Emma waved happily.

"Bye, Auntie A!" Hermon called before shouting out in fright and delight at the game monster about to catch him.

A GROUP OF SERIOUS-LOOKING, suited individuals watched Anna waddle into the massive boardroom like tourists observing the social habits of an ungainly hippopotamus— or so it felt to her.

Please don't collapse, she mentally pleaded the delicate-looking seat as she lowered herself into it at the head of the elegant table. *Houston, the heffalump has landed!* she thought, relieved to find herself not sprawled on the floor.

"Good afternoon," she said, her voice sounding tiny to her own ears.

The grim group nodded in unison. Anna suspected she would require a crowbar to lever a smile onto the lips of the pale-faced, severe women to her left. Greta, efficient as ever, handed out papers to the steely-eyed department heads and directed them to review the agenda on the first page.

Anna was about to read out the first item when the older woman interjected.

"So, I believe the first item relates to our," Pale Face paused, as if considering her words, "speculative research into quantum management systems."

Oh boy, here comes the nerd attack. I'm gonna look so dumb, Anna thought.

"Not speculative, May. As the board is aware, QMS is a huge opportunity for us. With the invention of quantum computing, power distribution could be infinitely more flexible. I say we divert resource into QMS right now," a middle-aged man with a tweed jacket and slicked hair objected. Anna noticed he'd managed to say the whole thing without pausing for breath, which was a pity, because her brain required several moments to digest what he'd just said. "Fail to do that and we all know what the consequences could be," he added, giving them all a solemn nod.

Anna didn't have a clue what those consequences might be. The only thing she recalled from the briefing notes was something about traditional fossil fuel companies investigating this QMS thing with the sole interest of keeping it from the market, because more efficiently-managed power equaled less need for energy and hence less profit.

"I'd be interested to hear what your thoughts are, Mrs. Price," Mr. Tweed suddenly asked her, in what felt like a barely-concealed test of her knowledge. There was no chance of riding out the meeting in silence, now. The entire board swiveled their heads in her direction.

"That's Jonathan Nightman, head of research," Greta added helpfully.

Suppressing the urge to run screaming from the room, crying about swollen ankles and sore breasts, she instead nodded sagely, as if mulling over the concept. "Of course," Anna replied, a tad more assertively than intended. *Thank you, Greta. I have no idea who this dude is!* she added mentally.

"Mrs. Price," Pale Face interrupted her again.

"Anna, please," Anna replied, trying on her warmest smile, despite wanting to punch her. In response, the woman gave the briefest of twitches at the corner of her mouth. Even this minimal effort looked dangerously close to breaking her face in the process.

"May Vilkes, director of the third gen project," Greta introduced her.

"Development of our third generation power cells is at the core of our business. It's critical we don't divert from our current efforts, or there's a significant risk of failing to deliver." May Vilkes looked around the room as if daring anyone to disagree. "As I'm sure you're aware, Mrs. Price, any failure to honor our contract will trigger a penalty clause for hundreds of millions."

Despite Anna's natural tendency to dislike the sour-faced prune, she had to agree with the logic. "Why not just buy in more people? We're good for cash, right?" she suggested, only to have the idea greeted by a wave of shaking heads.

"Extra money isn't the issue. We use highly skilled engineers—the best in the world," May replied dismissively with a smug edge to her tone. "We cannot simply ship them in like, well, like kitchen staff."

Anna felt her cheeks redden, sure the pointed jibe was a deliberate reference to her previous employment. It never ceased to disappoint her that life's journey always brought those special snowflakes who got a kick out of making others feel small. The board switched their heads back her way, like spectators at a tennis match. *Guess who's losing...*

"Any other suggestions?" Anna asked, trying to buy some time to think. Her brain was a swirl of technical questions she didn't understand.

"With respect, that's why we've asked you to attend. The board cannot agree," the head of research replied far too quickly. It seemed the two business rivals were not above putting their differences aside to give her a joint kicking.

Anna nodded again while mentally groping for something, knowing humiliation was about to follow. *Manage the people, not the problem.* "Are you telling me it's impossible to progress the research?" she asked Nightman.

"Well, nothing is impossible, but it has a serious impact on the number of man days we can resource. It doubles the schedule."

I *wonder how a man day differs from a woman day?* Anna thought. "How long is that?"

"Roughly, three months," he replied reluctantly. "That extra time could see our competition develop the technology before we do." He crossed his arms, like a child who was asked if they were responsible for stealing the chocolate cake.

"May, where are we on the schedule with the third gen cell?"

"The briefing notes explain all that," Vilkes shot back, looking around at the others, as if to emphasize how stupid the question was.

"Notes can be misinterpreted. I'm asking you for an answer," Anna countered, causing the tiniest bit of color to appear in the other woman's cheeks.

"We are on schedule, but—"

"Ahead of schedule by six weeks," Jonathan interrupted his suddenly-wary colleague.

"Well done!" Anna said happily, not caring if it sounded patronizing. "That's what I like to hear."

"But," May began.

"So, let's give Jonathan five weeks of support. That still leaves us a week ahead with the third gen stuff."

"I really must p—"

"Would you make a note of that please, Greta?" Anna said, cutting off the protest again.

"Certainly, Anna." Greta typed away.

Anna turned back to them all, beaming. "I'd call that progress."

"It will help, but it still leaves us seven weeks short," Jonathan said.

Jesus, give me a friggin' break, fella! "Good point." She

pursed her lips. "How much is this research worth to us? If we get the patent, I mean?"

"Billions. I do agree with May, however, that we can't just bring in extra resources. There are no short cuts," he replied.

Anna mulled it over. "What about a bonus?"

The head of research puffed his cheeks out, seeming to consider the point. "These are well-paid men."

"And women," Anna added.

He nodded, "Of course. Like I said, though, we pay them well, already: six figures for a senior engineer."

Anna decided to throw caution to the wind. There was no way she was going to gain their respect without stamping her mark. "Tell them I'll offer fifty million dollars to the employee who drops a viable patent on my desk." *Not that you have a desk, kiddo.*

Anna noticed the large man sitting beside Vilkes begin to furiously scribble sums on a notepad. She guessed he was some kind of moneyman or accountant. "Did you say fifteen million dollars?" he asked with wide-eyed concern.

"No, I said fifty. Five-O." She felt a sudden urge to giggle at the shocked expressions before her. Mr. Moneybags, in particular, seemed close to having a stroke.

Loud speculation followed the hasty announcement, including one comment to her left that sounded like, "Can she really do that without Corey's agreement?"

"Excuse me, all," she said to quiet them, which was

ignored. "Please everyone," Anna asked a bit louder this time. There was no change. "Shut it!" They stopped. "Listen, I know this is an unusual situation," she began, trying to placate them.

"To say the least," May Vilkes muttered loudly. This earned her an icy don't-fuck-with-a-pregnant-lady gaze.

"Corey didn't build this business by being a big pussy." That got their attention. "We need to speculate to..." she paused, at a total loss for how the phrase went. A foggy memory appeared to be another symptom of her present condition. She began to whirl her finger slightly to indicate she was thinking.

"Accumulate?" suggested a bearded man who hadn't spoken until now.

"Exactly," she agreed, starting to get a minor kick from this power trip thing. With a final flurry of inspiration, she added, "Just remember, guys: who dares wins." She wasn't sure where she'd heard the phrase before—probably in a documentary—but she felt sure the British wouldn't have heard the obscure reference and would attribute it to her, instead. The coughed chuckle she got in return from several board members, however, didn't fill her with confidence. "So, do we agree?" she asked, secretly crossing her fingers under the table.

The flustered chief researcher raised his hands in a gesture of supplication. "You're the boss, and frankly, if I said no and the team got wind of it, they'd probably tear me apart."

Hell, yeah! Anna thought in triumph.

"Next item on the agenda, please, Greta," she said as her cell began to ring. Cursing herself for not turning it off before the meeting, she waited for the caller to give in. After a few seconds of listening to the persistent noise, however, she reached into her pocket and glanced down at the screen.

Inspector Raymond. The name felt like a bucket of water being thrown in her face. She'd had no contact from the detective for months. With a shiver, she recalled that his interventions were never a trivial matter.

"Excuse me, I need to take this," she said, rising from her chair then stepping through to the adjoining lobby. Although the glass between her and the boardroom was clear, it would be enough to keep the conversation private.

GRETA WATCHED her employer with admiration as she strolled from the room with the phone to her ear. Not only had she handled the notoriously difficult May Vilkes like a pro, but she'd also come up with a novel approach to dealing with the resource issue. She hadn't told her beforehand, but there'd been a real risk that the encounter would turn into a disaster. Instead of being crushed under the scrutiny of the most insightful minds in business, however, Anna had stamped her own authority. With a flash of insight, Greta began to see why Corey had fallen for this remarkable person.

While she handed out papers, she noticed the concerned

look on Anna's face as she spoke into her cell. A moment later, the color drained from the face of her new boss. Something was wrong—very wrong. Greta dropped the documents and ran to the lobby, reaching Anna's side just in time to catch her fall.

Chapter 7

CALL ME GRIM

R andy Chambers reflected on the irony of having the name of a porn star while also working in the dreariest, soul-sucking job a guy could have. He sat in his tellers' booth, staring at the clock for what must have been the hundredth time during that long morning, fantasizing about what his alter ego would be up to right now in his world of erotic adventure.

Maybe a breakfast of pancakes with syrup followed by an orgy in the swimming pool. Three of them: a blond, a Latino, and an Asian girl. Oh, yeah! We start on the lounge chairs and I persuade them to remove their—

The prudish face of Mrs. Deacon appeared before his counter, her beady eyes narrowed at him in a gesture indicating she was in no mood to be trifled with. The erection that'd been growing in his pants instantly shriveled at the prospect of his daily interchange with the rancid old cow.

She was truly a person put on Earth for the sole purpose of making others as miserable as she was.

"Good morning, Mrs. Deacon. How may I help you today?" he said, wishing he could reach through the glass and punch the old lady in her ugly dentures.

His daily ritual of being publicly humiliated was postponed for a second by the brass bell above the bank's green doors announcing the arrival of another customer.

Randy hated that fucking bell almost as much as he hated old Freaky Deac. It seemed the morning rush, if that's what it could be called, had already started. A guy in leathers wearing a visored motorcycle helmet came in and joined the queue behind Mrs. Deacon. Judging by the bib of the Roma Pizza Co. on his chest and the cloth bag dangling from his gloved hand, he'd come to cash some coin.

Great, twenty minutes of counting nickels. Today just gets better.

"Where's my checkbook?" Mrs. Deacon demanded by way of greeting.

"I'm sorry, Mrs. Deacon, I don't understand." Randy inwardly sighed, trying to imagine the old woman as she would've looked forty years ago. Perhaps she'd have looked similar to the blonde he'd been about to mentally strip beside the pool. The leap of imagination failed, however, at the sight of the wart perched on her over-generous chin.

"Don't pretend you don't know what I'm talking about, you greasy little weasel!" she said, raising her dog-headed cane and tapping it on the glass in a gesture she reserved for when a truly mortal sin had been committed by his employer.

"Mrs. Deacon, I really don't appreciate—"

"Where is my God damn checkbook? You said it would take no longer than a week and it's been nearly two."

With a profound sinking sensation in the pit of his stomach, Randy realized he'd made a monumental screw-up. He'd agreed to place the order, but in a fog of Deacon-induced anxiety, he'd forgotten to input the request in the system.

There was no getting around this one—she would complain to the manager for sure, and said manager happened to be a spineless asshole who carried a barely-disguised dislike for Randy. There was no doubt the little prick would take great pleasure in making him suffer.

"Erm, Mrs. Deacon, I—I'm terribly sorry, but it seems there was an oversight."

Her eyes narrowed like crosshairs zeroing in on a dancing rabbit. "What the hell do—"

"Excuse me, I think I may be able to help." The male voice came from behind the dark visor of the motorcyclist. The figure now stood close behind Mrs. Deacon.

"Wha—" she turned and started to say before the biker smashed his bag against her jaw, causing a blood-covered set of dentures to fly from her mouth. They landed with a squelch on the counter right under Randy's nose.

Old Deac, struck dumb—probably for the first time in her life—slumped to the polished wooden floor. The bank teller stared back and forth from the grinning, stained teeth to the smoked visor that now looked at the prone figure lying by his feet.

The man in the helmet reached down and came back into view again with her cane in hand. He began to swing the thick shaft methodically into the old woman.

Bile rose in Randy's throat. The extensive thirty-minute security training course he'd undertaken demanded that he press the alarm buzzer, but he remained rooted in fascinated horror as the dog's grinning head rose and fell, sometimes with a dull thud and sometimes with a crack that turned his veins to ice.

After what seemed an eternity, his new customer dropped the cane and turned to face him. "I don't know about you, but I can't abide crappy manners." The observation made Randy giggle in terror, and the rider tilted his head as if weighing the man before him. "Have you ever heard of a scalds mask?" The visor guy asked. Randy started to nod, but then he shook his head. His finger began to slide toward the buzzer. "Marvellous things—really did the trick and kept a woman in her place. I had to make do with this!" He gave a muffled laugh and raised the cane dripping with blood. Gray hairs were stuck to the gore. "Who pays by check these days, anyhow?"

Randy's bladder lost its contents and the hot liquid spattered on the cheap, green carpet below. He had his finger poised above the panic button, but something told him that pizza guy would end his life with as much consideration as his uncle Lester had when poisoning wild pigeons.

The delivery driver from hell turned the bag upside down and emptied a couple of bricks beneath him.

"Now, here's the thing: I need you to fill this bag with twenties. You got that? Nice and simple. No need for fuss, old boy. Do that and we can stay best buddies. What do ya' reckon?"

Randy didn't press the buzzer until after the visor guy strolled from the bank with as much care as a man who'd just opened a savings account. He hoped to have time to mop up the piss at his feet before the cops arrived.

DOCTOR NICK RAMIREZ hooked the cigar in his mouth and then looked down the length of the putter to gauge the distance between the golf ball and the artificial hole at the other side of his office. He tapped and the ball trundled along the drab office carpet then fell into the flashing mechanical box. A tiny beach babe shaking her bikini-clad tits heralded his effort from the gadget's electronic scoreboard.

He sighed, wishing the game were as challenging as it used to be in the larger space of his old office in LA. Back then, he could've afforded a real Bay Watch extra to jiggle her ass while he practiced. That'd been before he'd been tossed onto the shit heap of the medical profession, though.

Of course, he'd known the case would go against him the second he'd laid eyes on that bitch of a judge. Her over-taut cheeks and the poorly hidden scars beneath her ear lobes screamed back alley butcher. There was no doubt he'd proven the perfect gimp to pay the price for her stupidity.

How was he supposed to have known the silicone in the implants hadn't been medical-grade? Of course, he'd saved a few bucks by using a non-certified supplier, but that was just good business. Unfortunately, the financier husband of his most prolific client hadn't appreciated not being able to grope the breasts of his former Miss Russia bride after one of the implants ruptured and damn near killed her. The subsequent lawsuit and three-month stretch inside had finished him in the big league. The greedy son of a bitch had milked him for a cool two mill, and that money—his money—had been pissed up the wall during their inevitable divorce. The last Ramirez heard, the financier had spent what was left of his hard-earned cash on securing the love of the next Mrs. Fuck Face the Third.

Thanks to a loophole in the law, his ban had expired two years later. On paper, at least, he was cleared to practice again—not that it mattered. The only referrals he'd received so far came from government health programs, which meant scraping the barrel with genuine medical disfigurements. Although his new, nobler path was a great pussy magnet in the downtown bars he frequented, financially it was a disaster. The equation of poor plus sick equaled destitute surgeon. Nick sighed at the injustice of it all and went to retrieve his ball.

The intercom buzzed on his desk. "Nick, your 2:30 is here," the staccato sound of Stacey's voice drifted up from the old-fashioned nineties system.

His dumb PA had been another compromise. Usually, he would have picked a professional who could both take notes and give him the occasional blowjob. Stacey excelled at the latter, but sucked—and not in a good way—at the former. He suspected she regarded herself as his girlfriend. It was a delusion he was prepared to tolerate, as long as she continued to accept minimum wage.

"Very well," he replied, perking up at the news. He'd feared his much-anticipated 2:30 wouldn't turn up.

This particular patient would have the privilege of being his first paying customer since getting his license back. There would be no depressing stories of meningitis taking fingers or facial reconstruction after a hit and run. He hoped this would be a good old-fashioned case of body dysmorphia, his favorite affliction that only the rich seemed to contract.

Making the extra effort the occasion deserved, he pushed the golf machine to the corner of the room and then strode to his second-hand walnut desk and glanced over at his notes: a male—not so unusual, these days. It was a little odd that he hadn't wished to discuss his requirements before the consultation, though. Nick sat on the polished surface, then faced the door and adopted a reassuring smile.

Might be a buffalo bill, he speculated with a thrill. *Now, that would be an interesting challenge!*

He'd never performed a gender re-assignment. A small part of him wondered if the risky procedure was a wise move, considering his previous legal difficulties, but the payout would be substantial. Many people couldn't get medical approval for such drastic surgery due to mental health issues; that's when Doctor Nick Ramirez came in on his scalpel-shaped white Charger to do what the establishment didn't have the balls for. Who was he to deny free will, especially when it came with such a big check?

"If I don't do it, someone else will," he repeated his favorite mantra just before the door opened, and his new best friend entered.

Nick was careful not to show his disappointment at the sight of the eye patch on the other man's face. Facial reconstruction around the eye socket didn't pay half as well as a trim and tuck of the crown jewels. He paced toward his visitor with his hand outstretched; the other guy looked down before ignoring the gesture. Unperturbed, Nick gave his best no-need-to-worry-any-longer, I-can-take-it-from-here expression. The man said nothing. One good, bright blue eye regarded him without warmth. In fact, he reminded him of...

Jesus, please don't be another fucking husband. I've paid my dues on that score.

Putting aside his paranoia for a moment, he turned back

to his notes and made a show of reading them. "So... Mr. Reaper? May I ask your first name?"

"Call me Grim," came the casual reply.

Oh fuck, oh fuck. He is a husband! What if he has a gun?

"Listen, buddy, I don't want any trouble," he said unsteadily while laying the clipboard back on the table. He thought of pressing the intercom and alerting Stacey, but realized that, unless he intended to distract the guy with an extensive oral workout, it wouldn't achieve a great deal.

"Trouble, old boy? Oh no, I'm interested in your services." The man grinned, but the gesture didn't reach that ice-blue eye.

Frowning, Ramirez looked into the face of the man before him. He had a hungry, gaunt cast to his features—wild—and without any sign of the self-indulgent vanity his previous clients had displayed.

"What do you want?" he asked, dropping the salesman facade. This guy meant business, and putting on a front would make no difference to the outcome.

Grim reached into his jacket, at which point Nick dove for the intercom. Stacey might have been as much use as a chocolate coffee pot, but he figured she could be used as a distraction while he fled. Just as his finger touched the button, however, he noticed what the other man had removed from his jacket. Nick halted mid-action and frowned at the Polaroid image.

"I want you to make me look like this," Grim said.

Nick straightened his skewed tie, the thudding in his

heart lessening. He plucked up the picture and stared in horror.

"Hijo de perra!" Ramirez said, slipping into his native dialect. The man's face in the image had been carved—at least, he thought it was a man. A single terrified eye stared from the bloody mess with all the hopelessness of a pig in a slaughterhouse. This was not the work of any surgeon. *Who took the picture?*

He turned to face the still-smiling Grim. "You—you're a crazy man."

"Oh, the picture's not real—just me and my buddy messing around. I'd like to look the same, please."

"W—why?"

"Why not?"

Nick licked his lips, trying to figure out if he could take this guy out, himself, wrestle the insect-like creep to the ground, and then call the cops. His instinct, however, said that if he tried he'd find out what the other man meant by "messing around". "Well, it would be unethical," he heard himself say, despite his fear.

Grim gave a contempt-filled laugh into his face. "Unethical? Well, you shoulda' said that. My apologies—I musta' mixed you up with the doctor Ramirez who did a stretch for melting some whore's tits off."

For the first time, anger flared in Ramirez. "You can't blackmail me for something I've already been punished for. I did my time." The indignant statement only drew another scornful chuckle from his unwelcome visitor.

The man's eye twinkled with what looked like actual pleasure. "Oh no? Well, maybe I'm just gonna' say you stuck your finger up my ass." The black grin widened, as did the intensity of his contemptuous regard.

"How dare you!" Ramirez said without the conviction he sought. Just a hint of scandal would be a disaster for him, even if it amounted to the ravings of some loon.

"Oh, and if you do this for me, no questions asked, I'll give you this," Grim said, reaching into his biker jacket and producing the biggest bundle of twenties Nick had seen since his days in LA.

Ramirez weighed his options for declining, each ending with him back inside or stabbed to death in his own office. He contemplated agreeing to this loon's demands before quietly calling the cops, but the sight of those lovely green-backs trumped such lofty notions. Besides, even if he did the right thing, he could end up back in the pen, sharing a cell with Big Bubba the love sponge.

Nick put his head in his hands and pinched the bridge of his nose—a gesture he hadn't made since ditching the specs years ago in favor of contacts. Just that morning, he'd contemplated being forced back into being Mr. Four Eyes, because he couldn't afford the more expensive lenses.

"When?" he asked, feeling sorry for himself again.

TJ GODRAM T-BONE, or as he liked to think of himself, TJ

God Damn T-to-Da-Bone, watched the storekeeper count out five hundred in bills and then push them over with a sullen expression.

A year ago, the jumped-up little shit had decided paying off the Bone Dog was against his religion. It'd taken four armed robberies to enlighten the fool, who was God on this block.

"I want six hundred," TJ said, a grin appearing around his broad, metal-rimmed teeth.

"We agreed five! No more."

"Inflation, my man." The truth was everyone paid five, but this sneaky bastard needed a reminder of which big dog pissed on his flowerbed. "It will be six, my good friend Ting Tong. You ain't gettin' all uppity with the T-Bone, is you?" TJ laughed at his own wit.

"My name is Alex—I tell you before." The old man puffed his cheeks, venting his impotent fury. TJ leaned forward into the other man's face, enjoying the fear he saw, only to pull back at the smell of garlic. He suppressed the temptation to break his rule and snap the neck of his golden goose.

"Now, now, ain't no need to get your rice cakes in a twist, my man. Didn't we stop those brothers comin' in here and takin' your shit right from under your terrified bitch self? Hmm. Ain't that worth a few more dollars?" The comment didn't help the other man relax at all, which was good: TJ wanted to see him break.

After watching the trembling storekeeper count out the extra cash, TJ strolled from the store, only pausing to grab a bottle of tequila. He emerged from the flaking green door and contemplated whether to service his nose down at the late bar or service his dick at Big Molly's. His deliberation didn't stop him from noticing the slim white guy watching from an alley on the other side of the street.

Fuckin' five-O man.

He'd learned years before that it was usually better to make a big show when spotting one of the undercovers; it rattled their tiny minds and made them think twice. It was a puzzle, though, because he couldn't recall doing anything serious enough to force those fat, donut-eating fuckers to get off their lazy asses and tail him. He was sure they didn't give a flying monkey's crap about the protection racket and regarded half of his clients as little better than himself.

He swaggered across the busy road, hands in the pockets of his pants, all the time eyeing his admirer without giving away how unsettled he felt by the stillness of the man observing him. His face remained in shadow under a wide-brimmed hat.

Strange fuckin' disguise, you rookie mutha... "Evenin', Offica'. I's real glad to see you. Thing is, these freaky dudes keep watching me. I's thinkin they wanna' get their hands on my sweet ass. What you say, Offica'?" Usually, the recipient of his provocation would develop a sudden interest in anything other than him, but this guy didn't move an inch. TJ continued to approach the figure, subconsciously toning down his body language. "What you want?" he asked, for the first time noticing the bandage covering one side of the other man's face. Fresh blood spots had soaked through the gauze, framing a single blue eye that regarded him without emotion. He began to get the first inkling that this wasn't a cop.

"You TJ?" The voice was low, just above a whisper.

"Who wants to know?" TJ thrust his chin out. No way was he going to be intimidated by this Halloween freak. "You talk, or we gonna' have a serious disagreement," he said, opening his coat a notch to reveal a glance of the Glock.

"Rat Boy said you're a man who can get stuff."

TJ's eyes widened at the mention of his only true friend, the Rat. They'd known each other since they were kids selling dime bags on street corners. Fuck, they'd been friends so long that they even knew each other's real names. Reggie Rattle was the kind of guy who always had your back.

During a long stint for armed robbery, Reggie could've lived up to his name and spilled his guts about his non-convicted accomplice for a reduced sentence, but he hadn't. The Rat had served eight years without speaking a word now, while his partner built up the business. It was the clos-est TJ had ever come to genuine gratitude in his entire miserable life.

"You were inside with the Ratman?" he asked, his suspi-cion not fully gone. As stupid as the law was, they could've set this up. "So, what tales you got from Pickford? I hear it's a zoo in there, man." he said, knowing full-well Reggie had never been anywhere near the place. TJ's hand hung by the gun, not liking the way that single blue eye seemed to judge him. Still, a cop he was not—the whole bandage thing was way too elaborate for them.

"Never been in Pickford. Neither has he." First test passed.

"Who are you?" TJ asked, tiring of the game.

"He said that you, Junior, are a resourceful man."

Junior. He hadn't heard that name in a long time. His police records had been recorded wrong by some racist asshole pig back in the eighties, and Junior Jermaine had become Terrence Jermaine. No one called him Junior, anymore, except Reggie. TJ relaxed enough to do business with the guy, even if his instinct said it would be as much fun as having a root canal with a teaspoon.

"Well, why didn't you say so, my man? Step into my office," he said, gesturing at the one good car parked on the street. As the other man stepped forward, TJ placed a straining hand on his chest. "I warn you now, slim dude: my services don't come cheap."

He thought he saw the icy twitch of a half-smile touch the visible part of the other man's face. "I only need one thing," Slim replied, flashing him a fistful of twenties.

Chapter 8

FINDING STRNGTH

The fluttering remnants of Anna's terrible nightmare faded as she became aware of the soft bed beneath her. She'd been back at Julia's house on that morning, staggering along a hallway that'd become a wicked parody of reality, plastered with dripping blood and smeared handprints. She'd tried desperately to turn and run from the bedroom door, but even as she'd struggled to escape, a darkness pulled her back—back to where she would find Julia a cold and lifeless thing. Unable to fight any more, she'd been sucked, screaming and clawing, into that hellish vision. There, she'd found more bodies piled upon her sister: other women. Their voices had called to her through unmoving blue lips, asking why she hadn't stopped him and why he was free again to add to their number. Worst of all, they asked when she would join them.

The sensation of linen sheets on her chest and the

warmth of the sun's rays against her cheek gave her comfort. Relieved, she opened her eyes and found Claire staring down at her. Anna screamed.

"Anna, it's okay. It's me—it's Emma." Her sea-gray eyes looked alarmed, not angry.

Emma. Not Claire. A second wave of relief welled in Anna's breast, but it faded as she recalled the phone call from Raymond. Had that been a nightmare? No.

The answer made her breath catch. Tony was free to kill again. She vaguely recalled the detective speaking platitudes about her being safe in the UK before she'd passed out.

"Where am I?" Anna asked, her throat feeling parched.

"The hospital. You just fainted is all."

She saw the care in the young woman's face—a softness she couldn't recall seeing in the girl's troubled sibling. As she looked at Emma, she knew she'd made the right choice to invite her. Maybe she'd prove to be the friend that Claire never was.

"The baby?" Anna asked, raising a protective hand to her belly.

"The doc says she's fine. Don't worry." Emma looked worried, though, and again it struck Anna that she'd reverted to an almost childlike state, unable to face the world as an adult.

"She?" Anna asked. "Did you just say she?"

"Well, yes. Like I said, the doctor says, she..." Emma stopped and raised her hands to her mouth. "Oh my gosh, you don't know, do you?" She looked horrified now. Anna blinked at first in shock, but then she swelled with gratitude upon hearing something positive to counter the endless progression of bad news.

Emma lightened her expression at the sight of Anna's sudden joy.

"It's a girl?" Anna asked.

Emma smiled and nodded. "Did you want a girl?"

"Well, I wanted either a girl or a boy. At least I know I've got one, now." They both laughed.

"I won't let him hurt my baby," Anna said with sudden tears welling in eyes.

Emma laid a comforting hand on her shoulder. "You mean Tony Eckerman?" Anna nodded. Just the mention of his name sent a shiver down her spine. "Greta said she called the detective back after you fell. I'm so sorry, Anna. After what that animal did to those women and how he manipulated Cl—" Emma stopped herself, seeming to realize she must be on tricky ground.

Anna suppressed the anger rising inside her. In a sense, she was right to feel that way. Claire may have carried out the attack, but perhaps she'd been as much a victim of Tony as Julia. Only an evil creature would take advantage of someone so vulnerable.

"Is Greta here?"

"No, she's looking after Hermie. We've been taking it in shifts and I'm it," Emma said, pointing to herself self-consciously, as if afraid she'd overstepped the mark, somehow.

"Hey, that's fine. I like having you around." They both smiled. "How long have I been out?"

"Oh, about five hours. Greta left not long ago."

"Five hours? But it's the morning."

"Was the morning. The docs said not to disturb you, because you had a nasty shock. Looks like you needed to check out for a while."

It didn't surprise Anna. She'd barely gotten two hours of sleep last night, stressing about the board meeting. "I can't believe it, Emma. After everything I've been through, and now he's out again."

Emma squeezed her shoulder. "They'll get him, Anna. He won't be out for long, and you and the baby are safe here. He can't hurt either of you."

"I know, but..." She felt herself welling up again. "With Corey still... it's the last thing I need." The tears came in great racking sobs that prompted another hug from Emma.

"Hey, besides, I've got news for you, Mrs. Price," Emma said while Anna continued to cling to her.

"Please let it be good. I can't take any more crap."

"Well, that really depends," Emma said, sounding unsure. Anna glanced up with a please-don't-mess-with-the-pregnant-lady look. "If it's okay with you and Corey—when he's feeling better, that is—I'd like to stay here with you guys."

Anna blinked. "You mean...?"

It was Emma's turn to look vulnerable. "Please don't make me go back, Anna," she spoke with a note of pleading in her voice. "I want to stay here with you and Hermie." Her words came faster. "I've been so happy here, without all the guilt they lay on me, and I feel bad enough, anyhow." Her voice trailed off until they were crying together, comforted by the closeness of each other.

Anna looked her straight in the eye. "You're more than welcome."

"Thank you."

The two women sat for a moment, lost in their own private worries.

"What's the Church of the Serene Martyrs really like, Emma? What's the deal with them?" Anna could see the pain register.

"They're not much better than Dad was," she said with a sigh older than her years should have needed.

"Did they, you know, the same as..."

Emma shook her head. "No, not with me, at least, but I've heard rumors about the reverend when he was younger." Her gaze burned with hate. "He's a mean old bird —says God speaks to him alone, just like Father did." She went silent for a second. "I'm sick of hearing how bad I am, Anna. He called me a jezebel! I'm not a bad person, I swear!" Anna strengthened her hug in return. "Ever since I can remember, everyone's told me what to do, how to dress, and even what to think," she squeezed her back, "but you don't judge me."

The sincerity touched Anna, fighting her refusal to trust again. "Why do they want you and Hermon so badly,

Emma? With all the money I'm throwing at this, why don't they just give up?"

"I'm not sure." Emma bit her lip. "Clarence screamed hellfire at me for days after the video call. I'm sure that, if it hadn't been for the judge and you, he would've stopped me." She seemed to consider the point. "I've known other people to leave the church before. It wasn't easy for them. I know, because

the elders made us pester them night and day, calling to say their immortal souls were in peril if they didn't come back." She paused, thinking for a moment. "With me and Hermie, it does seem different, though."

"Did Clarence bother to get involved with chasing the others who left?" Anna asked.

Emma shook her head. "No, that was novice work." She paused. "Anna?" she asked, her face pale and drawn.

"Yes, hon?"

"Do you ever feel ashamed about what's happened to you, even if it's not your fault?"

"Sometimes, but then it makes me angry at the people who are really to blame. How about you?" Emma gave an almost imperceptible nod. She looked away, as if unable to meet her eye. Anna turned her by the chin and looked at her once more. "What you did—running away and calling the cops—was one of the bravest things I've ever heard of." The girl's gaze was wide and filled with tears. "If you hadn't, you and Hermie would still be there with that monster."

She could still see the shadow of resigned pain there—

the last vestiges of a daughter's love for her father. There was strength, though, too. These were the eyes of someone who'd been through the worst life could throw at them and still survive. She was sadder, sure, just like herself, but wiser for it, nonetheless.

"Listen, if there's anything else you can think of, let me know." *And I'll do some digging of my own,* Anna thought.

Emma nodded like a frightened little girl who'd just been offered a comforting word. Anna wished she had someone strong by her side, just then—someone who could be her own rock and tell her it was going to be okay. The only two people who could give her that reassurance, however, were both gone now: one murdered at the hands of the man who was free to continue his reign of terror and the other, her husband, a victim caught in the crossfire.

Maybe I should have just stayed with him. Stayed the waitress and let life eat me away, until I looked into that diner mirror and stopped caring, anymore. At least I could have prevented what happened to Julia and Corey.

ANNA SCROLLED down the list of sensationalist news articles about the misfortunes of the Pike family, finding herself shaking her head in anger at headlines like "Incest Cult Uncovered," alongside an image of a harried-looking Claire and Hermon being escorted from what must've been their former home. The lack of sensitivity displayed by the gutter press was staggering, as was the total lack of critical analysis written about the shadowy organization to which the family had belonged before Tom Pike embarked on his personal journey of sick delusion.

There were a few quotes from Clarence Riley, mouthing sound-bite platitudes like "we didn't know" and "this isn't our way." She had no doubt that sensitivity surrounding matters of faith played a part in skirting around the criticism of the secretive group.

"Fuck that," Anna murmured, taking another sip of coffee. Despite her fighting words, her heart sank at the slim prospect of uncovering something valuable from the salacious speculation and lack of scrutiny. Deciding to change course, she switched her efforts to researching the church, itself.

Clarence founded the Church of the Serene Martyrs, himself, in the eighties. It soon became clear, however, that the group had a longer history. The most interesting information came from the blog post of someone referring to herself as Heretic, who claimed to have fled the church she insisted was a cult. According to the anonymous blogger, the reverend had traveled east from San Francisco during the height of the hippie movement, and during a drug-fueled confession, had admitted to having connections with the infamous Manson family, albeit for a short time.

There was no suggestion that he'd been involved with the murders, but it still wasn't the kind of association any aspiring guru would want on their CV. Anna found a much younger photo of the man. He'd been handsome back then, with a Jesus-like beard and beatific smile that exuded charisma—nothing like the withered old crow who had greeted her in the court hearing.

Another ex-member of the church posted photos of the transformation from the original Lovers of Serenity, a communal band of poetry-reading potheads, to a cult formed along religious lines. Out went the flared trousers and flower power shirts and in went the Quaker-style tunics and bonnets from a bygone age.

Shit. Talk about a change of direction, Anna thought.

For years, the movement had barely registered on any public records. According to the accompanying testimony, the switch to God in the late eighties marked a change in fortunes for the collective. Before, their numbers had been declining, but as a redeemed sinner, Reverend Riley found it far easier to attract the simple rural folk of the surrounding towns into his congregation.

She didn't come across the name Pike until finding an outdated website bearing the name of the church. It hosted minutes from several meetings in which Brother Pike was listed as a senior member of the leadership, second only to Clarence himself. Anna couldn't help but gasp out loud at his outrageous title: Defender Against Sins of the Flesh.

No prizes for guessing why he volunteered for that post, she thought.

Anna nearly overlooked the evidence of Riley's special interest in the Pikes, so blinding was the hideous wallpapered background featuring line after line of textured crosses. The photo was of the now-aging reverend being handed an oversized check by none other than Tom Pike. At first, she thought they were sharing the limelight to accept a donation, but upon closer inspection, she could see the name on the check was 'The Pike Dairy Co." Anna leaned back in her chair, trying to read the amount on the grainy image.

"A hundred thousand! Wow!" she said aloud, feeling the old surge of exhilaration. That meant Pike had money—lots of it.

And guess who's his next of kin...

Anna did a search on the name of the dairy company and found a sleek, modern website, complete with the corporate-speak one would expect for a large company. At the center of the marketing material was a picture of the same ranch house she'd seen Claire and Hermon emerge from during the police raid on the farm. She guessed the Pikes must've sold out the wider business years ago, so she checked her hunch by clicking on the About tab on the site. There was nothing unusual about the company details, until she saw the phrase "managed in trust by the Church of Serene Martyrs."

But held in trust for whom? A growing suspicion led Anna to pick up the phone and call Howard Baines.

Chapter 9

THE LIGHT

Corey thrashed in his seat, screaming and clawing at the belt, while icy water lapped his chin. Still, the liquid death rose with hateful inevitability until it covered his nostrils and stopped his last wretched efforts to breathe.

Time to die.

Memories of Anna caused him to look over at the co-pilot seat again, and his panic deepened at the sight of Claire sitting there, with a great dress billowing around her in the swaying current. Her eyes remained closed, but they peered at him regardless, like that of a sightless worm. Blood oozed from a wound at her neck, seeping into the darkness until it colored the ocean a cloying red.

Corey's lungs burned for oxygen and he knew that, at any moment, he'd lose the battle and breathe in doom. Seeming to sense his defeat was close, a smile twitched across Claire's white lips. She would stay here, gloating, while his fight gave way and eternal entrapment followed here in the black depths. He lowered his head and closed his eyes, unable to go on.

"Corey?" His name was called by a soft voice, which came with a warm sensation that spread along the back of his freezing neck.

He gazed up through the murk to see dappled light penetrating the gloom. The light drew him, urging him to follow. He tugged with renewed vigor against the belt, but still, it refused to let him go. In frustration, he raised his arm toward the illumination, imploring it to come to his aid. As the last of his strength ebbed, a slender figure appeared in the light above: an angel. The ethereal swimmer glided further down, a warm glow penetrating the darkness around her.

"Corey, come back."

The light around the figure grew until it became a dazzling blaze. The growing heat of that radiance gave him will, urging him to renew his efforts. He tried again, but the more he did, the more twisted the belt became. He glanced to the left again to find that the blind Claire thing had opened its dead eyes and now drifted toward him, its withered, dead arms outstretched, ready to embrace him forever.

"Corey, please. We need you!" The voice he recognized didn't come from the dead creature, but from above—from the light.

Anna!

He looked up once more and recognized her for the first time. As he did so, the clasp at his waist slid away. Now free, he thrust his legs against the cockpit floor and sped toward her until their fingers touched. She clasped his hand and drew him up, and they drifted through the growing, twinkling warmth, until they broke the surface together and took a deep, cleansing breath.

THEY CAME ASHORE on a golden beach with a blue, vibrant sky blazing in all its glory above them. The lovers lay together in the surf while Corey looked upon her beautiful face. He needed her warmth—needed to be with her right then. He kissed the lips he thought he'd never be able to savor again. A hunger grew inside him, and he reached to pull aside the strap of her bikini, exposing her breast, which he sucked. Anna arched her back and moaned. Passion took him, then, and he ripped the remaining clothing from her. Within a moment, he'd thrust himself inside her and they made love under the sun, reveling in the touch of each other's embrace.

"COREY, PLEASE. WE NEED YOU," Anna implored her husband with all the desperation of a woman in the eighth month of her pregnancy. She squeezed his hand and wept at the prospect of birth without the man she loved. *Did I just see?* Corey's eyes gave a definite twitch, causing Anna's heart to hammer.

"Corey, I'm here!" She squeezed him harder. "Come back. Do you hear? Please, you can do this!"

There was more flickering and then the first glimpse of a brown iris, but he wasn't quite there, yet. Anna pressed the buzzer above his resting head.

Although her hopes soared, she found herself unable to believe the perceived movement was anything more than her own wishful thinking. That was right until the moment his eyes flicked open and he took a breath deep into his lungs.

He blinked for a second, and then scanned the room, as if seeking something. When his eyes fell on her face, she knew he'd found what he searched for. Anna rose from her bedside seat in a state of shock, not knowing how to process the powerful emotions sweeping through her. Corey's gaze traveled downward and came to rest on her swollen abdomen.

"Damn, hon. You've really been hitting the coffee and cake," he said in a rasping tone.

Corey was back.

Chapter 10

MASK

The check-in line snaked across the departure's hall toward Lorraine Mathews, the newest and quite possibly most bored member of the flight team inspecting boarding passes. She looked down at a smiling little girl who eagerly passed over her documents, probably on the trip of her young life to Europe.

She forced a smile, and scribbled a quick initial on the boarding slip while resenting the spoiled little brat. When she'd first started the job, she'd assumed it would be great to jet to exotic places while serving happy people fulfilling their dreams. In reality, it'd only reinforced her own disappointment at the vanishing prospect of ever being one of them. The drab interiors of tedious airport hotels were the only thing she got to see of the many cities she visited. Lorraine stifled a sigh at the thought of the long flight ahead and the miserly seven-hour break she'd get before doing it all again.

After watching the girl skip off to the security screening with her harried mother in tow, Lorraine reluctantly faced her next unwanted customer. Her interest grew, however, at the sight of the man dressed in full military uniform. Immediately, she found herself sympathetic toward the poor guy leaning on a cane as he limped forward. Although his face was partially bandaged, the bottom half of his bearded mouth revealed a warm smile that must have been masking a great deal of pain.

The forlorn figure reminded Lorraine of her uncle, a color sergeant in the famed 7th Armored Brigade. A once-proud member of the Desert Rats, he'd returned to England from Iraq as a broken shell of his former self after becoming another casualty of the roadside bombs blighting the campaign. She wondered where this American had been stationed; as far as she knew, there were only a few troops in the Middle East, these days.

Perhaps Afghanistan, she thought, watching as he fumbled in determination with his documents. *Maybe Special forces? Wow.*

"Good morning, sir. May I take your boarding pass, please?" she asked with only a hint of the broad Yorkshire accent her training had all but erased.

He smiled again, as if grateful for the fact that she hadn't offered to assist him. Lorraine ignored the stern glare from the frumpy woman in the suit behind him. She sensed the disapproval resulted from her seeming indifference to the man's plight, but she knew better when it came to handling proud veterans. To have offered help would've been a humiliation. Uncle Gary had once punched straight through a wooden door just because her mother handed him a pair of shoes.

Fuck that snotty old bitch. She hasn't got a clue.

The soldier gazed down at her with a single blue eye, the other hidden beneath the bandages. She saw a deep, sad loneliness in that brief glance. Looking more closely, she could see the dressing failed to completely cover his disfigurement, and tendrils of angry, red scar tissue crept out from under the gauze. She beamed back at him, wondering about his story and why he looked so alone, speculating that his wife or partner had rejected him because of the injury.

"Have a pleasant journey, sir," she said warmly.

"Thank you so much," he said with genuine gratitude. "It'll be the first time I've been to the UK."

"You deserve it," she replied, unashamed to praise a veteran in public.

"You'd be surprised what I've had to do to get here," he agreed with a short laugh, his tone low and rich. Lorraine guessed he was referring to some kind of treatment that wasn't available in the states. His single eye regarded her with interest and she noticed the handsome curve of his jaw line.

"I hope you enjoy your stay in the UK, Mr..." she looked

down at his passport and blushed, "Sorry, Captain Reaper." The miserable cow behind the military man frowned again, impatient at the delay. Lorraine couldn't give a shit, though.

"Say, I don't suppose you know London, by any chance?" he asked. She felt her heart quicken as she realized he'd just made a pass at her.

Chapter 11

EARLY DAYS

I n the days following what he liked to refer to as his "second coming," Corey made slow, but steady progress and was soon frustrated by his forced rest. Only Anna's stern-faced support for the medical team's advice had stopped him discharging himself. The result, however, had been one grumpy husband whose spirits were further dampened by the news of Tony Eckerman's escape. So it wasn't a great surprise to Anna that he reacted without his usual easy-going charm upon learning of her efforts to adopt Hermon and welcome Emma.

"You invited whom to live with us?" he asked one morning, pressing his hand to his temple. Corey had developed migraines since he'd awoken—something the staff assured him would pass.

"They've got no one, Corey," Anna replied as she

waddled to the drink dispenser and ran him some water to go with the pain-killers.

"What if she's the same as Claire? What if the boy is... you know..." he made a stabbing motion with his other hand.

Anna couldn't help but laugh. "He's a little boy, Corey— not Chuckie."

"Okay, maybe not the kid, but what about Emma?"

She didn't answer at first and handed over the drink and pills to him in silence before lowering herself ponderously into the chair. The sight of Anna struggling seemed to make him think twice about his uncharacteristic moaning and Corey leaned over to help her. In response, she held out a hand to say, "Don't you dare, Buster."

"I'm supposed to be helping you, not the other way round," he protested.

"I'm used to it," Anna said, her tone harsher than intended. "Sorry," she added, realizing it sounded like she was blaming him for being in a coma for the past eight months.

They sat in silence for a moment, lost in their own concerns.

"Will it be like this when we're old, do you think?" Corey asked.

"What, me as fat as a hippo, and you grumbling at the world?" she poked back.

"You're blooming," he countered.

At first, she had thought the shock of seeing her so large had tipped him back under, but after some initial exclamations, he'd come to love her motherly figure and his impending status as a father.

"Bloomin' humongous!" Anna wasn't ready to let him off the hook just yet.

"I still can't believe it when I see your belly."

"Do we have to have the birds and bees conversation again, hon?" she teased.

"It's just, well, most fellas get the chance to get used to it. I wake up, and there you are. It's amazing."

"That's not the word I'd choose some days."

"I just wish I could help. It's so frustrating." He reached out for her hand and gave it a squeeze.

"I know, hon. Trust me, you'll get plenty of chances to fuss over us when you're feeling better."

"Just you wait—I've already had an idea for a nursery at Clearwater. It's gonna have great lighting and a fish tank, which I read is calming..."

"Does your brain ever switch off?" Anna asked, unable to stop herself from smiling at his enthusiasm, even while fighting off a headache.

"Hey, I've been lying like a piece of meat for months. I want my life back." He winced again, though, as he spoke.

"You just need to be more patient with yourself. It's gonna' take time to get back to normal."

"I know, I know." He puffed his cheeks out in a juvenile gesture. "I get bored though, and I'm so excited!"

"I understand, babe," she said, patting him on the hand while starting to feel the thrill of the future, herself. Until now, it'd almost seemed like none of it was real without him. Since Corey had come back, all the things she'd mentally put on hold had suddenly become real again, like an image snapping back into focus after staying blurred for so long. There remained one elephant in the room, though, casting a shadow over everything else, and that was the bastard.

"I don't want to go back home while he's on the loose," she said. They'd hardly spoken of it before, but the knowledge of it must be playing on her husband's mind as much as her own.

"Sweetheart—whatever it takes to make you feel safe. London isn't such a bad place to stay, anyway," he said, gazing at her with a wan smile.

"It's a beautiful city," she agreed. In truth, she'd started to think of it as a second home, and in its own way, it was just as unique as Clearwater.

She'd dreaded the prospect of Corey declaring an immediate return, so it was a relief to hear he had no intention to go back to the States, yet. The thought of sharing the same continent with Eckerman was too much for her, especially in her present condition. She needed to concentrate on her family, and let the police do their job.

"He can't hide for much longer, can he?" Anna asked, seeking reassurance she knew he couldn't give with certainty.

"They'll get him," Corey said, a glint of steel in his eye, "and he'd better hope they get him instead of me, 'cause if I got my hands on that son of a bitch..." he trailed off. "I'm gonna' speak to the cops about offering a reward. I want him scared of his own shadow wherever he goes. How does ten million sound?"

She mulled it over. "If it helps. What about the publicity, though? We've been trying to get away from all that." Since they'd left the States, it felt like they'd left the public whirlwind surrounding the case behind. A reward, however, would only re-open that wound.

"I don't care. Your safety comes first and I'll do whatever it takes. A million, ten million..."

She could feel the mood sour once more as it inevitably did at the mention of Tony. She wanted to change the subject, not wishing to invoke the evil vibes that came from talk of their enemy.

"And it looks like we need to be close to the boardroom, judging by the emails I've seen flying around after your debut as the boss," Corey said, seeming to sense her wish to change the subject.

"You promised me no work!" she exclaimed, while secretly grateful to be discussing something else.

"Just checking my emails."

"So," she pressed.

"So what?" he replied.

Anna had to resist the temptation to punch him on the shoulder. "What do you think?"

The grin returned. "God, I wish I had the balls to take resource off May Vilkes."

"You wouldn't have?"

"Off that scary bitch? You're kidding, right? I've seen her make grown men cry." He took her hand and kissed it. "You, my dear, kicked her ass in front of the entire board."

Anna beamed. "Big pussy," she said, already leaning forward to return the kiss.

THE DOWNPOUR CONTINUED FROM A LEADEN, gray sky onto the busy road opposite the Tower of London. The engorged River Thames churned and swirled at the foot of the ancient battlements like a raw, vital creature ripping at the guts of the immovable walled palace. Across from Britain's most ancient castle, the red sign for the Tower Hill Tube station glowed in the gloom. Tourists in plastic ponchos hurried to its entrance to escape the fickle English weather while city financiers hurried by, wrestling umbrellas against the wind.

Tony strolled into the gale as if being embraced by an old friend. The presence of Motha had followed him, willing him on his quest. Indeed, his vengeful god had already rewarded him with that pretty, young flight attendant, and, my, had she proven a worthy distraction.

He'd left her corpse in the bath of the hotel room next to Heathrow. Choking the life from her had brought back all the old pleasures and then some. In years past, his secret passion had felt like something to be ashamed of, but not now. Through Motha, he served a higher, darker purpose that few mortals would ever understand or master. As he emerged from the underground and its bustling hive of activity, he could feel the throbbing veins of this city open before him like the willing throat of a splayed bitch.

He smiled upon seeing the poster, for he knew it to be the will of Motha expressed as clearly as the death rattle of a dying soul. "Ripper tours start here. Discover the grim story of Jack the Ripper in the heart of London's East End!"

His lord had shown him the path he must follow before being permitted to claim his ultimate prize. He knew his time would be limited here and that, even with the power of Motha behind him, they would eventually catch him—his destiny made that inevitable. He didn't care, though, because after searing the will of his master into the memories of every man, woman, and child in this land, he would find her.

Death had come to London once more.

DOWN RIVER, less than a mile from where Tony stood, Anna and Corey sat in a maternity ward, staring in joy at the 3D image of their unborn son. As Anna viewed the beautifully detailed representation of the child that would soon become her world, though, a momentary feeling of unease passed over her like a cloud drifting through the sky on a sunny day.

Chapter 12

MANHUNT

D I Jane McKenzie traced the line of the ligature mark with a gloved finger. She could see prints interspersed around the tell-tale garrotte marks that gave away the perpetrator's inability to resist grasping the victim's throat with uncovered hands. He was either stupid or didn't give a shit. The former possibility was desirable while the latter filled her heart with dread. It looked very likely that there was a sexual element to the attack, but whether it was consensual remained to be determined. She didn't need a lab report to understand this wasn't the tragic result of a row between lovers, though. No, this was the calling card of a deeper kind of evil.

"What do we know?" she asked DI William Dawkins who stood nearby, examining the scattered uniform of the woman whose remains now occupied the hotel room bathtub like a discarded towel.

"Lorraine Mathews, twenty-three years old, employee of the airline for six months. Last seen by the hotel receptionist with, and get this: a man with a bandaged head and dressed in the uniform of an American soldier." Will flashed her a ferret-like grin at the salacious bit of information. Her partner was a short, wiry man with a cynical mind that made him a depressing compliment to any crime scene.

"If he's our perp, we've got ourselves a problem," Jane said.

"How's that? Surely it'll make it easier to catch him?" Will tended to go with the obvious. "Assuming it's him, of course. For all we know, she got through a whole platoon last night."

Jane gave him the glare she reserved for those times he treaded on dangerous ground. He'd once made the mistake of cracking a joke about choir boys at the scene of a bishop's suicide. Considering the political sensitivities surrounding the death, an ambitious senior Metropolitan officer attended the scene. Of course, the high-flyer overheard the comment and Dawkins came within a hair's breadth of being suspended. It'd only been her intervention that had saved his skin. Since then, the look was all it took to make him wind his neck in.

"Sorry," he added, his cheeks reddening.

"You will be the next time a chief hears any of your shit, Will." Ignoring his guilty acknowledgment, she continued, "He doesn't care enough to cover his identity, which makes him dangerous. Either the whole uniform thing is a red herring, or he's stationed in the UK."

"Or he travelled here recently," Will added before she could.

"It's possible the location is a coincidence." Dawkins didn't look convinced, though, and neither was she. "What was her exact role?" Jane asked.

Will flipped through his notebook before answering. "Junior cabin crew."

"We'll need records for every flight she was on in the past week and a passenger manifest for all."

"Already on it."

"I want any camera footage from this place and surrounding streets, too."

She ignored his cheeky salute in reply and turned her attention back to examining the bruising on the victim. *A sex game?* She speculated. This was no kinky session that had gotten out of hand, though—it was brutal and calculated, and every part of her instinct told her this guy was more than capable of doing it again.

"Maybe the uniform is a misdirection," Jane said, biting her top lip. There was little doubt this guy was a predator, and he was probably the same man seen by the reception staff. "If he did come from the States, why would he come to another country and kill in a way that makes him stand out more? It makes no sense."

"Maybe he's got a hard-on for British women?" Will suggested.

Doesn't sound right. The thought was interrupted by forensics moving in to record the scene. Knowing better than to stick around and risk accusations of contamination, they stepped out of the bathroom and into the drab bedroom, where a rumpled bed quilt and two glasses on the bedside table gave the only signs of a disturbance.

"Do we know the victim's nationality?" Jane asked.

"One of us: Yorkshire lass from Leeds," he put on the northern accent and earned himself another withering look. "According to her HR file," he added in a more normal tone. "So, that's your theory? He's got a thing for Brits?"

"I'm not sure, but something isn't right with this one. He's too brazen."

"Well, here's my two pennies' worth: crime of passion. They met in a bar in the States. He's a handsome, but fucked-up veteran—watched too many of his buddies get their limbs blown off. He stalks her back here and then..." he made a motion across his neck.

"Then why take his time?" At first, Will's assumption had seemed most likely to her, but when she'd looked at the body more closely, the wounds looked too methodical. "It's not frenzied enough."

"You can't be certain about that," Dawkins replied. "Even if he did enjoy it, maybe it's still a revenge thing, especially if he's a nutter." Will made a twirling motion with his finger next to his temple. "I heard the Yanks radiate their tank shells. Who knows what that does to your average grunt?"

She gave him a look of barely-contained patience. "Have you ever punched someone slowly?"

"Well, no, but…"

"A jilted stalker is angry. They stab, they strangle, they Garrotte, but they don't do all three," Jane said," and they don't gag, either."

"What kind of big game are we after, then?"

She hated when he used that phrase. "I don't know, but our friend has some real psychopathy going on. I'll bet the lab reports show her injuries were inflicted for hours."

"You mean we've got our first jet-setting serial killer?"

"Let's hope not, because trying to coordinate a manhunt between ourselves is hard enough. Getting international cooperation..."

Chapter 13

DON'T MESS WITH THE PREGNANT LADY

nna had to stop herself from smiling at the reaction of the reverend upon hearing that Emma intended to stay in the UK. His chameleon-like eyeballs bulged from their sockets as Howard Baines read out the prepared statement.

Wait until you hear the rest, you shriveled, old rooster! Anna thought.

"Yar Honor, I must object!" Riley raised his arms, as if beseeching the almighty. "Just as I feared, my ward has been indoctrinated by this woman. See how Sister Emma dresses like a jezebel!" He half-rose from his sitting position while the matronly woman next to him crossed herself and shook her head.

In truth, it'd been Emma's idea to wear the low-cut T-shirt and the bright red lipstick. Although she'd actually dressed conservatively since her arrival, such was her anger that she insisted on the sultry display just to antagonize Clarence.

"Now, now, Reverend," Anna said, starting to enjoy their imminent victory, "don't be silly. It's not like she's joined the Manson family."

The reference to his murky past made the preacher splutter, caught between rage and mention of his unwelcome connection with the notorious cult.

"Enough, please," the judge interjected via the video link. "Reverend Riley, your so-called ward is a grown adult with every right to live wherever she pleases. More to the point, she is Hermon's closest living relative."

"But Yar Honor, Emma is a lost soul. The ghosts of her own incestuous debauchery have clearly blinded her to the love of her church."

"Reverend, you don't have to remind this court what Miss Pike was forced to endure. I, like many others, admire the courage she displayed," the judge replied in an icy tone.

The preacher composed himself then and even managed a half-nod, rather than spouting the hellfire and brimstone he obviously wanted to. He took his seat once more and then straightened his wispy hair before continuing. "As much as Sister Emma's fall from grace fills my heart with sorrow, our first care must be for the innocent." He placed his hands together, as if in prayer. "With great reluctance, I must put myself forward to adopt this cherub of the Lord."

Anna felt her bile rise.

"On what grounds?" the judge snapped back, clearly losing patience with him.

"Yar Honor, what young Hermon needs is stability." Old Mother Hubbard nodded in agreement beside him. "We pray daily that the ongoing rampage of Mrs. Price's murderous lover will not damage Hermon's impressionable, young mind. Surely the court can see the devastating effect this business will have on the child?"

Anna had feared this line of attack. The callous description of the person she hated most was a low blow, even for Riley, and the single venomous comment wiped away her growing sense of victory.

The ongoing manhunt in the States had ratcheted up the stakes for the police and heightened the hysteria surrounding the case. Phoenix held an unofficial curfew after dark every night with women throughout the city fearing the strangler would return to his old hunting grounds.

The judge seemed to consider this. "However inappropriately made, he does raise a valid point, Mrs. Price." She sounded reluctant to offer him any support. "I will have to factor this into my deliberations."

Anna felt her shoulders slump at the blow. The truth was that she'd also become concerned about the impact of ongoing publicity not only on Hermon, but on Emma, as well. They'd been through so much already, and it made her wonder if staying with her was the best thing for them.

"Hermon doesn't know anything about what's happening back home," Emma spoke up as she rested a comforting hand on Anna's shoulder. "We both make sure of that." The judge didn't speak, but nodded, her face unreadable.

Howard Baines coughed politely. "Your Honor, may I take this opportunity to raise the matter of the Pike Dairy Company?"

This seemed to get the attention of the judge. "Yes, I'm very concerned to hear that neither Emma nor Hermon were aware of this legal arrangement. Emma, is that true? Did the church inform you of your status as a trust beneficiary?"

Emma shook her head firmly while the reverend scowled at her in impotent rage. The judge turned her attention back to Riley and raised an eyebrow.

In response, out came the supplicating hands again, as if shocked by the accusation. "Yar Honor, these young people have been through much, and I—the church, that is—did not wish to burden them with such administrative details."

"I'm sure you didn't," the judge replied, actually managing to sound neutral, despite the outrageous nonsense coming from the man. "Tell me, Reverend, has the church also sought not to burden Emma and Hermon with any of the..." she looked down at a paper beside her, "two million dollars of profit the enterprise made last year?" she asked.

Riley coughed and reached for a glass of water before answering. "We are simple folk of the Lord and do not seek to glorify ourselves with trinkets of Babylon—only those funds that support our work for the Almighty," he said and then pointed at Emma. "As cherished members of our congregation, Sister Emma and young Hermon willingly give us their tithe." The prayer hands came back.

"That's not true!" Emma said, her voice ringing with indignation. "Where's my money, you smelly, old scarecrow?"

The judge had to turn the laugh emerging from her throat into a cough.

You go, girl! Anna thought. She knew all too well how afraid Emma had been of Riley, so to hear her speak out in the face of the beady-eyed tyrant was an unexpected pleasure.

The judge raised her hand in a gesture to calm the furious young woman. "Please, Miss Pike, I appreciate that you have strong feelings, but the question of your inheritance is not for this court. It's the custody of your nephew that we need to consider."

Emma sat again, although still visibly agitated. Not getting the hint, the preacher gestured at Emma, as if to point out she was self-evidently part of a satanic cult, presumably with Anna as the high priestess.

The judge ignored him. "I think now would be a good time to hear from Hermon," she said.

As planned, Greta rose from her position at the corner of the boardroom before exiting and returning with Hermon. The little boy looked toward the big screen apprehensively as he entered with Mr. Boo pressed under his arm. As usual, Anna's maternal instincts kicked in at the sight of the boy she'd come to regard as her son.

Without speaking, he sat in the far too large chair beside his aunt and stared, wide-eyed, at the judge before turning his gaze on the cadaverous form of the preacher and frowning. As he did so, it struck Anna how these two individuals represented such a complete contrast to the other. Hermon was the personification of youth and innocence, while Riley looked tired and cynical. When the preacher returned the boy's stare without any hint of warmth, Anna imagined with a shudder how, if given the chance, he would leech away his innocence until it left the kid as morally bankrupt as his enforced protector.

He won't get him, she vowed to herself.

The countenance of the judge lightened and she smiled at the boy, who self-consciously examined his toy. "Well, hello, Hermon. My name is Judge Reynolds."

"Hello," he replied, half-raising his hand to wave and then thinking better of it as he sensed the formal nature of his surroundings.

"Now, do you know why we're here today?" she asked. He nodded, still looking at the teddy. "Why is that?"

"To find out who my new mommy and daddy will be," he said. Anna's heart melted at the thought that this was what the case meant for him.

"Do you like living with Anna and Corey?" she asked.

He nodded enthusiastically. "And Auntie Em," he added, receiving a beaming smile from Emma.

"Do you remember Reverend Riley?" she asked. "He cares about you, also, Hermon, and he would like you to go live with him at the church."

Hermon looked confused and more than a little scared.

"You can be with God's people again, my dear child," the preacher interjected, the smile on his face seeming to hold all the genuine warmth of a cobra eyeing a juicy mouse.

"You're a bad man! You made my mommy sad!" Hermon cried before hopping down from his stool and running toward the door. Anna began to rise, the instinct to comfort him overwhelming. It was the first time he'd spoken of Claire, and it made Anna wonder what he'd meant by "made her sad".

"It's okay, I'll go," Greta said before going after the boy.

"Yar Honor, the boy has clearly been coached—"

The judge raised her hand. "I've heard enough." The following silence spoke for itself. "We also now have a report back from the social care team, so I believe I'm in a position to consider a ruling." Riley tried to intervene yet again, only to receive the same dismissal. "Please expect my findings to be mailed to all concerned parties within a fort-night. My thanks to all."

The reverend started to speak, but before he could utter a word, the view of the courtroom disappeared, leaving Anna staring straight at Riley. The moment the judge left, the shallow veneer of reason left his expression and was re-placed by raw hate.

"Those who stand in the way of the Lord's work should

expect the full wrath of his fury!" he said through clenched dentures.

Anna's anger flared in equal measure. "Spare me the crap, you fraud!" she snapped back. "You can't intimidate me like one of those poor fools you brainwash." She could feel her cheeks flush as her rage flowed. "It's you who should be afraid, so-called Reverend," she pointed at his wrinkled features. "You've upset my family, which means I'm going to crush your weird, little cult and make you pay every single penny you owe Emma and Hermon. You've got that, you withered, old cock-knocker?"

She thought Riley's silent companion would actually faint after hearing such harsh words. It gave Anna a warm glow of satisfaction to see a glimmer of fear in his eye.

"Maybe we should call it a day," Howard suggested. Even the consummate professional seemed shocked by the venom she'd just expelled.

Clarence began to splutter.

"I'm gonna' give you one chance to put right what your poisonous bullshit did to this family, and that's to give them their inheritance. If you don't, then mark my words, I'll have your past scoured for every misappropriated fund, every sexual perversion that's gone on under your roof, and every skeleton rattling in your closet." The reverend looked back at the furious mother-to-be in abject terror. "Cut the call," Anna said to Baines, who had the good sense to comply.

Chapter 14

NEEDLE IN A HAYSTACK

Detective Raymond had never seen so many FBI agents in one room. It amused him to think this was what a Men in Black convention must have been like. His mouth twitched at the thought, bored by the presentation of the lead agent who looked young enough to be his grandson. The slides flipped along with precise efficiency, a logo of the Bureau tucked away in the corner of every page. Physiological profile, known contacts, sexual orientation, demographic data...

Raymond rolled his eyes at a particularly unsurprising analysis of Eckerman's position on the psychopathy scale.

Great, we've spent the past hour establishing that the guy's a nut job, he thought, frustrated by such an endless process. Sure, it was meticulous, but they just didn't have time to jerk around with this shit while Eckerman could strike at any time. He raised his hand, despite knowing that pissing on their squeaky-clean parade risked getting him excluded from the investigation—a fact that had been expressed to him in no uncertain terms at the beginning of the hunt.

"What do we have on his whereabouts?" he asked, trying to sound as respectful as he could to the kid.

The agent gave him a patient look, as if a none-too-bright exchange student had just asked how many letter S's there were in "Mississippi." "We're following multiple leads to track him down. He's not a man with contacts, so we're certain he'll surface soon."

That means you have no clue.

Regardless of the agent's optimistic assessment, the presentation droned on with little in the way of any concrete leads. It appeared that Eckerman had disappeared from the face of the earth. It was possible he was laying low, maybe waiting for Anna Price to return from the UK before making another attempt on her life.

Raymond had spoken to Anna less than a week ago to check that she'd gotten over the initial shock of the news. He'd been pleased to hear Corey Price had regained consciousness and was making a swift recovery. She'd also assured him they would stay well away from the States until Eckerman was back in a cage.

The investigation was going nowhere, though, and they'd been left in the unenviable and all-too-common scenario of waiting for their man to screw up—an age-old tactic that worked on all but the most cunning of fugitives. Often, the sheer weight of paranoia would be enough to trigger a panicked mistake. What Raymond hadn't admitted to the worried mother-to-be, however, was that the process could take years.

"What's our intel on the possibility of him leaving the country?" Raymond asked. It was something he'd considered, however unlikely, considering the huge scale of the manhunt and his likeness being plastered on every airport and border crossing in the land.

"We've estimated that probability at less than five percent," replied the young agent.

"Five percent?" Raymond replied with a spontaneous grin. "I'd make it more like six." Back at the office, laughter would have greeted this healthy dose of cynicism. Here, however, it drew an uncomfortable silence.

"How so? Our profile says less than five," the agent countered, his tone deadly serious.

Raymond needed a cigarette. Although there was no logical argument to contradict the Bureau's analysis, his gut insisted that Eckerman was crazy enough to try anything. It gave him some comfort to know that if he did try, he'd fail.

Chapter 15
THE TEMPLE

Tony stared into the boy's dead face and marveled. Unlike the other specimens, this one had been injected with some kind of chemical to give it a life-like quality. Instead of washed-out gray, this boy had pink cheeks and brown eyebrows, capturing the moment his severed head had been preserved two hundred and thirty years ago.

He shifted his gaze around the contour of the glass tank and observed the intersection where they'd divided the skull in two, starting just to the left of the kid's nose. He'd seen fractured bone before—mangled and broken—but this was a thing of beauty, rendering his own efforts primitive by comparison.

Wandering the streets of London had proven a strain. The bright lights, incessant noise, and vibrant life mocked him wherever he went. The museum was different, however: a dark testament to torment and one man's cruelty to another. The modern world dared not intrude here, with its shiny distractions and baubles.

It struck him that the museum of surgery was a shrine—a palace dedicated to death—where the spirit of the great Motha dwelt in all his glory. Every misfortune and carbuncled remnant of Motha's hand in the world could be found here: a two-headed unborn, the syphilitic genitals of both sexes, and even the skeleton of an Irish giant who, after learning of his impending death, had attempted to flee the country just to prevent the surgeons from having his body as a specimen. The freak had failed to stop the hand of Motha, though, as had the other hundreds of individuals preserved in this place—just as Anna would fail.

While studying every vein and crease of the boy's features, he contemplated his quest to bring Anna's head to this shrine. To earn such a gift, however, meant further sacrifice for his master first, and that meant he needed somewhere to hide while he completed his work.

Here, my son, make my palace your refuge, the voice came to him.

Noticing a doorway marked "Private," Tony slipped out of the main gallery and into the labyrinthine inner bowels of the vast Georgian building. He instinctively followed the winding route, trusting his luck and the hand of his protector to find the place that would be his home. He didn't fear capture, for he knew Motha would protect him here, in his own house.

He found the storage room in the gloom of the basement, filled with boxes containing non-exhibited medical instruments. A thick layer of dust covered the flagstone floor, meaning it hadn't been visited for months, if not years. In its center, sitting flush against the bare flags, was a single chair, complete with straps and a folding steel tray. Motha had provided him with a bed. Now all he needed were tools befitting his chosen status. While his previous efforts were commendable, they lacked the flair needed to match the achievements of the one in whose steps he intended to follow. After searching through the stacked wooden crates, he found the Victorian doctor's satchel. Tony unclasped it via hinges still oiled and smiled at what he saw inside.

Now he could begin.

Chapter 16

BELINDA

Belinda zipped her coat against the chill and trudged with unsteady legs along St. Katherine's quayside, disappointed that all the bars had closed and with them, her last night of fun. One final day of numbing tedium loomed on the finance course, and the thought of having to sit through another eight hours of arse torture on cheap, plastic chairs while a charmless tit of a trainer droned on about asset management made her want to scream with boredom. She looked down at her watch and winced. Six hours from now, she would be there with the mother of all hangovers and a three-hour exam she'd done exactly zero prep for.

If she failed, her boss would be pissed off to the point that he may fire her. The boozy temptations of the big city had proven too much of an enticement for Belinda, though

—not that she was an alcoholic, of course, despite her overzealous doctor alluding to that on more than a few awkward occasions. She knew it wasn't true, because she'd spent twenty years living with her father, a real drinker. That man could sink a bottle of gin just to warm himself up before a night out, whereas she'd have half, at most.

Point in fact, she could've headed to the real party district in Soho and let her hair down proper, but she'd opted to be a good girl—well, sort of—and hung around the business center of town, instead. Most of the watering holes this side of town didn't even bother opening during the weekdays. Belinda, however, could sniff out a G and T from a mile away and had scouted several potential watering holes along the docks during her all-too-short lunch breaks earlier in the day.

She suspected the barman at the Perkin had allowed her to stay after the official closure time in the hope of getting into her knickers later on. Unfortunately, he'd been a spotty little oink, and the so-called favor he'd given was common manners back home in Rotherham. No, he could bugger off. Part of her wished she'd strung him along a bit longer, though, because she already felt like one last night cap before trying to fall asleep on her lumpy hotel bed.

"Cheapskate," she muttered of her employer while heading up concrete steps beside the glass-fronted office blocks that backed onto the docks. Already, a dull headache throbbed behind her temple, prompting her to recall if she'd packed Aspirin in her bag. With any luck, she'd feel okay due to still being drunk first thing, but she dreaded the real payback coming her way around midday tomorrow.

"Oh, well, I'll just have to spew up on that boring arsehole," she said with a giggle that ended in a hiccup.

Tower Bridge loomed to her left, but she wasn't in the mood to stand and admire it. The idea of getting one last drink on her way to the hotel at Whitechapel grew more appealing still, and maybe, just to reward herself for enduring a week of discomfort, she'd hit the mini-bar in her box-like room before braving the mattress from hell.

Belinda blinked against a sudden chill wind sweeping across the now-deserted junction that'd bustled with tourists only a few hours ago. She ignored the green traffic light, hurried over the series of crossings, and headed into the heart of the city. Her destination was no more than a thirty-minute stroll, yet to her booze-clouded judgment seemed much farther, somehow, like a trek for an explorer in an alien environment.

Heading down the road she'd memorized as Mansell Street, Belinda walked under the massive railway archways feeding into the nearby Tower rail hub. An eerie quiet accompanied her under the shadowed interior, accentuating the clicking of her heels and her own feelings of isolation. Earlier, this place had been a hive of activity, lined with businesses nestled in each arch recess. Now, they'd all been shuttered with steel security barriers against London's less productive inhabitants.

Just ahead, a piercing scream made Belinda freeze in her tracks, causing the boozy fog to disappear like an old friend scurrying off and leaving her to fend for herself.

Stay calm, silly B! Her father's saying flashed into her head without its usual calming influence.

A second later, the scream of alarm turned into laughter. "You bastard! Your hands are freezing!" the voice of a female echoed toward her, soon followed by a giggle.

Belinda rolled her eyes and hurried past the couple who'd decided to stop under the relative concealment of the arches and engage in extra social activities. She didn't bother to look into the doorway as she continued toward the welcoming light of the city.

Fifteen minutes later and she was on the home stretch, having reached the well-lit Whitechapel High Street and no more than ten minutes from the hotel. The tension she'd experienced under the rail arches was gone now, only to be replaced by annoyance at the vanishing prospect of finding a damn drink in one of Europe's largest cities. She'd pinned her hopes on a strip bar converted from an Old East End boozer, but when she reached the entrance, all that greeted her was a closed door and a poster of a pouting nurse with ginormous breasts.

"Men. Pfft," she tutted before continuing on to what her trainer would refer to as her "contingency plan". *Mini bar it is!*

With that thought in mind, she decided to take a shortcut through an alley leading off the main road and into the back lanes. She passed under an archway, noticing how it looked historic, with a single weird window peering into the alley. Walls pressed in on both sides with the darkened doorway of yet another pub on her left. Belinda wrinkled her nose at the smell of urine pervading the enclosed space and hoped she wasn't walking in whatever had caused the acidic reek.

To the relief of her nostrils, the alley soon opened into a road again, with offices and warehouses on either side. As she passed the darkened courtyard of a vacant office, a faint groaning emanated from her left. Belinda paused mid-stride upon hearing the unusual sound. The light of a flickering street lamp seemed to stop at the gloom-covered entrance, as if afraid to intrude further. The moaning came again; whoever was making the sound seemed to be in distress.

The hotel is just up there, silly B, she thought. *Probably just a wino sleeping it off.* Belinda turned, ready to do the sensible thing and leave. *It could be someone having a heart attack.*

She'd helped her mother care for her grandma in the last year of her life, and the pitiful noise reminded her of the old lady's pain-filled protests. *What if that was Gran, and some pissed-up bitch ignored her?*

With her sense of guilt now in the driving seat, she hesitantly stepped forward until standing parallel with a For Let sign before peering into the gloom. "Hello?" she called, her voice sounding high in her own head. "Are you okay?"

"Please," a hoarse male voice with an unusual lilt answered.

Belinda leaned toward the plea, her face becoming engulfed by the darkness. As her vision adjusted to the recess, she made out a pair of booted feet that began to jerk and skitter against the tarmac. The body of the figure stretched into the pitch-black space beyond. *Jesus, he's having a fit.*

Her caring instinct took over and she strode to the prone person, intent on helping. As she bent to get a better look at the figure, the jerking motion stopped. *That's odd...*

She didn't get a chance to finish the thought because a thudding agony suddenly bloomed in her gut, causing her to gasp and stagger backward. Instinctively, she clawed at the source of her distress, as if trying to swat away a bothersome fly, only to find a dark liquid dripping off her fingers.

In those last moments, she looked at the blood in confusion, wondering why it appeared black under the half-light. That's when the face of the pale, one-eyed demon emerged, its face an angry mess of hacked flesh.

Belinda wondered if her alarm clock would wake her soon. *Back home tomorrow...*

"Am I dreaming?" The question only half-came from her lips, sounding oddly drowned. "Can I go home?" She staggered, feeling her heel snap beneath her foot.

The creature grinned, shaking its head. "You have a new home now," it said, the wicked smile widening, "in our temple of pain."

The thing raised the blade before them. Belinda tried to scream, but the sound wouldn't come.

THE REWARD from Motha came almost immediately after, while he washed away the gore in a puddle near the scene of his latest hunt. A single page of newspaper lay within the filthy water; on it read a single headline that made him smile and clasp his hands in praise:

"American billionaire recovers from wedding stab horror." He didn't recognize the image of the hospital accompanying the piece, but he did recognize the looming presence of the Shard building rising above it, like a beacon pointing to his destiny.

His dark master helped him further that evening by revealing a back entrance to the museum storeroom via a floor-level window in the service courtyard. It was to the rear of the building where no cameras monitored the largely unused section, and it fell into shadow during the night—perfect for keeping his movements concealed.

With his appetite sated for now, Tony sat on the barber chair and read the next chapter of the dog-eared paperback entitled "The Whitechapel Murders," which he'd stolen from one of London's many homeless shelters. A small thrill of excitement ran down his spine in anticipation of the next challenge.

With a faint sense of guilt, he remembered feeling skeptical about the viability of the high demands of his master, but after completing the first step to enlightenment, he marveled at the power surging through his veins, willing him on to even greater deeds.

Chapter 17

A DISTURBING DEVELOPMENT

J ane McKenzie pondered the arrangement of the body. The skirt had been hoisted over the waist, leaving pale skin exposed to the elements in a display of careless contempt that bothered her more than she cared to admit. This was no robbery that had gotten out of hand, but a pre-meditated act of pure hatred. Her immediate thought was to make a mental link with the airport murder, but the MO was completely different.

"What have we got?" she asked Dawkins, who'd completed some preliminaries before her late arrival. These morning gigs were always an issue due to the school run her cheating ex-husband had left her to deal with alone.

"Multiple stab wounds. We've not got the exact number, yet, but at least thirty."

"Do we know who the victim is, yet?" she asked.

"Belinda Briarson, another Northern girl—Rotherham,

this time," Will replied, tucking his hands into his old-fashioned parka jacket and joining her to stare at the sad remains of the woman. Even he seemed uncharacteristically subdued today. "We checked the local hotels and the King's Charter confirmed she's a guest until tomorrow. We're in the middle of following up with her employer. Seems she was here on business."

"The King's Charter?" Jane asked, knowing the East End like the back of her hand, yet never hearing of it before.

"It's a shit hole. I stayed there once when Kim kicked me... well, when we went through a few issues."

No prizes for guessing why, Jane thought, not surprised in the slightest. "Looks like she was on her way back to the hotel," she interjected to head off any further unwanted insight into his personal life.

"Yep, our perp must've dragged her down Gunthorpe Street, somehow. What do you reckon? Robbery and..."

"Time of death?" she ignored the question, not in the mood for his usual brand of callous curiosity.

"Forensics reckon 2-ish."

"Speak to the local bars and restaurants."

"Yes, sir," he said sarcastically.

She ignored that, too. "I want to know where she went and who was with her. At that time on a weekday, she's not likely to have gone far."

Jane only half-listened to Dawkins explain his less plausible theories about where the woman could've been before the killing, because her attention became drawn to a short, fat man with a handlebar mustache and wearing a ridiculously outdated deerstalker hat, standing amongst the small crowd gathered beyond the cordon tape. Something about his odd attire and the way he spoke excitedly into a mobile phone while staring at the blue forensics tent made her curious enough to notice him.

Although there was no logical reason for her to take an interest in the guy other than his odd attire, there was something in his expression that implied he knew something she didn't. Jane approached the group, feigning a look of disapproval. "Come on folks, let's show a little respect, please," she said.

Most of the passers-by quickly dispersed at the prospect of being branded a ghoul. As she suspected, though, Sherlock's fat stunt double didn't move. If anything, he seemed encouraged by her presence.

"Is it a copycat killing?" he blurted, clearly unable to contain himself. His manner seemed theatrical, and she wondered if he was a performer of some kind. It would at least explain the weird clothing.

A frown appeared on her face—the copycat comment wasn't what she'd expected to hear. "I'm sorry, sir, but this is a police investigation, and I can't discuss anything with you. Please move along."

"Gunthorpe Street, the infamous George Yard," he said, his voice sounding inappropriately satisfied as he pointed at the tarmac, as if it were hallowed ground. His facial hair made him look older than he was, and she guessed he was no more than twenty—young enough to be her son.

Her blank expression prompted him to offer his hand in greeting. She didn't accept, but wasn't quite ready to dispense with him just yet. He dropped his arm with an awkward blush. McKenzie winced at the sound of her colleague's footsteps reaching her side.

"I'm Richard Smith, Ripperologist," he introduced himself with a solemn tone, as if addressing a fellow officer.

"Good for you," Jane replied, starting to regret her first instinct already. She had a mountain of work to do, not least of which was the still-open case of the air stewardess. Now she had the added nuisance of looking like she was clutching at straws in front of Will, a man who would no doubt relish telling tales of her hunt for Jack the Ripper for his own amusement in the canteen.

"You don't know, do you?" Sherlock asked with a jovial twinkle in his eye, as if they weren't just a few meters from a brutalized dead woman.

"Know what?"

"Detective, this is the very same place they found the Ripper's first victim." She didn't have time for this. "I stop the tour here every night," he added hopefully, as if that information was the clincher. McKenzie was far from being in the mood for this conversation. She had two complex murders to solve, and this fella was wetting his knickers at the thought of attracting more tourists to join his freak show.

"Wow, that's really fascinating," Will interjected before she had a chance to tell the guy where he could stick his tour. "Why don't you leave Detective McKenzie your details and I'm sure she'll be in touch to explore the whole Jack the Ripper scenario with you." He actually managed to sound serious.

She shot a poison-filled glare at the irritating little dickhead, and his corresponding smirk did nothing to improve her mood. The effect on the bearded pudding-face of young Sherlock, however, was dramatic. He looked like an enthusiastic puppy being handed a bone. With exaggerated care, he reached under his tweed jacket before retrieving a black business card that stated "Ripper Tours of London" in blood-red type. Mackenzie snatched the proffered card without a word and marched back toward the forensics tent with Dawkins on her heels.

"Wow, hunt for the new Ripper," he said merrily, tracing the imaginary headline with his finger. She turned to face him finally, her hand poised on the tent zipper.

"You know when your wife kicked you out?" the question was delivered in an icy tone.

"What about it?" his grin immediately dropped.

"How many fellas do you think she fucked while you were gone?"

Chapter 18

ANGEL

She appeared like an angel, gliding down the road with a swollen belly and an expensive handbag at her side. A young boy held her hand as she strolled past, seemingly without a care in the world. It was the first time he'd seen her since their dalliance together in Julia's kitchen.

He lay as still as death upon a bed of cardboard nestled in a disused doorway opposite the hospital entrance, peering from under his hood. He'd endured the water dripping from the corner of an overhanging roof onto his sodden sleeping bag for hours, but he didn't care. Anna had come.

The sight of her condition made him grip the cold, wet covers with barely-suppressed fury. How he wished to go to her then and kick the unclean thing from her body! But

Motha, in his wisdom, stayed his hand, counseling patience and reminding him of their pact. Gradually, the rage subsided, and he watched her disappear inside swinging doors.

"Three green bottles..." he continued the rhyme.

Chapter 19
HAPPY NEWS

Anna stifled a laugh as Corey swayed precariously along the physical therapy mat with Hermon in support beside him. The boy held a look of complete concentration as he guided her mischievous husband through his daily exercises. Every time Corey seemed close to toppling over, Hermon would scurry to his other side to assist. The patient, however, would tilt the other way, causing the boy to switch again in a heroic effort to keep him upright.

In reality, Corey was pretty steady on his feet now. The silly display was more for the benefit of Hermon, who had expressed a keen interest in getting to know the man they all hoped would become his adoptive father. In typical Corey style, he'd won the boy over with a mixture of theatrics and a love of all things tech—a combination no child could resist. The friendship had finally been clinched by a promise of a future flight in the HELA as co-pilot, no less.

After several seconds of the kid being remorselessly teased by the older man's antics, Hermon seemed to understand. He paused in the middle of rescuing yet another impending disaster and put his hands on his hips, instead.

"Hold on a minute. You're not really going to fall over, are you?" He looked to Anna, seeking agreement with his suspicion. She replied with a look of wide-eyed innocence, biting her lip to quell the mirth threatening to leave her. While Hermon did this, Corey began to swing his arms in a protracted gesture to show he was losing his balance again.

"Hermie, help!" he called.

The dramatic action was enough to pull Hermon back into the routine and he obediently went back to Corey's side. The moment he did so, though, her husband revealed the full extent of his dastardly plan by placing his left hand on top of the boy's curly blond hair and doing a quick dance around him while making a jazz hand with his right. Anna laughed then—a full, happy sound that set the two boys off, too.

"That was mean!" she declared as Corey took a bow. "Don't trust him; he's a silly man!"

Hermon was too busy laughing to agree, but his face soon took on an excited expression when the implication seemed to hit. "Does this mean you can come home?" he asked in obvious joy at the prospect, warming Anna's heart.

At the same time, she felt bad that he'd come to regard a temporary place as home. It emphasized just how unstable his short life must have been.

"A week, the doc said," Corey replied with a grin.

"Wow, that's so amazing! Just wait 'til we play my VR games!"

"We'll see what the doctors say next week," Anna interjected, recalling the actual phrase the medic had used was "at least a week."

Just before the baby is due she thought with a small thrill as she rubbed her hands protectively around her belly again. Miss Bump had become her very own stress ball of late.

"Hmm, VR, eh?" Corey pondered, stroking his chin. "What's that stand for?"

"OMG, Corey, you don't know what VR is?" Hermon asked. "It stands for Very Real, 'cause everything you see through the helmet looks very real, even though it's not. Cool or what?"

"Wow, that does sound great!" Corey agreed, giving Anna a sly wink.

"Hey, why don't we get something to eat?" she suggested to divert them from Corey's over-optimistic view of his impending discharge.

"Pizza?" Hermon piped up.

Anna realized that, in her quest to win him and Emma over, she'd been a little too happy to indulge their appetite for food an average dietician would throw holy water at. Her own odd cravings hadn't helped matters, either. Her latest fad was for a strong-tasting veggie extract called Marmite—a British condiment she'd found in the hospital canteen. After falling in love with the stuff, she'd forced Corey to try some, only to watch him feign falling back into a coma.

Just as Anna was about to suggest sushi, Nurse Jessie entered through the swinging ward doors. "Hey, guys," she greeted them all. "How are we doing today?"

"Corey can come home soon!" Hermon declared before rushing to her and giving her a hug.

"Oh, is that right?" she asked, returning his embrace with one arm while giving the suddenly sheepish Corey a stern stare. "I tell you what, Mister, why don't you draw me a picture while I have a quick word with your Auntie A, honey?"

Hermon gave her a curious look, but was used to allowing grown-up talk, so he skipped to the children's area in the corner of the brightly lit room.

"There's a Howard Baines waiting for you outside," she said after the boy had left. The smile on Anna's face froze, and Corey strolled to them, noticing the change in atmosphere. The significance of the lawyer turning up at the hospital unannounced could only mean one thing.

They'd been waiting for the ruling for two weeks now, but it seemed as though the limbo was about to end. The thought of losing Hermon while on the verge of becoming a full family had been an unbearable concept for Anna, not least because of the impact it would have on the boy.

After Emma withdrew her adoption claim, it'd only left a straight fight with Clarence Riley. The press back home had been in a frenzy over the news of her attempt to adopt the son of the woman who'd tried to kill Corey. There was no doubt the preacher's organization had taken advantage of their absence to sow lies about her.

"Will you keep an eye on Hermie?" she asked Jessie, who nodded with her usual warmth.

"Good luck," the nurse added, giving them both a squeeze on the arm before joining the boy playing in the corner.

Howard looked out of place as he sat in the waiting room wearing his designer suit. He rose with a broad grin that made Anna's heart leap. "We won," he said immediately, causing her to gasp in joy and turn to give Corey a fierce hug.

"We can be a family now," she said, sobbing with relief that Hermon would no longer be threatened with going back to a life of fear and manipulation. Still, her anger at the so-called reverend and his organization hadn't been sated. Anna wanted to make sure their corrupting influence couldn't destroy families like the Pikes ever again.

"Tell that snake, Riley, I want Emma and Hermon's inheritance transferred to them yesterday, or we're gonna come after him with everything we've got," she said with passion.

"That might be..." Howard looked to Corey.

"Hey, you heard the lady," Corey said, putting an arm

around Anna to show he meant it. "Tell that freaky old dude to cough up the dough, or we're gonna' squeeze his balls!"

"Fine," Howard replied, rolling his eyes, clearly knowing when he was outgunned. After promising to follow up straight away, he strode off for another of his endless procession of meetings.

"Squeeze his balls?" Anna asked after the lawyer had hurried away.

"It was all I could think of at the time," Corey replied, kissing her hand and giving her one of those grins she'd come to love. "I'm not sure I'd enjoy it, though—they're probably gray, small, and leathery."

"Thank you for backing me up," Anna said. When she noticed no one else was around, she planted a slow kiss on his cheek.

"Wow, all this talk of balls is having an effect, I see," Corey said with a glint in his eye.

"Yeah, right. Maybe if you're into humping Humpty Dumpty." She looked down at the swollen abdomen between them.

"You're a very sexy Humpty," he replied with undisguised mirth. "Except for when you eat that Marmite stuff—then I'd have to go with the rev's shriveled old coconuts, instead."

The resulting laughter felt good; it was just what she needed.

Chapter 20

ANN

"I told you I'll fackin' pay next week! Now fack off, you smelly, fat twat!" Ann Smeaton screamed into the sweating face of her landlord while two high court bailiffs changed the lock.

"Miss, if you continue to threaten, we will call the police, and you won't be able to collect your things," the burly bailiff spoke on behalf of his client, who wisely chose to remain silent. A look of supreme indifference stretched across the jowls of Abbas, however.

Ann knew the sneaky, Turkish bastard charged her more than the other tenants in the block just because she was a street girl. His smug face, the sure knowledge he was ripping her off, and the fact that she'd not yet had a fix made her blood boil.

"Pay me the rent and you can stay," he added, taking a

half-shuffle back from the fiery redhead. "I've been more than patient, Ann."

"Oh yeah, real old sweetheart, you." She spat in his face, causing him to turn crimson with fury. "So kind of you to stick your cock in my arse for rent money—how very generous."

"Enough!" the fat man shouted. Ann took a small amount of pleasure at the fleeting look of amusement that passed over the face of the bailiff as he drilled screws into the new lock.

"Probably decided he don't wanna' do that again, 'cause I'm not a boy. What do you reckon, fellas?" she added. The professionals, however, remained stoic in their refusal to engage with her.

Ann wasn't making it up. She'd noticed how he got all cow-eyed whenever Gazelle, her pre-op friend, visited. His tussle with her had been a substitute for the forbidden fruit he really craved.

"Filthy whore!" he shouted, now rattled. Ann realized her moment of payback had also just removed any prospect of being able to stay in her home.

The next ten minutes became a blur of screaming, crying, and begging before she finally accepted the inevitable and marched down the narrow staircase, not bothering to collect her worthless possessions from inside.

Emerging into the chill November air, she let out the sob she'd kept locked inside. The harsh reality of her predicament came thudding home, along with the freezing drizzle.

Although it wasn't the first time she'd been homeless, she'd been younger on both previous occasions and it'd been during the summer, when at least the weather wasn't an issue. Even back then, though, she'd known older women to come to a bad end. That triggered the depressing thought that at almost forty, she was no longer a youth, herself.

"Fucking Turkish bastard," she muttered under her breath, cursing him one last time and wishing she'd kicked him in the balls. If she had, at least a warm cell at the police station could have been hers.

Pulling her thin jacket close to her body, she headed off into the night to spend her last twenty pounds on some gear before heading to the homeless shelter near Spitalfields in the hope of a bed. She recalled they didn't like taking people on at short notice, but females were generally given a little more leeway than the fellas. With a bit of luck, she wouldn't freeze.

Ann passed the empty market stalls of Petticoat Lane that'd bustled with bargain-seekers earlier in the day. Sure, it wasn't as impressive as the big market in Camden, but to her, it was home. She still remembered walking the street as a girl when London was very different and the remains of the old warehouses and mills still loomed. Now, she barely recognized the place or its inhabitants.

Most of the old pubs were gone and those that did remain sold gin to tourists for five quid a shot. She remembered a time when there was a proper boozer on every corner and she'd spend long Sunday afternoons sipping on

Coke while her dad played darts all afternoon with his drinking pals. It seemed to her that the Old East End had died around the same time he had.

Jesus, I'm an old woman, she contemplated after calling her dealer and pressing on toward Vallance Gardens, where he would greet her with his usual disdain for females. She'd only made the mistake of offering to trade sex for drugs once before—the black eye he'd left her with made sure of that. It made her wonder if he would've accepted when she was twenty.

As she turned onto the main road, a man wearing a dark coat and hat approached her from the shuttered doorway of an electrical shop.

"Hey, you know where a guy can get some fun around here?" The American accent got her attention. The Yanks had money—lots of it. She'd not had the good fortune of picking up any in years, but her mate Franky reckoned she'd been tipped two hundred notes by a fat guy from Texas a few months ago. She immediately put on her best eager-to-please smile, only to falter at the sight of the bandages.

"Might be," she said, wanting to sound more enthusiastic, but his obscured features made her apprehensive.

"Oh, sorry, didn't mean to scare ya'. I've had surgery at Harley Street." His tone was friendly, and her smile returned.

"Harley Street, indeed. So, you look handsome under there, then?" she asked, trying to suppress the thrill running through her. A rich American who'd come over for surgery.

Play her cards right and this punter could top Franky's haul and maybe even earn her enough to get the apartment back.

"I'm kinda at a loose end tonight, and it's been one helluva week," he replied, pointing at his face.

"So, what do you want to do, then, Mr. American?" Ann turned on her female charm, putting one hand on her hip and running her finger down the lapel of his dark coat. It looked curiously old-fashioned, and she smelled something musty and not altogether pleasant about it, but she ignored the warning at the back of her head—this guy could turn a bad night into a great one.

"Lead on, my good man. Where'd you like to go?" she asked, tucking her arm in his. He seemed to recoil from the affectionate gesture for a moment before allowing it.

"Not far at all," he replied, taking them east.

Chapter 21

RIPPER

The woman lay in a pool of blood with her skirt yanked up around her waist. She had a slashed throat, and a deep gouge ran from her abdomen to her breastbone. McKenzie chewed the side of her thumb while her mind raced at the implications. Two murders, both involving women, both mutilations.

She opened the case file of Belinda Briarson and laid the two images side by side. On the surface, they appeared to be a different MO: one a frenzied stabbing and the second the deliberate opening of the woman's abdomen. When she compared the pictures of the victims, however, both females seemed to have been carefully arranged post-mortem.

The removal of clothing suggested a sexual motive, yet the lab said there was no evidence of intercourse. And there was the stewardess, as well. Could it be a coincidence that three brutal killers were operating at the same time in

London? It was statistically possible, but her experience told her there was no such thing as coincidence.

So, if they are linked, why such differing methods? The answer didn't come—only the creeping ache of a growing migraine.

She stood and grabbed her coat from the back of the office door before searching through the pockets for painkillers. As she did so, the black card of the pudgy Ripper tour guy fell out. Rubbing her neck against the growing throb, she turned it over in her hand speculatively. Deciding she needed a distraction for a moment, Jane logged into her workstation and typed the words:

"Jack the Ripper."

As expected, the search results for the most famous murderer in history presented an avalanche of information. Most was speculation about the identity of the culprit, ranging from outlandish claims that Jack was a member of the Royal Family to the more conventional weight of evidence pointing to a Polish immigrant named Aaron Kosminski.

Her attention turned to the victims and locations of the murders. A cold finger of ice ran down her spine when she read a body had been discovered in Buck's Row (now Durward Street), Whitechapel. The throat had been severed by two cuts and the lower part of the abdomen had been partly ripped open by a deep, jagged wound. Stunned, she picked up the file on the redhead.

I'll be. "Durward Street," she said aloud.

Jane picked up the phone and dialed the number on the card. The line rang several times before a sleep-filled voice answered in a curt tone that implied, unless the caller had a good reason for calling at this hour, they could most definitely fuck off.

"It's DI Jane McKenzie. We spoke yesterday at the scene of the murder," she said, her head bursting with implications.

"Hello again, Detective," the voice perked up immediately. "How can I help?"

"Can you meet me in Whitechapel?"

There was a pause. "Absolutely. How about nine tomorrow? If it's about the murder location, I can give you my tour, if you'd like?"

"No, now."

"Now? It's nearly eleven."

She frowned with irritation. "I know what time it is. Do you want to help me or not? You're not the only—"

"No, no. Please, I'd be happy—"

"Good. I'll meet you outside the Whitechapel Tube station in thirty minutes." She put the handset down, cutting off a stammered "but," and turned her attention back to the screen before her. Even a suggestion that the police were considering a Ripper connection would cause a feeding frenzy in the press, and if proven wrong, she was certain to lose her job. She knew the significance of the locations couldn't be ignored, though, so after taking a deep breath, she picked up the phone receiver a second time and prepared to put her career on the line.

JANE STOOD in the drizzle underneath the red sign for the Tube, wishing the thumping ache in her head would clear and allow her to focus her racing thoughts. Even at this late hour, Whitechapel High Street remained busy with a steady stream of traffic splashing through puddles left by a heavy rain earlier that day.

After more hurried research, she'd begun to understand why the Old East End had been such a perfect hunting ground for the original Ripper. Over a hundred years ago, this now cosmopolitan part of town had been a degrading slum filled with poorly-lit back streets and vulnerable prostitutes for the notorious killer to pray upon. Modern London, by contrast, was one the safest cities in the world, monitored by an army of security cameras and a dedicated police force.

There was no doubt in her mind that whoever was doing this was reckless to the point of insanity. The fact that this improved the chances of a quick resolution gave her little comfort, though. Even with all the advantages of technology at their disposal, it still took time to sift through evidence and question suspects. With the second attack happening within only a day of the first, however, it appeared that their man was in no mood to play fair and allow them what they needed most: time. It was proving a terrible irony that the killer's lack of caution was proving his biggest ally and forcing her team onto the back foot.

Jane felt a presence beside her and turned to find the man who called himself Richard Smith on the business card. He gave a wary nod of his head by way of greeting, again wearing the ridiculous-looking Deerstalker hat.

"Just us?" he asked.

"For now," she replied, in no mood for pleasantries. "Before we start, you need to understand this is an official investigation. Breathe a word to anyone, and I'll make sure you face a charge of perverting the course of justice. You got that?" Although she wouldn't normally be this blunt, the circumstances demanded it.

He turned bright red at the undisguised threat. "There's no need to—"

"There is a need—people's lives are at stake. Do you understand?" He nodded again, this time with wide-eyed concern that indicated her point was made. "Follow me," she said.

They walked the short distance from the Tube station to the narrow entrance to Gunthorpe Street. She led them into the alley, noting the old arch above them was likely one of the last vestiges of the alley the original Ripper and his victim would've recognized. They carried on past the row of businesses on the left until reaching the scene of Belinda Briarson's murder in the courtyard of a vacant office. The only remaining sign of the horror committed here was a stray fragment of police tape attached to the iron bars on the windows.

"This used to be called George Yard?" she asked.

"Yes. Some people think this is the location of the first murder."

"Some people?"

"Well, yes. Because the modus operandi was not the same, many experts believe it wasn't Jack's work. It was a frenzied attack to be sure, but none of the throat-slashing or abdominal mutilations of the later canonical five, as they became known."

She pondered the information, having read something similar on the web. "So, why would our killer copy this one?"

He seemed to become excited by the question as he stared at her through metal-rimmed glasses that had steamed up from the cold. "Wow. You think there's a copycat?"

"It's possible. Like I said, if you speak one word to the press—"

The young man raised his hands in supplication. "You have my word from one professional to another."

Jane wasn't quite sure what he meant by that, but it would do. "So, why copy this one?" she asked again.

"It's possible she was one of Jack's, although it's not a theory I'd agree with, myself," he seemed to hesitate, "but perhaps this new Ripper does." Jane nodded, unable to glean anything of value from the information. "If you don't mind me asking, Detective, why did you ask to come here at this hour?"

She gave him a flat stare back, knowing that to take him any further on this midnight tour risked making her a laughing stock in front of her peers. "What kind of man was the Ripper?" she ignored his question for the moment.

"Like I said, it all depends on what theory you subscribe to. For example, was the 'from hell' letter to the police a hoax? Some think—"

"What do you think?"

He sighed, as if being asked a million dollar question. "A madman with a pathological hatred of women," he replied eventually.

"Careful? Ritualistic?" she pressed.

He shook his head. "No. His motivation was pure rage. All five confirmed victims were killed in a frenzy, which is the only real reason they connected the stabbing of Martha Tabram, here, with the others." He pointed at the crime scene. "Stabbing someone thirty-nine times takes real anger."

Thirty-nine times. She cast her mind back to the report on Belinda Briarson, in which the hurried coroner's examination reported thirty-nine separate wounds.

Her thoughts turned to the concept of a copycat killer. It sounded more like a Hollywood movie than reality. To kill someone in such a brutal manner was a deeply personal act that most human beings were incapable of, unless pushed to extremes. People just didn't copy serial killers. By their very nature, they were rare freaks of nature and abhorrent to all but their own kind. *Their own kind...*

"Jack wasn't the only murderer around at the time," Richard added. "The Ripper sucks up all the publicity, but the East End was such a cesspit that there were similar murders to this, just before and after the five."

"The Ripper could've killed more, then?"

"Possibly, but not likely," he shook his head. "It's been proven that people used him as a red herring. We know of at least one robber who cut the throat of his victims to confuse the police into thinking the Ripper was still on the prowl."

The thought had crossed her mind, already: could someone be using the notorious murders as a distraction to cover another agenda? So far, though, they'd failed to find any obvious connections between the victims either online or via their work connections, which included the air stewardess, who remained a question mark. A lab report due the following day should have helped rule her in or out.

Just like the other aspects of the case, their perp was moving too fast for the normal processes to be effective. Frustratingly, the fact that two of the women were of northern origin had proven a coincidence, and the latest victim was barely cold. They had, however, established that she was a local sex worker. That's where the similarities between their man and the Ripper differed again: all the original victims were prostitutes, whereas only one of the victims in the present case fit the profile.

"Follow me," she said, striding to the end of Gunthorpe Street and into the back lanes leading to their next destination. Taking him wasn't a prospect she relished in the slightest, but her mind was made up." How long you been doing this Ripper stuff?" she asked him, realizing she hadn't even checked the experience of the self-professed expert.

"Three years—since I started my undergrad course at UCL."

"What are you studying?" she asked, mentally plotting the quickest path and bracing herself against the sudden gust of chill wind.

"Forensics science."

Well, that's something, at least, she thought. "You're called Richard, right?"

"I prefer Dick."

Jane made a mental note not to call him that in front of Dawkins. "Listen, Dick, can you do me a favor?"

"Of course. What's that?"

"Take off the Deerstalker," she said without even a hint of humor.

"Oh, why? Where are we going?" he asked, sounding confused and already a little out of breath by the pace she'd set.

Jane sighed. "So I don't look like I've engaged the services of Sherlock Holmes when we get to the scene."

"What scene?"

It seemed that her instructions to keep the full extent of the attack at Spitalfields from the press had paid off, for now. By morning, however, London would be waking to the news that they had a new Ripper among them.

"The crime scene at Durward Street," she answered.

He halted dead in his tracks, forcing her to stop.

"Oh, you mean…?" At that moment, he looked every inch the fluff-faced student. Jane was beginning to regret not having time to find an alternative guide.

THE RIPPEROLOGIST HAD FALLEN silent as they trudged through the grim night. Like her, his initial curiosity had given way to the contemplation of the true magnitude of the unfolding events. The familiar sights seemed different to her tonight—darker and more sinister, somehow.

"It's too soon," Dick said suddenly, voicing the conclusion she'd already come to. "It's only been two days, and the murders of Tabram and Nichols were three weeks apart in 1888. Why would he be so..."

"Reckless," she finished for him.

"Yes, exactly."

"I'm not sure, but we need to find out quickly. He could kill again tonight," she replied, cursing a timeline that made it all but impossible to get the upper hand.

If the killer was so unprecise about the timeframe and victims, what other predictable factors would he ignore? Perhaps the whole Ripper angle really was a smoke screen for someone to carve out a vendetta for reasons they'd yet to establish.

"What about Hanbury Street and Mitre Square? Shouldn't you have colleagues there?" he asked.

"That's if he sticks to this pattern, which isn't certain."

"But still…"

"We've got it covered." This was true. The hurried call she'd made to the assistant commissioner had been one of the most uncomfortable ten minutes of her life, but his initial disbelief at the request for emergency resource had soon given way to wary agreement after she'd explained the unarguable similarities and aggressive time frame.

Dozens more undercover units should be in Whitechapel and the surrounding area by now. She'd also requested all CCTV operators in a mile radius to be on high alert. If their man went anywhere near the six original locations, they'd get him.

They soon reached the hive of activity on the corner of Durward Street. Several teams, including one from the Mets, had gathered, no doubt as a result of the senior intervention. Jane guessed it likely that, at this very moment, they'd be weighing her career in the balance.

"Just fucking great," she said aloud at the sight of Will Dawkins, hands folded into the pockets of his parka. As if sensing the opportunity to mock, he turned in their direction, his bored expression transforming to one of sly amusement.

"Is everything okay? Would you like me to wait here?"

Richard asked, sounding discomfited by her muttered curse.

"No, just keep your mouth shut, unless I have a question," she replied in a low tone before striding over to her colleague, projecting a confidence she didn't feel.

"You weren't kidding, then?" Will asked, eyeing the younger man with a look of morbid curiosity. He was attempting to sound casual, but the strain in his expression was clear. This latest killing had rung alarm bells up and down the chain of command, putting pressure on everyone to get results in the face of the unholy shit storm about to descend. "What makes you think this is a copycat?" He lowered his voice, giving the other figures nearby a surreptitious look. "I've had to 'ma'am' and 'sir' so much tonight, you'd think I was a fucking butler!"

"Tough! Deal with it, Will," she whispered through gritted teeth.

"Both locations are identical to the original murders. That's if we include Martha Tabram, of course." It was Dick who answered Will's original question, as if being quizzed by a tourist. Dawkins gave him a look that spoke volumes about his thoughts on the subject.

"Do the research," Jane interjected, not having time to allow a pissing contest between the two. "Do you have any more on her yet?" she asked Will, nodding in the direction of the covered area surrounding the body.

Will continued to eye the blinking, bespectacled student, seeming unsure if he should go along with her apparent acceptance of the flamboyant addition to their team. "Not really—just what we put in the initial report: two cuts to the neck confirmed and abdomen slashed open," he said to Jane, rather than Dick.

"Exactly the same as Mary Ann Nichols," Dick added excitedly. "I'll bet it was the lower part of the stomach," he added. "We should check." He looked at them both like a dog looking for a pat on the head.

Dawkins looked to Jane, seeming to dare her to support such outlandish nonsense. She responded with a curt nod. He shook his head and sighed, but strolled to one of the suited forensics team and spoke into her ear. The SOCO looked at him curiously for a moment, then unzipped the front of the protective canvas and stepped inside. Jane caught a brief flash of a pale body with an angry-looking red crescent gouged into it before the flap dropped. The sharp intake of breath beside her indicated Dick had also seen the corpse. A second later, the suited figure re-emerged and nodded at Will, who seemed surprised by the confirmation.

"Jesus," he said, returning to them. "This is going to be huge."

"Do you reckon?" she agreed with sarcasm born from her own anxiety.

"Where's the next location? Have we secured it?" Will asked.

"Hanbury Street off Brick Lane, and, yes, of course. I

want to see if Di—Richard, here, can give us anything else of value."

"Great, you get to have a Chicken Bhuna while I stand around here, freezing my nuts off," he grumbled, referring to the many Indian restaurants located in the famed curry capital of London.

"I'll save you a papadum," Jane replied, thinking the chance would be a fine thing. It'd been days since she'd last had the time to eat a good meal.

"I'd wish you good luck, but I'm sure Mr. Holmes, here, will crack the case, by Jove!" he said, by way of goodbye.

"You're an arse, Dawkins," she replied.

A SHORT TIME LATER, they'd passed the many curry houses and accompanying sales staff who stood at the entrance of each establishment, trying to entice late evening revelers with promises of special meal deals. Like much of the East End, the areas around Brick Lane were now a vibrant mix of different cultures. Almost every business along that congested, busy road was dedicated to the provision of food from all over the world.

The competitive hustle of the city at night was a welcome relief from the revelations of the past few days. Jane felt a strange sense of guilt that she would soon be the messenger placing a cloud over these people and their lives when the news broke.

All the more reason to catch him as soon as we can.

Despite the proximity to the main thoroughfare of Brick Lane, Hanbury Street was far quieter and residential in nature. Street art obscured by shadow covered the brick wall isolating the two-storey apartments from the road. At this time of night, most of the occupants had turned in, leaving their dwellings lightless and seemingly devoid of human presence. Something about the stillness of the hour made Jane slow their pace while her senses became inextricably more alert. A freezing rain began, numbing her exposed forehead.

About halfway along the route, she spotted a figure standing opposite the children's play area.

"Wait here," she whispered to Dick before approaching the stranger in the dark jacket who seemed to be facing the gloom of an overgrown tree-lined area near the swings.

She was sure the observer was a man, judging by his muscular frame outlined by the weak street light. With her heart pounding, she approached the distracted male who turned at the sound of her footsteps. The familiar face of Paul Jacobs, one of the plain-clothed units sent to keep watch on the target area, was revealed.

He stepped back in surprise and then let out a relieved breath. "Shit..." he muttered. "I mean, sorry, Detective." She saw a brief flash of guilt directed at her. Jane didn't know him well, but enough to exchange a greeting in passing.

"Everything okay?" she asked, copying his hushed tone.

"I thought I heard something in those trees," he replied,

wiping a rivulet of the increasingly heavy downpour from his brow.

"Do you want to call it?"

"No, not yet. I want to go look, first. It's probably a rat." He didn't sound certain, however. As a precaution, she'd ensured the surveillance team was briefed enough to understand that they were looking for a dangerous perp, although she'd stopped at full disclosure of the situation.

She nodded in agreement, subconsciously tapping the comforting bulge of her radio tucked into her coat pocket.

Jacobs reached into his inner jacket and removed a standard issue ASP baton before extending it. Despite being a non-descript tool, it was nevertheless an effective weapon capable of breaking a man's arm, if used in the right way. He swiped the water from his face once more, then crept across the play yard toward the copse at the far end.

Jane held her breath, straining to hear any sound from that dark triangle. Other than the sound of raindrops hitting pavement, though, the world seemed silent. Jacobs inched forward, the baton held in the attack position. Finally, he reached the trees and pulled a branch aside before disappearing and becoming another shadow amongst many. The seconds dragged on until Jane became unnerved enough to reach for the radio in her pocket.

Footsteps approaching from behind interrupted the action, and her irritation rose when she glanced up to see the wide-eyed form of Dick Smith. His whiskered face looked even more anxious than before, and she guessed the tension of the moment was becoming too much for him.

Not so fun in the field, eh, she thought, regretting her invite.

"Detective," he whispered urgently.

"Not now," she hissed back, flicking rain off her brow and turning back to watch the copse. Was that movement?

"Detective, the number of the house opposite us—"

"Shush!" she saw a flicker of movement. With no small measure of relief, the figure of Jacobs appeared once more. He didn't seem to be creeping, anymore, and instead, was making a gesture she couldn't quite make out.

"Detective, it's number twenty-nine. They found Annie Chapman in the backyard of a house right here."

"What?" Her attention was caught between the two.

A noise came from the direction of Jacobs and the signal he'd made before became more pronounced, almost as if he were raising his hands to his...

Sweet Jesus!

Even as he began to stagger and collapse against the children's slide, she was already sprinting to help while pulling out her radio. Jane approached her stricken colleague to see a sudden gush of what looked like black liquid spraying from his throat into the night air. With her instincts torn between duty and giving aid, she raced to his side, looking for a way to stop the lethal bleed.

Get a grip, Jane!

Jacobs' pleading gaze burned into her conscience with

such ferocity that she almost staggered back from his grasping hand that reached out to her in an act of hopeless desperation. Even as she pressed her palm against the appalling gash in his neck, trying to quell the ebbing force, her own inner voice screamed a warning that coincided with a shrill call from the street.

"Detective!"

But Jane McKenzie didn't have time to react because from the corner of her vision, she saw death approach. Pain bloomed and she could only look on as her own blood sprinkled and then poured onto the still face of Jacobs. The world seemed to flicker like a bulb casting a light between this world and another place. She wanted to stay, but her strength failed within seconds, and blackness covered all.

Chapter 22

CELEBRATION

A nna stared out at the rain-shrouded city below and marveled at the beauty surrounding her. In the distance, she could make out the winking lights atop the shard building, the only thing higher than her position in one of Canada Square's equally impressive skyscrapers. From so far up, the vista appeared like a child's model being drenched under racing clouds skittering across an iron-clad sky. Her position felt so remote up here that the only visible sign she wasn't experiencing an optical illusion came from the faint sound of rain lashing against the sheer glass panes of the tall viewing window. In the months since her arrival, Anna had never tired of the view and loved the privilege of watching the seasons pass while the life inside her grew.

Despite the happy occasion, she'd needed a moment to step away from the party to gather her thoughts and consider the journey ahead. For the rest of the team, this represented a reward for what they'd achieved as a company, but for her, it was just a pit stop before plunging into the real task that still lay ahead.

Anna set her hand on Miss Bump once more and gave her a quick rub for luck. Even though the doc assured her everything was fine, the prospect of squeezing something the size of a melon out of her private parts was hardly welcome. What would come after, however, was a different matter.

The reflection of a tuxedo-wearing Corey appeared behind her nightgowned figure. "It's time," he said, kissing her ear and slipping his arm around her belly. She hadn't been the only one to develop the habit. "What are you doing over here? The party just started."

"I'm just having a moment," she replied, patting his hand. They'd come to use the term to describe the frequent bouts of emotional turmoil that'd dogged her for weeks. "Besides, there's only so much orange juice a girl can take," she added. "I think when this little man comes out, she's gonna' be a piece of fruit! What I'd do for a glass of wine..." she paused, noticing the half-full glass in his hand. "Shouldn't you be laying off the sauce, too, fella'?" she said, turning and poking him in the gut playfully.

"Come on, hon, I've been looking forward to this for weeks—and it's more to thank the guys than anything," he replied with a slight slur. It all sounded very reasonable, but she wasn't quite ready to let him off the hook just yet, especially considering her present condition was down to his wicked charms.

"So, I suppose the old baby machine can look forward to being locked in the kitchen while you disappear down to the pub with your mates?" she asked, adopting the British lingo and making him laugh. "Not that I'd blame you. It looks like I've grown a pair of udders." Anna looked down at her swollen assets with a sigh.

"You look great," he retorted, ignoring her obvious teasing. "I promise not to have any more after this one," he added, although she wasn't sure he'd keep that particular vow. "They want you to cut the cake, by the way."

"Me? I thought you were going to do the honors?"

"I was, but apparently they want you to do it—something about Anna getting credit for this one," he said, giving his own mock sigh.

She couldn't help but smile. "You're shitting me."

"Nope, this project is all down to you, hon."

"Yes, but surely you get to cut the cake? You're the boss."

"I told you not to call me Shirley." That earned him a slap on the arm. "Ouch! I have many talents, but directing a multinational while being in a coma is beyond even my considerable abilities."

She returned his grin and they stepped down from the viewing platform to re-join the other guests mingling around the bar.

Taking her by the hand, Corey led her to the leaf-shaped cake at the center of the extravagant spread. The original plan had been to buy the services of a catering team to produce the spongy treat, but Anna had insisted on baking it herself with the help of Emma and Hermon. She took her place beside her beaming husband and smiled at the gathered team accompanied by their families. On a prearranged signal, the music from the band stopped and everyone turned to look at her. A polite applause followed, interspersed with the odd whoop.

Anna felt genuine warmth toward this group of people who'd put aside their own justified reservations to make her feel welcome. At first, many of them had treated her with a polite, yet skeptical deference, but in time they'd come to respect her, as she did them. While she stood there, warming to the smiling faces and looks of shared achievement, it occurred to her that, if she hadn't proven her worth, they would've found a way to quietly remove her, regardless of Corey's wishes. She couldn't blame them if they had—their shared mission had been too important for that. Anna allowed herself a little mental pat on the back.

"Go on, speak. I want to try that cake, Misses," Corey whispered in her ear.

She stepped to the small microphone built into the table and gave them all a demure wave before blushing.

"Hey, guys!" she said down the mic, too happy to be put off by the initial sound of distorted feedback.

There was more cheering, and that's when she spotted Greta in her stunning evening dress. She blew the other woman an appreciative kiss, much to her enthusiastic acknowledgment.

"We—I just wanted to say a few words." There was a big round of applause, and she smiled in gratitude before continuing. "It hasn't been the easiest year for us."

"I slept through most of it," Corey said while putting an arm around her, bringing muted laughter. He often joked about his enforced departure, but it made others uneasy to be reminded of how close they'd come to losing their brilliant friend and leader.

"Seriously, though, Green Gen took me in, even when I didn't have a clue," Anna said. "Now we haven't just delivered the third gen cells, but we're also about to kick some serious ass with our research." This brought more applause. "Those with vested interests say green energy will always be more expensive than their poisonous crap, and we're proving how wrong they are." This was greeted by a thunderous reception.

"So, without boring you further, let's hope this cake of mine is edible!" she declared before picking up the silver knife and poising it over the icing while camera phones flashed across the grand room. She sliced the blade down into the lemon sponge interior and everyone gave a cheer. With the ceremony complete, the music started up again and the guests began to mingle once more.

As she turned to plant a firm kiss on the cheek of her husband, Anna felt a sudden wet, gushing sensation down her legs. She kept her lips pressed against his face while her mind raced in panic.

"Steady on, babe—there's time for that later," he joked, as she seemed to enjoy the affectionate moment a little too long.

"I'm not sure anyone will want my cake," she whispered into his ear.

"Don't be silly, hon—it's beautiful. Best lemon cake ever."

"Corey."

"Yes, babe?"

"My water just broke."

There was a pause. "Holy shit!"

Chapter 23

TOO LATE?

Raymond stared at the security camera footage, knowing without a shadow of a doubt that he was looking at Tony Eckerman. The height and the way the grainy figure moved with the same slinking ease he'd seen during the trail all fit. In his very bones he knew it, and the fact that Eckerman had obscured his face only made the detective more certain.

The tip-off came from the British Metropolitan Police hunting an American in connection with the murder of an air hostess just a stone's throw from Heathrow Airport. It had been a strangulation typical of Eckerman. It seemed some of his Federal colleagues, at least, had been capable of connecting the dots, because the intel had eventually reached the task force.

"It's him," he said immediately, causing a stir in the exhausted agents around him. "We need forensics."

"How do—"

"If we don't warn the police in the UK right now, more are going to die, including Anna Price."

"Anna Price?" The lead agent asked, as if the name shouldn't already be etched in his brain.

"His ex-fiancée—the one he tried to kill. She's living in London right now to avoid that evil fucker."

He took no pleasure in the look of outright panic passing over the face of the young agent as cold realization struck. Raymond began to dial on his cell and nobody tried to stop him.

Chapter 24

SHADOW

Tony darted between the shadows, feeling power and triumph surge through his body even as the gore dripped from his fingers. He'd found the woman easily enough—middle-aged admittedly, but, hey, it wasn't bad under the circumstances.

The ploy had been a simple one: he'd asked for help in the same strangled voice that'd worked so well with the first bitch, loud enough to get her attention. Like a moth to the flame, she'd responded to the call and it'd proven easy to drive cold steel into her throat and watch her terror bloom. He recalled with relish that even someone with her skin color could turn pale like a fish plucked from its tank and laid upon the slab of Motha.

He'd been quiet, of course, and she'd been too shocked to scream while he opened her up. The sound of footsteps coming to a halt on the pavement opposite his position amongst the trees, however, had halted his work. The fish had been in its death throes by that point, so there was nothing he could do to stop the violent spasms rustling the foliage.

It'd taken just a few moments to finish her, but Mr. Steps had made no move to leave, so with one hand still buried deep within her guts, he'd risked moving aside the undergrowth to better observe his foolish visitor.

Half the lights along the street were out, in presumably an energy-saving scheme, so the meager backlight only revealed the bulky frame of a male. Tony had remained still, praying for guidance. His suspicions about his unwelcome observer became firmer when two other people joined the figure. The woman must've known him, because he could hear them talk. Their hurried words, however, had been lost amidst the hiss of rain. It'd all come so close to ending before he'd completed his quest.

He'd prayed harder, stirring the guts of the fish while he did so, vowing with all his soul to bring a mighty prize to his god, just as the book said he should. In return, he begged Motha to free him to claim his reward, sensing that he only had hours at most. Tony raised the blade and kissed it, allowing the rain to cleanse it for the next offering.

After he'd slit the throat of the undercover pig, he'd finished the woman cop. The second man had tried to run, but had the agility of a dead cockroach and died like one, begging and squealing. Next came Motha's prize, a mighty gift, indeed. He'd gone back to the woman's body to find she was a detective, according to her ID. Even old Jack, himself, hadn't managed that. He'd removed her uterus in seconds, just as the book instructed, while hoping Motha would forgive his haste. Now, the bloody trophy nestled within his pocket.

He'd planned his return route the previous day, choosing roads that gave him the best chance of evading capture. Still, it was far from easy in a city that never slept, especially when he'd stirred them up like a fox in the henhouse. He paused and shrank into a shop doorway as a police car and then ambulance sped by, perhaps for one of his victims.

The minutes passed in a blur of darkness and shadowed wandering while the downpour washed his body clean. He'd learned weeks ago that his disheveled appearance gave him a ready way to make himself invisible; few people noticed the silent ones stretched out in doorways or slumped on a bench. In this way, he stalked through London, pausing and hiding when he needed, lying low until each threat passed. After a time, he came to the yard of the Museum and slipped in.

Tony carefully removed his bloody prize from the trench coat, then threw off the soiled garment, leaving him naked. He placed his prize in the specimen jar he'd prepared earlier and knelt before it, suppressing the urge to shiver in the near-freezing temperature. Motha didn't tolerate weakness—his Lord was a shepherd of wolves, not of the meek cattle infesting this Earth. He clasped his hands together before him in prayer with flecks of diluted blood still clinging to his fingers.

"Lord, I bring a great prize to your shrine of pain. I beg of you, release me to claim my reward. Please, Motha! Let me go to her now and bring her into your embrace." *Must not shiver. Must show strength.*

The moments ticked by while his body screamed for warmth. No matter—tonight, he would either succeed or his own cage of flesh would perish in the failure. Finally, the words he longed for came.

You have done well, my child. Yes, I see your black heart is worthy. Go with my blessings and take them.

Tony roared his triumph before wrapping himself in a second old, but clean coat he'd found stuffed in storage.

He would make their ending the stuff of nightmares, forcing them into the meat grinder of the Motha's maw slowly, until they begged for death. He'd only grant that wish, however, when his toll was paid in full. Even then, they would find him waiting on the other side, hand in hand with his god. There, they would kneel by the stone where he would eviscerate them for all eternity.

Chapter 25

ANYONE FOR CAKE?

U nsurprisingly, the cake wasn't very popular with the guests, but that wasn't Anna's main concern as another contraction racked her abdomen. It hurt a lot, and the prospect that it would only get worse didn't appeal to her in the slightest. The ambulance staff had been fantastic during the short ride across town, however, and they were now completing their brief journey. Corey laid a comforting hand on her shoulder, which she had a sudden urge to bite in a most unreasonable manner.

"Would you like something for the pain?" the ponytailed medic asked as she lowered the gurney onto the tarmac outside the maternity ward entrance. Her colleague stood beside Anna with a large umbrella covering her from the almighty downpour surrounding them.

"Just gas and air," Corey said, no doubt trying to be helpful. It was true that they'd agreed to try for as natural of a birth as possible, but that was three weeks ago when she didn't feel like a watermelon was about to burst out of her.

"Screw that, Corey. Give me drugs!" she gasped.

"You heard the lady," he agreed sensibly.

EVERYONE HAD EVIDENTLY BEEN PREPPED for her arrival, because to her delight, Nurse Jessie greeted her in the spacious private room set aside for the special day. An older woman with gray hair and motherly demeanor stood beside her, smiling in a way that Anna found reassuring.

"Jessie!" Anna exclaimed. "What are you doing here? I thought you were on a day shift?"

"I made him promise to call me the minute you went into labor," she said with a grin. "This is Maria, your midwife," she added, introducing her colleague and then looking around in a conspiratorial manner, as if checking that they were out of earshot. "She's the best."

"I don't know about that," the gray-haired woman said with a warm smile, her gaze assessing Anna in a professional manner.

"Hey," Corey greeted them with clear relief at the sight of the trained professionals. "Looks like we're gonna' go with pain relief, after all."

"Good," the midwife approved. She came close to Anna

and spoke in a low tone. "Birth hurts like hell, and I don't care what the latest fad says, a shot does the trick every time." She patted her patient on the hand. "It's usually men who say otherwise."

Anna liked her already.

Chapter 26

ALL OR NOTHING

Finding them had been easy. He'd monitored the glossy website of the company since his escape, noting the announcement of the party days ago. After watching the entrance of the lobby for what only seemed like minutes, well-dressed, but drunken figures emerged, talking excitedly about the ambulance and Anna's impending labor. Tony smiled, because he knew exactly where they would take her for the birth. It would be a risky journey on foot and would take more than an hour, but he'd take that chance and trust in his own hate to get him there.

So be it.

A scout at the maternity ward entrance forced him to

rethink. The chances of getting past security without being stopped were vanishingly small. He needed a plan—something that would ensure he could get in without raising the alarm.

Give me an offering, my child, and you shall enter.

Darting into the shadow of a nearby alley, Tony removed the exquisite knife from its nest within his coat pocket and stared into its gleaming surface, admiring the shining steel like an old friend. As always, its mirrored surface made him feel calm. He took the handle, rose to a squatting position, and then thrust the razor-sharp blade deep into his thigh.

THE SECURITY GUARD had reported finding the stab victim staggering toward the entrance of A & E before collapsing outside. Doctor Vaughn peeled back the man's eyelids and noted with surprise that the gaunt man was conscious. Although unusual, it wasn't unheard of for patients in shock.

He guessed the patient was a vagrant, from his appearance, while his horrific facial scarring told a tale of serious trauma in the recent past. At the removal of the patient's clothing, he couldn't help but whistle at the many old lacerations he'd suffered.

Fuck, is that a bullet wound?

Vaughn's professional curiosity piqued. Wounding by firearm was rare in this country, so it pointed to the man possibly being ex-forces. Even so, the facial wounds looked odd and not as random as one would expect from explosive damage.

"Can you hear me?" he asked, feeling an odd reluctance to disturb him.

The man moaned, his eyes rolling in their sockets. Either he was faking the state, or there was something else going on—maybe drugs. The doc bit his lip, wondering if he should involve the consultant. The case appeared a-typical, and although he'd been a junior for almost a year, there were still times when he needed extra support. This guy, well, there was something fucking weird about him.

After inspecting the fresh wound, he re-applied the gauze and bandaging before pondering his options. "Can you open your eyes for me?" he asked, trying to assess his level of awareness.

There was more groaning and no response to the command.

"He's tachycardic, the nurse said, drawing his attention to the EKG reading.

"Yeah, he's lost a lot of blood," he said, ordering an ABO type test.

The blonde-haired patient began to blow great gasps.

Schizophrenia? he pondered.

"We'll need to clean the wound," he said, observing the

filthy condition of the man's skin, "and can you page Mr. Kelling, please?"

"Mr. Kelling? Are you sure?" the nurse asked. He could sense the morbid curiosity in the question. Kelling had a fearsome reputation for verbally flaying over-zealous juniors who bothered him without good reason. On the surface, he would agree this patient wasn't in any immediate danger, as the wound was deep, but nowhere near an artery. And there was no evidence of other fresh injuries, but the man's odd reactions were a concern not entirely explained by shock.

"I'm not happy..." he paused, tapping his stethoscope against his chin. "Actually, I'll get him," he added, changing his mind.

At least she won't see the drubbing I'm about to get, he thought, not enjoying the prospect of being embarrassed in front of the pretty nurse he hoped to date. "Keep him under close obs and he'll need more pain relief—the same dose again," Vaughn said, pulling aside the cubicle curtain before striding toward his superior's office.

As soon as the nurse left, presumably to get more morphine, Tony forced himself into a sitting position and strained against the throbbing wave of agony threatening to knock him into unconsciousness. The mention of pain relief had triggered a physical yearning in his body that had been close to overwhelming his will. It would've been so easy to give up the fight against his own body, then, and allow them to treat him, but he knew that would be the end of his quest, failure in the eyes of Motha, and a fate worse than the one he planned for Anna. No, even if he had to saw off his own leg to get to her, he wouldn't allow that to pass.

Tony pulled on the hospital gown lying beside the bed and then rummaged through the medical instruments nearby. He took a roll of the surgical gauze before using it as a rudimentary strap to fix a scalpel against his leg. It'd been a real shame to ditch the beautiful barber's knife, but the risk would've been too great when he was so close to his goal.

He tested the weight on his leg and became light-headed as fresh agony shot up his side, forcing him to lean on his good hip. Sucking his teeth, Tony hopped to a nearby wall and grabbed a pair of waiting crutches. Hooking them under his arms, he propelled himself out of the cubicle, trusting to luck that the nurse wasn't already returning.

Praise be to Motha, she stood a few meters away with her back turned and vial in hand, while talking to a gown-wearing pensioner in mid-rant about a three-hour wait for an X-ray. Just behind the arguing couple lay salvation in the form of the ward doors. Tony limped past them and out while the older man droned on in an accent he could barely recognize. No call followed him, and he found himself in a warren of interconnecting corridors.

After a few meters, he came to wall sign listing directions to various departments. He started toward an arrow pointing to Maternity before noticing another labelled Plant Room.

An idea began to form in his mind—one that could create the perfect distraction.

Chapter 27

TOGETHER

The lights dimmed as Corey reached out to rub her hand again, not that the gesture seemed to help much.

Great, that's all we need, he thought.

"What's that?" Anna panted, her legs pulled up to her chest. The contractions had become frequent now, with only a few minutes between them. He recalled from their antenatal clinic visits that it meant the baby was about to make an entrance. His stomach flipped again in both terror and anticipation.

He'd made all sorts of arrangements for their new arrival in London and back home at Clearwater. The little one and its mother didn't know, yet, but he'd built a whole new atrium at the estate complete with a stargazing room and a sci-fi themed soft play area. He hoped the kid would love it as much as his father had while designing it. The strain of keeping it a secret had driven him crazy.

"Just a power cut. The generators cut in, so nothing for you to worry about, my love," the midwife said, although Corey noticed she raised an eyebrow at Jessie, indicating this was not ordinary.

A second later, Corey's phone began to ring. He cursed himself for not turning it off, but he reached for the vibrating device and saw Detective Raymond's name on the screen.

"Corey, if you answer that fucking call, this baby will be the last you'll ever be able to make," Anna growled through clenched teeth. "You promised to turn it off!"

He was about to say "but," until he thought better of it and cut Raymond off, while making a mental apology to the man and promising to call him back after the birth. It conjured a wild hope that the detective had called to say they'd finally captured Eckerman, preferably with a bullet through his forehead. Corey forced his thoughts away from negativity— he needed to be here for them both. Screw that evil creep.

The lights dimmed again, this time followed by a thudding boom from the other side of the hospital grounds. The floor trembled beneath them, accompanied by strangled beeps emerging from machinery unused to being starved of juice.

Instinctively, Corey covered Anna's body with his own, fearing they'd been subjected to some kind of terrorist attack. The initial thundering rumble ebbed, followed by several more loud bangs, until the lights flicked out completely. An eerie red glow replaced the reassuring brightness and surrounded them in shadow. Anna shouted in alarm, even during the extremity of her exertion. Corey held her, listening to her labored breaths, while silently cursing their poor luck on such an important night.

"Mary, mother of..." the gray-haired midwife said, her Irish accent becoming thicker for a moment.

Jessie rushed to the window and peered through the blinds, allowing Corey to catch a flash of orange reflected through the slats. "It's the plant block," she said in shock, seeming to momentarily lose her professional demeanor.

"What do we do?" Corey asked, needing them to focus on his wife despite whatever crazy shit was going down outside the room.

"It looks like we'll be doing this the old-fashioned way," she replied in a light tone, appearing to regain her composure, but not before shooting a worried frown at her colleague.

"Will it be okay?" Anna gasped with a terrified cast to her face.

"You'll do just fine, I reckon," the big Irish woman replied. "I've helped smaller girls than you without any of this fancy stuff." Her levity had a forced ring to it.

"I've seen Maria deliver twins in the back of a bus before, honey," Jessie came back to support a clearly flagging Anna. Corey could see she was doing her best to keep it together, but she'd been through so much in her life already that he worried this could be the final straw.

"I need to pop out for a few minutes. Okay, hon?" Jessie said. At that point, he knew the loyalty of the nurse was torn between Anna and the possible injuries or worse caused by the blast.

"No! Must push!" Anna screamed, grasping Corey's arm in a vice-like grip.

"Don't you worry, honey, Maria will be with you the whole time," the nurse said. At that prompt, the midwife began to rub Anna's back and utter words of comfort. As Jessie turned to leave, Corey grasped her arm before shaking his head at her conflicted expression. "I'm sorry," she mouthed, then hurried out.

When she left the small birthing room, Corey saw other medical staff gather in the corridor outside, scrambling to enact various disaster recovery strategies on an evening that only moments ago had seemed so full of light and joy. Deep in the pit of his being, dread began to form in him. It was an omen he couldn't quite put his finger on, but it left him cold and filled with fear.

Several minutes passed before Maria inspected Anna again. "I think we need to give the baby some help," she concluded.

"Help?" Anna gasped, her face taut with pain.

"I just need the forceps, is all, hon." She looked around, irritation appearing on her face. "How many times have I told them to leave the..." the rest was a grumbled mutter.

"Is something wrong?" Corey asked, frowning with concern.

"No, not at all. My numbskull students have taken the forceps. Not a problem—there will be more in the other delivery suite." She grasped Anna's hand, "I'll be back in two minutes, sweetheart."

"Don't you leave me, as well!" Anna was clearly in no mood for more complications.

"Two minutes, I promise."

"IT HURTS, COREY! OH... MY... WORD!" Anna screamed.

"Maria will be back in a second." He tried to comfort her, feeling more than a passing measure of guilt that he was partly to blame for her pain. He looked down, hoping to see the baby's head crown, but that wasn't to be. With a sinking sensation, he realized they weren't at the end, yet.

"Remember your breathing, honey," he suggested, wishing he'd taken up Bob Vicker's advice at the party and indulged in a few shots of vodka while waiting for the ambulance. The father of four claimed his selfish approach to the big event actually made him appear calm, pretty much the opposite of how Corey felt right now.

"Fuck breathing! I want morphine!" Anna cried with a definite slur to her words, whether from the medication she'd already taken or from sheer adrenalin, he couldn't tell. He puffed his cheeks in and out, as she'd been taught during her antenatal classes, in an effort to encourage her. "Quit with the goldfish impression!" Despite the venomous reply, she did attempt the exercise and it seemed to calm her.

Another loud bang sounded from outside that he did his best to ignore.

"Just our luck to have a baby when World War III is breaking out," he joked. Unsurprisingly, it didn't resonate with her.

An almighty 'whoomp' blasted into the night, followed by the shattering crash of a thousand glass shards. Corey turned to see that one of the thick, double glazing panes in the suite had smashed, such was the force of the blast. The sounds of a chaos flooded into the usually-tranquil environment, accompanied by a roar he recognized as flame. From the distance came the eerie wail of approaching sirens.

Another strong contraction racked his wife's slender frame and brought his attention back to where it should be. Anna clung to him, moaning in terror while he tried to comfort her, despite his own fears. It was with some relief to hear the ward door flap behind them.

"Thank Christ!" he shouted above the cacophony of wind, fire, and cries from outside. "I think she's ready to push, the contractions are—"

A blinding, white flash cut off the words before he could speak.

ANNA SAW the presence through a fog of pain, as she looked up to Corey for some much-needed reassurance. Everything had become so confusing so quickly. She'd been so happy when they'd arrived, and now a thin veil of worry had ballooned into a black shroud around her awareness with every passing moment. The safest place in the world had transformed into a nightmare, leaving her reeling with worry for the baby.

Fear became a clamp of crushing horror as she saw the shadowy form swing a long object into Corey's temple. He fell. The sight was like a blow to her own body, and she watched on, rendered helpless by her unstoppable urge to push.

When she saw the creature who stood in place of her loving husband, she didn't recognize its grinning face at first, thinking Corey's joke about the end of the world had literally come true and one of hell's angels stared down at her. The scar tissue couldn't hide the true nightmare for long, though, because she recognized Tony, even as her mind refused to accept the crushing truth. He had come for her again, and this time there was nothing she could do to stop him.

"I must say, dear, I was a little sad you didn't write to me," he said, tilting his head like a curious cat observing its prey.

She wailed, flicking her wrist at him, as if trying to shoo away a bad memory induced by pain and meds. "Can't be real, can't be real," she closed her eyes and muttered again and again. The wraith didn't evaporate when she opened them, though. It looked all too real, nodding its head while still at that oddly-cocked angle.

"Oh yes, I am real, my love, and I've come a very long way to find you."

Her own screaming sounded removed now—a tremor in the life of another person. She was back to that place she'd thought was behind her forever, where she opened the bedroom door to find Julia on the bed in all its sadistic color. It was a sightless thing—not Big Bird, but a husk where a soul used to be.

Corey!

Although Anna tried to move, her body refused to obey, as if paralyzed, while a giant, black spider crawled up her arm. She forced her quivering gaze away from the creature calling itself Tony for a moment and looked down at her husband. A crutch lay beside him, its padded base covered in a dark liquid. A dim part of her realized that it must've been the same thing she'd seen flashing toward Corey's temple.

No, no...

A primal urge of self-preservation demanded she turn back to face Tony, who now posed in a wicked parody of her anguish, jutting his bottom lip and sniffing. She found nothing human left to appeal to in that single crazy eye glittering with pure malice.

"So..." he raised a hand gripping a scalpel, "as much as I'd like to... chat..." he snarled then, grasping her hair.

Anna waited for the end to come.

The sound of the room door flapping intervened. "Excuse me, sir, you can't be..." the stern command from Maria trailed off the moment she must've seen their dire situation.

"Please help," Anna's voice came out as a trembled whisper from her throat. It was a desperate plea coming from the center of her being.

"Won't be a second, dear," Tony whispered, licking her face and then hobbling toward the midwife, silhouetted against the brighter red light of the corridor.

"Ma'am, thank God you're here! I'm wounded and need help. Please help me!" he rasped, tucking the scalpel behind his back, where its deadly blade glittered in the red-tinged gloom.

The ruse must've been enough to make Maria hesitate, because the creeping form of Tony reached her, and in the half-light, appeared to envelop the woman in a strangely sensual manner. A heartbeat later, Anna's would-be savior lay jerking on the floor.

Another contraction came then, forcing her body into a spasm that even approaching death couldn't halt. Rage and despair fought for equal prominence within her until utter hopelessness forced Anna to make an inner appeal to time, itself, begging it to delay the inevitable.

"Now, where were we?" Tony rasped, lurching closer again before slicing the scalpel across his own bristled chin, causing blood to well against his filthy skin.

Anna couldn't breathe and was unable to avert her gaze from the maniacal stare. The sheer cruel injustice of it broke her, sending her to another place in her head. For a moment, she remained there, alone and curled in the dark, lost in her pain. The end approached.

Move, Little Bird! The voice was Julia's, calm, strong, and defiant.

I can't! she replied from her dark place.

You must, for the baby.

Anna pulled her legs to her belly and cradled it in her arms before rolling off the side of the bed. She hit the cold linoleum on her side, and even through the resulting jolt of pain, she felt relief at not falling on her front.

She tried to stand, but her strength didn't come. For all the effort she'd expended, the desperate act had saved her for a few seconds, but no more. Desperately, she looked around for something—anything—to use as a weapon, but saw only shadow in the dusky glow surrounding her. She heard the sliding drag of Tony wrenching his leg behind him as he made his way around the bed. When that sound stopped, she knew the scalpel would follow, taking her child and the future with it.

The hospital bed had no solid base, and as she lay there, her gaze fell on Corey's face. At the end, it gave her a small measure of comfort to see him one last time and look upon those lips she'd kissed.

At least the three of us will be together.

"Thank you, Motha," the creature muttered as it approached. "I will make this one worthy of you."

She waited as a single tear rolled down her cheek. She kept her view on her husband, drawing every memory she could, to the last.

Just then, Corey's eyes flicked open.

A calloused finger ran down her naked arm like a snake ready to bite, causing the paralyzing terror to set in once more. Any moment now, the blow would follow.

Corey!

"You're a fucking coward," Corey said, his voice choked. The strain on his face appeared superhuman as he clambered to his feet like a man pushing a monumental weight up a mountain. His features shuddered in agony and outrage.

The finger stopped its slow progress toward her throat. "Even better, Motha, I see. Yes, we can make him watch. Oh yes, make him watch as we cut out the brat and flay it."

Anna began to crawl away, her loins screeching in protest as she inched forward on her elbows. She didn't look back, but focused on the billowing drapes framing the growing red carnage outside. Shards of glass littered the way to the opening, and her heart sank at the thought that she would not be able to go much further without risking the baby's life.

She looked back to see Tony start toward her, but she could also make out Corey staring at the other man, as if in a fog of confusion as he tried to reset his senses. The terrible truth was that she didn't know what to fear most: Tony turning to finish her love or continuing on to…

What did he say? To…

She screamed again, a thing straight from her soul—a plea to whatever forces of good were left in her moment of need.

"Take one more step toward her and I'll kill you," Corey said.

Tony began to hum. She recognized the tune, hating it for its shared meaning. It was the sound of coming rage—another slap—the music accompanying the gradual erosion of herself under his thumb. Now its significance was even bleaker.

"Three green bottles hanging on the wall..." he began.

Another slide of the foot.

"And if one green bottle…"

She desperately pulled forward onto the first scattered shards of the window.

"should accidentally fall…"

A hot lick of fire bloomed up her leg. She stopped, pinned by some unyielding force, and turned to find the blade buried in her thigh, held firm by the grinning creature poised above her. It reached for her throat.

Suddenly, Tony's satanic smile faded as another shadow loomed behind him. She watched as her charging husband carried himself and her attacker forward, over her, toward the window aperture. The momentum didn't last, though, because Tony turned to fight back. They strained against each other, silhouetted against the broiling inferno outside.

Anna's heart rose and then sank again as she saw that, despite her man's resolve, Tony was like a reptile, lithe and hard, gaining the upper hand like a thing that'd learned to fight for its existence powered by hate alone. Corey's legs began to buckle and she knew he would fail. Tony howled with pleasure before reaching out and grasping her love's neck to choke him.

"Fight, Corey!" she screamed. "We need you!"

He heard the plea and found the strength to shove the hated fucker square in the chest. The look of demon-like glee on the deformed face of Tony faltered and then became a frown as he fell back across the window frame. At first, he thought the body of his opponent would go straight through and disappear into the night, but it remained pressed at an odd angle against the ledge, un-moving.

Corey stumbled forward and peered into the face of the thing that'd plagued their lives and watched as the black light powering its evil began to leave. He saw fury in that fixed gaze and something else resembling fear. Cold hate mixed with the bitterness of failure emanated from that look. He glanced down at the large sliver of blood-smeared glass protruding from the nape of the man's neck where life pumped from a hideous wound. It filled Corey with incredible joy to know the monster would face whatever dark force he served, having let his ultimate prize slip between his fingers.

He lowered himself toward the body and the single blue pupil of Eckerman focused on his lips. "I'm going to make her so happy." Corey smiled at the growing terror registering back at him. "Go tell them in hell how you failed."

The single eye widened in horror and then fixed in position.

Corey turned and hurried to his wife. Anna looked up at him as if unable to believe he was real. Gently, he reached down and lifted her shivering frame to the bed.

"We can do this together," he said.

EPILOGUE

TWELVE MONTHS LATER

The SUV was almost too big for the narrow country road as they approached their destination. A moment before, Hermon had spotted a glimpse of blue between the green, rolling hills of Yorkshire and the sun-filled sky, triggering a dozen excited questions about the sea. A few minutes later and the ocean could be seen on all sides as they came to the end of the peninsula jutting into the North Sea.

"Look," Hermon cried, "I can see a lighthouse!" He pointed at the majestic white tower looming above them beyond the small visitor's car park.

"Wow, that's cool," Corey agreed as he turned his head above the steering wheel to get a better view of the structure.

"Keep your eyes on the road, please," Anna chided from

the back seat before glancing to the car seat beside her to check if little Julia was still asleep, as she had been for the best part of two hours. They'd been lucky to avoid any rosy-cheeked tantrums caused by the poor mite's long journey.

In typically unpredictable Corey fashion, he'd declared he wanted to end their extended stay in the UK by visiting the seaside, where they would have a picnic and build the best sandcastle in the world. Also in the infuriating manner of her husband, he'd decided a trip to the beaches of northern England was a must after Bob Vickers insisted they were by far the best. Anna suspected the fact that Yorkshire also happened to be the UK CEO's home county had more than a little to do with the recommendation.

Of course, Corey considered the small matter of a four-hour drive with two young children a minor issue. So, after loading the car with what seemed half of a toy store and enough movies to keep Hermon occupied until he graduated from college, they'd set off on their grand expedition.

Julia woke with a grumpy face on her otherwise impossibly cute face, just as the car pulled into its spot opposite the cliff edge a few hundred meters away.

"Looks like madam has woken hungry," Anna said, as Corey stepped out and stretched his legs.

"Sorry hon, I'm not the one with the boobs," he replied with a cheeky wink toward the boy.

Hermon laughed loudly because his dad had just said the B-word again.

"Hey, Mister," she said, pretending to be angry.

"Dad said 'boobs,'" Hermon emphasized.

"Hey!" the two adults said in unison. Corey, it seemed, was not above a little hypocrisy with his parenting skills.

They set out the picnic blanket on a spot with a stunning view of the bay below. Seagulls swooped above and beneath them, calling into the warm summer air. Anna could see a tanker ship on the horizon appearing to travel at an impossibly slow pace across the sea. Waves crashed far below, and for a second she closed her eyes and took in all the sensations before letting out a sigh of contented bliss.

They'd brought far too much food, of course: sandwiches, rolls, and cakes that she'd pulled, still-warm, from the oven only that morning. After setting all the dishes out, they began to enjoy their bounty while gazing around at a world that couldn't have felt more alive right then. Anna looked at her happy family and drank in the moment. It was the happiest day of her life.

THE END

Manufactured by Amazon.ca
Bolton, ON